JANE CARVER of WAAR

nathan long

night shade books
san francisco

First Edition

ISBN: 978-1-59780-396-0

Night Shade Books
http://www.nightshadebooks.com

For my mom and dad,
who never stopped believing in me.

AUTHOR'S FOREWORD

Years ago I used to go with my friend Anthony Balsley to see this Irish punk band called The Troubles at a bar on Fairfax known as Molly Malone's. Anthony was a burly, Harley-riding tough guy with a pompadour and a broken nose. We shared a love for rock-a-billy, punk, ska, and all things rowdy and loud.

One night as I was walking toward Molly's green door, I saw Anthony at the curb comparing Harleys with a big, red-headed biker chick. Anthony is around five eleven, and this girl was a good three inches taller than him and as broad in the shoulder. He introduced her as Jane and me as Nathan, his Hollywood screenwriter pal, and she gave me a disinterested handshake. I didn't blame her. Next to Anthony I looked as fascinating as a glass of lukewarm water.

Anyway, Jane came in with us and we spent the night singing and drinking along with the band and having a blast. At the end of the evening Jane went home with Anthony and I never saw her again: just another of Anthony's one night stands. She passed completely out of my mind until last year when I got a strange package at my PO box. It was full of cheap cassettes, numbered one through fifteen, along with a nearly illegible note written on a piece of Motel 6 stationary. This is what it said.

I got yr address from Anthony. Maybe U can make a story out of this. If it makes any $ send half to PO Box _____, Coral Gables, Fla. Don't try and cheat me about it either. If U do I'll know and U don't want that.

J. Carver

I groaned. The writer's curse is to be constantly approached by well-meaning idiots who say, "Hey man, you're a writer. I got a great idea for a story. You write it and we'll split the money," not realizing that having ideas is less than one percent of the work in writing.

I put off listening to the cassettes for months, but one night the cable was on the fritz and I was feeling too lazy to read a book, so I popped the first tape into an old boom box I've had lying around since the '80s. I didn't stop listening until I'd finished the last tape at eleven the next morning. Yes, Jane, I thought, I might be able to make some "$" from this.

At first I was tempted to do a total rewrite: tell it in a more traditional style, but every time I tried, it lost the original punch of Jane's voice and died. In the end I let it stand, doing little more than excising the "ah"s and "um"s and the occasional mispronounced word. I left her colorful and sometimes non-grammatical prose the way I found it. I *did* rearrange a bit. I've spared you most of the "No, wait, I forgot, before that we were already…" stuff and put it all in chronological order.

Jane is remarkably honest in her admissions of her failings, but sometimes I wonder if she isn't being too modest. She says throughout the tapes how ugly she is. Well, I met her, and though she was no Scarlett Johansson, she was by no means ugly. She had the kind of broad-faced, rugged good looks you associate with frontierswomen and female fire-fighters.

Other than that, the document is what it is. If you choose to think of it as a work of fiction, I'm sure my publishers won't mind. If you take it as fact, well then, maybe you too will find a cave in the hills one day and have an amazing adventure.

And if you do, send me a tape.

Nathan Long
Hollywood, CA
March 2011

PS. No, her name isn't really Jane Carver, so don't go digging in the Coral Gables phone book.

CHAPTER ONE

HUNTED!

'd just killed a man in Panorama City and the cops were on my trail.

No wait. Let me go back a bit. I'd been having a drink at the Fly By Nightclub, this biker joint just the Panorama City-side of the 405 from Van Nuys airport. Panorama City is nothing but ten square blocks of North Valley strip-mall hell, but I liked the Fly By Night: Merle Haggard and AC/DC on the jukebox, a guy named Mike behind the bar, a couple of pool tables, and signs on the bathroom doors that said Pointers and Setters. Homey, relaxing.

At least it was until this damn fool started trying to get into my jeans. You can't hate a guy for asking, not the way I look, and sometimes, some days, with the right guy, with the right line of bullshit, I can be mighty obliging. Hell, I'll even help him with the buttons. But this was the wrong guy, on the wrong day, with entirely the wrong line of bullshit. So I told him, politely, but with a look in my eye that a sober man should have read, no thank you. Well, he didn't listen, and *that* you can hate a man for.

He kept piling it on. "Come on, sweetcheeks, who you kiddin'? When you had better'n me? I'll take you outta this world."

"Brother, I said no."

"Damnit girl, you got enough ass for every man in this bar with some left over for seconds. You can't spare ol' Dutch a piece?"

I don't mind telling you my teeth were beginning to set a little on edge. But this being California and the Three Strikes law being in effect, and me having two strikes and a foul tip against me, I put my hands in my pockets and tried to dodge him for the rest of the night.

Some things you just can't dodge. A little later I went out to the parking lot for a smoke, since you can't smoke inside in California anymore, not even in a biker bar. The fool followed me out. There I was, sitting on my fat-boy, Baby, smoking what I didn't know was going to be the last Marlboro of my life, when Digby the Idiot Boy comes up behind me, slides his hand down the back of my jeans, and squeezes my ass.

Now you can say all you want to me. Sticks and stones and all that, but no man, or woman for that matter, puts hands on me without an invitation. It's not a code or a creed or something I even think about. It just sets me off, and when I get my mad-on the world turns red and hot and Jane isn't driving the bus anymore. I punched him once. Once.

I swear I was aiming for his face. He just jumped or something. I caught him in the throat instead, a picture perfect kill strike just like they taught me in Airborne Ranger training. It worked. I heard something crack and red spit sprayed out of his mouth. He hit the ground like a pair of empty jeans.

"Fuck." I knelt beside him, shook him. "Hey, buddy. Hey Dutch." I checked his pulse, but I knew he was dead. You see it once, it stays with you.

I'm just too fucking big for this world. Any other girl would have hit that guy and maybe bruised his neck a little, or if she was lucky, and really connected, she might have sent him to the hospital. Me, I killed him. A murder rap. My life was over. And just when I was getting things back together.

Somebody was shouting. I looked up. In the parking lot of the 7-Eleven a street guy with a squeegee and a bottle of Windex was pointing at me. "Hey, bitch! Hey! Leave him be! I saw you! You robbin' him now too?"

Behind him some rich kids standing next to their SUV were staring at me. The girl was tugging on the guy, trying to pull him into the truck, but he waved her off, dialing his cell-phone, all jittery. "It's okay. It's okay. I'm calling the cops."

People on the street were turning. A couple of guys stepped out of the bar, coming toward me. It just wasn't going to look like self defense. Not with the dead guy unarmed and me with my record. I fired up Baby and rode.

**

The cops got the dragnet on me before I made fifteen blocks. Gum-ball lights were flashing down every street I turned on. Pretty quick they had me hemmed in south of Ventura Boulevard, chasing my tail in the twisty suburban hills of Tarzana.

They almost caught me near Winnetka and Wells. I was burning down a side street when a prowler with his lights off roared out of an alley, right on my tail pipe. He was trying to nudge me, which the cops ain't supposed to do with bikes, but hey, bikers ain't citizens, right? Two more black and whites cut off the street ahead of me.

I was boxed in but good. There was only one chance. I laid Baby over so flat I shredded my left knee—denim and skin—and fishtailed into a driveway, missing a parked car by a gnat's ass. I almost ditched when Baby's back wheel slipped on the front lawn, but I muscled him back under control and gunned it along the side of the house. I heard crunching metal behind me. Guess the cop didn't have a gnat's ass to spare.

I barreled into a back yard, ducked a clothesline and swerved to miss a swingset, then rode down a flimsy, white picket fence. I hit an alley and lit out again.

I kept taking the up-turns, hoping to find some little rabbit-run that would take me over the mountains and down onto Highway One where I'd hitch a ride to Mexico and points south. What I found was a dead end, way at the top of Vanalden. Before I had time to turn around and find a better street, I heard the sirens coming up the hill behind me.

I ditched Baby in some yuppie's kidney-shaped pool. It was a tearful good-bye. I kissed him on the gas cap and lowered him into the deep end without a splash. That bike had taken me back and forth across this country more times than I could remember and had been more faithful than any lover or friend had ever been, even Big Don. Don had died on me, the fucker.

I ran into the scrub and dirt of the Topanga mountains.

With a little luck I might have made it. If a swamp-trash country girl like me couldn't elude LA flatfoots in the biggest chunk of wild land inside the city, I'd give up all my merit badges. Unfortunately, I don't have any luck. Never have. They brought dogs. And helicopters.

I nearly pissed myself. Too many episodes of *COPS* I guess. You know it's over when they bring the choppers. Two big whirly-birds came up from the valley and started cutting a huge grid pattern over my head. Their search-lights criss-crossed the scrubby hills, turning 'em white as sugar. It looked like the lights at a big Hollywood premier, only upside down. I didn't want to be the star of this premier.

I ran, splashing through streams so the dogs would lose me, keeping under trees so the choppers wouldn't see me, but pretty soon those years of Marlbo-ros caught up with me and my lungs felt like some midget with a chainsaw was trying to cut his way out of my chest. The choppers were way off and I couldn't hear the dogs so I ducked into a thick clump of bushes to catch my breath.

Funny, as soon as I stopped, that dead guy caught up to me. I guess I'd been running so fast my brain had lagged behind like a trailer hitched to a car with a piece of rope. Now that I slowed down that trailer slammed into my brain.

I'd killed a guy! I shook like I had a fever, like his corpse had just wrapped its cold, dead arms around me. That poor slob didn't have his life anymore because of me. Sure I owed him a punch in the mouth for what he did, but he didn't deserve to die.

I started to choke up. Then I got mad. How could I feel sorry for some dumb, drunk, grab-ass son-of-a-bitch? Fuck him. Fuck him for not ducking. Fuck him for dying so easy. And most of all, fuck him for *ruining my life!*

Shit, I was going to cry after all.

Barking bounced off the rocks. The dogs had my scent again. I peeked out. Flashlights were swinging through the trees about twenty yards away. The choppers were turning my way. I guess I could have just stayed where I was and waited for the dogs to find me. I mean, what was I running to anyway? But giving up never occurred to me. Just the *idea* of being cooped up in prison for the rest of my life made my chest tighten up. I'd done juvie time and county time, but hard time? I'd never survive. I'd rather die right here, swinging and shouting, than be trapped inside four walls for forty years.

I searched around, shaking with panic, looking for a tree, a big rock, any-thing. A shadow caught my eye up the hill from me. Fifteen feet up was a long, narrow patch of dark, sandwiched between two slanting slabs of rock. A cave? Probably not, but I was all out of options. I scrambled up the slope as fast as my shaking arms and legs could carry me.

It *was* a cave. I stopped at the entrance even though I could smell the dogs behind me. It was pretty cramped in there, and dark. I don't like cramped, dark places. Then again, jail is pretty cramped and dark. Still I hemmed and hawed. It was like cutting off my head to stop gangrene from spreading to my body. I couldn't do it. I couldn't go in there.

I heard cop shoes, dogs and radios behind me. Decision made. I dove in.

The tunnel wound up and back, shrinking as it went. I was sweating stink like yesterday's fish. I clawed my way through the dark, wishing, not for the first time, that I was a flat-chested, no-assed little pipsqueak that nobody ever paid any attention to.

Ten feet in, the entrance disappeared back around a twist in the passage. The light went with it. Pitch black. I couldn't see forward or back. I could barely turn my head to look. It was tighter than a coffin in there. I couldn't breathe. I couldn't think. I couldn't move. If it hadn't been for the sound of dogs snuffling behind me I think I might have froze there forever, but the thought of sharp teeth tearing into my ankles got me moving again.

A few feet later the darkness wasn't so total anymore. Above and ahead I saw a pale green light, or almost saw it. It was so faint it disappeared when you looked right at it. Moonlight? No moon tonight. Street light? Was I coming up in somebody's basement? Whatever it was, I was all for light. Trapped is bad. Trapped and blind gives me the crawlies.

I followed the ghost light and finally pushed through a keyhole opening halfway up a rock wall. The tightest squeeze yet. I had to get my shoulders in one at a time, and then my tits and hips, but finally I popped out the other side into a low, tent-shaped space with a sandy floor, which I could see 'cause it was lit by a strange glow coming from the far end. It was some kind of gadget, half buried in the sand. I crawled closer. It looked like a little clock. It was silver, with hood-ornament fins curving out from its sides, but where the clock face should have been it had a round, glowing jewel the color of lemonade.

I didn't get much time to look at it. Suddenly the tiny space was full of barking echoes, ping-ponging off the walls and the inside of my brain. I turned. German Shepherds were squeezing through the keyhole and jumping at me.

I stepped back.

They leaped.

I fell.

My hand touched the glowing silver clock thing.

Somebody hit me with a building. No, it just felt that way, like a giant had grabbed me by the leather jacket and yanked me through a thick velvet curtain, into... where? It was ice cold, and blacker than ten caves. Weird voices were jabbering at me in some gobbledygook I couldn't understand, and that giant kept yanking at me, harder, and harder, and...

And then I blacked out.

CHAPTER TWO

STRANDED!

I woke up flat on my back with the bed-spins so bad it reminded me of the time in high school my friend Briana made piña coladas with Southern Comfort and we drank two pitchers.

Where was I, anyway? Did the cops put me in a body bag? It felt like it. It was hot, and the air was thick and dusty in my nose. The color above me couldn't be the sky. It was blue, but the kind of deep blue you get with sapphires or bottles of fancy water… or plastic tarps.

I started to panic. I was weak, but I had to thrash around and let 'em know I wasn't dead. Being buried alive was right up there with caves and prison in my catalog of claustrophobic no-nos.

Just as I lifted my hands to start pushing at the body bag an insect buzzed past my nose, and a fluffy white cloud edged into the corner of my vision. That Ty-D-Bol blue *was* the sky. What the hell?

I struggled up, rubbing my eyes. Maybe my vision was fucked up. That glowing gem could have damaged… I looked around and seized up like an engine block with sand in the pistons. My eyeballs did a slow right-to-left over the scariest landscape I'd ever seen. Not that there was actually anything outright horrifying about it; as far as visuals went it was pretty easy on the

9

eyes, but, well, let me lay it out.

I was lying on a stone disk the size of a helicopter landing pad, in the middle of a wide prairie of knee high grass with stalks the blue of a junkie's veins and pointy flowers the size and color of a match flame. Stones stuck up out of the grass, some in straight lines that made me think there must have been a building or a town built around the disk a few centuries back. Beyond the stones, the prairie humped over some low hills to the horizon, where white-capped mountains faded away to purple.

Like I said, pretty. The thing that scared the living piss out of me was that every single piece of it was wrong. All wrong. I couldn't say exactly how. I ain't a scientist. But I knew, like you know your red 1987 Ford pick-up from somebody else's red 1987 Ford pick-up without having to look twice, that I wasn't on good old terra firma anymore.

The sun was wrong: too big, too orange. The horizon was wrong: it didn't go far enough away. The plants—I know there are blue plants on earth, but not these plants. Even the air was wrong. It filled my lungs too much. And it smelled off, sharp, like a gun battle in a swimming pool. It wasn't right, none of it, and it made me shake so hard my teeth rattled.

After a while my brain unlocked a little, and let me notice more than just the scenery. First off, I was naked. I looked around for my clothes. Not there. But I found something else. Right behind me, sunk into the center of the stone disk, was a platter-sized, lemonade-colored gem, big brother to the one in the clock thing in the cave.

Well, I can put two and two together. I'd touched the green gem on the clock and *poof*, I landed here. Maybe the thing was a teleporter, like in *Star Trek*. Was it going to be that easy? I reached down for it, then stopped. Did I really want to go back to that cave with the cops and the dogs? If the alternative was staying… wherever the fuck this was? Hell yes! I slapped the gem and waited to get yanked back to earth.

Another fly zipped past my ear. The too-big sun kept toasting my shoulders. I was still here, wherever here was. I took a closer look at the gem, cupping my hands around my eyes to block out the sun. It didn't glow. Not even a little. It was dead.

I haven't cried since my first week in boot-camp. My friends call me Iron Jane because nothing gets to me, not death, not loss, not old movies, but as I looked around at that big, empty prairie and it sunk in how alone I was and how far from home, I ain't ashamed to say that I curled up with my cheek on the smooth face of that gem and bawled like a baby.

***

I must have cried myself to sleep, 'cause I woke up to a ground-shaking rumble that was getting louder by the second. I snapped my head up and looked around, blinking the sleep out of my eyes and scanning for what was making the racket.

A big dust cloud was racing my way, filled with—I didn't know what. I could see what looked like ostriches with giant parrot beaks, people with funny-shaped heads and right arms twice as big as their left ones, a chunky thing on wheels, splotches of red and purple, and bright flashes of steel. And it was all coming right at me.

I hopped up—and nearly had a coronary. My leap lifted me nearly six feet in the air! I face-planted in the tall grass beside the stone disk and lay there, heart jackhammering. What the fuck? No one could jump that high! Not without a running start and special sneakers!

I didn't have time to think about it. The crowd of whatever-they-were was so close I could smell 'em; a weird mix of man sweat and birdcage funk. I peeked over the edge of the disk in time to see the whole circus roar past not ten feet from my hiding place. They weren't coming for me after all. They were too busy fighting each other.

Now I could sort all the parts out. It was a bunch of purple guys swinging swords and riding big, two-legged birds. Sure, why not. Happens every day.

Except for being purple, the guys weren't quite as weird as I'd first thought. Their funny-shaped heads turned out to be funny hair-cuts: sumo top-knots, mohawks, braids and fancy shave-jobs. What I'd thought were giant, mutated right arms were actually thick sleeves of scaly, bronze-looking armor that covered their sword arms. Besides that they were nearly naked. Just the sleeve and a few other scraps of armor covering their groins, shins and knees, all held in place by leather harnesses like something out of an SM club. Capes of red or gold flapped around their shoulders, and they waved around long thin swords with lots of curly metal bits protecting the grip. Most of the swords were red with blood.

Their mounts were like emus on steroids, shaggy monsters with gray and black feathers, and powerful legs that ended in heavy claws big enough to close around my chest. They had useless little wings almost hidden under their saddles, and mean-eyed, turtle-beaked heads as big as air condition-ers. And to make them look even more like a cross between a T-rex and an ostrich, they had shrunken little arms dangling from their chests like broken doll parts, as weak and pointless as their wings.

Men and birds were kicking the crap out of each other, claws slashing, beaks snapping, swords clashing. It took me a second to make a guess at what was happening, and by then it was almost over.

The guys in the red cloaks were protecting a fancy coach drawn by four of the massive birds. The guys in the gold cloaks were trying to stop the coach, and were handing the red-cloaks their collective asses. There were more of the gold-cloaks, and they knew their stuff, turning their big birds on a dime and tagging the poor red-cloaks at will. I looked back the way they'd come. Dead red-cloaks all the way to the horizon. No gold.

I turned back in time to catch the big finish. The coach's four harnessed birds, panicking in the middle of the brawl, turned too sharply. The coach heeled over on a big rock and slammed to the ground on its side. The wooden tang holding the birds to it snapped and, still harnessed together, they ripped free and sprinted for the horizon.

After that it was a slaughter. The gold-cloaks weren't going to let the red-cloaks off with just a whipping. They rode down every last one of those poor bastards and chopped them to pieces. It turned my stomach. They might have been purple aliens, but their screams were plenty human.

While his riders finished mopping up, the leader of the gold-cloaks, a square-jawed superhero with a pencil-thin moustache, a flopped-over mo-hawk, and two pigtails hanging down in front of his ears like a yeshiva boy, climbed onto the coach. You could tell he was the leader. One, 'cause his guys ducked their heads whenever he gave an order, and two, 'cause his shit was flashier: zigzag designs on his cloak, gold sleeve armor instead of bronze, jewels all over his sword.

When he got to the top of the coach—which was the side, if you see what I'm saying—he wrenched open the door. A little long-haired purple guy in white popped up like a jack-in-the-box and flailed around with a dagger. Square-Jaw hardly blinked; a casual backhand with his sword and Long-Hair dropped back into the coach with a thump.

Square-Jaw grinned. His teeth were as white and straight as a row of sugar cubes. He reached down into the coach and lifted somebody out by the wrist. For a second I thought it was Long-Hair again, 'cause this one had long hair too, but when square-jaw lifted her a little higher I saw there were one or two differences.

She was your standard-issue hot babe, except in purple. Not exactly my type. When I go for gals, which ain't that often—I'd been gay-for-the-stay in a couple of young women's correctionals in my youth—I tend to go for big-ass, baby's-got-back chicks. This gal was a mite too delicate for me, but it wasn't hard to figure why Square-Jaw had the hots for her. Even screaming and trying to kick his teeth in, I could see she had the goods: pin-up body in a tiny yellow bikini-top and loin-cloth outfit, long black hair, pouty lips. The whole package in a handy, carry-out size.

Square-Jaw laughed off her attacks and threw her over his shoulder. He looked down into the coach again, like he was making sure Long-Hair was dead, then shot a glance around at the empty prairie. He shrugged. I read him like he was Marcel Marceau: "Why bother, he's a dead man anyway." He hopped back on his mount, signaled his gang, and off they rode, back the way they'd come.

Maybe you're wondering why I didn't leap into the fray and rescue the damsel in distress. Well, I'll tell you. I'm not an idiot, that's why. I've never minded a scrap, but naked and unarmed against the Ginsu clan wasn't my idea of good odds, and besides, it was all coming over the plate a bit fast, new planet, new gravity, giant birds, guys out of an episode of *Xena: Warrior Princess*. And anyway, I hardly had a chance to react. It was over in less than a minute.

The part I don't have an excuse for is why I didn't try to help the dying red-cloaks as soon as Square-Jaw and his posse had giddi-upped off back the way they came. I could hear the poor guys moaning and sobbing, but I just stayed where I was, crouched behind the stone disk with my jaw hanging open.

Maybe I'd seen too many movies where the hero thinks the monster's dead and then something rips out of its stomach and eats the guy's face off. Whatever. I was chicken, and some of those guys probably died because of it. By the time I finally got myself moving, clouds of alien flies were settling over them for a mid-day blood binge.

Getting to the guys was like trying to walk on a trampoline. I kept springing up twice as high as I expected, and crashing on every part of my anatomy except my feet. At least I fell down as lightly as I stepped, so I didn't get more than a few cuts and scratches. By the time I'd reached the killing ground, I'd adjusted my walk to a wobbly glide.

I was way too late. The one guy who was still breathing when I found him died by the time I found anything to bind the gushing wound in his leg with. I felt like a fucking idiot.

Up close the dead guys looked pretty damn human. Too human. Back in the rangers I'd had to help clean up a helicopter crash after a training exercise went wrong. A lot of these guys were just as young as those kids had been, and they'd died just as scared. I decided I didn't like Square-Jaw too much.

What made it worse was that they looked like kids I knew. Hell, back in my punk-rock run-away days most of my friends had haircuts just like these guys. Except for the purple skin and pointed ears, I wouldn't have given any of them a second look walking down Hollywood Boulevard. Their eyes were a little longer, their canines a little sharper, and they were a tad shorter than the average American guy, but they had hair where we have hair, and five fingers on each hand and five toes on each foot, and everything else where you'd expect to find it.

This nearly freaked me out more than all the rest of it. Weren't aliens supposed to be more, uh, alien? They always were in the movies. Shows you how much I know about the universe.

I looked at the coach. There was one guy left to check on. Long-Hair. What was I supposed to do if he was still alive? Help him out? He probably still had that dagger on him. I didn't want him stabbing first and asking questions later. On the other hand, if I was stuck here, I'd have to meet the natives sooner or later, and one-on-one with some wounded sap with a dagger was probably better odds then alone against a healthy, well-armed posse. I snatched up one of the fancy swords and hopped up onto the overturned coach.

Or at least I tried to. My leap overshot it and I hit the ground on the far side. At least I was getting better at landing. I tried again with a more controlled leap and dropped softly beside the open coach door.

I looked down inside. Overstuffed red leather benches, scads of throw pillows in rich fabrics, candleholders on the side panels. Of course everything was topsy turvy; the pillows thrown against the opposite wall and smeared with food from a bronze tray that had been dented in the wreck.

Lying in the middle of all this high-class debris, with a bloody hand to his wounded head like one of the tortured saints from the stained-glass windows back at Saint Sebastian's, was the most beautiful boy I'd ever seen.

His mane of black hair was spread out like a halo around the face of some

Roman emperor's boy-toy; high cheekbones, straight nose, and lips like Elvis at nineteen. His body continued the beauty parade. He was built like a ballet dancer, with flawless skin a shade darker than the chick Square-Jaw had dragged off, and he covered it only a little more than she did. He wore a flimsy white, ankle-length, sleeveless vest thing, open in front, and a tiny white silk loincloth that made it pretty clear that these guys were human all the way down to the important parts. And how!

He wasn't my usual type anymore than the gal was. I tend to like a guy who can make me feel delicate. Big Don had been six four and about a yard and a half wide, and when I was in his arms I'd felt protected from the whole rotten world. But I've got what you might call varied tastes. I like to sample the whole buffet, and sometimes I want to be the one who wraps her arms around some poor little boy and tells him everything's going to be alright.

And then screw his brains out.

The kid moaned. His long lashes fluttered and a pair of pale violet eyes looked up at me. That gaze was like an electric shock. It made my mouth dry. It made my skin prickle. It made my... well I'll spare you the gory details. Let's just say that any worries I'd had about making friends with the natives went right out the window.

I gave a little wave, just to show I was friendly. "You okay?"

He frowned like he didn't understand. "Who are you?" His voice was soft and clear, like a choir boy's. "Come you to aid me or to kill me?"

Well, of course he didn't understand. The odds of him speaking English were... But wait a minute. I'd just understood him. It wasn't English, but I knew what he was saying.

Suddenly I realized that I had a whole new language in my head just waiting for me to take it out of the box and plug it in. Where the hell did that come from? Then I remembered the babble of voices that went rushing through my mind after I'd touched the jewel in the cave. That gizmo wasn't just a transporter, it was a translator too, a goddamn tourist's dream! Instant travel, and you speak the language perfectly when you get there. Who the hell thought this stuff up? It sure wasn't these sword swinging refugees from a Conan movie. What was up with this place?

Long-Hair started groping around for his dagger without taking his eyes off me. "Speak, sir. You alarm me with your silence."

I snapped out of it, "Uh, aid. I mean I'm here to aid you." That jabber tumbled out of my lips like I'd been born speaking it. It was like that sensation when you realize you no longer have to think about all the steps of shifting gears, you're just doing it automatically.

I dropped into the coach and knelt beside him. It was dark in there. It took me a second to adjust. I squinted at his eyes first. A concussion would have been the icing on the cake. He looked okay. Both pupils were the same size.

I could see why Square-Jaw had left him for dead though. He was as bloody as a pro wrestler at the end of a steel cage match—head wounds always look like a splatter movie—but the cut didn't go all the way to the bone and he'd slowed the bleeding by keeping his hand pressed over it. He was seeping, not gushing. That was a good thing.

I breathed again. "How you feelin'? Any other wounds?"

"I…" Suddenly he jerked like somebody'd zapped him with a cattle prod. He tried to sit up. "Wen-Jhai! Beloved! Where—"

I pushed him back down. "Sorry, brother. She's gone. The big guy with the teeth took her."

He struggled against my hand. "But then we must—"

"You ain't doin' nothin'. You're too hurt and… and your pals…" I didn't know how to say it.

He did. "Dead?"

I nodded. He closed his eyes in pain. "The butcher."

"The quicker we get you patched up, the quicker you can go after him. Now, you hurt anywhere else?" I almost laughed, listening to myself. All of a sudden I was coming on like some super para-med, like I knew what I was doing. Stupid, I know, but the minute I started to take care of this guy I calmed down. Works every time, doesn't it? As soon as you've got somebody else worse off than you, you start trying to solve all their problems and forget about your own. Probably why so many fucked-up people become guidance counselors and psychiatrists.

He sighed. "You are kind, sir." He raised a feeble hand. "Only my arm. I seem to have fallen on it…" He stopped, staring at my boobs. "Sir! You are a woman! And… unclothed."

"Uh-huh. Good eyes."

"But…but… My apologies, mistress. My wound must have disturbed my sight. I thought…"

"It ain't the first time, pal. Don't worry about it."

"No no, forgive me for mistaking you. 'Tis unpardonable. And you are in distress. Did those ruffians…?" He turned his head so he wouldn't have to look at me. "Please mistress, help yourself to a garment."

"Hey, I ain't freezin'. We gotta fix you up first."

He bumped his arm and turned several shades lighter than his girlfriend. He gasped. "Very well. Is there a man in your party who might assist me?"

What was I, chopped liver? "You don't want my help?"

"I'm afraid I require more than tender words and gentle ministrations, mistress. With my head and this arm, I may not be able to climb out of the coach on my own."

"Pal, I could probably fold you up and put you in my pocket, if I had a pocket. I'm the only one here, so maybe you should let me have a look at you." I reached across him to pull his matted hair away from his wound. He jumped again, this time looking at my arm.

"By the Seven, *are* you a woman?"

So my arms were bigger than his. My arms are bigger than a lot of guys'. Hitting the iron relaxes me. "Brother, what planet are you from?"

Well, duh. Now that I thought about it, I was the one from another planet, and if all the chicks around here looked like Miss Teeny-Bikini, I guess I could see why he was a trifle confused. I sighed. "Sorry. Don't freak out. I'm not from around here, but I am a woman, and I'm here to help you. You got a needle and thread?"

"In my lady's baggage, perhaps, but you don't mean to…"

"Relax pal, I used to sew leather wallets in juvie crafts class. This ain't much different."

I jumped back out of the coach and searched through the jumble of luggage that had fallen from the roof-rack during the crash. There were big wooden trunks wrapped with iron bands, and fancier chests made of polished woods and decorated with six-sided symbols. Most had smashed, and all kinds of rich fabrics and fine china were spilling out. I dug through clothes, jewelry, funny-shaped crockery. Finally I found a little gold sewing kit in the shape of some cute animal I'd never seen before.

Back in the coach I cleaned Long-Hair's cut with water from a cracked clay jug, doused my needle and thread in some liquor that smelled like cranberries and Everclear, and sewed him up, then tore his gauzy kaftan into wide strips and tied it around his head. It made an ugly turban that unfortunately hid a lot of that beautiful hair. I made the splint by smashing up a fancy wooden make-up box and binding two long slats to his arm.

He was pretty brave under my "tender ministrations," only flinching and whimpering a little, and never complaining. He reminded me of a kid too proud to let on how scared he was, though he thinks his life's blood is spilling out of him—which in his case it was.

He was less co-operative when it came time to get him out of the coach. "I cannot allow it, mistress. No true Dhanan would permit a woman to lift a burden as heavy as myself. And am I so poor a man that I must beg assistance in the first place?"

Well, nobody can say I butt in when I'm not wanted. I shrugged. "Hey, I ain't stoppin' you. Go on, take a crack at it."

He stood up, jaw set—and sat right back down again, sheet-white, his eyes rolling up in his head. "A passing weakness. If you will allow me a moment to recover."

I crossed my arms. "Dude, you need a week in bed watching game shows, with someone who knows a hell of a lot more than me takin' care of you. We gotta get you home."

I put an arm around his waist. He flinched from my bare skin. "Mistress, I protest. I weigh too much…"

What a little priss. I slung him over my shoulder, pulled myself out of the coach one-handed, then eased us both down to the ground and sat him down, his back propped against one of the trunks. His eyes were as round as poker chips.

"By the Seven, mistress, such strength is impossible! Why, you carry me like so many bedclothes. How do you come by this…" He gasped and looked around at the carnage. His face sagged like somebody had pulled the bones out of it. "Lau. Sil. Cousins." He put his head in his hands.

I didn't know where to look. I never do when people get all emotional. After a while he stopped snorfing and wiped his nose on the back of his hand. "My apologies, mistress. I dishonor brave men with these tears. They were true Dhanans. They would never have wept…"

He stopped, staring at me in the sunlight. "Mistress, you are…" He went pale and started trying to back away from me, eyes wide, but since he was already pressed against one of the trunks, so all he did was dig grooves in the dirt with his heels.

I raised an eyebrow. "What's the matter now?"

He made a weird hand motion at me. He put his thumb and middle finger together and touched them to his left eye, his right eye and then his mouth. "Begone, mistress demon. I do not wish to travel yet to the lands of the dead."

"Demon? I ain't no demon. I ain't even a Hell's Angel."

"Tease me not, tormentor. Have you not a demon's dead pink skin, its hair of flame, it's green eyes? Do you not have a demon's unnatural strength and size?"

I laughed. Maybe I should have been insulted at the less than flattering description, but it was too funny. So hell on this planet was full of big, pink, red-headed chicks? Pretty much what Father Flanagan always told me. "Buddy, calm down. I promise I'm no demon. I'm flesh and blood, just like you." Well, okay, not just like him. He was an alien, but you know what I mean. I held out my arm. "Go on. Pinch me."

He shrank away. "If you be no demon, explain yourself. What are you? From where do you come?"

That was a tricky one. Did I tell him I was an alien from outer space? Not smart. I'd probably be taken to the local version of Area 51 and get dissected. But telling him I came from "across the big water" was risky too. These guys probably knew exactly who lived across the big water, and it was a good bet it wasn't dixie-fried biker gals. I decided to play dumb. "I don't know. I woke up on that stone there, right before you were attacked, and I can't remember anything before that. Do you know where I came from?"

He looked toward the stone disk and froze, then the weird eye-touching motion again. "So strong. Could you be...? By the Seven, that is worse even than..." He trailed off.

I stepped forward. "Come on, pal. Don't leave me hanging. What do you mean? What's worse? Worse than what?"

He shook his head. "No man speaks of this."

He wasn't putting me off that easily. He knew what the stone disk was. My heart thumped. Maybe he knew how to get me back home. "Bro, if you know something, some way to get me back to my own people..."

Suddenly there was an edge in his voice. "I know nothing. Be silent."

"Listen, you little pipsqueak. I'm only asking a civil..."

"Do you dare speak to me this way?"

"I just saved your life, pal. I'll talk to you anyway I damn well please."

That made him pause. He nodded. "Forgive me, mistress, you are correct. That was ungracious. I owe you a debt I cannot repay. But there is danger here. We must leave quickly."

"Not unless your house is right around the corner. You need to eat and rest first. You lost a lot of blood."

He scanned the horizon. "Impossible. We cannot wait. There is food in that chest. Help me fill a pack and I will eat as we walk."

We? That was twice now he'd said we. "Uh… I'm coming with you?"

"You may go where you wish, but in exchange for your assistance, I will gladly offer you what meager hospitality I can, though as things stand, this may be the extent of it."

I dragged the chest he'd pointed to from the pile. He looked sadly around at the wreckage and the slaughter. "'Tis unthinkable to leave good men unburied, but if we stay we will soon join them. Kedac-Zir will pay for this."

I took a pack from a bird saddle and started filling it with stuff from the chest; strange fruits—or vegetables maybe, I couldn't tell—little round yellow ones, long twisty white ones, like curly-cue string beans, sweet- smelling bread, cold cuts, little meat pies with crust the color of boiled lobster, a clay jar sealed with wax that sloshed when I moved it. "So what was all this about, anyway?" I asked. "Why did those guys attack you and take that girl?"

"She is no mere girl. She is the Aldhanshai Wen-Jhai, daughter of our Aldhanan, Kor-Har, the ruler of Ora, the greatest nation on Waar. She is…was, my betrothed. The love of my life. He who stole her is Kedac-Zir, Dhanan of Kalnah, and Kir-Dhanan of all Ora. I am Sai-Far, son of Shen-Far, Dhanan of Sensa."

Well, that all went in one ear and out the other. The only thing that stuck was that his name was Sai something. I stuck out a hand. "Jane Carver, of…" I remembered just in time. "Of I don't know."

Sai bowed where he was sitting and crossed his wrists like they were chained. "Your servant."

"But why did he attack you?"

He sighed. "Uncivilized barbarians that we are in Ora, we continue an old custom that should have died out in the dark ages; "The Sanfallah", or to give it a truer name, the bride-napping. Though my family and Wen-Jhai's had both approved the marriage, custom dictates that I must come to her father's castle like a brigand, duel with her father—the Aldhanan no less—and drag her off to my lands, defending my right to have her against all comers."

I passed him some of the meat pies and veggies. "Eat. You gotta get your strength back."

He took the chow, but offered some back to me. "And you? Do you not hunger?"

I hadn't realized it 'til then, but I did hunger. I hungered like dammit.

Traveling light-years in a second, or whatever I'd done, sure built up a powerful appetite.

I was worried that the grub might kill me, being from another planet and all, but I was going to die slow and painful anyway if I didn't eat. I'll take quick and painful any day. I nibbled one of the meat pies. The meat tasted like pumpkin. I mean it tasted like meat, but like pumpkin meat. Like cows that had been eating pumpkins. Ah hell, forget it. You try and describe a taste. I dare you. Whatever it was, it was food. I wolfed down four little pies as Sai continued his story.

"Usually the ordeal is purely ceremonial. The groom and the father touch swords, the father falls back, the groom departs with his bride as the women wail the traditional laments, and all that went as arranged. But this Kedac-Zir, the animal, decided to exercise the other part of the ritual and take Wen-Jhai from me before I brought her safely to my home."

I stopped chewing. "This was all part of some ritual? Killing all these guys? Can't you sic the law on him?"

Sai made a face. "No no. Kedac-Zir is perfectly within his rights. Here in benighted Ora we believe that a man who can't hold onto his bride doesn't deserve to keep her. Wen-Jhai is Kedac-Zir's betrothed now, unless I can reach him before the wedding and defeat him in single combat. Then she would be mine again. But as you can see, I unfortunately am a man of words, not actions. And a wounded man of words at that. She is lost to me, forever."

"Man, that blows chunks." Poor kid. I guess it doesn't matter where you go in the universe, the jocks still pick on the brains.

He nodded. "I know not this phrase, but your meaning is clear, and true. When news of this defeat reaches home I will not be welcome in my father's house. To have lost my bride is one thing. Not to have died defending her is unforgivable. I will be scorned by society. Perhaps I will enter the priesthood."

He closed his eyes. I worried for a second, but he was still breathing, so I let him be. I guess talking so much had worn him out.

It was at that moment, sitting in the middle of a bunch of dead purple guys and their luggage, eating strange food and talking to an honest-to-god alien that it all caught up to me. I thought, "Well I guess I ain't goin' to jail any time soon," and that was it. I started laughing so hard I couldn't breathe, that laughter where your chest hurts and no sound comes out.

I guess you had to be there. Okay, maybe it wasn't funny, not even then.

Maybe I was just hysterical. Sai sure didn't appreciate it. He opened his eyes and raised an eyebrow. "Does my plight amuse you?"

I shook my head and tried to talk through the spasms. "My plight... Not yours... My plight's amusing the hell out of me."

It took me a second to stop chuckling. I could see Sai steal a look at all my jiggling flesh. He looked away, as embarrassed, and waved toward the trunks. "Mistress, it pains me to see you... distressed in this way. Please. My lady's garments will only go to waste in this desert. Take whatever you like."

He was right. I needed some duds. If we were heading for polite society I couldn't be walking around with my skin hanging out—not all of it anyway. "Good plan, bro. You just rest up a bit and I'll make myself decent."

He nodded wearily and closed his eyes.

I glanced through Sai's fiancée's stuff. Not a chance. The waist of one of her fancy loincloths wouldn't have fit around one of my thighs, let alone my hips. And the tops? Forget it. It would have been like trying to fit footballs into egg cups. Time to get practical. This planet seemed to be a place where fights happened at the drop of a hat. I gave up on the frilly stuff and turned to the dead guys.

First I tried out some of the swords. I didn't know bad from good. I just picked the one that felt best in my hand. They were all as light as toys. More gravity problems. I'd just have to get used to it. Next I found a dead guy close to my build and stripped off his harness, armor and loincloth. It was all a little sticky and stinky. There wasn't much to do about the armor or the harness, but I rinsed the loincloth in water from a little wooden keg. I have *some* standards.

The harness went on no problem. It was adjustable, with buckles and cinches and rawhide ties. The armored sleeve was a good fit too. It was leather, sewn over with overlapping metal scales, and covered my arm up to my neck and all of my right boob. Or at least it would have if I'd been a man. As it was I had to leave a strap loose to make room.

And speaking of boobs, while I was making my adjustments, I noticed that the lighter gravity had an unforeseen plus; my breasts now sat higher than they'd been when I was sixteen and the envy of the girl's locker room. I smiled. I might be living in some bad sci-fi nightmare, but this I could get used to.

I was finishing off my outfit with a pair of boots and shin guards from another, smaller guy, when Sai woke up. He choked. "Mistress Jae-En, what

JANE CARVER OF WAAR « 23

have you…? Please, mistress. This is unseemly. You cannot…" He stopped, lifting his head, listening. I heard it too. A rumble, like the one I'd woken up to earlier. We looked up. Coming across the plain at a run were the four harnessed birds from the coach. They'd come back.

I smiled. "How's that for luck. We've got a ride."

"No, Mistress Jae-En, this is no luck at all. This is our doom." He was looking past the approaching birds. I followed his gaze.

Far off, but closing on us fast, was a churning dust cloud, shot through with glints of steel and half hiding the forms of massive galloping beasts.

CHAPTER THREE

MONSTERS!

At first I thought they were horses and riders—okay, not horses, but some kind of powerful animals carrying big, shaggy riders. There were definitely things with four legs galloping in the dust cloud, and hairy arms hefting big-ass spears and swords, but as they got closer I got the next big shock in a long day of big shocks. Horse—or whatever—and rider were all one animal!

They reminded me of those horse-man things in *Fantasia*. Whaddaya call 'em? Cen-somethings. Except these weren't cute. Not by a country mile. The horse-part was more like an extra large tiger, low to the ground and striped yellow and eggplant purple. It had a thick, Komodo dragon tail at one end, and a squat, upright man-body at the other. Their back legs were like a cat's, strong and springy, with padded paws that left footprints bigger around than a Frisbee. Their front legs had what looked like big, lumpy clubs on the ends. I couldn't make out any more detail than that with all the dust and movement.

Their heads were huge, with wide, blunt faces like a bear's, except tiger-striped like their bodies. The striping went up into thick dreadlocks, some yellow, some purple, that hung down their wide backs.

Even with the swords and spears in their hands it took a minute for it to sink in that these weren't animals. I mean they were, but they were people too. Okay, not people, but another race. You know what I mean. *Real* aliens this time. Not guys who looked like some guy in a band with a little purple make-up. I got it when I noticed the beads and bones woven into their dreads. Apes might pick up clubs, but jewelry don't interest them much. For a second I thought that might be a good thing. If they weren't animals maybe we could negotiate, right? Then I saw some very human-looking skulls around the waist of one mean-ass mother. So much for the "We're all cousins under the skin" approach.

I'll give Sai credit. He didn't run or burst into tears. He took a sword from one of his dead buddies and painfully got to his feet. He could hardly stay upright he was so weak, but he set his jaw, used the sword for a prop and made like he wasn't going to budge.

The cen-tigers slowed as they neared us, circling us and the coach like a bunch of bikers intimidating some nice couple who've broken down in the middle of nowhere—not that I know anything about that kind of thing. The leader, a huge, scarred thug with a leather eye-patch over one eye, stopped in front of us. He was about eight feet tall, and smelled like the world's dirtiest cat box. Then, like we weren't already impressed, he reared up on his hind legs and dropped his tail to the ground to make a stable-looking tripod. Now I got why his front "legs" looked different than his back ones, and why some of these boys had two, three and even four swords strapped to their backs. Their middle limbs were some kind of multi-purpose leg/arm, and those lumpy clubs they ran on were fists with thick, callused knuckles.

Pretty snazzy—four legs when you needed speed, and four hands to swing swords with when you needed to fight. If I hadn't been so worried about keeping my skin intact right then, it would have been fascinating. As it was, I spent the time multiplying hands and swords and cen-tigers and coming up with some really depressing numbers.

Sai stepped forward, raising an open hand in what would seem to be a universal sign of peaceful intentions. "Hail, noble Aarurrh. Forgive our trespass. We were forced into your lands by our enemies. Please take what you will of our supplies and… and our dead, but leave us to withdraw and seek vengeance on these cowards who drove us to violate your borders."

It seemed like a pretty good speech to me, but One-Eye didn't think much of it. He spat insultingly close to Sai's feet and scratched himself with his left middle hand. "Aarurrh not care why you here, insect. This Aarurrh land. You pay." He had a hard time talking Sai's talk. It was like his mouth wasn't shaped right to make those kinds of noises. "You be slave for women until die. Then meat like these."

And with that he signaled to two flunkies and turned away to supervise the looting. He barked at his men in some lingo that sounded like a bear gargling razor blades. I didn't understand a word. So, my universal translator wasn't universal after all. That sucked.

Not that I needed a translator to tell me what he was saying. He motioned to some guys to grab boxes and armor, and had others start cutting up carcasses. I almost lost my cookies when I saw that they were choosing their chops and spare-ribs from both birds and men.

I tried to catch Sai's eye while our guards were putting away their swords and unhitching coils of rope. If we were going to try something now was the time, but Sai was already putting down his sword and holding out his wrists. Wounded and out of it like he was I guess that was the smart thing to do, but I felt a little let down.

The flunkies tied him up first. Nobody was watching me. These guys had no idea what my earth-strong muscles could do. If I jumped, and kept jumping, I just might get away. But while trying to decide if I could live with myself if I left poor Sai behind, and wondering how much he'd weigh me down if I slung him over my shoulder, the flunkies finished him up and grabbed me.

It probably saved my life. As they were making me look like something from Bondage Babes Monthly, I noticed some nasty little bolo-thingies hanging from their belts. I might have got a jump or two on them, but it was a good bet they would have brought me down, maybe permanently. I decided I should keep my jack-rabbit impersonation to myself. I played meek and mild as they threw me and Sai face down over the haunches of two junior members and cinched us in place with belts.

Soon after that all the baggage and dressed meat were loaded up and tied down. One-Eye gave a roar and we were loping in double file over the endless blue prairie.

***

There's a way to ride a cen-whatever-they-are. I've seen pictures. This wasn't it. My arms and face hung down one side of the smelly bastard's flanks, my legs down the other, all getting whipped by the springy stalks of the blue grass while my nose and eyes filled with gritty, alien dust and my internal organs got a brutal shiatsu from bouncing up and down on the cen-tiger's butt.

It was a long ride. The too-big sun was burning the snow caps of the far mountains candy-apple red when we finally cantered past a pair of armed Aarurrh look outs and down a trail into a wide ravine with a stream winding through it.

I was barely conscious. The endless pounding gallop had jumbled my brains to cream of wheat, so I only got impressions: trees like droopy palms hanging over the creek, a sea of leather tents spreading to the canyon walls, the smell of meat and shit, pony-sized cen-tiger kids and cen-tiger chicks with four boobs to go with their four arms trotting alongside the column staring at us, the feel of cool air as we left the dry dust of the plains. I couldn't imagine how Sai felt. Maybe he didn't feel anything. Maybe he was dead.

We stopped in the middle of the camp so One-Eye could report in with some cen-tigers standing outside a big tent. I should have been taking in details. This was the enemy's camp. I should have been noting defenses and escape routes, figuring out the chain of command, but it was dark and I could barely turn my head, let alone focus my eyes. I got nothing. My old CO, Captain MacFerson, would have been disgusted with me.

When One-Eye was done gabbing he dragged us off to a pen filled with animals that looked like those jungle pig things with the floppy snouts, only orange and shaggy and with six legs. They backed into the far corner of the pen, making an annoying "Keee keee keee!" sound and rolling their eyes. One of One-Eye's flunkies untied my bonds, which started an agonizing attack of pins and needles, and left us alone.

Finally a chance to check on Sai. His bandage was solid with dried blood and he was out cold, but he was still breathing. I couldn't do much to help him. I could hardly help myself. In fact, blissful unconsciousness was about the only thing that held my interest just then, even though, with all my aches and pains, I didn't think it would be possible to sleep.

**

The next thing I knew I was being rudely awakened. It was morning. One-Eye was dragging me and Sai out of the cage by our ankles. He turned us right-way-up, knocked the dust and pig shit—or whatever it was—off us with his big paws and shoved us ahead of him. "Go."

I could barely walk, I was so stiff and sore, but Sai could barely crawl. I got an arm around him and limped him through the crowded camp, leaning in to whisper in his ear. "How you doing, Sai? Anything broken? I mean anything new?"

He didn't look up. "It matters not."

I didn't like his attitude, but we couldn't talk anymore. We'd reached a tent. The tents of the camp were pretty much all the same, tall, five sided teepees made of a patchwork of stitched together skins (some of them too purple and human-looking for my liking) with various bits of caveman decoration, bones, skulls, feathers, painted stick figure symbols. This tent was like all the rest, if maybe a little better taken care of.

One-Eye pushed us through the flap into the smoky dimness and I found myself face to face, or actually face to boobs with my first up-close she-centiger.

CHAPTER FOUR

CAPTIVES!

Funny, even though she was a monster and all, I liked her right off. Maybe because her face reminded me of a fat old tabby named Queenie that my Aunt Cici had when I was a kid. Whatever it was, the big she-beast who was smirking at me like Mama Bear finding Goldilocks in her bed made me feel more relaxed than anything I'd come across so far on this nasty-ass planet.

Not that I had any time to bask in her warmth. One-Eye pushed in behind us, made a quick speech to Queenie, shoved Sai at her like he was a pound puppy, and fast as he could, steered me toward the back of the tent.

There, facing away from us, her four legs tucked up under her on a bed of straw and her gold and purple fur tinged red by the light of a skin lamp, was a younger, skinnier Aarurrh chick, braiding her long mane as if there were nobody in the tent but herself. One-Eye didn't like this much and got pretty stiff. He made some sort of demand, which she pointedly ignored. He repeated it, roaring, and she at last consented to look around.

I guess she was the goods as far as Aarurrh went; a face like a naughty kitten under a peek-a-boo fringe of dreads, a slim upper torso, and four perky breasts. One-Eye quivered beside me. Kitten played snooty to the limit. She gave us a lazy, half-lidded once over, then looked past us to where Queenie was squeezing Sai's muscles and checking his teeth and his head wound. I thought I saw an evil little look in Kitten's eye, and then she squealed like a school girl at a Justin Beiber concert and sprang to her feet. She rushed across the tent, snatched Sai off the ground as easy as you'd pick up a sack of groceries, and crushed him to her.

One-Eye seemed to think this wasn't part of the plan at all. He tried to get Sai away from her, pointing at me and then at Queenie. Kitten turned her hindquarters on him and started cooing to Sai and smoothing his hair and checking out his clothes like he was a new Barbie. One-Eye began complaining to Queenie. She just shrugged, as if to say, "Girls will be girls."

One-Eye glared at Kitten, but she was done with him. Growling, he stalked to the tent flap and threw it open. Standing right outside with a hand up like he was about to come in was a young, handsome—at least by giant, tiger-headed monster standards—Aarurrh. I could tell he was heart-throb material: trim, strong, and half a head taller than One-Eye. He had a face like the MGM lion and a swoop of dreadlocks that hung down over his big, brown eyes and made him look shy and sweet. Hell, if I'd been an Aarurrh, *I'd* have let him take me to the spring dance.

His magic wasn't working on One-Eye. With a roar like a Harley at full throttle, One-Eye decked Handsome with a pair of simultaneous lefts. Handsome staggered, yelping. I backed up, expecting the fur to start flying, but instead of fighting back, Handsome went down on all fours and bowed his head.

One-Eye growled and and cuffed him on the ear, then started dragging him off by the dreadlocks.

Kitten cried out and started forward, but Queenie held her back. One-Eye stopped and roared something over his shoulder that was definitely a threat, then headed off, Handsome in tow. The kid looked back and exchanged forlorn looks with Kitten as the tent flap swung shut, then Kitten exploded into tears and threw herself onto her straw bed, Sai flopping over her arm like a Raggedy Andy with half the sawdust missing.

Queenie hugged Kitten with a couple of arms and stroked her with the rest, but she didn't spend too long on it. I got the feeling this happened a lot.

I was beginning to think that everybody had forgot about me and that it might be time for a quick sneak out the door, Sai or no Sai, when Queenie turned and beckoned to me with a paw and a grin. I hesitated. Was I here to be a slave or a pet or lunch? I wanted to pick "none of the above." Queenie snagged me with a long arm and pulled me close. She started pinching my arms and both of my legs all at once. You know how I feel about being manhandled. I pushed one of her huge hands away with my little one. She laughed, impressed. She spoke the purple guys' language worse than One-Eye. "Rmmm. Damn strong, hin? Good. Get much work from you…"

Great. Warm, friendly, but still a slave driver.

***

Slave driver wasn't just a figure of speech, neither. Half an hour later I was out on the prairie digging in the dirt like I was on an Alabama chain gang.

Sai wasn't with me. Queenie'd had another look at his head wound, smeared some green muck on it and put him to bed on a pile of straw out behind her tent. I guess they didn't get slaves so often that they could afford to let one die on them.

No spa treatment for me. After a five-minute breakfast of some meat I prayed wasn't breast of purple guy, and a bitter lump of some kind of grain mash, I was trudging through the camp in a line of slaves and Aarurrh females. I checked out the other slaves. All purple guys like Sai. They didn't check me out. They just stared straight ahead, glassy-eyed.

This time I was awake enough to case the camp, and came to the conclusion that Sai and me were gonna have our work cut out for us when it came time to escape. Almost every Aarurrh male I saw was a warrior. Even the kids were armed, and the population of the camp looked close to a thousand. It filled a wide section of the canyon all the way to both sheer walls. I liked those walls. I didn't figure the Aarurrh for good climbers, even with all those arms. Their back ends were just too heavy. With my new leaping ability, I could probably scale those walls like they were so many ladders. But what about Sai? Maybe with a rope. Maybe not even then. Okay then, plan B, whatever that was.

The little creek cut the camp in half. We walked beside it, heading upstream. There were a couple narrow bridges scattered along it, even though the creek was slow and shallow enough that a kid could have waded through it. Maybe the Aarurrh didn't like getting their fur wet. Maybe that was another way out.

The only easy way up to the prairie was the trail we'd come down when they brought us in. Beyond that the canyon walls narrowed down until they were no wider than the stream. They might have opened up further on, but the canyon took a left turn about a quarter mile up and I couldn't see past it. I'd have to try to sneak out and go exploring later.

As we slogged up the trail Queenie introduced herself and Kitten. "I Hranan of Hirrarah tribe. That my daughter, Murrah. You say Hur-Hranan and Hur-Murrah when speak, hin?"

I nodded. "Hur-Hranan. Hur-Murrah. Got it. I'm Jane..."

She stopped me with a laugh and a cuff on the shoulder that was like being hit with a sofa. "That not your name. You got only two name: 'good girl' and 'bad girl,' hin?"

I ground my teeth. "Yeah, I hin alright." I don't deal with authority real well. If somebody tells me I gotta go one way, I want to go the other way, just on principle, but all my juvie time, prison time, and my stint in the rangers, and all the beatings, ass-kickings, and "disciplinary measures" that went along with 'em, have taught me that fighting back don't get you nothing but more lumps and more supervision. If you keep your head down and your eyes open, sooner or later they're going to forget about you and let down their guard. You just gotta be patient and not ruin everything by tearing some big bitch's head off with your bare hands.

I rubbed my shoulder and followed along with the other slaves like a "good girl."

***

The work was boring and backbreaking, but nothing I couldn't handle. That first day we dug for tubers under the blue grass. They were fat black things, like a cross between a carrot and an eggplant, but they smelled like garlic and dirt. The Aarurrh chicks worked right along with us slaves, doing the same work, but not as much of it. We dug with sharp sticks—the Aarurrh chicks used their claws—wherever we found a little blue plant with circular leaves, prying the thing out of the ground, knocking the dirt off of it and tossing it in a sack. Thrilling.

There were forty or so Aarurrh women, and only about fifteen slaves. I got the idea that slaves were quite the status symbol. Most women didn't have them. Queenie had her nose in the air like a Beverly Hills mom with a new Mercedes SUV.

As the day went on I tried to talk to my fellow slaves. They were all purple-skins, almost all male, all burned a leathery maroon, and as dull-eyed as cows, but more than half of them spoke languages my translator didn't understand. I don't know why I was surprised. Not everybody on Earth speaks English, do they?

When I finally found a guy who spoke Sai's language he shoved me away. "Quiet! Speak not!"

"What? Why?"

"Foolish woman, we are not allowed to speak."

"But you gotta help me. I gotta get out of here. Where are we? Where's the nearest..."

Something clobbered me on the back of the head. I hit the ground eight feet away and looked up, my eyes going in and out of focus.

Queenie was scowling down at me. "Bad girl."

Another Aarurrh mama started slapping around the guy I'd talked to. He squealed for mercy.

For the rest of the day all the other slaves gave me dirty looks.

***

The day wasn't done when we got back home. Queenie showed me how to kebab some of the tubers we'd dug that day, and how to chop up meat with a cooking blade shaped like half a circle. It looked a bit like an Eskimo's chopper. I breathed a sigh of relief when I saw that the meat had feathers on it. Giant bird I could stomach. I've had worse chow. Giant bird tasted like a combination of wild duck and alligator—yes I've had gator; I grew up in Florida—and once the tubers cooked up they tasted a little more like garlic and a little less like dirt.

After dinner Queenie sent me down to the river to rinse off the skewers and the chopper. There were no plates, they just chewed everything right off the kebabs. I thought she was crazy sending me off on my own like that, and armed with blades and pointy pieces of metal no less. What was she thinking? All I had to do was slip into the river, float downstream 'til I was below the camp, climb out of the canyon and...

And go where?

I sighed. I finished cleaning the skewers and chopper and walked back to Queenie's tent.

My bed was the same pile of straw Queenie had laid Sai on. I flopped down beside him, more wiped out than I'd been since boot camp. All I wanted to do was close my eyes, but first I checked Sai's wound. Queenie's goop seemed to be working. The edges of the cut were starting to knit together and there was no redness or puss.

Sai opened his eyes. "We still live?" He almost sounded disappointed.

"You're doin' fine, Sai. You'll be up and around in no time."

He was less than thrilled. He closed his eyes again. I should have let him sleep, but I had a question. "Sai, what's up with these furry fucks, anyway? Why do they hate your guys so much? What did you ever do to them?"

He sighed. "The myths of the Aarurrh tell them that they once ruled all of Waar, until the Tae stole it from them and forced them to live in the wastelands."

"The Tae?"

"The Tae. My people." He closed his eyes again. "The Aarurrh religion is pure superstition of course. We Tae have been here since the Seven created the world and placed us upon it to serve as their custodians."

"Custodians? You gotta mop the floors and fix the plumbing?"

"Pardon?"

"Nothin'. Never mind. Just bein' a jerk."

Sai lay back, but I had something else on my mind. I dropped my voice to a whisper. "Listen, Sai, I know you ain't feelin' so good right now, but shouldn't we be thinkin' about bustin' outta this joint and hightailin' it after your fiancée? You got a wedding to stop."

He shook his head without opening his eyes. "There is no escape from the Aarurrh. It is hopeless. We are dead."

"No escape? What are you talkin' about? We're not even chained up. We get down to that creek, I can get us up to the plains in twenty minutes. As long as you know your way home from there…"

"Unfortunately, I do not." He opened his eyes and looked directly at me for the first time since we were taken. "Mistress Jae-En, your enthusiasm is admirable, but useless. Even if I did know my way home we would not survive the journey. If by some miracle we managed to elude the Aarurrh, who are only the greatest trackers and hunters on Waar, we would not escape the savage packs of Shikes, capable of stripping us to our bones in the blink of an eye, nor the dreadful Vurlak, the jaw of which can crush stone, nor the wild Skelsha, which can——"

"Okay okay okay. I get the picture. But does that mean you're just going to give up? Are you gonna let that four-armed teenybopper play dollies with you 'til you grow old and die?"

Sai shuddered. "No. That I will not do. I am praying to the Seven for the courage to find a way out. An honorable man would rather die than submit to such indignities."

I squeezed his shoulder. "That's the spirit."

I lay back, feeling better. Sure, Sai said it was impossible, but at least he wasn't giving up. That was half the battle. If I had to drag him around like a sack of potatoes we'd get nowhere fast.

There were two moons overhead. Well, if nothing else was going to convince me this wasn't all some big prank Steven Spielberg had decided to pull on me, that would. I don't care how big your special effects budget is, nobody launches another moon just to make a fool out of some big, dumb biker chick. There was a fat blue moon peeking over the sawtooth skyline of the tents, and a little bright one that zipped across the sky so fast you could see it move. They gave everything around me two shadows. Kind of pretty, but all I could think was that all that light made making a break for it that much harder.

Beyond the moons were stars I'd never seen. Riding cross country on my bike and sleeping rough all those years, I'd gotten pretty good at picking out the constellations. They were all gone. I got hit with another wave of homesickness. Not even the stars were right. Where was I? Where was Earth? I started wondering if any of those little pinpricks out there was the Sun. My sun. Man, I sure went from happy to depressed awful fast, huh? Being stranded on another planet'll do that to you.

***

From then on things slipped into a routine; not exactly comfortable or happy, but not torture either, at least not for me. Queenie gave Sai about three days to get back on his feet. After that we'd either go up to the plains to dig for the tubers, or along the creek upstream from the camp to hunt in the shallows and under rocks for snails with finned shells and emerald green crawdad things.

The crawdads only had four legs. I began to notice that all the bugs, from winged biters to crawly collectors to hopping blood-suckers, had only four legs. Maybe One-Eye wasn't just being an asshole when he called me and Sai insects.

Once I got into the rhythm of the life I actually didn't mind it. I've always been more physical than mental, and heavy labor makes me feel useful. It toughened me up too. They didn't let us wear anything more than loin-cloths—just another way to remind us we were animals—so after a bad week of pink peeling, I ended up covered in so many freckles I looked like a drop-cloth—which is as close as I ever come to getting a tan. After two weeks, I'd built up and thinned down enough that you could see my abs and biceps, even when I wasn't flexing. I felt better and stronger than I had in years. I even stopped craving Marlboros, mostly.

But I made sure I didn't show my true strength. I held back; digging and lifting just a little bit more than the others, just enough for Queenie to appreciate me, but not enough for anyone to take me for a threat. I was a "good girl" and a happy little worker, and I kept an eye out for the main chance.

Sai didn't take to it like I did. Even though physically he recovered pretty quickly, mentally he was about as lively as a sloth with a barbiturate problem.

After what he'd said I kept expecting him to snap out of it, but he never did. I didn't know what to think. Was he playing possum like me? If he was, he had an Oscar coming his way. He stumbled through each day in a sleep-walk fog, shuffling and staring at his feet and harvesting about half what the rest of us did. Not that he was allowed to work that much anyway. Kitten, who seemed to spend more time gossiping with her girlfriends than she did working, led him around like a lap dog, petting him, dressing him up in cast-offs that must have come from other slaves, both male and female, tying colorful strings and ribbons in his hair. He took it all with the same rag doll stupor he showed for everything else. He didn't eat. He didn't clean himself. He hardly noticed when I tried to cheer him up.

The only thing that woke him up was once when Kitten tried to take off this thin silver chain he wore around his waist. It had a medallion dangling from it that I hadn't noticed before, probably because he kept it tucked down in his loincloth. When she grabbed it he started fighting like a wild animal. She decked him when he chomped down on her thumb and threw him into a corner, but she let him keep the chain.

I helped him up. "What was that all about?"

"She tried to take my Balurra. 'Tis the token of a man's love for his lady. He makes it with his own hands in the shape of her family crest, and only reveals it to his beloved or at his death."

I got a look at it before he put it away. It was a silver circle with a design of green and black diamonds inside. I'd seen the same mark inlaid on some of the luggage from Sai's coach. Must have been his sweetheart's stuff.

***

After a while I noticed that there were some intra-camp rivalries going on. There was another clique of Aarurrh chicks who gave our gang the cold shoulder. We'd always make sure we did our gathering as far from them as possible. Queenie sneered at them, "They from One-Eye's clan. Too good to dig 'cause their men best hunters. Hrrn! They steal kills from other men."

"So how come nobody says something, Hur-Hranan?"

"Best hunters protect chief. Nobody can talk to him."

Yup, just like trying to see the boss when his secretary hates you. Not gonna happen.

One-Eye's clan had most of the top spots in the tribe, and lorded it over everybody. One-Eye was the worst. We used to pass him and his men most mornings on the way out of camp. He always gave Handsome, who was part of his squad, the shit detail, sometimes literally. The Aarurrh used the stream as one big combined dumpster and toilet, and sometimes they threw in so much stuff that somebody had to go dredge it out. Handsome was always the guy, and One-Eye made sure to let Kitten see. It was a funny way to try to impress her, but hell, I'd seen bikers pull the same shit back home.

One day after Kitten had been moping all morning, I asked Queenie why she didn't dump One-Eye's ass for good. Queenie grunted, angry. "Can't do. Chief give her to Hruthar." Hruthar was One-Eye's real name. "They join at pregnant moon festival, next moon. Too soon."

"The chief's giving her to Hruthar, Hur-Hranan? You don't get a say in it?"

She sighed. "When I girl, I leave Hirrarah tribe and join warrior from Yurrahah tribe. Yurrahah wiped out by Unrarach Clan and my man die, so I come back here. But too old to have babies now. No use they say. Won't feed me. Har! I best digger here, but they want warriors. Chief say he take me back if I promise daughter to him to do what he want. I got no place to go so I say okay." She ripped a tuber out of the ground, angry. "When cheater Hruthar make top man, chief promise Murrah to him when she joining age. Now she is."

Man, and I thought chicks had it tough back home. I saw how One-Eye treated Kitten. I couldn't see him changing when they tied the knot. I felt sorry for her and Queenie. But then something happened that made me put their troubles on the back burner.

*****

One night Queenie and Kitten left us alone at the tent to go do some secret tribal women stuff. No slaves allowed. Sai was his usual talkative self, so I'd gone down to the creek to rinse the grain for the next day's breakfast. When I got back to the tent Sai was teetering on top of Queenie's cooking tripod, the tallest piece of furniture in the tent. Getting up there must have been the most athletic thing he'd done since we got here.

"Sai? What the hell…" Then I noticed the rope around his neck, knotted to one of the tent's cross poles. "Sai! Don't!"

He looked down at me. The smeared mess of Kitten's last rouge and eye make-up experiment made him look like an abused doll. "At last I find hope of escape."

And with that he pitched forward, tipping over the cooking tripod and falling free. The rope jerked tight and swung as he reached its limit. The whole tent shook.

"Sai!" I leaped up to the cross pole and tore at the knot as Sai made hideous dying fish noises below me. Thank god he hadn't dropped far enough to break his neck, but if I didn't untie that knot he was going to choke to death.

It was too tight, and my fingernails were worn to the quick from digging tubers. I looked around, desperate. Queenie's cooking blade hung "out of reach" on the center pole just below my feet. I snatched it up and chopped down on the knot. The blade bit through the rope and Sai hit the ground like a sack of shark bait. I was next to him in a second, digging my finger under the rope and tugging it lose none too gently. "You stupid butt-smack! What the fuck do you think you were doing?"

It took a minute for him to stop retching enough to answer. When he did it wasn't to thank me. "How dare you? After shaming myself for these long days, too much the coward to do what must be done, I finally summon the strength and do the deed, and… and you ruin it!"

"Ruin it? I saved your life!" Then it hit me. "Wait a minute. Hope of escape? Is this what you meant by 'finding a way out?' You sorry-ass loser!"

He pouted. "And now you make it doubly hard. Now that I know the pain and fear of it first hand, how much more difficult will it be to find the courage a second time?"

I'm sorry to say I bitch-slapped him. Somebody had to. "You whiny little puke. You think you're being brave by committing suicide? All that crap about honor and courage. You're just giving up. Sure your life sucks right now, but you're alive. You've got all your arms and legs. They work. As long as you've got all that there's still a chance."

Sai tried to push me away. I grabbed his jaw and forced him to look at me. "Can you save your fiancée from that dumb jock when you're dead? Can you fix things with your dad? And what about me? You're gonna leave me here to fend for myself?"

He flushed at that, turning from lavender to magenta. "Mistress Jae-En, I am ashamed that an outlander should show me the path of honor. You are correct. I have strayed, forgetting in my misery your plight and that of my beloved Wen-Jhai. Ending my own wretched life is a luxury I can not indulge in until I have done my all to deliver you both from your fates. I crave your forgiveness."

Man, I hated when he got all gushy on me. "Forget it."

From outside the tent we heard Queenie's alto purr and Kitten's soprano whine. They were coming back. I leaped up.

"Quick! The hibachi!" Good thing I pointed too. I had a tendency to mix my old dictionary with my new one when I got excited and half the time Sai didn't know what I was talking about. He righted the cooking tripod as I shoved the rope under a trunk and leaped for the cross pole, yanked the chopper out of the wood, hung it back on its hook, and was down again sweeping the rug with a straw broom just as the tent flap started to open.

Sai, in a flash of inspiration that made me hope he'd gotten over his suicidal funk, tied one of kitten's brightly colored scarves over the raw rope marks on his neck. It make him look like a sixties stereotype of an interior decorator, but it hid the evidence. Queenie and Kitten were busy talking and paid even less attention to us than usual. Probably more Hatfield and McCoy stuff.

After we finished making and serving our mistresses their vittles and cleaning up, we were finally allowed to lie down on our straw to sleep.

Sai whispered in my ear, "Again I apologize, Mistress Jae-En. I have been so long absorbed in my own despair that I have ignored you. Have you a plan?"

I hated to disappoint him. "Sorry, Sai, not yet. But stay strong and stay ready. Something will happen."

And something did.

CHAPTER FIVE

SNEAK ATTACK!

For about half a big moon... Now, wait. I guess I gotta explain about that first. I already said about the two moons—the big slow one and the little fast one. Well, the Aarurrh used them to tell time and keep track of the days. I picked it up just being around them.

The little moon went by so fast it lapped the big one twice a night—and twice a day too—you just couldn't see it so well then. The Aarurrh called the time that the little guy was in the sky a crossing, and the time it was on the other side of the planet a dark, so the day was cut up into First Crossing, First Dark—sunrise to noon—Second Crossing, Second Dark—noon to sunset—Third Crossing, Third Dark—sunset to midnight—and Fourth Crossing, Fourth Dark —midnight to sunrise.

They kept track of the passing days by the quarters of the big moon, which went from full to dark to full in about twenty days by my count, so each quarter was five days long. Got it? Okay. Where was I?

Right. For about half a big moon, things had been getting tenser and tenser in the camp. Even Sai felt it. It was like somebody was winding a guitar string too tight. Any minute something was going to pop, you just didn't know exactly when. There were high level councils around the men's fire most nights, with the big chief and all his captains arguing long into the Fourth Crossing. Queenie and Kitten talked in hushed tones with the other females. One-Eye was crankier than ever, and more than once caught Kitten and Handsome meeting in secret and making like the last act of *Romeo and Juliet*. I thought he was going to kill poor Handsome, but though he whaled the tar out of him he was careful not to do any serious damage, though it sure looked like he wanted to.

Every day, raiding parties returned to camp with severed heads of Aarurrh stuck on the points of their spears. When they passed, the women howled and snarled like a wolf pack. Queenie would grin and point. "See how ugly? Disgusting. Barahir thieves. Poach our meat-birds. We make pay, hin? Ugly dung eaters."

I guess you had to be an Aarurrh to see it. The junk jewelry they wove into their dreads was a little different, but other than that they looked just like the guys from Queenie's tribe to me.

Ugly or not, our tribe, I mean Queenie's tribe, the Hirrarah, had a major beef with these guys, the Barahir, and things were heating up big time. Everywhere we went in the camp I could pick out that name, "Barahir" from all the usual Aarurrh cat yowling. I noticed a lot of spear sharpening going on too. Defenses around the camp were doubled, and Queenie and Kitten were going to funerals for young Hirrarah warriors almost every night. Sai and I watched it all and started getting excited. War means chaos, and chaos is good for opportunities. Of course, when it came, it didn't work out exactly the way I wanted it to, but that's chaos for you.

***

It all started as just another day of hunting and gathering. Sai and I were out with Queenie's work party about a half mile from the ravine, digging the black tubers, and also picking little sapphire-blue weeds which were in season. If you dried and crushed them, they made a sour, orange-rindy type seasoning. A hunting party had passed us on our way up to the plains, and rode off east at first light.

Sai was finally pulling his weight, and actually seemed to be getting used to the life, or at least not actively hating it. He was even interacting with Kitten a little. Not that he pretended to like her petting on him, but at least now he'd get pissed and wipe off the make-up she put on him instead of just sitting there like a lump. Kitten thought this was cute, and called him "bad baby." Poor guy just couldn't win.

We had armed guards with us these days. They'd been coming out ever since things got tense with the Barahir. They were supposed to be keeping an eye out, but mostly they talked to the girls. That little breach of duty almost got us all killed.

Less than a mile away a huge herd of those big birds, which Sai called krae, wild cousins of the big-headed bastards that had pulled his coach, were grazing in the blue grass. That was pretty common. The krae were a prime source of meat for the tribe and hunters went out every few days to bring down a dozen or so. They weren't dangerous if you kept your distance and didn't provoke them. They looked like crazed carnivores, but they were really more like cows. They used those big snapping turtle beaks to steam-shovel up the same tubers we were digging for. We ignored them. Most of the time they ignored us. Not today.

I had just filled my first sack of tubers when I heard a rumble. The guards looked up from their flirting. The heads of the slaves and the women came up like prairie dogs. The krae were stampeding right for us. My heart jumped like a frog in a bread box. A big, gray wave of huge, shaggy birds a mile wide was about to crash down and drown us.

The krae are fast. Real fast. The tribe's hunters almost never try to cut them down them on the fly. They get most of their kills sneaking up on them and using their bolos to bring them down, or trapping them in blind canyons and spearing them like fish in a barrel. In a straight race the birds win every time. We were in big trouble.

The guards, those brain-dead, bootie-blinded bone-heads, shouted a command—about two minutes too late—but we were already running, the Aarurrh girls screaming, the older, wiser women saving their breath.

Some of the slaves got left behind in the confusion, pumping away on their scrawny legs without a chance in hell. I would have revealed my leaping ability right then and there, but Queenie, the sweetheart, slung me up on her back and we raced for the ravine trailhead. I looked over and saw Kitten scoop up Sai and tuck him under her arm like a running back with the pigskin. Whew!

The birds were gaining. They'd been at a full run when we noticed them, a half mile away, and by the time we'd all got up to speed, the gap was closed by half, and the ravine didn't seem any closer. I looked back, just in time to see a slave go down under the tide, claws wider than he was crushing him to the ground and ripping giant divots out of his back. I could make out individual feathers on the big bastards now, and the red of their wild eyes.

Then a glint made me look beyond them. I squinted into the huge cloud of dust those big chicken feet were kicking up and saw something back there that wasn't a bird—a spear head, a spangle of jewelry, the silhouettes of broad shoulders and dreadlocks.

"Hur-Hranan! Look! There are Aarurrh back there! Behind the krae!"

Queenie shot a look back and growled low in her throat. She barked to the guards. "Barahir!"

They looked back too.

The ravine was only a hundred yards away now, but the krae were only fifty. The guards were dropping back and urging us ahead. Queenie was doing the same, shoving the other females ahead of her. I broke out in a cold sweat. It's fine to play the noble den mother, but not when you've got a passenger. The first girls were sweeping into the hairpin turn of the steep trail down to the floor of the ravine. The trail hugs the cliff pretty tight in some places. The Aarurrh don't usually go down it more than two abreast. The girls were taking it full tilt three and four at a time.

The first krae were twenty feet away when we all suddenly realized that they weren't going to stop! Whatever the Aarurrh behind them had scared them with, it was enough to do a total lemming trip on them. Forget gravity. Forget flightless wings. The krae herd was about to become a mindless krae avalanche.

Queenie wheeled down into the trail as the first of the krae hit the edge and did the old Wile E. Coyote step into thin air. A dozen more were right behind them. The air was filled with squawking screeching plummeting bodies. Looking back I saw our four guards bulldozed off the cliff by a tidal wave of unstoppable bird-flesh. Ahead of us, down the trail, krae were bouncing off the path between sprinting Aarurrh girls.

We were actually lucky that the damn things ran so fast, because momentum arced most of them over the narrow trail and straight into the ravine. It was like riding behind a solid, feathered waterfall. Unfortunately, a lot of the birdbrained things tripped at the edge. It reminded me of that Indiana Jones movie where the temple collapses and big chunks of stone drop all around the hero, only with giant birds. Far down the path an Aarurrh mama was punched off the trail like an eight ball getting knocked into a corner pocket.

Right in front of us a young Aarurrh girl got clobbered on the hindquarters and went down all splay-legged and half off the trail.

Queenie, the idiot, stopped to help her up. Krae were hitting like depth charges all around us. One grazed Queenie's shoulder, and mine. Queenie didn't flinch. She got the poor girl's hind legs back on the trail and had her halfway to her feet when we heard a roaring behind us.

A Barahir warrior, some crazed berserker who couldn't wait for the rain of krae to stop, charged down on us in full, four-legged gallop mode, two swords held high. Queenie shoved the wounded girl down the trail and tried to follow, but Two-Swords was on us way too fast. One sword slashed Queenie low on the left back leg. The other would have took my head off, except I ducked.

Queenie went down, howling. I got thrown clear and crashed into some low scrub. Good old low gravity. I hopped up, unhurt except for a few scrapes, and looked around. Two-Swords was raising his blades for the killing blow.

If I'd thought about it, I'd have remembered that Queenie was my enemy and I was her slave. After all that "good girl" and "bad girl" stuff I should have been happy to see her buy the farm. I wasn't. I still liked her. So I didn't think at all.

My hand grabbed a rock. My legs sprang. I landed right between Two-Swords' shoulder blades and swung with the rock. I put it inside his skull easier than breaking an egg. Two-Swords dropped, his head a concave half-moon, red and wet. My hand was drenched in blood. I'd killed a guy. Another one. I wanted to call a time out and wash myself before I puked.

I looked up. Queenie was staring, amazed. She'd seen my leap, and probably had a better idea than I did what it took to crush an Aarurrh's skull. I shrugged, still dazed.

No time for interrogation though. A full company of Barahir was barreling down at us. Queenie snatched me up again and we galloped down the trail. Queenie cried out in pain from her slashed leg every time we leaped the body of a dying krae or dead Aarurrh girl.

Before us, down in the ravine, I saw that the alarm had been raised, but maybe not soon enough. Our boys were still scrambling into their harnesses and galloping up to form a ragged line of defense, snatching up swords and spears as they came. But the double line of Baharir charging behind us was like a railroad spike shot from a bazooka. Nothing short of a steel wall was going to stop it. Ours was barely under construction.

The front line parted as we roared through, then closed up again behind us, but it wasn't enough. Not even close. I could hear the smack of flesh on flesh as the two fronts met. It sounded like the Packers and the Jets coming together after the snap, except with a car wreck mixed in.

Queenie pulled up near Kitten and a cluster of other Hirrarah women and started to herd them further into the camp. Hirrarah men raced past us toward the front, which had crumbled almost instantly. The Barahir had plowed through the center and done end-run plays around the edges. Now they were fanning through the camp, swiping at anything that moved, kicking over cooking tripods, and starting fires in a dozen places. And as if that wasn't enough chaos, maimed, terrified krae were running around like panicked, half-ton chickens, crashing into tents and clawing good guys, bad guys, everybody.

Snatching up a spear somebody had left behind, Queenie led her flock through the camp and into a narrow arroyo in the ravine wall. It was a tight squeeze at the mouth; we had to go in single file, but further in it opened up like a wine bottle. There was hardly any room for us. The place was already sardine tight with Hirrarah gals and kids. This was a planned safe hole for the women-folk, the most easily defended place in the ravine. Only problem was, it wasn't defended. Whatever males were supposed to hold the entrance weren't there. It was pretty obvious they were either dead or real busy right about now.

Queenie grunted, then whistled up a few of the heftiest gals to back her up. She planted herself dead center in the arroyo's tiny opening, spear at parade rest.

I was ready to help out. My blood was up. I generally try to avoid fights, not because I don't like them, more because I find it kind of hard to stop once I get going. Queenie had other ideas. She nodded up to the peak of a nearby teepee, and mimed me jumping up there for a look around. "Up."

I tried to look like I didn't know what she meant, but it was no good. She'd seen me brain Two-Swords at the end of a fifteen-foot jump. The cat was out of the bag. She smirked and raised a sly eyebrow at me.

I shrugged, sheepish, and leaped to the top of the tent like a cat jumping onto a fence post. Queenie was right. It was a good vantage point. I had a clear view of almost the whole camp.

Man, what a mess.

There was one good thing. Our guys had finally gotten themselves together. It wasn't looking like quite the massacre it had when it started, but even now it wasn't pretty. The damn krae were still running around, some on fire, and the tent fires were spreading. The fighting was all over the camp. There was no front anymore, just a bunch of isolated ass-kickings and bloodlettings wherever there was room to swing a sword.

Recon training took over. I was assessing threats and preparing contingencies just like Captain MacPherson had taught me. The nearest fight was four tents away, a swirling mosh pit of snarling, slashing Aarurrh and flashing steel. It took me a second to sort out the two sides, and another to recognize One-Eye and Handsome in the thick of the scrum. It was One-Eye's squad, fighting a gang of Barahir and separated from any other action by at least fifty yards and any number of tents. It looked like they'd stopped to rescue a downed Hirrarah gal from some Barahir and got caught up in a scrape they couldn't disengage from.

One-Eye, like the coward I'd always figured him to be, was leading from the rear, shouting insults and encouragement from behind his men and waving his sword around a lot, while Handsome was fighting like a demon at the front. As I watched, he ran through two all by himself with a desperate double-sword lunge, and he paid for it. He'd left himself wide open. He parried a slash at his gut, but took a slobberknocker crack on the temple from the butt of a spear. He screamed and wheeled, doing the boxers' rubber-leg dance on his hind legs, then fell back, crashing heavily on his flank.

His pals closed up the gap like good soldiers, and pressed the advantage he'd created. The bad guys were starting to retreat. One-Eye cheered his men on, but I saw him shoot a glance down at Handsome, still in dreamland beside him, then look over his shoulder. I got a sinking feeling in my stomach. Something was brewing behind One-Eye's one eye and he didn't wait long to act on it. He bent his middle arms/legs to kneel by Handsome like he was going to check his wounds. It was perfect. Nobody around, all his men looking the other way, fighting for their lives. It would look like Handsome had died in battle. One-Eye pulled his hunting knife from its sheath.

I said before that my blood was up. Now it was boiling like a gumbo pot. I launched from the tent. I have a vague idea that Queenie shouted something, but it could have been me. Two tents away I hit dirt and sprang forward again like a kung-fu kangaroo.

One-Eye was just laying his knife against Handsome's helpless throat when he caught my motion out of the corner of his eye. He looked up, guilty. I hit him in the numbers with a cross body block.

It didn't go so well. The problem with living on a planet with less gravity than Earth is that, for the same reason I can leap ridiculous distances and not hurt myself much when I crash, I don't make much of an impact when I hit something—particularly not something four times my size. So it was more surprise than power that knocked One-Eye back on his haunches.

I careened past him into a rack of drying bird meat and was up and flying at him again before he could get his multi-purpose limbs back under him. The impact thing was a bust, so this time I hopped on his back and got him around the neck with a triangle choke.

Now this was where that alien, strength/mass thing worked out. This wasn't weight against weight. This was strength against strength. There we were an even match, and I was in the one place he couldn't get a good grip on me.

One-Eye's eyes and tongue were popping out in seconds. He shredded my arms with his big, clawed paws. I took the pain. I didn't even feel it. I had a mad on, blind, red, and roaring, and when I have a mad on, everything goes away—pain, cold, hunger, exhaustion.

There was shouting in the distance. One-Eye's squad was turning, winners of the rumble, just in time to see their leader getting punked by a pink midget. Someone clipped me on the head. The next thing I remember I was flat on my back, staring up at rising spear points and sword blades. I was dead. Then there was a shout, and a big body leaped over me, scattering the swords and spears.

Queenie! There were growls of protest as she yanked me up and crushed me in a hug. For a second it was a stand off—One-Eye and his squad demanding that Queenie hand me over, and Queenie refusing, but then another gang of Barahir veered into view and One-Eye's squad had to get busy again.

Handsome, shaking off the cobwebs, was about to join them, but Queenie, an odd look on her face, called him back and ordered him to come with her. He didn't put up much of a fight.

***

We won. I mean they won. I mean the Hirrarah won. Barely. I didn't see any more of the battle. Queenie kept me by her side until it was over—I wasn't sure if she was worried about my safety or One-Eye's—but I learned later that it had been a hell of a close call. The only reason we came out on top was that that big hunting party of ours that had gone out early had felt the rumble of the stampede through their feet and raced home, thinking more about meat on the hoof than danger. But when they saw the smoke from the burning tents rising from the ravine they breaknecked it down the trail, fresh as daisies, just as the Barahir thought they had us licked.

After that it was all putting out fires, clearing wreckage, repairing tents, burning our dead and carting theirs away. Plus, there was the logistical nightmare of what to do with more dead krae-flesh than the tribe could eat in ten years. Most of the slaves helped out, but not me. Once the all-clear blew and the women came out from their hidey-hole, Queenie took me straight to her tent and tied me to the king post with leather thongs that I couldn't have broke with twice my strength.

I looked up at her. "I'm up shit creek here, ain't I, Hur-Hranan?"

"Hin?"

"Trouble. I'm in trouble, right? Bad girl?"

She looked me in the eye and stroked my cheek sadly. "You good girl. Good girl."

Then she turned and walked out.

Yup. Shit creek. Big time.

CHAPTER SIX

CONDEMNED!

After a day when nobody but Queenie came into the tent—and she only came in to feed me and didn't say a word—two tough looking hardcases, wearing the Chief's colors of orange and green woven into their dreads, stepped in, cut me loose, and led me out.

I'd had plenty of time to think about what I'd done and what kind of shit storm paying the piper was going to involve—time enough to go from dead certain I was going to die to optimistic and back again. It was automatic death for a slave to strike or even lip-off to an Aarurrh, so I knew I was fucked. But then I started thinking. If they were going to kill me why wasn't I dead already? Had Queenie put in a good word for me? Had she seen One-Eye try to ice Handsome? Maybe I'd get a pardon. Maybe they'd even let me go. Yeah right. On Queenie's say so? Females, even wise old mamas like Queenie, didn't get much respect in a testosterone boy's club like an Aarurrh tribe. And with One-Eye's clan practically running things? The men would probably just laugh at her and kill me anyway. But I wasn't dead yet, so...

A big crowd surrounded a square of open space in front of the chief's tent. The camp, as they dragged me through it, was only half repaired. The teepee skyline had more gaps in it than a shark with dental problems, but it looked like everybody had downed tools to see the pink chick get the axe.

The chief was impressive—a massive, white-muzzled silverback with a head full of gray dreadlocks and so many white scars criss-crossing his fur it looked like somebody had written on him in Chinese. He sat on a low-slung, upholstered hassock, built to fit an Aarurrh's lower body. It was the biggest piece of furniture I'd seen in the camp.

He was flanked by a bunch of other higher-ups. They didn't get couches. Under their feet was a beautiful rug decorated with twisting purple and black lines that looked like a cross between Arab stuff and the Celtic knot-work from a biker's tattoo. It was big enough to cover a basketball court. I wondered who the sucker was who had to lug that thing from camp to camp. Some poor slave most likely.

Standing before the bigwigs, in the open space in front of the rug, were Queenie, Kitten and Handsome on one side, and One-Eye and a couple of his clan homies on the other, like plaintiffs and defendants in a trial—which I began to suspect this was. The space was square, with wooden posts pounded into the ground at the corners and roped off to keep the crowd back. The posts were taller than me and carved to look like big swords sticking into the ground. I didn't care much for the symbolism.

My two guards ducked me under the rope and pushed me to the center of the square, then stood at my shoulders. They carried battle-axes as tall as stop signs, with huge double blades nearly as big around.

The chief gave me a skeptical once over while his mouthpiece, a thin Aarurrh with a face like a stuck-up bobcat and some kind of official necklace, got the show started with a long loud roar and a little ceremonial semaphore. Once the crowd simmered down he introduced the players, giving the two sides big build-ups like the ring announcer at a wrestling match, while the chief continued to look from me to One-Eye and back again like we were a nut and a bolt that just wouldn't fit together. Then the mouthpiece finished speechifying and we got down to business.

I was still at square one when it came to understanding Aarurrh yakking—it just sounded like cats in heat to me—but I could get the gist of the arguments that went back and forth from everybody's gestures and tone of voice. First One-Eye said his piece, pointing at me and growling something fierce. He had to have been saying that I'd struck an Aarurrh with intent to kill and that was all there was to it.

Handsome spoke next. It should have been Queenie, but apparently only males were allowed to speak at these things, so Handsome spoke for her. You could almost see her pulling his strings. He told 'em that I'd saved Queenie's life and had only attacked One-Eye because One-Eye'd tried to kill him, miming the whole thing so I could almost see it happening.

One-Eye jumped in, waving all four arms and shaking his head. He hadn't tried to kill Handsome, and he dared anyone to come forward and prove that he had. Handsome interrupted One-Eye's interruption, gesturing again, with lots of looks back at Queenie to make sure he was getting it all right. He gave her testimony, acting out her running after me and seeing One-Eye leaning over Handsome with a knife. To back that up, Handsome showed everyone a small cut on his neck.

One-Eye laughed at this. Of course he'd had his knife out. He mimed being in the middle of battle—and giving himself a lot more action than he'd really seen, by the way. He motioned to the guys from his squad, showing all the cuts they'd picked up during the fighting. Then he crossed to Handsome and pointed out all *his* cuts. He was playing the jury like Johnnie Cochran. How could Handsome prove that he hadn't got that little cut in battle along with all the rest?

I could see a lot of the big-wigs leaning his way, but the chief still looked undecided. He asked Queenie and Handsome if they had actually seen the attack. Because it was a direct question from the chief, Queenie was allowed to speak, but unfortunately she couldn't give a good answer. She'd seen the knife and One-Eye's position, but from her angle she couldn't be certain if he was stabbing Handsome. Handsome said he'd still been knocked loopy and couldn't remember exactly what happened. Triumphant, One-Eye again demanded my death.

That seemed to convince the last of the doubters, but the chief was still frowning. He called One-Eye's squad forward and asked them something. From all the leaping and choking gestures they made—and believe me, you haven't seen gesturing until you've seen a guy with four arms tell a story—I could tell they were telling him about my fight with One-Eye.

They were the last witnesses. After that we all stood around and waited for the chief to make a decision. It was a bit of a wait. The Chief rubbed his furry chest for what seemed to me, who had the most to lose in all this, a half an hour or more, but was probably under a minute. The crowd got so quiet I could hear the "skritch skritch" of his claws scratching his skin.

Finally he spoke. This part I couldn't figure out from hand gestures, but everybody took it big. The crowd gasped. One-Eye bellowed in anger. Queenie and the kids talked among themselves and looked over at me, faces going back and forth between relief and worry.

After a gesture from the mouthpiece, my escort dragged me over to Handsome and dropped me at his feet. Queenie came out from behind him and scooped me up into a hug that could have killed a grizzly bear.

"So, am I free?"

Queenie shook her head. "Almost not yet. Chief think One-Eye weak not to kill you first time. Aarurrh not win fight with insect? And only a she-insect?" She laughed. I wasn't sure if she was insulting One-Eye or me. "Now he think One-Eye coward too, asking chief to settle his fights." She leaned in, rolling her eyes like I was supposed to get her meaning. "One-Eye ask for you execute, not trial."

I was confused. "Wasn't this the trial?"

Queenie shook her head. "Not trial like that. Like this." She drew her dagger meaningfully. I still wasn't exactly following, but I didn't like the gist.

"One-Eye say trial only for Aarurrh. He no fight animals. But chief, he hear how you jump. He want to see a good fight. Now, stay. We find armor."

Queenie and Kitten trotted off, leaving me and Sai with Handsome. My heart dropped into my colon. Now I got it. Trial by combat with a twelve foot, four armed monster. That was the chief's idea of a good fight.

Sai was beside himself. "Mistress Jae-En, you mustn't. 'Tis naught but suicide." This from the bone-head who tried to hang himself.

"I don't exactly have a choice, do I?"

"But how does this chief know of your abilities? You have been so careful to keep them secret."

"Nobody knew but…" It hit me. Only Queenie and One-Eye had seen me leap, and One-Eye sure as hell wouldn't have said anything. "Sly old bitch. No wonder she was grinning like the cat that ate the canary. She knew old Silver-Dreads would rather see a fight than a boring old execution any day of the week."

Sai raised a worried eyebrow. "But is this a victory? Surely you have but exchanged one death for another."

"Hey, I'll take any fight over face-down on the chopping block. But I don't think this has much to do with helping me out. I may be her favorite slave, but I'm still just a slave. Queenie's got other fish to fry."

"You baffle me, mistress."

Poor Sai, born without a devious bone in his body. I spelled it out for him. "This is all about Kitten and Handsome. Sure I killed that Barahir bozo and nearly choked out One-Eye, but Queenie knows I got as much chance of beating him in a stand-up fight as the Cubs have of winning the World Series."

"Pardon, mistress?"

"I'm saying she knows the odds of my winning are about a million to one and she doesn't care. She's covered any way it goes." I started ticking options off on my fingers. "If One-Eye kills me she's no worse off than before. If, by some miracle I kill One-Eye, Queenie's troubles are over. Kitten can marry Handsome and everything's happily ever after."

"But, Mistress Jae-En, you are guaranteed to lose! Why would she trouble herself for such a slim chance?"

"Because—and thanks for the vote of confidence by the way—because if I give One-Eye even the slightest bit of trouble before he takes me out, his rep is in the shitter for being the guy who had a hard time killing an insect."

The light bulb went on over Sai's head. "Of course. His abilities as a warrior would be in question, thus lowering his standing in the matrimonial race."

"Bingo. All of a sudden One-Eye's low man on the totem pole and Handsome walks right in."

Sai was round-eyed. "By the Seven, the subtlety of the creature. Who would have thought these animals capable of such guile?"

I sneered. "Yeah, well, two can play at that game."

"Mistress, you are hardly in a position to…"

"I don't care. I ain't fighting Queenie's battles for her unless there's something in it for me."

I saw Queenie and Kitten coming back, loaded down with weapons and armor. They dropped it all in front of me.

Queenie nudged me. "Hurry. Try quick. No time."

I held up a hand. It was brass balls time. "Sorry, Hur-Hranan, I don't suit up 'til I know what I get if I win."

Queenie looked like she was going to hit me for sassing back, then she laughed. "You get life."

That's what I was afraid of. "No deal. I want freedom for me and Sai."

Sai looked shocked. "Mistress Jae-En."

"Zip it, Sai. I know what I'm doing." Sure I did. I was shaking like a paint mixer.

Queenie glared at me. "Chief no deal. Chief speak."

"Well, you go speak right back. No deal, no fight. He'll have to settle for a plain old beheading. Whaddaya think the crowd's going to say about that after all the build up?"

Handsome looked toward the chief, then at the excited crowd. He saw my point. Aarurrh chiefs have absolute rule, but if they piss off the mob one time too many they get the absolute chop. He turned to me, gravely. "You die for this?"

"No offense. You guys have been real nice and all, but as long as I'm a slave, I'm already dead. The only reason I haven't killed myself is that I still think I can escape."

Queenie looked a little hurt, but Handsome nodded. He seemed to be impressed by my honesty.

"I tell chief."

He crossed to the carpet and knelt like he was about to get the wafer and the wine. The chief grumbled when Handsome gave his spiel, but I saw him shoot an uneasy glance at the crowd, then back at me. His eyes were pure murder. Being manipulated by an insect seemed to stick in his craw, but in the end he shrugged and waved Handsome away with a nod. It was pretty obvious he figured that the chances of me winning were so slim that it wouldn't matter anyway.

The crowd started yakking big time when the mouthpiece announced the new conditions. One-Eye threw down one of his swords in disgust, but the chief's word was law, so that was that.

CHAPTER SEVEN

SINGLE COMBAT!

Sai helped Kitten and Queenie strap me into a purple-guy fighting harness, complete with arm and shin guards. Not that he was much help. He was still shaking like a leaf about my gambit. It made him all thumbs.

"You should not have risked so much, Mistress Jae-En. You might have lost your head had the Chief been of another mind."

"I still got plenty of chances to lose my head. Sometimes you've got to take a chance to get a chance."

Sai looked across to where One-Eye was preparing. "Is there a chance?"

I shrugged. "I'm alive. I've got all my arms and legs, and they all work."

"'Tis still two fewer than your nemesis." Good old Sai. Always the encouraging word.

"So, any tips on fighting these guys?"

"Be where his blades are not."

I sighed. "Thanks for the ancient wisdom, Master Po. When was the last time you were in a fight?"

Sai put his nose in the air and got all defensive. "I've studied under the finest weapons masters in Ora."

I knew what that meant. He'd never been in a real scrap in his life. "Great."

By now the crowd around the roped off square was ten deep. A fight between a warrior of the Aarurrh and a pink insect drew a crowd just like those guys down in Florida who wrestle alligators. It was geek show stuff.

I don't know where Queenie and Kitten dug up my armor. Probably from some Aarurrh warrior's trophy case. There weren't any human-size swords around, though. The Aarurrh are nomads. They don't do their own mining. Not when there are civilized pushovers to steal from. That meant that any purple-guy swords that came into the camp were immediately melted down to forge Aarurrh weapons. So Aarurrh weapons were what I had to choose from. This was a problem.

I could see One-Eye laughing as I tried out various giant weapons. He knew he had it in the bag right there. His own weapons fit him like extensions of his four arms. I was like a pee-wee leaguer trying to swing Mark McGuire's bat. The spears and axes were just ridiculous. Twelve foot monsters with balance points higher than I could reach. I nearly chopped Queenie's head off trying to get the feel for one.

The sword was a surprise though. It was huge—I was eye to eye with the pommel when I stuck the point in the ground—and built to size. The blade was wider across than my palm, and curved a little at the tip. The grip was a foot and a half long and way too thick. But it was balanced like a miser's checkbook, and the weight of it, which would have had Sai gasping and weaving after two swings, felt just right to my Earth muscles; like a sawed off pool cue. I'd found my weapon.

I tried to hide how comfy I was with it. I made sure One-Eye saw me take a few clumsy, off-balance swings. They weren't too hard to fake. First off, I'd never fought with a sword before. Second, the grip had to be fixed. It was like gripping a can of spray paint. One hit from One-Eye's sword and mine was going flying.

Handsome noticed this and quickly cut the leather binding that wound around the grip. Under that was a thick wooden dowel. With a few quick scrapes of his knife, Handsome whittled the grip down to fit a human hand. Not perfect, but there wasn't time for anything else. The crowd was getting antsy. One-Eye complained to the chief and the guards came over and told me I was ready. Now.

Sai clasped my hand as they dragged me off. "Good fortune, mistress. I pray to the Seven for your victory."

"Tell 'em to send along a Smith and Wesson."

It wasn't until I was facing One-Eye across the packed earth, with a couple hundred rowdy monsters howling behind the ropes and sword-posts, that I realized how scared I was. I've been in bad spots before, but this was crazy. This wasn't, "Oh shit, I fucked up. I'm going to jail." If I fucked up here I was going to die, and not in one piece.

My stomach seemed to be pushing up against my lungs. I couldn't take a breath. The damn sword was squirming around in my sweaty palms like a wet bar of soap. I realized with a rising wave of panic that I should have put the leather wrapping back on the grip. I wanted to call king's X, time out. I wanted to do that on this whole fucking adventure. Hit the reset button. Start over. I wanted to go back and not kill that poor guy in Panorama City. Shit, right about now I would have gladly thanked him for squeezing my ass.

The chief clapped his four hands. The crowd roared. One-Eye charged out of his corner on his back legs, three flashing swords in his four hands.

I back-pedaled like crazy trying to keep track of all that steel. He had a big sword in his top two hands, and two smaller ones in his bottom two, which he waved in front of him like an umpire calling safe. I jumped over them easy, then saw the big sword coming at me like a girder with a guillotine edge. On pure flinch instinct I got my sword up, wrong way around, and took the hit on the flat of the blade. I've taken softer hits in bike wrecks. The impact knocked my blade into my face, smacking me on the temple, and sent me flying fifteen feet to land on my neck in the third row.

The Aarurrh laughed like yowling tigers and picked me up. My head was ringing like a time-keepers' bell at a boxing match. Everything was too bright and out of focus. They passed me forward with good-natured backslaps and dumped me back over the rope. Swell.

Before I could pull myself together again, One-Eye's three swords came at me like something out of a cheap 3-D movie. My legs were still all jumbled up. At the last second I got my left foot—my off foot—under me and launched. Not exactly a thing of beauty, that leap. I flew off sideways, out of control, and one of my ears popped as his big blade whistled by it, sucking air like a Concorde.

I landed on my tits across the square, inhaling a mouthful of dirt and pebbles as I skidded to a stop. The impact knocked the wind out of me, but at least the breastplate kept me from getting roadrash on my nipples. The tigers gasped at my leap, the first one they'd had a good look at. They started murmuring like the crowd in a courtroom just before the judge bangs his gavel.

I got to my feet. My head was clearing, but not fast enough. One-Eye was closing fast, and looking annoyed that I was making him walk so far to kill me. Well, he was going to be even more annoyed before I was through. Until the wind chimes in my head stopped I wasn't about to go toe to toe with him. I leaped again, and kept leaping. My equilibrium was still outta whack. I kept landing funny, but at least I was staying ahead of him.

One-Eye growled. "Stand still, insect."

The crowd didn't like it either. They started making a high "keee keee keee" sound; the noise their pig/sheep/goat things made when they were scared.

I let 'em razz me. I wasn't fighting until I was good and ready. Leaping around was helping in two ways. My head was slowly clearing, and I was getting some practice testing my limits. All this time I'd had to pretend I couldn't jump higher or lift more than a regular old purple guy, so I hadn't had a chance to see what I could do, and it felt good to let go and use my muscles. I felt like a balloon that had slipped out of some kid's fist at a birthday party.

I was getting used to the sword too, adjusting for its weight, using its mass to sling my body around in the air. But I couldn't stall forever. I saw the chief squirming on his couch and realized that if he didn't like the show he could cancel it—and me—without a word. There were guards with spears and bolos and battle axes all around the square, just waiting for him to yawn. Time to make my move.

One-Eye had continued to try and close with me, hoping, I guess, to wear me out. Fat chance. Even when I smoked I had decent endurance. On this planet, with its clean air and the field hand exercise and the gravity deal, I felt like I could run a hundred miles and not get tired. I sprang again, straight at him this time. He'd got so used to me running away it took him by surprise.

I swung my sword like a baseball bat, the only way I knew how, right at his head. He ducked to one side, smooth as silk, and parried the blow with the big sword, then turned like a ballerina, all one thousand pounds of him, and snaked out one of his small swords after me. It caught me on the shin guard and spun me around. Luckily my head was clear now, and I had my balance back, so I landed on my feet. Okay. So I dropped to my knees pretty quick, but waddaya want? My leg hurt like I'd kicked a fire hydrant.

I looked down. The shin guard had a dent in it the size of a cereal bowl and was cutting into my leg something fierce. Blood was running down my leg and mixing with the dirt on my toes.

One-Eye inhaled and licked his lips. "Hrmmmm. Blood. Smell good."

Okay, now *that* pissed me off. He was going to eat me after he killed me? That was just plain rude. I got mad enough to forget I was scared.

One-Eye swung down at me. This time I noticed something. I'd been so panicked before by all that sharp steel that I'd just jumped. Anywhere. Now that I was a little calmer, I could see where all those swords were going to go, with just enough time to go somewhere else. Fucking Sai and his, "Be where his blades are not." Maybe he was right after all.

I jumped forward and right, getting my legs up just as his left blade cut underneath them, and dove between his upper and lower right arms, so close to his body that his fur brushed my legs.

I swung backhanded as I passed him. The fucking grip twisted in my hand and I didn't hit him edge on, but I did some damage. The tip of the blade was trailing red drops like rubies hanging in the air. One-Eye roared.

I hit the ground and launched again like a Super Ball with a brain, another frontal assault. But even wounded and disoriented, One-Eye didn't lose his balance. My blade shrieked off two of his and I had to twist like a contortionist to dodge another of his backhands.

It was his tail! That's why I could never catch him leaning. The most stable structure in the universe is a tripod—I remembered that from junior high science class—and the Aarurrh, when they reared up on their hind legs, were walking tripods. I was no swordsman, or swordswoman, or whatever. I didn't know a parry from a periwinkle or any of that Three Musketeers crap, and against a guy with three swords? With balance like that? If it wasn't for my jackrabbit routine I'd have been in five easy pieces by now. I had to even the odds, fast. Already I saw One-Eye tightening up his guard. He hadn't expected me to be able to tag him. He wasn't going to make the same mistake twice. I'd just have to find another mistake for him to make.

He came at me, more cautious this time, like a dog catcher edging up on a rabid Chihuahua. The sun was right over his head, stabbing me in the eyes. A blade came out of the glare and nearly sheared off my right arm. I jumped left, barely in time, but came away with an idea. Crazy, but—

I started circling him until the sun was on my neck, then backed up into a corner, acting scared. One-Eye took the bait. He came after me. My back touched the rope. One of the sword-posts was at my right shoulder. If this didn't work I'd just trapped myself. One-Eye would be tearing chunks off of a Jane kebab in an hour.

I jumped. Most of my leaps so far had been long and low, trying to keep plenty of distance between me an ol' One-Eye. Now I hopped straight up and kicked off the sword post, pushing for as much height as I could. One-Eye was a good twelve feet tall on his hind legs. At the top of the jump my toes hung over him by about three feet. He looked up, following me, right into the sun, and cringed, blinded.

Even then, if I'd come straight down I would have been dead meat. One-Eye was like Andre Aggassi waiting for the ball to drop so he could ace another serve. He didn't need to see me to know where I was. But what if I was someplace else? While One-Eye was still blinded, I swung my sword, not down, where his big blade was waiting to block, but straight out, hard as I could, letting the weight jerk me sideways in the air, over One-Eye's head.

I slid down his back like a kid on a water slide. One-Eye flailed with his swords nowhere near me. He started to turn. Too late. I brought my sword down like a cleaver and chopped through his tail like it was a three hundred pound salami.

Poor One-Eye went from tomcat to Manx in one swell foop. The crowd shrieked. So did One-Eye. He lost his balance and fell, bleeding like Niagara and dropping his two small swords to try to catch himself.

I didn't let him. I jumped on his back, drove my sword through his ribs and pinned him to the ground.

CHAPTER EIGHT

INTERROGATED!

That shut 'em up. The crowd of Aarurrh was as silent as a congregation when somebody farts in church. They couldn't take their eyes off One-Eye's body, like they were waiting for him to get up and wave and say, "Only a joke, folks. All part of the show." They couldn't believe that a little pink bug could kill a brave Aarurrh warrior.

A murmur started, soft at first, then rising, like a summer shower whipping up into a gullywasher. Pretty soon it sounded like feeding time at the predator house. Boy howdy, were those cen-tigers worked up. I was shaking so hard from reaction that I didn't pay 'em much mind at first. I'd only ever killed two people before, that guy back in Panorama City, and the Barahir Aarurrh who had attacked Queenie, and both them had been blind instinct. One-Eye was the first person I'd ever set out to kill on purpose. Sure, it was self-defense, but you try it sometime and see how you like it. I felt kind of sick and weepy. I wanted to curl up go to sleep for a while, but the crowd, who were pretty ugly to begin with, were getting downright hideous.

Queenie's gang, the smaller clans and loners, were cheering, but they were way outnumbered. The rest of the crowd was howling for my blood, surging forward so the ropes bulged in and the sword-posts started to tip. It didn't matter that One-Eye had been a bully, even by Aarurrh standards. He was an Aarurrh. I was an outsider—an animal.

Fights were breaking out. Queenie's pals versus everybody else. A pack of thugs ducked under the rope and started toward me. I thought I was done for, but just as I started trying to tug my sword out of One-Eye's rib cage, I was surrounded by four of the chief's big elite guard and the bobcat-faced living megaphone started shouting for everybody to shut up. It took a minute, but finally the volume dropped to a low grumble.

The chief stood up. He spoke. I couldn't understand what he said, but his voice stayed calm so I hoped for the best. I searched the crowd for Queenie. She gave me a reassuring nod.

The chief finished his speech and Bobcat broke up the meeting. As the crowd wandered off, the chief's guards marched me toward his tent. I got worried again. The chief might not want to murder me in public with part of his tribe giving me the hip-hip-hooray, but a little accident in the tent? I felt a little better when I saw that Handsome, Queenie and Sai were getting the invite too. You don't bring witnesses to a murder.

We filed through the flap. The details faded in as my eyes adjusted to the low light. Weapons and shields and wooden masks hung from the tent poles. Rugs were overlapped on the ground. Blankets and wicker baskets and trunks were tucked close to the leather walls. Four purple-guy slaves brought the Chief's couch back in and he settled stiffly into it. I suddenly realized that the couch wasn't just a chief's right. The guy couldn't stand too long without it. A young Aarurrh girl poured him a drink in a jeweled cup that had obviously been made for much smaller hands, and he took a long sip.

Sai and I were held back as the Chief had a pow-wow with Queenie and Handsome. Sai whispered a sketchy translation. "He promises that we shall be escorted to civilized lands at first light tomorrow. Handsome wishes to be part of the escort but the chief refuses. Now they speak of Handsome and Kitten's betrothal."

That didn't need any translation. I could see the happiness in Handsome and Queenie's faces. They bowed and stepped back and the chief turned to me and Sai, giving us a cold once over, especially me. He called over his shoulder.

A skin curtain at the back of the room was pulled aside and an Aarurrh like a blind ghost stepped out of the shadows.

He was a shrimp by Aarurrh standards, almost as small as the pony-size kids, but he still scared the pants off me. First, he was an albino. His tiger-striping was almost white on white, like the pattern on a fancy dress shirt, and his dreads were like fat white grubs. Second, he couldn't see. His eyes were filmed over with a milky membrane, the purple-black of the pupil showing through as lavender, like a grape drowning in liquid soap. And finally, he was sniffing like a bloodhound, his head hanging to one side like his neck was broken, mouth gaping.

Queenie and Handsome shifted uneasily as he shuffled in. They didn't like him any better than I did. The chief grunted something and that wobbly head rolled around, snout taking in a long breath, until that unseeing gaze settled on me.

I flinched back and bumped into my guards. Blind Ghost's four hands snaked out like they had eyes of their own, then slid around me with nauseating gentleness, closing around my arms, my neck and my waist, pulling me in. That snuffling snout started probing everywhere, my mouth, my hair, my armpits, my crotch. I tried to struggle away, but my guards' hands clamped down on me. I wanted to heave, but he probably would have sniffed that too. Finally he pulled back, staring at my forehead like he thought he was fixing me in the eye.

"A new smell." His voice was as creepy as the rest of him, a high, thin wheeze like a cat with a cut throat. He turned and hissed at the chief in his own language. He didn't sound any better that way.

They talked back and forth for a bit. Then the chief turned to me and Blind Ghost stuck his schnozz in my pit again.

I looked over at Sai. "What the hell is this?"

"He's a diviner. He can smell when you lie."

"Bullshit."

My guard wrenched my head around and pointed me at the chief. The chief spoke Sai's language even worse than Queenie, but he got his point across. "Where from?"

"I don't know."

Blind Ghost barked. "Lie!"

Crack! My guard belted me with a paw. It was like being crowned with a fur-covered frying pan. I hit the carpet. The boys picked me up again and we started all over.

"Where from?"

I shook my brain back into place. Maybe this guy *could* tell if I was lying.

I'd just have to tell the truth then. "Coral Gables, Florida."

Blind Ghost sniffed, then sniffed again. He frowned. "Truth."

"Where that?"

"America."

"Truth."

The chief growled, annoyed. He tried another tack. "Where that from here?"

"I don't know."

Blind Ghost was looking really unhappy. "Truth."

The chief started forming another question, but I continued. "I don't know how I got here. I woke up on…" I saw Sai twitch and something told me mentioning the teleport stone to these guys was not a good idea. "…on the plain. Near a battle between the red cloaks and the gold cloaks. That's the first thing I remember."

"Truth."

"No memory?"

"I remember where I was before, but I don't know how I got here, or where there is from here… or how to get back."

"Truth."

Blind Ghost and the Chief jawwed again, then…

"Alone?"

There's one I could answer without hesitation. "I am the only one of my, uh, tribe within five thousand…" I hunted through my built-in alien diction-ary for a word that meant a really long haul. "…Five thousand *ilns* of here."

My guard floored me again for sassing back, but Blind Ghost just stared. "Truth."

The chief stared too. I don't know how much these guys knew about their planet. They might have thought it was flat for all I know, but if an iln was anything like a mile they'd have to see I was pretty damn alone.

They talked again, for longer this time. Queenie and Handsome were start-ing to look worried. After a bit, the chief turned to Sai and grilled him about me, with Blind Ghost snuffing at him the whole time. Sai backed me up, tell-ing the truth, but also leaving out the part about the stone disk. After that, the chief had me pick up chests and his couch, all easy one-hand lifts, which amazed them all over again. It was only after I finished that I saw Queenie shaking her head at me like I'd fucked up.

Finally the Chief signalled the guards to take us outside again. The crowd was gone, but One-Eye's clan and the higher-ups were still there, chatting and waiting around. They came to attention and the chief had his mouthpiece make an announcement.

This time it was One-Eye's gang who were all smiles and Queenie's gang who were upset. I could see Handsome and Queenie wanted to speak, but they held their tongues. I wondered what was wrong.

I got my first inkling when the guards led me and Sai away. Instead of going with Queenie, we were put in some kind of supply tent with guards posted outside. "What is this bullshit? We're supposed to be free. Why are we shut up in here instead of over at Queenie's, packing?"

Sai shrugged. "I know not, mistress. Perhaps we are here for our protection. One-Eye's compatriots seemed less than pleased at your victory."

It seemed a little thin to me. "Yeah, well maybe. What did that snooty bastard say? The chief's mouthpiece? Queenie sure looked down in the mouth about it."

"My knowledge of the language of these savages is limited, but from what I could decipher it seemed nothing untoward. He merely named the warriors who would escort us out of Aarurrh lands."

Well, we could have wondered back and forth all night, but I was beat. Killing giant, four-armed tigers takes it out of a girl. I found myself a nice comfy stretch of floor and sacked out.

***

Me and Sai woke up before daylight the next morning to the sound of Queenie's purr outside the tent. She was talking to the guards, and laying on the charm with a trowel. I could smell cooked meat and sweet roots through the tent and the clink of crockery. After a bit there was a grunt and the tent flap opened, revealing Queenie carrying a bag full of breakfast and the guards chowing down on more of it behind her.

She hugged us and greeted us in a loud voice, laughing and setting out the bowls of food. As we started eating she stole a glance back to the tent flap and lowered her voice.

"They kill you. First night out. The guards who take are clan brothers of Hruthar. Wait for you sleep and…" She made a throat slitting motion.

The food turned to dirt in my mouth. Sai sighed, like he knew this was coming all along. One-Eye's pals had the escort job. We were dead meat.

Queenie patted my arm. "No worry. Raohah and Murrah save you." She meant Handsome and Kitten. "That night, you camp Black Rocks. Always first stop on long trip East. You lay down. Guards lay down. Then quick, you get up, carry," She pointed at Sai. "And…" She made a hopping motion with a hand. "Find rock like uklan's head. Raohah and Murrah wait. Take you."

"What's an uklan?"

Sai spoke up. "A desert lizard. Fear not, mistress. I know its shape."

I had a lot of other questions. Were these guys really going to wait until we were asleep to kill us? What if they didn't camp in the usual spot? What if they caught me before I got Sai to the uklan rock? I didn't get to ask them. One of the guards looked in and barked at Queenie to get out.

She barked back, gathered up the bowls and the bones, then gave me a sad motherly look and one of her rib-cracking hugs. She put me down and touched my cheek. "Keep eye open and claw sharp, Jae-yin."

She was out of the tent before I could do anything more than nod. She'd knocked me for a loop. She'd used my name. I didn't know she even knew it. After all that stuff about "good girl" and "bad girl."

Sai got all nosy. "Is something wrong, Mistress Jae-En?"

"Mind your own business. Just dusty around here, that's all."

CHAPTER NINE

ESCAPE!

I had to hand it to the chief. He'd solved his little problem neater than a CIA cover-up. By agreeing to let me go he'd satisfied Queenie's faction, but by naming One-Eye's pals as our escorts, he'd let the other side know that we were going to die once we got out of camp. Sure Queenie's side realized what was going on, but you can't just call the chief a liar. He'd tied them up but good. Luckily, Queenie was one smart, brave mama, or Sai and I wouldn't have known the score until their swords were halfway through our necks.

About an hour after Queenie's goodbye breakfast, just as dawn was seeping through the seams of the patchwork tent, the door flapped open and our two escorts popped their heads in, grinning, and motioned us out.

The ugly bastards acted like a couple of pederasts taking cub scouts to a football game. They led us to their pack krae with way too much chuckling and backslapping. They couldn't wait to get us out of camp. Sai and I exchanged uneasy glances, but what could we do?

You'd think that the Aarurrh would be their own mules, being built like they are, but they're too proud. They don't like to carry more than their weapons and a light pack and they never take riders. Queenie had been going

way out of her way putting me on her back during the krae stampede. No
warrior would have done it. The Aarurrh use the krae the way the purple guys
do, for meat and as pack animals and cart horses. Our escort saddled up two
of them for us, but hobbled them so that we couldn't high-tail it.

Sai had no problem mounting up; he'd been riding these things all his life,
but I was a little nervous. I remembered the whole wild-eyed herd of them
going off the cliff and thought maybe I'd just walk. When I stalled, one of our
guards picked me up under the armpits and plopped me on the saddle like a
dad putting a kid on a horsey ride outside a supermarket. I flailed around for
a second before I found the reins and stirrups and settled in.

Riding a krae felt kinda odd to somebody who's only rode horses before.
The saddle sat in front of the wings, practically on the krae's neck. And since
the thing only had two legs, the stride was more like a human's side-to-side
stroll than a horse's four beat roll. It wasn't bad, just different and it took a
little getting used to.

As far as the big birds being temperamental, turned out I had nothing to
worry about. These were pack animals, and pretty beat-down pack animals
at that. Our captors didn't treat their livestock any better than they treated
their slaves.

There was no official send off. Queenie was there, sad and quiet, but Kitten
and Handsome weren't, and neither was the chief or Blind Ghost. We trailed
out of the dark, silent camp and up to the rosey light that spread across the
plains and tinted the flowers of the blue-stemmed grasses the electric pink of
a hooker's hot pants.

***

Nothing happened during the day. We rode into the sun all morning, until
it was right on top of us, then rode away from it all afternoon. After a while
Sai started recognizing some far off mountains. "That is Shar-Vet, and that
the Tooth of Zavyan. We travel homeward. Think you they mean to honor
their bargain after all?"

I snorted. "You believe that, I got some Florida real estate I'd like to show
you."

"Flo-rida, Mistress?"

"It's an Earth thing. You wouldn't understand."

Our escorts kept up their palsy-walsy bullshit, pointing out landmarks, translating dirty Aarurrh jokes with the few scraps of purple-guy talk they knew, piling on the food and drink and exchanging knowing looks and private jokes that Sai, who had a Dick and Jane level vocabulary in Aarurrh, couldn't begin to understand.

I like to think that even without Queenie's warning we might have figured out what these bozos were up to from the food thing: they were feeding us way too much. If we were going to be travelling for three days we would have run out of food on day two the way they were shoving it down our throats. They knew they'd have two less mouths to feed after tonight. But even if we'd figured it out and escaped, I'm not sure we'd have made it.

From our weeks of hunting and gathering, Sai and me knew enough of the local veggies that we wouldn't have starved, but water was harder to find than an honest politician in Washington DC, and there were predators. We saw them in the distance a few times; vurlaks, Chevy van-sized six-legged hulks that looked like a cross between a Gila-monster and a pit bull with skin like velvet over concrete; and shikes, spindly, two-legged, four-armed tiger-monkeys with teeth too big for their heads. They hunted in packs and looked like they were distant cousins of the Aarurrh. Between those guys and a whole damn menagerie of other horrors I only heard about, Sai and I would have been lunch meat before sunrise.

We reached the outcropping of black rocks just as the sun was setting behind us in a sky like raw meat. They were a jumbled collection of natural stone towers sticking out of the top of a low hill like teeth growing from a tumor. They ranged from tree height to higher than a five story walk-up, and were split and crumbled like rotten wood. Boulder crumbs the size of Volkswagens were piled up all around their bases.

Tweedledum and Tweedledee wound us through the rocky maze to a wide clearing somewhere in the middle. There was a scorched ring of stones in the center filled with blackened wood and ash, and surrounded by sun-bleached bones. This was obviously a regular campsite.

I could see Sai scanning for the rock that looked like an uklan's head, and I let out a breath I didn't know I was holding when I saw him relax. He nodded subtly off to the east and I snuck a look. One house-sized rock did kind of look like a lizard's noggin. We spent the rest of sundown trying not to look in that direction.

Our murderous buddies made a big show of setting up the camp, building the fire, helping us with our bedrolls, and cooking up another big feast. It occurred to me that the fuckers were fattening us up, and that tomorrow night *we* were going to be the main course. Tweedledee grinned at me. "You eat good. Long trip tomorrow."

Yeah, through his lower intestine. I suddenly knew how Hansel and Gretel felt when the wicked witch gave them the grand tour of the oven. I wasn't hungry anymore.

Pretty soon, too soon, it was time for bed. As I lay down, an army of doubts invaded my mind. What if we'd beat Handsome and Kitten here? What if Sai had picked the wrong rock? What if I couldn't carry Sai and jump at the same time? Panic rose. I was sure our boys would hear my heart beating, even over the crackle of the fire and the train whistle of the wind through the rocks.

It wasn't my heart that gave me away. I forgot these guys were animals. They weren't all experts like Blind Ghost, but they could smell fear.

"Why you scare?"

Tweedledum had been banking down the fire when he turned. He took me by surprise.

"I… Animals. I thought I heard an animal."

He laughed, showing too many teeth. "Animal not what you need be scare." He went back to his side of the fire, still chuckling. I let out a sigh of relief.

Sai and I lay down and waited for the perfect opportunity, though what that was supposed to be I don't know. It was like a bad comedy. The Aarurrh were faking sleep on their side of the fire. We were faking sleep on ours, both of us waiting for the other to drop off. Finally I couldn't take it anymore. I needed to do something or I was going to scream. The perfect opportunity wasn't coming. I'd have to make an imperfect opportunity.

I rolled a little toward Sai. "Go pee."

"I beg your pardon?"

"Go piss, dammit! Then wait for me."

"Ah, a ruse. I understand."

An Aarurrh head raised. Damn animal hearing. Sai stood up. The Aarurrh were on their knees instantly, grabbing for weapons. Tweedledee barked. "What?"

Sai motioned to the dark beyond our low fire and said the Aarurrh equivalent of "I gotta go drain the lizard."

Tweedledee and Tweedledum exchanged a look, then waved him off. He wasn't the one they were worried about. He shuffled off. The Aarurrh didn't lie down again, but after a bit they tucked their legs under themselves and set down their weapons, talking quietly. I figured that was as good a chance as I was going to get.

I rolled onto my stomach and gradually got into a pushup position, pointed directly where Sai had disappeared. I prayed that the fire between me and the Aarurrh was hiding some of what I was doing. My heart was pounding like the subwoofers on a cholo's Chevy. Now or never. I pushed up, got a leg under me and launched like a sprinter coming off the blocks.

Tweedledee and Tweedledum yelped. I could hear them clattering to their feet. I didn't look back.

I landed fifteen feet from my launch point. Sai was tucked behind a rock the size of a toll booth. A spear whizzed by my shoulder and chipped sparks off a rock wall beside me. The heavy thud of paws shook the ground.

I flinched to Sai's side. "Come on, fancy boy! Mount up!"

Yeah, okay, I'd fantasized about saying that to him before, but in slightly different circumstances. He hopped on my back and I leaped for the stars. I didn't make it.

That first leap wasn't so good. I didn't adjust for Sai's weight, and ended up tripping on a refrigerator-sized rock I meant to go over. Luckily we crashed down into the shadows on the far side and the Aarurrh thundered past.

I got up with bleeding scrapes all down my left arm and hip. Sai didn't have a scratch on him, the fucker. I'd broken his fall.

The Aarurrh spotted us again as soon as I made my next leap, but I had the balance down this time and stuck my landing, a rock ledge higher than they could reach. They tossed their spears, but I jumped away and hopped from rock to rock like a mountain goat, staying off the ground entirely as Sai shouted directions in my ear.

Tweedledee and Tweedledum tried to keep me in sight, but the monoliths were a maze. They had to swing around huge blocks and double back from dead ends that I floated over.

Now I knew why Queenie had told us to wait until we got here to make our escape. This was the perfect place for someone who could leap to get away from someone who could run. On the plains the Aarurrh's bolos would have brought me down before I got a hundred yards. Here I lost them in seconds. Suckers.

I touched down by the uklan's head and looked around, nervous. All this was going to be for nothing if the kids weren't here to do their part.

We heard footfalls behind us and spun, terrified that it was Tweedledee and

Tweedledum. Kitten and Handsome came out of the Uklan's shadow.

Handsome motioned to us. "Hurry!"

We ran to them. They hauled us onto their backs and started galloping hell-for-leather down the hill toward the moonlit plains. Behind us we heard the frustrated howls of Tweedles Dee and Dum echoing from inside the maze of rocks.

We didn't stop running until daylight. I drifted in and out of sleep on Handsome's back and I'm pretty sure Sai did the same on Kitten's. I had a dream where I was back on the Greyhound my first time running away, trying to get comfortable lying against the window with the metal frame vibrating against my forehead and the skanky guy in the seat next to me breathing tuna salad all over me as he told me how he'd personally killed Pol Pot back in Nam.

I woke up feeling a slightly seasick when I felt Handsome slowing down. My head had been bumping against a buckle on one of his sword straps. Not exactly where I wanted to wake up, but better than that Greyhound.

The landscape had changed. It was hillier and lusher. There were twisty little bushes with dusty blue leaves, and tall aspen-like things that I thought were trees until I got closer and saw that they were more like giant, stretched-out pine cones.

We stopped at a stream and Handsome and Kitten gulped down water, sides heaving. Sai and I dismounted and had a drink and a splash ourselves. When the kids caught their breath they lead us up a path to a pass between hills that looked over a fertile river valley.

Handsome waved a paw. "Tae land. You safe there."

It was a landscape painting on acid. A patchwork quilt of fields straight out of a Jolly Green Giant commercial, except with purple plants, pink and safety-orange bushes, crayon-red dirt roads, a glint of river between bushy trees with black leaves, clusters of little six-sided huts, and far off in the distance a bulky castle, sandstone orange, all under a Pepsi-blue sky. It hurt my eyes.

Handsome turned to me. "Sorry you must run, back then. I want to kill Aarurrh men, but chief can't know we help you."

"Isn't he gonna guess? How are you gonna explain being missing from camp?"

Handsome and Kitten exchanged a sly glance. Handsome grinned and said an Aarurrh word I didn't understand. I frowned and turned to Sai. He looked embarrassed.

"Er… honeymoon."

I laughed and grinned back at Handsome. I swear he and Kitten were blushing under their fur.

After that we had a little food. Then the kids gave us some lovely parting gifts. Handsome undid his pack and took out the battle gear I'd worn in my fight with One-Eye. He'd even gone to the trouble of banging out the dent in the shin guard. Before I could thank him he'd unslung one of his swords and handed it to me, hilt first. "You have sharp eye. Now you have sharp claw too."

It was the sword he'd whittled down for me, but he'd smoothed out his rough hack job on the handle and wrapped it with new leather braiding. It fit my hand like it was made for me.

I was embarrassed. "Aw, man, Handsome—I mean, Raohah—this is great. I don't know what to say."

"You do favor for I. Say nothing."

I guess I'd solved his romance problems for him, but still.

"Well, thanks anyway. You already did plenty helping us get away and letting us ride on your backs. Now, how the hell do I wear this thing without tripping over it every five seconds?"

Sai wasn't quite as happy with his gifts. Kitten had brought him a bunch of froofy clothes, as usual not all male, and was happily trying to help him decide which to wear.

Sai tried to be diplomatic. "Thank you, mistress Murrah. But this really isn't necessary. Yes, very beautiful, but perhaps not practical for… Er, I'm afraid I don't have the correct anatomy for that particular…"

Finally he gave up. "Mistress, forgive me. These clothes are much too beautiful for me to make a rash decision now. With your permission, I will take all and decide later which to keep. Clothes as fine as these should not be worn for hard travel. I will continue to wear this sturdy shift for the rest of our journey and save these treasures for some grand occasion."

Kitten blinked. I knew just how she felt. Sometimes Sai used so many words you didn't know what he was saying. "Take all?"

Sai bowed like a maitre'd. "If that accords with your wishes."

Kitten giggled, sounding like a cat trying to swallow a fish bone sideways, and gave him a goodbye hug that made him squeak. I offered Handsome my hand. He'd never seen the gesture before, but got the hang of it when I took his paw and shook it. He shook back and nearly ripped my arm off.

Finally Sai and I waved goodbye and trudged down the path toward the psychedelic farmland as Handsome and Kitten started heading back to the plains, with plenty of "honeymoon" stops along the way, I'm guessing.

CHAPTER TEN

CIVILIZATION!

We were halfway down the hill before Sai remembered what I looked like. After so much time together wearing nothing but dirty loincloths he'd started taking me for granted. Now with civilization only a mile away, it occurred to him that he was walking with a giant, half-naked pink chick whose boobs were peeking out from under her armor.

He stopped. "Mistress Jae-En, er…"

"What's up?"

"Er, below us are the lands of my people. Civilized lands. You cannot… 'Tisn't proper for you to… We must make you decent."

He started digging through Kitten's scraps, looking for something that fit. The only thing that came close was a flimsy, green peignoir kind of thing that must have originally been worn by the Waar version of the half ton German soprano. It hung around my waist like a muumuu and didn't make it all the way to my knees.

"I ain't wearin' this. I look like Sophie Tucker."

"Mistress, once we are among friends, I will find you more suitable raiment, but until then naught else will cover your… your…" He motioned helplessly at my height and general hugeness.

I smirked. "Go on silver-tongue, see if you can end that sentence without me clobberin' you."

"Er, your… statuesque proportions."

I grinned. "Nice save, bubba. Alright, I'll wear it, but you gotta let me fix it up a bit."

"As you will, mistress."

He didn't say anything when I ripped the muumuu's sleeves off, or when I cinched the waist tight with a belt, but when I started strapping the armor on over it he had conniptions. "Mistress, please, in Ora a lady does not fight. She neither bears arms nor wears armor. It would be unseemly to appear in Oran society this way."

I turned on him. "Was it *unseemly* when I killed One-Eye and bought our way out of camp? Was it *unseemly* when I threw you over my shoulder and leapfrogged our asses away from those cannibal killers back there?"

Sai backed off. "I…"

I stayed nose to nose with him. "I don't trust this planet. Ass-kickings happen way too frequently around here for my liking. You say it's civilized down there? Well, until I see a 7-Eleven and a Kentucky Fried Chicken I ain't takin' any chances. I'm keepin' the armor and the sword, and if you don't like it I'll be glad to take you back to the Aarurrh and you can fight your own way out of the stew pot."

"Mistress Jae-En, forgive me. I meant no slight. You have been the soul of valor and are entitled to wear anything you please. I merely hoped to save you the embarrassment of becoming a spectacle. Dressed this way, you may be stared at, even mocked."

I snorted. "Sai, look at me. I ain't exactly gonna blend in with the crowd down at the local bar and grill no matter what I wear." Then I got it. "Wait. You're not worried about me. You think *you're* going to be mocked. You don't want to be seen with me."

Sai opened his mouth, but nothing came out. He didn't know where to look. "I… I…"

Poor little idiot. He looked so pathetic I couldn't hold on to my mad. All of a sudden I wanted to cuddle him and pet his little head, among other things. I sighed. "Aw Sai, I ain't mad at you. I just feel safer with this stuff on, okay."

He tried a smile. "I… I shouldn't have thought that you would be afraid of anything, Mistress."

I laughed. "I'm a million light-years from home, bro. I'm afraid of every-thing."

***

Sai was right. We got plenty of stares. And no wonder. We looked like a comedy act. I could have passed for a halfback at a toga party, and Sai looked like the movie poster for "Male Models in Distress." Slogging down the long, red dirt roads, we caught all kinds of gapes and gawks from the local yokels. It reminded me of my punk rock days, with my green mohawk and black lips, asking the normals, "What are you looking at?" And not getting the irony at all.

The hicks were poking what looked like short sections of bamboo into the dry dirt of the fields that spread out around us.

I pointed. "What are those?"

Sai looked around. "Lasi shoots. They grow into tall stalks with delicious leaves. A perfect compliment for krae meat."

"Huh. You cook too?"

"I? Cooking is servant's work."

"That so? You got somebody to wash your back for you too?"

Sai was insulted. "I left the nursery years ago, Mistress."

***

After a while we came to a bunch of the little hexagonal huts huddled around a well. There weren't any shops, so I'm not going to call it a town. The huts were covered in piss-yellow plaster, with beam ends sticking out through the walls. Single room huts were one hexagon. Bigger places were a bunch of hexagons stuck together. Dirty purple kids in grimy smocks stared at me like a tree had walked into town. Scrawny purple women peered out through glassless windows and made the same touching the eyes and mouth gesture Sai had made when he first saw me.

Sai got a couple doors closed in his face at first. It steamed him up. "Peas-ants! Know they not a Dhan when they see one?"

"Maybe if you scraped off a couple layers of dirt."

When the villagers realized we weren't leaving until someone talked to us, a scared, scarred old hard-case with a bulldog face and working man's muscles came out holding a hoe like it was a spear. He was looking at me as much as he was at Sai.

"What want ye here?"

Sai glared him up and down. "Do you threaten me, lout? I am Dhan Sai-Far, son of Shen-Far, Dhanan of Sensa. Lower your weapon."

The hick's jaw dropped. "A… a Dhan? But…" He shot another look at Sai's loincloth, then a scared one at me.

Sai went livid. "Dare you insult me as well? A Dhan wears what he chooses. And travels with who he chooses."

The attitude did it. The hick dropped the hoe and did the bow-and-crossed-wrists gesture as fast as he could. Poor guy. How could he expect to meet the upper crust out here in East Bumfuck. "Beg pardon, sir Dhan. Us blind, sir Dhan, not to see it."

Now that he'd had his ass properly kissed, Sai relented. "Come now, enough. Rise, please. I mean you no ill. My temper has been frayed by recent adventures. Merely tell me whose lands these are and we will no longer trouble you."

I stared at Sai, my jaw almost as slack as the hick's. I'd never seen him like this. Our whole time with the Aarurrh he'd either been mopey and suicidal, or terrified and apologetic. Now that we were on his home turf he was suddenly all lord-of-the-manor. Not even his ratty hair and dirty rags could hide it.

He had the whole village bowing and scraping in five minutes. He knew where we were and where we should go. He also managed to talk the hicks out of a skin of water and some dry little cakes that tasted like the paste I wasn't supposed to eat in kindergarten. We hit the trail again, this time with a spring in our step.

Sai was smiling like a Hare Krishna. "These are the lands of Dhanan Zhae-Gar. I have not the honor of his acquaintance, but by incredible good fortune, I am best of friends with the scion of the Dhanan whose lands border these. If Lhan-Lar is home we will be welcome and safe."

I had to burn brain cells to unravel all that. "So, you don't know this guy, but we're going to your buddy's dad's place, which is next door."

"Succinctly put, Mistress Jae-En."

"Thanks. It's a gift." We walked a few more steps. "Uh, Sai?"

"Mistress?"

"What's this mean? I saw the villagers doing it." I did the touching the eyes and mouth thing.

Sai looked embarrassed. "It means 'I do not see and will not speak.' One

makes the sign when one sees something unholy. 'Tis one of the command-
ments of the seven not to see or speak of evil."

"Evil, huh?"

"They mistook you for a demon, as I did, mistress. Take no offence."

"None taken." I was used to scaring hicks. Back home a bunch of bikers
rolling into some little burg always had the locals slamming doors.

***

Getting to the place next door took another day. These Oran nobles had
estates like Texans have ranches. We passed through endless fields and count-
less little clumps of houses. Most of the time we traveled on the little red
dirt roads, but once we came across a highway that looked like the Ventura
Freeway—eight lanes wide and made of rubbery gray stuff without any seams
or potholes in it. It was smoother than the highway to Vegas.

Looking down that long, straight stretch made me ache to have my old
Harley between my legs; traveling down a wide open road, new countryside
to explore. If only Big Don was here riding beside me, seeing all this. Suddenly I had another ache. Big Don would have loved this. While the other
bros would just roar from rally to rally, Big Don would pull off the road now
and then, just to look at the scenery.

We met like that, actually. Up in the Dakotas. I thought he was broken
down. He told me to turn off my bike and listen to the night. I thought he
was crazy. Then I heard the wolves howling and fell for him like a ton of
bricks.

Poor Don. Even if I got back to Earth, I still couldn't have brought him
here, not unless Sai's people had some kind of magic that could bring a man
back from being a hundred yard smear of red under a speeding semi.

I swallowed. My throat was rough. Fucker. For a dead guy, Don sure had a
hell of a long reach.

Sai seemed to think the road was something special too. He touched it with
his finger tips before we stepped up on it, then touched those fingers to his
heart and forehead.

I frowned and poked at the road surface. Hard as a Super Ball. "Damn.
What is this thing, Sai?"

He turned. "This is the road to Ormolu."

"Yeah, okay, but I mean what's the deal with it. You guys never built this.

You haven't even gotten around to inventing flintlocks or sliced bread."

Sai looked insulted. "You suggest that mere tae built this wonder? This is a gift of the Seven. We are blessed merely by walking upon it." He made the chest to forehead gesture again.

I'd heard him mention the Seven a few times back in the Aarurrh camp. I'd figured them for the local gods and forgot about 'em, but no gods back on Earth had ever come across with a turnpike.

"Who are the Seven?"

He gave me a strange look. "You truly are from far away, Mistress Jae-En. The Seven are Ora's gods, who made this world and all that is in it. They made the sky and the land, the Tae and the beasts, the roads and the Seven temples, the holy weapons and divine relics."

Holy weapons? Divine relics? Was this just religious hoo-haa, or was there more stuff like this road? "Where are the Seven now? Are they still making goodies like this?"

Sai shook his head. "The Seven warred, long ago, against The One, and we, their children, betrayed them. They have retreated to heaven and left us behind as punishment."

Typical religious bullshit. Make the rubes feel guilty. Yadda yadda yadda, but maybe there was something to it. Maybe these guys were in some kind of dark ages. Maybe I'd landed in some Road Warrior time when everybody'd forgot how to make the factories go. That would suck, because I was guessing the teleport disk that got me here was one of the Seven's ancient wonders and there weren't going to be any mechanics around to get the thing up and running again.

***

We made it to Sai's pal's house around noon the next day. It was the size of your average mental institution, with thirty foot high walls built out of dusty orange stone. There were six-sided towers at the corners, and domed roofs and pointy steeples inside, but no windows on the outside. Nice place, if you've got a thing for prison architecture. It made me nervous. Too many bad associations.

Sai had me wait out of sight while he presented his bonafides to the muscle at the main gate. They looked down their noses like he was street trash, but eventually sent a message inside. When word came back the gorillas changed their tune, bowing and kissing ass and throwing the doors wide open. Sai waved me forward.

The guards saw me and looked like they were going to change their minds, but Sai barked at them. They stepped back uneasily, like dogs who don't agree with their master's decision to let a stranger into the house. A servant led us across a flagstoned yard toward a long, narrow building butted up against the inside of the thick outer wall.

Sai frowned. "Where do you take us? We are here to see Lhan-Lar."

"Dhan Lhan-Lar is in the stables, sir. There has been an accident."

"An accident! What has he done this time?" Sai hurried forward. I followed. There was a mournful hooting coming from the stables that sounded familiar.

We went in. A wooden loft built over the stalls had collapsed and stable-hands were clearing away wood and bags of black tubers. Other guys were trying to raise the fallen beams. There was a dead krae pinned under the cave-in, and one that wasn't dead, but wasn't in good shape either. That was where the hooting was coming from.

A man was kneeling at the krae's head, stroking the thing's neck and whispering to it as workers tried to lever a heavy joist off its back. The guy was covered to the knees in krae shit and straw, and blood was drying to a sticky brown on his hands.

Sai ran toward him. "Lhan! Are you hurt?"

The man looked up at Sai, then glanced over at me. One glance wasn't enough. He did a double take and gave me a long head-to-toe, but otherwise kept his cool. He was handsome, not in Sai's league, but enough to get him a job on the soaps, and more bright-eyed than Sai. He had the rubbery face of a born class clown, but with a goatee and a ponytailed mohawk to keep him up with Waar fashion.

He turned back to the krae. "One moment, Sai. Old Chirrit needs a little peace and quiet just now."

We waited as the workers lifted the beam enough for Lhan to guide the nervous krae forward. The poor thing stood up with a cry. Lhan immediately felt along its legs, then stood to check out its back. He scowled. "Well, 'tis a life of loafing and lovemaking for you my lad. You'll heal all right, but your racing days…"

While he finished checking out the krae I gave him the once over he'd given me: swimmer's body, broad shoulders, narrow waist, zero body fat. He'd do in a pinch.

Lhan handed the bird over to a servant, then turned to us, a dazzling smile breaking through his blues like a jump cut. I could tell he was curious about me, but he wasn't going to get all googly-eyed about it. "Your pardon, Sai. A disaster of my own making. I became bored with country life and decided to redesign the loft to provide more room down here. I thought if I cantilevered... Well, there it is."

Sai was still anxious. "But you're not hurt?"

"What? You can't tell krae blood from noble blood? No, I am wounded in my pride only. You however, were walking in the lands of the dead the last I heard." He flashed a sidelong look at me. "I see you have brought a spirit back with you."

Sai glanced at me, obviously seeing me with Lhan's eyes. "Er, Mistress Jae-En, this is Lhan-Lar of Herva, my dearest friend. Lhan, this is Mistress Jae-En of... well, she..."

Lhan held up a hand and motioned us out of the stables. "She is a story that deserves our full attention, and therefore will wait until we have washed away the blood and dust of our recent adventures." He hustled us across the yard to the castle.

It wasn't nearly as prison-like on the inside as on the outside. The entryway was a high, wide hall with a big curving stairway and lots of jumbo doorways. The ceiling was a bunch of criss-crossing arches, like a cathedral, except they reached down almost to the floor, and sat on stubby painted pillars that bulged out in the middle like they couldn't take the weight. The walls were hung with colorful tapestries showing big battles happening under a sky with seven stars in it. Between the tapestries, they'd mounted wild saw-toothed and spiked weapons like they were art.

We breezed through one of the archways and then down a twisting spiral staircase. The lower we went, the warmer and damper it got, until we stepped out into an echoey hallway with tiled walls that dripped with sweat. Servants appeared out of clouds of mist. Lhan-Lar turned to me.

"Mistress Jae-En, if you will follow Li-Tin, she will lead you to the ladies' baths."

Li-Tin, a mousy little serving girl, looked like she was afraid I was going to eat her whole as soon as we were alone, but after a glare from Lhan she meekly led me left down the hall into the mist as Sai and Lhan went right.

The ladies' baths were a low, hexagonal room, half natural rock, half beautiful blue and orange tiles. This was where all the steam was coming from. It rose off the water in a round stone tub as big as a backyard pool but not so deep. The tub had been carved into the floor and polished smooth. It was fed by hot water that seeped out of the bare rock on the far wall.

Li-Tin help me out of my dirty muumuu and armor with reluctant fingers and stole peeks at my naked, alien hugeness with horrified eyes. I was looking around for the soap, and realizing that the new language in my head didn't seem to have a word for it, when she handed me a flat oval of flexible material like a spatula head. "What's this?"

She looked revolted. "You don't clean yourself?" She mimed scraping the little oval across her arms and stomach.

"Oh. Yeah. Right." It wasn't exactly Oil of Olay with eight essential moisturizers, but I guessed it would work.

As Li-Tin staggered off under the weight of my clothes, armor and sword, I stuck a toe in the pool. I nearly hit the roof. You could have boiled a lobster in that gumbo pot. After about ten minutes of eeking and ouching, I was in up to my neck and practically crying like a baby it felt so good. I'd splashed in a couple of streams since I'd come to Waar, but this was luxury. This was the damn Ritz. I let myself drift for a few minutes, brain locked firmly in the off position, until I started to get dizzy from the heat. Then I scraped myself with the little scraper. I was afraid my skin was going to come off in strips, like when you boil a fish too long, but it worked just fine. Of course water that hot would have steamed an oilfield roughneck clean without any help. I undid my hair and rinsed it as best I could. It turned two shades brighter. I felt really clean for the first time since I stepped out of my shower back in my one-bedroom in Reseda.

When I couldn't stand it anymore I heaved myself out and slapped around on the tiles looking for a towel. I was red as a cartoon devil. No towels. There was a door in the right wall. I opened it, thinking it might be a linen closet. It was a little room which was as dry as the rest of the basement was steamy. Warm dry air blew up through vents in the floor. I was dry in less than a minute.

As I was braiding my hair, Li-Tin came back, looking scared and embarrassed. She had a pudgy grandmother with her who cackled at me. Li-Tin shushed her. "Your clothes were… uncleanable. The Dhan has ordered clothes made for you. If you will allow…"

She motioned the old woman forward. Granny had a piece of string with lines marked on it. She used it to take my measurements, giggling at each ridiculous number. When she was done Li-Tin held out a big, thick, embroidered robe. "This is all we could find that…" She seemed really embarrassed to mention my size. I took the robe and gave her a friendly grin. She flinched anyway. It was like trying to make friends with a deer. "Don't worry about it. This'll do."

It did. Barely. The robe was roomy, but like the muumuu, a little short. It was obviously supposed to sweep the floor like a judge's robe, but on me it didn't quite come to my knees. Barefoot, I followed Li-Tin and granny out and up the stairs.

CHAPTER ELEVEN

QUEST!

Sai and Lhan were waiting for me on the second floor in Lhan's apartments, which were downright swanky—rich draperies, embroidered chaise lounges in deep maroons and blues, little dark wood tables with marble tops, vases, sculptures of naked people looking snooty, metal lamps with holes punched in them in complicated patterns, swords crossed on the wall. Tall windows looked out onto a tiny garden surrounded by the castle walls. There was a big, tasty-looking spread laid out on a circular table in the middle of three chaises. Lhan and Sai were digging in with their fingers when I came in.

Sai was talking. "But I *must* go. Though I die I must face him. Love and honor compel me."

I didn't really hear him. I was too busy staring. Sai and Lhan were totally transformed. Other than when I first met Sai, I hadn't seen him in anything but grubby cast-offs, with make-up smeared on his face and dirt and dried blood dreading up his hair. He was heartstopping now; black hair glossy and thick, his body lean and relaxed, and almost totally nude.

The fashion with the in crowd on Waar this year was apparently bare-ass naked. I've seen male strippers who ended their act wearing more. Sai wore a royal blue silk g-string straight out of International Male which barely covered his equipment, a couple of belts and straps, and a matching silk sleeve and half-chest piece that seemed to be modeled on the armor men wore in battle. This version wouldn't have stopped a butter knife, but it looked just fine. Lhan was decked out the same way in maroon. He didn't look bad either. A devil to Sai's angel. I wondered what they wore when it snowed. Maybe it didn't.

Lhan saw me hesitating and waved me in. "Ah, mistress Jae-En. You do my father's robe more justice than ever he has, the fat ruktug. Come. Sit. Eat. We will be but a moment."

I sat. I ate, more than happy to be left out of the conversation as I stuffed my face. This was the first civilized meal I'd had here on Waar and it was delicious. Chunks of red meat in a peppery sauce that you grabbed with little folds of bread, fruits that looked like sea anemones and tasted like sugary string beans, some kind of bitter wine that I got used to after four or five cups, little pastries, some with meat, some with spicy jam.

Lhan turned back to Sai. "If you are determined to go, then we must make haste. Kedac-Zir and Wen-Jhai travel for the wedding in Ormolu in three days at most. We must depart at dawn to reach them before they leave."

Sai looked up. "We? You join me in my folly?"

Lhan smirked. "Better folly than boredom. Father sent me here to supervise the spring planting, as if Dir-Var needs my help. I don't know one end of a plow from the other and do not intend to learn. 'Tis plain banishment. He approves not of the reputation I gain at court, or my appetites."

I saw the look in his eye when he said appetites and wondered what he was hungry for. He continued. "Your adventures sound much more entertaining. I'll not allow my youth to be squandered on lasi shoots and rodoc bulbs."

Sai looked relieved, and at the same time guilty to be relieved. "The Seven bless you, Lhan. You boost my flagging courage."

Lhan waved this away, embarrassed, and turned to me. "And what of you, Mistress Jae-En? Where go you?"

The question took me by surprise. From the minute I'd got here I'd spent all my time either hiding, fighting, or running away. Suddenly I had the luxury of making a decision about what I wanted to do next, and I was stumped.

Sai and Lhan waited politely while I let it all percolate. Did I go with them? Did I go exploring? Did I get married and settle down? Did I try to figure a way to get… "Home. I want to go home."

I didn't think about it realistically. I didn't think about what was waiting for me when I got back. There was just a sudden lump in my throat, and a squeezing in my chest. For all the amazing things I'd seen—four armed tiger-men, giant birds, castles, beautiful boys in porn star undies—what I really wanted more than anything was a beer and a Marlboro, and a wet November blowing around me to make me appreciate my leather jacket. Asphalt, car horns, FM radio, chop suey out of a Styrofoam box, the smell of paint, big hairy guys who knew the words to the songs in my head. I tried to shake the image of Big Don out my head. He wasn't back home waiting for me anymore.

Sai and Lhan were looking at me.

"I think I got here on some sort of..." No word for teleporter came to my head. "Transport device. A stone disk with a gem in it. But it was burnt out. If I could find a live one—"

Lhan interrupted me. "Sai has told me about your... curious history. He made much of your daring and your extraordinary prowess. You seem to have been his constant savior." Both Sai and I blushed at this. "And slaying an Aarurrh in single combat. Few men can claim to have done that. Not since the days of the War God have there been such stories."

"Lhan!" Sai snapped at him.

Lhan grinned. "Dear me, do I blaspheme?"

What was Sai upset about now? I turned to Lhan. "Who's the War God?"

Sai and Lhan exchanged a glance. Lhan raised an eyebrow at me. "That is a good question. Over a hundred years ago, a man appeared on Waar—tall, like you, and with impossible strength, like yours, but with tan skin and brown hair rather than your demonic hues. He claimed to be a warrior god, come from the heavens, but there have been a few who have said that it was some gift of the Seven that brought him here."

"You mean like my gem thing?"

Lhan shrugged like he didn't want to commit himself. "Perhaps. There are rumors of such things. The War God was a great leader. He swiftly became the ruler of Ora, then most of the known world. But as the years passed, his rule became despotic. He made himself High Priest of the Church of the Seven, and using the Church, he hoarded the holy weapons, and destroyed many holy sites as false icons, claiming they belonged to The One. All this under the guise of protecting us."

"Sounds like he just wanted to keep it all for himself."

"So his client kings thought. They believed he was attempting to consolidate his power and take from us the weapons that might overthrow him. They began to foment war, but just as the armies were on the march, the War God disappeared. The church says that we disappointed him and he abandoned us like The Seven before him. They daily pray for his return. Others say he died, or that he returned to where he came from. The peasants think he still watches over us like some benevolent guardian from some hidden retreat." Lhan laughed at this.

My heart was pounding. This War God guy sounded like another Earthman! Maybe he knew how to get me back home, but… "A hundred thirty years ago? And people think he's still alive?"

Lhan shrugged. "No one knows, but he didn't age as other men. Only in the last years of his fifty-year reign did he seem to approach middle age."

That weirdness was only a sidebar to me. "So, you think the same thing happened to me as happened to him…"

Lhan and Sai exchanged another look. Lhan coughed. "The Church of The Seven would have something to say about that, and we dare not suggest any such thing. The War God is an official Demi-God, but… a rational woman can certainly make up her own mind, can she not?"

I didn't like the sound of what he wasn't saying. "These church guys aren't going to come gunning for me for impersonating a god, are they?"

Sai started. "By the Seven! Do you think…?"

Lhan shook his head. "With your hair and coloring you are more likely to be mistaken for a demon than a god, but even were you His twin, to pay notice to you would mean acknowledging a comparison between you and He, and thus throw into question His divinity. They wouldn't dare."

I wasn't entirely easy in my mind about the whole thing. Maybe it's just that I've never really got on with organized religion, not since Father Flanagan tried to infuse me with the holy spirit in the confessional and I kicked him right in the chasuble.

"So does *anybody* know how to get me home?"

They hemmed and hawed, then Sai spoke. "The knowledge of holy relics is jealously guarded by the church. But I may be able to help. In the future. Wen-Jhai, my bride, is the daughter of the Aldhanan, our king. As the Seven's emissary on Waar, the Aldhanan could tell you what you need to know, and once I am tied to him by blood I might intercede with him on your behalf, if it were done discretely, of course."

My head was spinning. The way he said things! Sheesh! "Did you just say your father-in-law might know and you could ask him once you got married?"

Lhan laughed. "Brevity, Sai. An admirable trait. We must learn it."

Sai ignored him. "I'm afraid this provides no immediate solution to your problem, but if you could bear to wait here while I attempt to win back my bride, I'm sure Lhan would extend his hospitality indefinitely."

Wait here while frail little Sai got himself killed and I lost my chance to get home? Wait here while Mr. Body Beautiful Lhan took his extendable hospitality with him? "Sorry, Charlie, I got too much at stake in getting you married. Let's hit the trail."

I was all for leaving right that minute, but as Sai and Lhan tried to convince me that we needed a night to prepare, that fifth glass of sour wine hit me. That, on top of a whole day on foot under the big orange sun, and getting boiled in that stew pot they called a bath. Suddenly I could barely keep my head up. I think I remember Li-Tin guiding me through some dark passageways, but I'm not sure.

***

I woke up feeling better than I had in… I didn't know how long. The room I was in beat any place I'd slept so far on Waar. Hell, it topped the nine-hundred-dollar-a-month shit-box I'd been calling home since I'd moved to California.

I was on some kind of futon: a soft, firm pad that rustled a little when I moved, and a thick blanket made out of some woven material that kept me just the right temperature. The room was cool and dim, with a knife-edge of pink light cutting through a gap in the heavy curtains. I could make out the shapes of bulky furniture against the plaster walls. Everything was cozy and rounded, like the stuff in Snow White's room when she was shacking up with the seven dwarves.

I was practically purring. Even the pressure in my head from the wine felt right. A little pain to let me know how nice the pleasure was. I lay there awhile. Maybe staying here wouldn't be so bad after all; hot baths, comfy beds, good food. Who could hate that?

Well I could, after a while. Even in heaven I'd get restless. And there weren't any cell-phones here to keep me up to date on Sai's progress. Not knowing and having to sit and do nothing? That wouldn't be heaven. That would be hell.

I yawned and stretched and rolled out of bed. The flags were cool on the soles of my feet as I crossed to the window and threw back the curtain. The sun was peeking over the castle walls. I could see men down in the yard getting kraes and packs together.

I turned, wondering what the hell they'd done with my clothes, and stopped. Laid out with my sword on a backless chair was a brand new outfit. Grandma and the other elves had been busy last night, and they did good work.

They'd made me the standard Oran hot-babe get up: a bikini top and loincloth, but of some heavy green weave instead of the usual semi-see-through stuff. The cloth was reinforced with leather and rivets at the stress points, and all the bits were connected by leather straps. I also noticed that the loincloth, which on most gals trailed almost to the ground, was cut above the knees, probably to make it easier to ride. I had sturdy boots too, a perfect fit. My armor had been cleaned and polished and, most amazing of all, the breastplate had been banged out and reshaped so that there was actually room for my breast.

There was also a pair of leather saddlebags packed with two more outfits, one in deep purple and one in black, a bone comb for my hair, and one of those scrapey bath things.

I was ridiculously happy about all this. Ugly as I am, I've always taken pride in my appearance, and it wasn't until this minute that I realized how embarrassed I'd felt about the hand-me-downs and cast-offs I'd been wearing.

You think it's funny for a biker chick to be vain about her clothes? How much fuss can you make about jeans and a t-shirt, right? Just ask your neighborhood cholo. You know, the guy who irons his t-shirts and takes an hour pleating his baggy pants so they hang just right. Back home I spent hours on my leather jacket, oiling it, massaging it. I threw my Harley t-shirts out at the first stain. My jeans might have holes in them, but they were always Downy fresh.

I put the clothes on, amazed how grandma had got my cup size right without a fitting, and looked around for a mirror. There was one in the hall, a big polished yellow metal circle between two pillars. My reflection was a little on the brassy side, but then so am I.

I liked what I saw. A big, strong, half-naked, bad-ass chick in armor with a sword sticking up over one shoulder. I wouldn't have kicked me out of bed for eating crackers.

***

Riding one of Lhan's thoroughbred kraes was a lot different than moping along on the tired old pack birds the Aarurrh had given us. These were leaner and longer in the leg, with an evil gleam in their eyes.

Lhan picked out a high-stepping she-krae named Moonlight. "As gentle as a summer day."

A summer day in Death Valley, maybe. She held still enough when Sai made her kneel so I could climb on, but as soon as she stood up and Lhan let go it was another story. She skipped and sidestepped like a pigeon in a room full of cats. She craned her neck around and tried to bite me off her back.

Lhan called out. "Your knees, mistress Jae-En. One controls a krae with the knees."

I clamped down, hard. Maybe too hard. Moonlight yakked like a dog on a choke collar, then stood still, panting.

Lhan raised an eyebrow. "Please, Mistress, little Moonlight has many good years left in her. Use her gently."

I shrugged, embarrassed. "She started it."

Lhan smirked at Sai. "Perhaps your stories of Mistress Jae-En's strength were not exaggerations after all."

Sai grunted. He wasn't paying attention. He had his head bowed, lost in thought. Thinking about mister shiny-teeth Kedac-Zir was my guess.

We rode through the castle gates and hit the road.

***

It was a long boring day in the saddle, so I'm not going to tell you about it. The next interesting bit happened after we set up camp on the first night and Sai asked Lhan for a refresher in fencing. He was nervous about his throwdown with Kedac-Zir, and I didn't blame him. I'd seen the guy. Lhan said sure, so they took out their swords and started hacking back and forth beside the fire.

At first it looked like a bunch of flailing around, mostly on Sai's part, but after a while I started to see the science of it. It was a little like bayonet training back in Airborne school, but more complicated.

Lhan was a first round draft pick at this shit. He did everything as easy as taking a walk—no wasted motion, no effort—but his blade was always where it needed to be, always slipping through Sai's defenses. Not that that was hard. Lhan was constantly holding back, pulling thrusts that would have kebabed poor Sai six ways to Sunday.

It's not like Sai sucked, exactly. He did and he didn't. It looked like he really had trained under the finest masters, because he knew his stuff. When he was going through the drills he was fine; fast and smooth. But when they started to spar, when it started to matter, he fought like a spastic duck.

It was like he was thinking too hard. He'd forget easy moves he'd done right seconds before. He'd freeze up when he had an opening and miss parries he should have seen from miles away. Pretty soon he was as frustrated as a one-armed man trying to hang wallpaper, stomping around and cursing himself, calling himself a fool.

I knew what he was doing. It had happened to me plenty back when I was racing bikes. I'd be at the starting line, thinking over and over again, "Don't let out the clutch too fast. Don't let out the clutch too fast," and when the tree turned green I was thinking so hard I'd let the clutch out too fast. He was choking. He was trying to make his brain do the work he should have let his body do.

Lhan said the same thing. "Let the sword lead you, Sai. Do not lead the sword."

Sai got worse and worse. He could barely hold onto his blade, let alone use it. Finally, when he almost impaled himself on Lhan's sword after a wild, blind stab at nothing, Lhan stopped. He wasn't even breathing hard. "Enough, Sai. Let's call an end before we do ourselves injury. Our long ride today has wearied us both. Let us resume in the morning when we are both refreshed."

Sai gestured angrily with his sword. "How can I rest when I must face Kedac-Zir so soon? I am not prepared. My life depends on my skill and my skill is sorely lacking."

Lhan's voice hardened. "Forgive me, Sai, if I quote my old Master of the Sword, Eshen-Gar. 'One cannot teach a sleeping krae.' You are too fatigued. We will start again tomorrow."

Sai slumped, miserable. "As you say, Lhan. I only hope tomorrow is not too late." He dragged himself off to the stream to dunk his head. Lhan started to sheath his sword, but I wanted a try.

"Mind if I go a few rounds with you? I may look the part now, but I don't know move one of this crap."

Lhan grinned. "Certainly, Mistress Jae-En. It would be a pleasure. The first lesson is: the art is not, as you so delicately put it, crap." I blushed, but he was only funnin'. "Come, let us see what you have to work with."

He laughed when I unslung my huge Aarurrh blade. "Perhaps at first we should use less fatal weapons." He stepped to a tree and cut us some sword-sized sticks.

Sai came back as we were getting started. He seemed a little miffed. "Your weariness has left you, Lhan?"

Lhan just smiled. "I quote Master Gar again. 'One can often learn as much from observation as from participation.'"

Sai curled his lip. "Was Master Gar a teacher of the sword or of the platitude?" He went off to his bedroll and sulked.

Lhan took me slowly through the basics. Very slowly. There were seven guards and seven attacks, and a shitload of combinations to learn; beat-lunge, parry-riposte, disengage. No big surprise that he had it all over me on technique, but I did have a couple things on him. The first time we brought it up to speed and crossed sticks I nearly knocked him flat. The second time I remembered to pull my swings, but I got carried away escaping a lunge and jumped over his head.

He was too stunned to block and I whacked him hard on the arm. He hit the ground in a heap.

I ran to him. "Oh shit! Lhan, are you alright?"

He sat up, grinning and rubbing his arm. "By the Seven, Sai spoke of your leaps, but hearing of a miracle and seeing one with one's own eyes are two different things. I can scarcely credit it."

I helped him up. "Sorry 'bout that. That's cheating, huh?"

"There is no such thing as cheating in a fight to the death. Use whatever advantage you have."

I smirked. "That's why I want to learn all your fancy tricks."

He laughed. "You may never have much need of finesse, Mistress Jae-En. Your strength will more than suffice for most of the louts you face. But strength does not always win. Skill can often defeat strength, and skill and strength together? That is nigh unbeatable. Shall I demonstrate?"

"Sure. Go nuts."

He nodded. "Good. Now attack. As hard as you like."

I wasn't crazy about the idea. I'd cut the tail off an Aarurrh with one chop, and that was thicker around than Lhan's waist. Even with just a stick I could bash his brains in without trying. "You sure? I already put you on your ass a couple of times."

"Fear not. It will not happen again. Now come."

I shrugged. "You asked for it." I wound up baseball bat style and charged, swinging like Paul Bunyan.

I didn't have a chance. Lhan was like a cobra. I couldn't touch him, even with all my leaping around and dropping out of the sky. I couldn't even see him half the time. He was like water in a stream slipping around a boulder; sliding past my stick, ducking under my arm, dodging around my back, then slapping his stick against my skin or touching me with the tip with the precision of a kung fu acupuncturist.

It was my turn to be red-faced and frustrated, but when he finally called a time-out, I noticed that I'd at least raised a sweat on him. "Very good, Mistress Jae-En. You have a natural facility. Once your skill equals your strength you will be a formidable fighter indeed."

I nodded, still catching my breath. "Thanks. Er, listen. I don't want to beg or nothing, but, uh, this sword stuff seems pretty important around here, so…"

Lhan bowed, hands out and wrists crossed. "I would be honored."

Our eyes caught, and for a second I thought he was going to offer to teach me another kind of swordplay, then he looked away and the tension faded. We got ready for bed, separately.

Who knows, maybe all the tension was on my end. I wasn't going to blame him for not having the hots for me. I wasn't exactly the ideal of Waarian femininity, even without the freckles and red hair. I tried to shrug it off, but I couldn't stop thinking about it. What if I never got home? Was I ever going to find a local with a thing for big pink chicks?

Once we were all laid out around the campfire Lhan dropped off instantly, like a Christian with a get-out-of-hell free card, but Sai tossed and turned like a kid with his first dose of crabs. I couldn't sleep either. I had a couple questions about Waarian honor that were keeping me up.

I whispered to Sai. "Why fight this Kedac guy if you know he's gonna kill you? Why don't you just grab Wen-Jhai and head for the hills?"

Sai looked shocked, but then relaxed. "I forget sometimes that you are a woman, and know little of honor."

I bristled, but let it pass, remembering that Sai was an ignorant barbarian who knew little of girl power. He put on his patient voice. "Honor is the shackle that chains we Orans to the warrior tradition where strength of arms is held in higher regard than strength of intellect. Thankfully Wen-Jhai shares my modern philosophy and our marriage will be free of these backward notions. But barbaric though it may be, honor is still the law. I had but two options when Kedac-Zir attacked me: defend Wen-Jhai or die."

"But you tried, didn't you?"

"To try is nothing. Lhan informed me that when news of my defeat by Kedac reached Ormolu, my reputation actually rose because they believed I had died fighting bravely against overwhelming odds."

He sighed. "Alive I am a coward, and will not be able to show my face in court or country until I win Wen-Jhai back honorably, or die trying."

It sounded whack to me. "But this guy's like Errol Flynn times ten. You're gonna buy it!"

Sai sighed. "I don't understand your words, but I parse your meaning, and share your apprehension. I am reluctant to face this challenge. If there was another way…"

CHAPTER TWELVE

DISSENSION!

Early the second day we hit a forest. Lhan and I were pretty chipper, but Sai had woke up even glummer than he'd been the day before, and it just got worse with every mile.

This was the first time on Waar I'd seen more than twenty trees together in one place. They looked like giant Q-tips: tall and thin, with a fuzzy clump of branches and leaves way at the top. At ground level it was more like riding through a field of telephone poles than being in a woods. "This must be the only forest on Waar."

Lhan smiled. "In Ora, certainly. Kalnah, the city we ride to, exists because of this forest. The shipyards of the Oran Navy are there. They fell these trees for their lumber. To fell one without the Aldhanan's order is death."

I gave Lhan a look. "You guys have a navy? I haven't seen enough water around here to drown a rat in."

Before he could answer a shadow covered us, like a cloud blocking out the sun. I looked up.

Hanging high in the sky above us, exactly the way boulders don't, was a big, wooden pirate ship-looking thing with a huge leather Goodyear blimp plopped on top instead of sails. Actually, that's wrong. They did have sails, little ones, stuck on each side of the gas bag like fins on a fat fish.

"Jesus H Christ on a ten speed bike! What the hell is that?"

Lhan smiled. "An Oran man-of-war. You see, we have no need of water."

"But you guys never…! Oh, wait. This is another Seven thing, huh?"

Lhan nodded. "The secret of the levitating air was the closest-guarded mysteries of the Oran empire. It made us invincible. But in the wars that followed the War God's departure, Ora lost its empire, and with it many of our secrets. Now all our former colonies have navies of the air."

I watched as the bulky airship lumbered into a turn, pulling one of its sails in and letting the other fill with wind. What a way to travel. Not exactly the SST, but I bet the view was terrific.

About an hour later we rode out of the woods at the crest of a hill. I stopped to take in the scenery.

A wide plain stretched away from us for about two miles until it hit a high cliff. At the base of the cliff was an honest-to-god city. It wasn't big by LA standards. Hell, it wasn't even big by Albuquerque standards, but it was definitely a city. Towers and domes and spiky steeples stuck up over the walls and smoke rose into the air from a thousand chimneys.

I followed the smoke up with my eyes. The sky was filled with airships going every which way. I wished I had a camera.

Lhan pulled up beside me. "Kalnah, city of the sky." He started pointing out things like a tour guide. "To the south, by the river Kal, is—"

I laughed. "River? Back home that trickle wouldn't qualify as a creek."

Lhan coughed. "By the *river* Kal, is the Navy's shipfield and stockade."

He pointed where the airships were thickest: an open field next to a stone fort between the river and Kalnah proper. Docked airships floated above it like a fleet of Porky Pig balloons from the Macy's parade.

Lhan pointed straight ahead. "On the cliff over the city…" He looked over at me, sly. "You have no objection to the designation 'cliff?' Perhaps this would only qualify as a stepping stone back home?"

"No no, that's a cliff alright, wise-ass. Go on."

"You are most gracious. On the cliff over the city is Kedac-Zir's ancestral castle, which also serves as quarters for his high-ranking officers."

I had to squint to see the castle. I hadn't even noticed it before. With the sun behind it, it looked like part of the cliff. It was black and blocky, and the walls seemed to spread out wide along the edge like the wings of a vulture, hovering over the city.

"Cheerful place."

Lhan laughed. "Like its master."

Sai groaned. First sound he'd made all morning.

***

The streets of Kalnah were all hustle and bustle and a stink like an open sewer. Crowds of sky-sailors—they called them Kir-Dhans, which basically meant airmen—were everywhere: soldiers too, army and marines, in uniform versions of Sai and Lhan's fighting harnesses, unit insignia and symbols of rank on their breastplates and shoulder guards. There were shipyards and sail makers and rope makers, and a huge, heavily guarded enclosure with walls so high I couldn't see in. Something inside was roaring like a turbine.

I turned to Lhan and raised my voice. "What's in there?"

Lhan shouted back. "That is the temple of flight, where the priests make the levitating air."

"Priests, huh? Not engineers?"

"I know not the word."

We passed through streets full of bars and food stalls and shops and houses and apartment buildings, some as high as eight stories tall, all using the hexagon floor plan, and painted like candy wrappers—reds, oranges, yellows, purples.

This was where the reality of Waar really started to sink in. I mean, I knew it was all real before. I'd been cut, bruised, gone hungry and eaten like a queen, but this is where I started to feel it.

Before it had all been like some fairy tale—a really violent fairy tale: all castles and princesses and four-armed ogres. Now I was around people who were just making a living. Women slapping clothes on the lip of a fountain in a courtyard laundry, guys carrying big loads around on their backs, boot makers, brick makers, butchers, millers, fruit-and-vegetable sellers, street kids, merchants with snooty wives, a dentist fixing a tooth using something that looked like a railroad spike. Beggars, acrobats, pickpockets, hookers, and guys who, with a change of clothes and a Harley between their legs, could have joined the Angels no questions asked.

I liked it. I got it. I understood these people. The guys were just guys. The chicks were just chicks. They wouldn't die for some sucker's idea of honor if you told them heaven was an eternal blowjob. They might die for love, or friendship or even their country, but they wouldn't throw their lives away because it was more honorable to be dead.

Sorry. I guess Sai was pissing me off a little at that point. I bet he could have ditched his title, got the girl and lived down here on Sailcloth Street and nobody here would have given him a second glance. But with his upbringing that would probably have been harder for him than dying. Oh well, fuck it.

About ten blocks in, Sai snapped out of his funk and looked around. "Lhan, where do you take us?"

Lhan motioned ahead. "Kalnah was my home for two years while I served in the Navy. I roomed with relatives of my mother's: the Dhan Dal-Var and his family."

Sai cringed. "Please, Lhan. I would not stay where I would be recognized. Could we not instead find an inn?"

Lhan looked shocked. "You would ask an Aldhanshai to stay at an inn?"

"No, of course not. If I succeed, I will gladly accept your relative's hospitality for Wen-Jhai and myself, but since I have no hope of succeeding, I would not suffer the pity of good-hearted people who know that I go to die."

Lhan waved a hand, impatient. "Sai, enough. If you continue to speak like this you will defeat yourself long before Kedac-Zir ever has his chance."

"I only speak the truth."

Lhan turned his krae with a shrug. He was pretending not to care, but I could tell he wasn't happy. "Then away to the Nightflower ward with us, where beds are cheap and discretion is an industry."

Lhan led us into a neighborhood of dirty streets and shabby buildings. Slutty chicks laid their boobs out on windowsills like grocers showing off grapefruits. Shady guys talked in groups on the corners, watching us as we passed. I'd been in plenty of places like this, the Tenderloin, the Bowery, the Combat Zone. Every city on Earth has one. It looked like Waar was no different.

We stopped in a square surrounded by sketchy-looking inns and filthy food shops. Lhan dismounted. "Wait here. I shall inquire after a room."

Sai looked around in horror. "How do you know of such places, Lhan?"

Lhan grinned. "I was a Kir-Dhan when I lived here, Sai. Not a priest."

He crossed to the nearest inn. I wondered if he'd picked this area as some kind of revenge against Sai for being such a goober.

Sai looked up over the crumbling adobe skyline at Kedac-Zir's castle, which you could see from just about any point in the city. He swallowed, nervous.

He was looking more gray than purple. Now, after dragging us all the way here with his, "I must, 'tis the only honorable course," he was staring his destiny in the face and not liking it much.

"You alright there, Sai?"

He shook his head. "No, Mistress. I fear I am not." He didn't look at me. He couldn't take his eyes off the castle.

Lhan came back. "We have a room, and I have discovered that we arrive not a moment too soon. Out host informs me of gossip that Kedac leaves with Wen-Jhai for Ormolu tomorrow at dawn. You have only tonight to challenge him."

Sai paled. He turned suddenly to Lhan. "What... what if she's content, Lhan? Kedac is Kir-Dhanan of all Ora, the commander of a thousand airships. What would she want with a mere Dhanan's son? I don't want to ruin her happiness." He was practically begging Lhan to agree with him.

Lhan fiddled with his krae's harness, embarrassed. "A charitable thought, Dhan Sai. Perhaps you should ask her."

Sai caught the sarcasm and flushed a deep maroon, but even Lhan's disgust couldn't cure him of his cold feet. He played it off like Lhan had meant it. "Yes, yes! I must do exactly that. I must reach Wen-Jhai somehow and ask her the way of her heart. We must find a way into the keep."

Lhan jerked his mount toward the tavern. "Come. The stables are this way."

Sai was practically melting from shame, but he didn't call Lhan back. I felt as uncomfortable as a kid when mom and dad are fighting.

***

Things were a little strained in our room. It wasn't exactly a big room in the first place: a ten-by-ten box with two beds and a table, and with all the tension and hostility Sai and Lhan were throwing off, it felt like a matchbox. At least it beat the roost, which is where most people stayed. That was a big open room with cots all over like in a flop house, and a stink like the bunkroom of a biker's clubhouse after a week-long beer bash.

Sai kept trying to catch Lhan's eye, but Lhan just polished his sword and wouldn't look up.

Sai wailed. "But, Lhan, how horrible if I win Wen-Jhai only to find she preferred Kedac all along."

"Do you know her as little as that?"

"But I must be sure, must I not?"

Lhan's sword flexed he was rubbing it so hard. "Unless you go through the main gate with an honorable challenge, you go alone."

Sai sagged like he'd been punched in the chest. "If that is what you must do, I understand. I know how this appears. But... but could you not at least help me to prepare? You have been in Kedac's keep before. Is there some way to gain entrance without detection?"

Lhan's voice hardened like concrete. "Unless you go through the main gate with an honorable challenge, you go alone. I will wait here in case you repent of this folly."

Sai looked at Lhan for a long second, then sniffed. He stood, jaw out. "Come mistress Jae-En. If Dhan Lhan-Lar chooses to forget the many times in his youth that his steadfast companion Sai-Far followed him into folly, we do not need him. We are not helpless. We will reconnoiter the castle ourselves, despite the dangers."

He was obviously hoping to shame Lhan into coming along, but Lhan wasn't rising to the bait. He just glared at the sword in his lap as Sai walked out the door.

I rolled my eyes. What a pair of boneheads. They were like passive aggressive newlyweds having their first tiff. Disgusting.

I went after Sai. Not that I felt much like going. I didn't feel much better about this trip than Lhan did, but my future was sort of tied up with Sai's, so I felt obliged.

The crazy part was that what Sai was planning was as suicidal as facing Kedac one on one. I guess the difference was that, although he knew raiding the castle was dangerous, he wasn't absolutely positive it would kill him. He was absolutely positive Kedac would kill him.

CHAPTER THIRTEEN

VIOLATED!

It was sundown when Sai and me left the seedy inn and headed across the city to case the approaches to the castle. We got plenty of good looks at it along the way. The red sunset lit the place up like a picture postcard, a postcard that said "wish you were somewhere else."

What I had thought were long, low walls that morning when the the sun had been behind the castle turned out to be hundreds of dark brown tents that seemed to surround the castle on three sides. The side facing us butted against the sheer cliff. The place was wrapped up tighter than Fort Knox.

Sai sagged. "We shall never penetrate all that."

I agreed with him, but I wasn't going to say it. I knew if I pushed him he'd get all stubborn and try it just because I said it couldn't be done. If I wanted him to give up, I'd have to play along and let him figure out for himself how impossible it was. "Maybe there's another way. Come on, lets go see what the front door looks like first."

***

The front door looked like the gates of hell. The road up to the castle was a shallow zigzag carved into the face of the cliff just to the south of town. The only access to the road was through the navy base at the bottom of the cliff. Not exactly promising.

We peeked at the gates from behind the hull of a boat—a plain old float-on-the-water boat—turned upside down in a shipyard by the river Kal. The navy base was on the far side of the river, across a stone bridge. The walls of the base were thirty feet high, ten feet thick, and crawling with archers.

A squad of marines stood outside the gate checking a line of carriages and pedestrians waiting to get through. The line was an odd mix. There were fancy coaches with uniformed drivers that got waved through right away, but there were also lots of people in funny costumes. As we watched, a bunch of short, muscly guys in matching tights were being let in. They looked like the Oran National Gymnastics Team. Right behind them was a gaggle of cooch dancers in g-string loincloths and pasties.

I didn't pay them much mind. I was too busy trying to see around them through the gate. As the gymnastic team went in I got a look. It was grim. Right inside, four burly marines were patrolling with vicious, six-legged monsters that looked a cross between a bear and a panther: low and slinky, with powerful muscles and glossy, purple black fur.

"What are those?"

Sai shuddered. "Ki-tens. From the jungles of the south."

I snapped my head around. "Kittens? Are you shitting me? If those are kittens I'd hate to see your cats."

Sai pursed his lips. He wasn't in the mood. "You say it incorrectly. Ki-tens. The most ferocious animals on Waar."

"Go figure."

I looked above the walls to the cliff. The approach didn't get any easier once you got to the zig-zag road. There were stone guard towers, chock full of bowmen, set every fifty feet along it, with a gate house at every switchback.

I could hear Sai swallow. "It does look formidable, does it not?"

I nodded. "And I ain't got a clue how we get through that once we get up there."

"Could we perhaps—climb the cliff and go over the wall?"

I broke out in a sweat. I probably could, damn it. "Uh, well, I might be able to get up the cliff, but look at the wall. It's as smooth as glass."

Sai's face dropped. "Yes, I see that."

Now was my chance. If I pulled this off I could get him to forget the whole thing right here.

I sighed, playing it big. "I'm sorry, Sai. I'm all outta ideas. Since we're here, maybe you should just go announce yourself and face Kedac the way you meant to from the beginning."

Of course I didn't expect Sai to agree with that. What I hoped was that mentioning Kedac would push him over the edge and send him scurrying back to the inn with his tail between his legs. And I think it might have too, except that just then we got handed our ticket in on a silver platter.

Sai was just saying "Yes yes, perhaps 'tis for the best to abandon…" When he trailed off. He was looking along the riverbank. I followed his gaze.

A string of brightly colored wagons was parked in front of a dockside tavern, and as we watched, a crowd of bizarros in wacky hats and masks straggled out of the joint, yawning and stretching. A balding old guy as thin and wrinkly as a stick of jerky followed them out, shouting. "Hurry now, you lazy lamlots. We've near to slept though our entrance."

A midget in what looked like a yellow mini-skirt and tarantula dreadlocks bitched back at him. "'Tis your own fault, you miser. If you hadn't booked us in Rivi last night and Saen-Lat this morning with a thirty iln march between we'd be fresh as new paint."

Sai looked from the freaks to the gate, then slowly turned and gave me the once over like he was seeing me for the first time. He got a wild look in his eyes and licked his lips. Oh hell, I thought. Here it comes.

"Mistress Jae-En, I think for once your… er, unique nature may be an advantage. It appears that Kedac holds an entertainment this evening, no doubt for the amusement of Wen-Jhai. And these mad-cap fellows…"

"Yeah yeah, I get it. I'll fit right in with the freak show. Thanks."

Sai blushed. "My apologies, mistress. I meant no offence, but, er, you must admit…"

"Give it up before you swallow your whole leg, Sai. I already said I was in. But are these guys are just going to let us join up with them? I'd be a mite suspicious about some joker who wanted to use me to sneak into a castle."

Sai shook his head. "I was not suggesting we approach them, but merely…" He finger walked his two hands, one tip-toeing up behind the other. "…become part of their train."

"You think the guards are just gonna figure we're part of the circus?"

Sai looked uncomfortable. "Once again, Mistress Jae-En, I draw your attention reluctantly to your appearance. You will forgive me, but I doubt they will give us a second look."

Damnit, he wasn't wrong. There had to be some excuse. "But, uh, what about you? And our clothes? And our swords? We're not dressed like freaks, and they're not gonna let us in armed to the teeth."

Sai frowned. "You are correct. These are indeed obstacles. Well, hmmm, we shall hide our weapons here, and…"

"Hide our…! Are you nuts? This is crazy enough as it is. Without our weapons it's suicide."

Sai raised a finger like he was making a point in debating club. "You forget, Mistress, that I have no intention of fighting. I merely wish to speak to my beloved and retire."

"And if somebody spots us you'll be retired permanently! Things go wrong, Sai. Happens everyday."

Sai swallowed. "Well then, we will just have to take extra care. Now come, place your sword here with mine under this skiff, and as to our clothes… You will do as you are, while I…"

I stared at him as he started to unbuckle the straps that held his sleeve in place. The little bonehead was insane. Scared out of his wits to face one guy, but totally oblivious to the dangers of walking into hostile territory unarmed. He was like one of those idiots you read about in the news who go splat on the sidewalk climbing out a tenth floor bedroom window because they didn't want to face some jealous husband. Sometimes what you're afraid of has nothing to do with what's actually dangerous.

Of course, the real crazy one was me. At this point I should have let him go join the freaks and gone back for a couple of drinks with Lhan, but I'm a different kind of idiot—the kind that doesn't go back on her word, even when the other guy changes all the rules halfway through the game.

Sai pulled off his sleeve so that he was naked to the waist—and nearly naked below it, as usual. He took out his dagger and cut two holes in the shoulder end of the sleeve, then pulled it down over his head like a stick-up punk putting a pair of panty-hose on his head. He tugged the holes down until they were over his eyes. The rest of the bright yellow sleeve flopped over his back like a windsock. He looked like a gay Klansman with erectile problems. He did a little dance and looked up at me. "Well? Will I pass as a clown?"

"Oh, you'll do more than pass."

Sai looked relieved. It went right over his head. "Then we have some hope of success."

I groaned. "Sai, we've got a snowball's chance in hell."

"Snowball? I know not..." He stopped. We heard the creak and jingle of the circus wagons as they passed our hiding place. Sai made some Oran holy sign with his fingers and stepped forward. "Come, mistress. 'Tis now or never."

"How about never?"

He ignored me and stepped in behind the last wagon. I sighed and followed him. I felt naked without my sword.

***

Amazingly, it went just like he said it would—at least the getting-through-the-gate part did. It helped that as we were waiting in line, a gang of cross-dressing tumblers pulled up behind us and we got lost in the shuffle. The guards just waved us through all together.

But getting in so easy didn't make me feel any better. Walking up the cliffside switchbacks and seeing all the marines and ki-tens and crossbows and iron gates, all I could think about was how the hell we were going to get back out when everything went south. Notice I said when, not if. With Sai involved I couldn't see how we'd manage to pull this off without a hitch.

The picture didn't get any brighter when we walked into the castle itself. Security was tighter than a flounder's sphincter. The main entrance into the castle courtyard had a double set of drop-down iron gates with big spikes on the bottom. There were guards every five feet and crossbow guys all along the tops of the walls.

Sai was checking them out too. He swallowed. "Perhaps... perhaps..."

I put an arm around his shoulders. "If you say you're getting cold feet now I'm going to throw you off the cliff."

He gave me a sick little smile. "I was going to say nothing of the kind."

"Good."

We could see the fancy carriages dropping off fancy people at a pair of tall gold doors at the far end of the courtyard. That's not where we went. The guards steered all the acts to a small door around a corner where a fat guy in a deep purple robe waved us into line. He looked like a snooty eggplant. "Hurry now, hurry. You're late as it is already. They've begun the second meat course."

The freaks parked their wagons and unloaded their gear as quick as they could while Eggplant bustled around with a list, checking people off. This is it, I thought. This is where they pull off our fake moustaches and feed us to the ki-tens. We tried to stay as close to the wagons as we could, but that wasn't enough. We needed to look busy. I caught the midget's eye. "Need any help?"

He scowled at me. "Look to your own kit... er, lass."

Eggplant found us a minute later. "And you are?"

I could see the sweat popping out on Sai's forehead. I was a little damp myself. I jerked a thumb over my shoulder at Slim-Jim's crew. "We're with them."

Eggplant raised an eyebrow. He called to Slim-Jim. "Are these yours, Jit-Bur?"

Slim-Jim gave us the once over. "Never seen them before in my life."

My whole body tensed, ready to fight. It would have been pointless with so many guards around. But instinct doesn't know from pointless. I heard Sai whimper beside me.

Eggplant turned on me, glaring. He put his hands on his hips. "Coin catchers, eh? Well, no-one gets paid who isn't on this list, so you might as well start walking. And if I didn't have such a kind heart I'd throw you out on your hindquarters."

I almost melted with relief. He thought we were just angling for a spot on the show, not trying to sneak into Kedac's bride's boudoir. The plan had tanked, just like I'd thought, but at least we weren't going to end up as ki-ten kibble. Now we could go back to the inn and drink ourselves stupid like I'd wanted to all along.

I hadn't counted on Sai.

He crossed his wrists and bowed his head to Eggplant. "Please, noble master? We ask for no pay, just the opportunity to perform before his most benevolent excellency the Kir-Dhanan."

Eggplant laughed. "An opportunity to pass the hat is more like it." He harrumphed and made a big show of checking his list as I died inside for about the tenth time that night. Finally he looked up. "Well, you're in luck. The Vinkolt sword-divers haven't shown and the axe juggler had a little mishap while warming up, so we have a place open. What do you do?"

I had no idea what we did. I was a big pink freak. Wasn't that enough? Fortunately—or maybe, now that I think about it, unfortunately—Sai, for once in his life, was firing on all cylinders. "She... she is, Mistress Jae-En, the demon giantess of far Oompaloo. The strongest being, man or woman, on all Waar."

Eggplant shrugged, unimpressed. "A strength act?" He gave me another look. "Well, at least you have *some* novelty going for you." He turned to Sai. "And what do you do, besides beg?"

Sai picked that moment to run out of ideas. "I... I, er... I. That is..."

I grabbed him by the belt and lifted him over my head one-handed. Sai squeaked like a kid getting a wedgie, which is exactly what he was. I smirked at Eggplant. "He makes funny noises."

Eggplant and a lot of the other acts gaped. Eggplant opened and closed his mouth like a goldfish. "Astonishing. You... You may do very well. Very well indeed."

I set Sai down. He collapsed to his knees, moaning. Eggplant pulled himself together and gave us a hard look. "You are welcome to any coin that freely comes your way, but if I catch you turning up your palms..." He made a chopping motion. "You'll have no hands to count your riches with, comprehend?"

I nodded. Sai was too busy groaning.

The freaks had finished unloading their props, so Eggplant motioned for everybody to follow him through the door. I helped Sai up and we got in line. He was kinda pale. "Mistress, that was most... uncomfortable."

"Sorry, Sai. It was all I could think of."

We started down a tight hallway. Eggplant called back down the line. "You'll be staged in the servants' dining hall until your turn is called. Do not wander off. Anyone found in a forbidden area will be killed."

Nobody else batted an eye. They probably heard it in every castle they gigged in, but Sai and I exchanged uneasy glances. Forbidden areas were exactly where we were going to wander off to.

The mess area was so low I had to duck my head every five feet so I wouldn't knock myself loco on the heavy wood beams that held up the ceiling. It was hot and smelly too. Too many show folk packed into too little space: contortionists twisting themselves into pretzels, acrobats turning handsprings, jugglers, singers and acts I couldn't even begin to guess at, all talking and sweating at once.

A woman in a dress that looked like she was being attacked by cheerleader pom-poms wasn't helping any. She had some kind of dog act. They weren't dogs, of course. They were little piggy six-legged red things, cat size, but with heads like a fruit bat's: huge ears and noses that looked like they'd been turned inside out. It wasn't their looks that drove me nuts. They made a noise like a pack of dentist drills gone feral, and of course everybody was trying to shout over them so it all got louder and louder. My little problem with enclosed spaces started to come on pretty quick.

I shouted in Sai's ear. "What's the deal? This fucking castle is huge. Why is this place so cramped?"

Sai looked at me like I'd asked why wheels weren't square. "Why, to make room for the spaces where people actually live."

"Don't the servants live here?"

"Yes." He looked toward the door we had come in and changed the subject like he'd answered my question. "Have you a plan, Mistress Jane? We have done remarkably well so far, but you see that both doors are guarded."

I stared at him. He'd just blown off half the population of his country with one word and he didn't seem to notice. Servants weren't people. Nice to know. I had half a mind to give him an earful about it, but this really wasn't the time. Some day when we weren't up shit creek without a canoe. I checked out the doors.

There were two—the one we came in, back to the narrow hallway, and another one that led to a flight of stairs. Every ten minutes or so, Eggplant would pop out of that one and call for the next act, so it probably went up to the banquet room.

We didn't have swords anymore, so fighting our way out would be a little tough, and even if we did have swords, fighting wasn't the smartest option. People were going to notice if I just walked over and decapitated one of the guards, and the whole point of this shindig was to get in, talk to Wen-Jhai, and get out without anybody in the castle the wiser.

We needed a distraction—some kind of craziness that would pull the guards away from the doors. I looked around the room again. It was pretty crazy in there already. People were getting hot under the collar everywhere I turned. Everybody was in everybody else's way. You couldn't turn around without tripping over somebody's feet or bumping somebody's elbow. It wouldn't take much to push it over the edge. If only those damn bat-pig things would shut up and let me think.

I almost smacked myself in the forehead. Duh! The bat-pigs. I turned to Sai. "Okay, I got it. Get ready to move."

A whistle stabbed me in the ear. I looked up. Eggplant was waving at Sai and me from the stairs. "Strength act! Wake yourselves. Bring your giantess, little man. You're on."

Sai shot a glance at me. "Oh, but…"

I stood up. "We're not ready."

Eggplant laughed. "If you're not ready you don't go on at all. I'll turn you over to the guards for wasting my time. Now hurry. Quick step, quick step."

What the hell could we do? I started for the door. Sai hung back. I grabbed his arm and pulled him along.

He squeaked. "But how can we…?"

I hissed in his ear. "Our only chance is to go do our song and dance, then come back here and hope we'll still get to pull the fire alarm when we get back."

"But we have no act! What are we going to do?"

"This was your idea. You tell me."

"But I never expected…"

We reached Eggplant. He gave me a once over. "You go out like that?"

I looked down at my self. "Like what?"

He rolled his eyes. "Amateurs! You lose half your mystery before you start." He called to one of the freaks. "Stiltwalker, lend this giant infant a cloak."

The guy tossed Eggplant a long, green cloak, and Eggplant threw it at me. "Mystery. You see?"

I didn't really, but I put the thing on anyway as he turned and waddled up the stairs. We followed his double-wide behind up two flights into a huge, steaming kitchen. The ceiling was as low as the mess hall. The cooks ran around with their heads hunched down, sweating into hot tub-sized kettles. At least it smelled nicer up here. Whole carcasses turned on spits in fireplaces bigger than New York apartments. Pots boiled on charcoal grills and nearly-naked serving girls took heaping platters of fancy grub from the cooks and ran out through a curtained door.

Eggplant waved us on. "This way. This way."

We tiptoed through the chaos, dodging trays and carts and meat cleavers. I got a few stares along the way and heard one of the cooks say "fell in the flour bin" when he thought I was out of earshot.

I was too worried to take much in. What the hell were we going to do? I've never been real good in front of big groups of people. I've got no problem racing bikes or riding rodeo. That's different. That's a contest. I don't think about the crowd. All I worry about is beating my opponent or the eight second bell. Here I was supposed to entertain people. I got the heebie-jeebies just thinking about it. I mean, I can be the life of the party and tell a joke or two when I'm with people I know, but this... I had to pull a whole circus act out of my ass on the fly, for Christ's sake.

And as if that wasn't enough pressure, it had to be good too. If we just stood there with our faces hanging out somebody might peg us as fakes and, hello ki-tens. Even if that didn't happen, Eggplant would probably boot us back down the cliff so fast we wouldn't get a chance to try our sneak.

Eggplant led us out of the kitchen and across a wide hall to another doorway. Orange light came around the sides of a curtain and we could hear voices and laughter. He turned to us. "Wait here. I shall return for you when it is time." He stepped through the curtain.

Sai and I looked around, there were guards posted at both ends of the corridor and serving girls walking through constantly. I shrugged. "Not yet."

We peeked through the curtain. I shouldn't have. My insides turned to ice. Through the door was a big room with high ceilings and too much decoration. Armor and weapons cluttered the walls along with animal heads out of an acid trip—chupacabras, jackalopes, flying purple people eaters, you name it, they were all there. And anywhere there was any leftover space there were big murals of studly guys hunting more unlucky livestock.

Below the tapestries the place was wall to wall people, all lying down on couches and stuffing themselves from little tables set in front of them. The couches were laid out in a big "U," three deep on the two long sides with a single row on a raised platform at the curve, all facing into an open area in the center.

The platform was where all the big shots sat—sorry, lay—and looked down on all the not-so-big-shots. Everybody there was *some* kind of big shot. Even the guys furthest away from the platform were duded up like Mardi Gras floats. Over half the guys were navy brass, decked out in dress kilts and capes, with chests inches deep in medals. The women either wore the usual Oran bikini loincloth if they had the bod for it—or at least thought they did—or a less revealing toga deal if they needed to cover up.

Men and women shared couches. Most of the time the guy would lie with his head at one end and the gal with her head down the other so they could both reach the grub and watch the show, but some of the younger couples laid side by side and I could see a lot of groping going on in the dark.

The crowd was watching a couple guys in the center of the "U" who were doing a goofy Three Stooges sword fight act. There was a lot of butt-smacking and eye-gouging and snappy patter going on. They ate it up, laughing every time one guy's harness dropped around his ankles and he fell flat on his face, or the other guy got a cut on his finger and cried like a baby. I cringed at the thought of having to go out there and follow them.

Sai pulled his eye from the curtain and looked at me, upset. "She is not there!"

"Who?"

"Wen-Jhai. I fail to see her."

I looked again. I'd been so freaked by the size of the crowd that I'd forgot to search for our target. I found Kedac easy enough. His teeth were the brightest thing in the room. He was front and center on the platform, on an extra-fancy couch. Wen-Jhai wasn't with him. There was another broad sharing his loveseat, a sultry, Sigourney Weaver type, tall, slinky, and as cold-looking as Ilsa, She-Wolf of the SS.

I raised an eyebrow at Sai. "Who's the dragon lady?"

"Pardon?"

"The ice queen. Sitting with Kedac."

He looked again. "Yes. Kedac's cousin, the Dhanshai Mai-Mar. She runs his household. She..." He stopped and squinted. "How odd."

"No shit. If this knees-up is all for Wen-Jhai, what's Kedac's cousin doing in the place of honor?"

Sai kept his eye to the curtain. "Eh? Yes, that too is odd, but there is something else. Why is my future brother-in-law here?"

"Wen-Jhai's brother?" That didn't sound so odd, considering.

"No no. My sister's betrothed, Vawa-Sar. He sits just left of Kedac. What does he here? And dressed like an Ormolu dandy?"

I took a gander at the guy, a decked-out drip with trying-too-hard written all over him. His hair was too oily, his moustache too thin, his harness loaded down with too much gold. If he'd just relaxed he would have been decent looking. He was plenty tall and buff, but right now he looked like the guy who thought it was supposed to be a costume party.

"Uh-huh. He's a dude alright." I didn't really care who he was. I just wanted to find Wen-Jhai and get this cluster-fuck over with. "But listen, Wen-Jhai not being here is a good thing, right? If she's somewhere else in the castle it'll make it a hell of a lot easier getting her alone for a little heart to heart."

"You speak the truth, mistress, but none the less I am concerned. Could she be unwell? Hurt?"

"Maybe she's got a couple of black eyes."

Sai stared at me. "Mistress Jae-En, Kedac may be my rival, but to suggest that any Oran Dhan…"

"Yeah yeah, forget it. She probably just has gas or something."

Sai looked like he was ready to slap me, but just then a wave of clapping and cheering came from behind the curtain and Eggplant poked his head through. "'Tis time, coincatchers. Do not make me regret my charity."

My heart did a flip-flop. I'd almost forgot that we were supposed to go on. Eggplant held the curtain open and the two sword clowns stumbled into the hall, flushed and grinning. Their hands and hats were full of coins. Sai started forward, but I couldn't move. Eggplant waved impatiently. "Come on, come on."

Sai touched my shoulder. "Mistress Jae-En?"

It broke the spell. I blew out a breath like a horse and followed him out, heart hammering.

The crowd got quiet as Eggplant pushed us to the center of the "U." I heard whispering all around me. "Demon." "Giant." When he got us into position before Kedac's couch, Eggplant stepped in front of us and raised his arms. "Dhans, Kir-Dhans, Dhanans and Dhanshai, and most benevolent, generous Kir-Dhanan, we present to you now a surprise; an oddity so unique as to verge on the fictitious."

The audience chuckled.

"And yet she exists. She waits eagerly to astound you with her extraordinary powers. Munificent Kir-Dhanan and nobles all, I give you Mistress Jae-En, demon giantess of far Oompaloo, the strongest being, man or woman, on all Waar!"

The applause from the crowd was just polite. They were going to wait and see. Eggplant turned to us. "Luck, coincatchers. The Seven be with you." He stepped between us and headed for the curtain.

I stood there.

Sai stood there.

I stood there some more.

A woman giggled out in the darkness.

Sai elbowed me. "Do something."

I nudged him back. "You do something. You're supposed to do the talking."

"Oh. Oh yes." He coughed and stepped forward. "Er…" He stopped. Somebody else giggled. Sai blushed. I could see it even from behind him. It covered his whole back. He tried again. "Dhan's and Dhanshai, Noble

Kir-Dhanan, may I present to you Mistress Jae-En, the demon, er, the *terrible* demon giantess of far... of far..."

I hissed out of the side of my mouth. "Oompaloo."

"Of far Oompaloo. The strongest woman, or man for that matter, on all Waar!"

Silence. Some joker spoke up. "Yin-Yir said that already. And better."

Sai was sweating buckets. He swallowed. "Er... yes. Well... then the time for words it done!" He turned to me, holding out his arms like Vanna White showing off a leatherette livingroom set. "Mistress Jae-En, show us your strength."

The whole room looked at me, wondering what I was going to do. I was wondering that myself. Well, first of all, I was boiling in the damn cloak Eggplant had saddled me with. I untied the strings from around my neck and shrugged it off.

The crowd gasped. I stopped. Oh yeah, I forgot. I was a freak. I didn't need to do anything to make an impression. Now I got what Eggplant had been saying. Mystery. I'd been standing there letting the crowd wonder what I looked like without even knowing what I was doing.

Well, I could probably kill a few minutes just letting them look at me. I stood up straight and turned around. I felt like a bodybuilder. Ah-ha! Idea! I was still ripped from all the slave labor Queenie had put me through. I made a bicep. The crowd 'oohed.' I made the other one. The crowd 'ahhed.'

My brain raced, trying to remember all the bodybuilding poses. One of my biker boyfriends had been into that shit—making up for other shortcomings—and I'd gone to a few of his contests: double biceps, side triceps, lat spread, front quads. I ran out way too fast. I could hear the crowd getting restless when I started going into reruns, so I ended it with the Schwarzenegger "drawing-the-bow" pose and the Steve Reeves victory pose. The crowd clapped, but I could tell my novelty was wearing off fast. I was going to have to actually do something.

"Sai, come here."

He looked suspicious. "Mistress?"

"Just come here, damnit."

"For what purpose?"

I growled. He was pissing me off. "You told them I did a strong man act. I gotta lift something, don't I?"

"Me?"

"Yes, you. Come on."

"I... I don't care to."

I made a swipe for him. He danced away. "But it hurts."

The audience chuckled.

That gave me another idea. I hissed at Sai. "That's good. Keep away from me. Pretend you're scared."

"Pretend?"

He dodged another swipe. I made my grabs bigger, tripping and cursing when I missed. Sai skipped away from me like a bunny, his sleeve-mask flapping around behind him. I couldn't tell if he was acting or not. Whichever, the audience ate it up. I played it for as long as I could, then made a real grab and caught Sai around the neck. He yelped.

The crowd laughed. I swatted him on the head. They laughed harder. "Hold still!" Another swat. Another laugh. Sai didn't move. I think I may have dazed him.

I raised my free hand like a gymnast before a routine, grabbed Sai by the belt, then hoisted him one-handed over my head.

The crowd gasped. They'd been pretty sure I was going to lift him eventually, but they weren't expecting that.

Sai squealed and squirmed. I was losing him. I set him down fast. He bounced. The crowd cheered. Sai crumpled to his knees, clutching himself. The crowd loved it. After all, what's funnier than a guy getting it in the nuts?

I was feeling better. I knew how to play this now. These guys had all the class and sophistication of rubes at an Arkansas cooch show. As long as I was smacking somebody around or making a fool out of somebody they'd eat out of the palm of my hand.

I looked at the crowd. "Not heavy enough." I shaded my eyes like I was searching for a victim. The audience laughed. Everywhere I turned people shrank away, waving their arms like they were fending me off.

I spotted a guy one row back who would make an impressive lift: a burly marine with a forest of medals hanging off his harness. He looked about six-two—tall for a purple guy—and two-fiftyish—at least that's what I figured he'd weigh on Earth. Here it would feel like he weighed half that. I wouldn't be able to lift him one-handed, but I'd benched his earth-weight in my time, so I'd be able to do something with him.

But I didn't want to lift him right away. If I did, I'd have to come up with something else after that. I needed a way to kill time. That way I could end the act with him and get the hell out of here.

I hauled Sai up and clipped him on the noggin again. His knees buckled. The crowd laughed: bloodthirsty sons-of-bitches.

Sai whimpered. "Please, Mistress Jae-En, desist with this abuse."

"Sorry, Sai. They love it. You're knocking them dead."

"Precisely what you do to me."

"Don't be a wimp. Now come on. I want you to bring me three guys. The last guy is that big marine with the broken nose. You see him?"

"Yes."

"Good. The other two should be smaller than him." I raised my voice so the rubes could here. "Now go! Find me a big man! Big!"

I shoved him. He stumbled forward and scanned the crowd. They laughed and pulled away from him like he had cooties. I stood with my arms folded like Mr. Clean until he finally found a guy and dragged him off his couch. The crowd hooted and gave the guy shit as Sai brought him in front of me.

I gave the guy the once over like I was in a meat market, then shook my head. "Too small. Throw him back. Bring me a bigger one."

The crowd laughed. The guy looked relieved. Sai took him back to his couch and hunted around again.

We went through the whole deal again with another dude, this one a little bigger than the one before, and again I waved him off. "Still not heavy enough. Aren't there any men here?" That got another round of laughs and Sai went searching again.

This time he picked my big marine. The guy had a bit of a macho problem, and if I'd had any idea how big that problem was I would have left him alone, but you never know. Some big guys are pussy cats. This guy obviously didn't want some chick lifting him, but the more he said no, the more shit the crowd gave him: his girlfriend was pushing at him, his pals were riding him. Finally he turned to Kedac. "Kir-Dhanan, please. This is beneath my dignity. I am a man of rank."

Kedac grinned, nasty. "Tonight you are a man of rank. Tomorrow it may be that nothing is beneath your dignity. Go on, Lut-Gar. Unbend for once in your life."

Lut-Gar hesitated for a second, pissed, then bowed. "As you wish, my Kir-Dhanan."

He followed Sai through the crowd as stiff as a starched collar, and stopped in front of me, staring me down. I gave him the once over and nodded. "Yes.

This is the one."

I stepped up to him and whispered. "Don't worry. I can't lift you like I did him. I'll make it look tough."

He growled through his teeth. "You'll make it impossible, freak, or you'll not see tomorrow."

I looked in his eyes. He was dead serious. I could feel my blood start to fizz. I hadn't planned on making a fool out of this guy. I was going to take it easy on him, but now... I don't like being threatened. I don't like macho assholes. The gloves were off.

I smiled as sweet as pie. "You're right. I probably couldn't lift you anyway, you're so big and strong."

The guy relaxed a little. I put a hand on his shoulder. "But I gotta make a show of it, so I'm going to try to get you on my shoulders. Just stay still."

He nodded and let me squat down next to him. I set the back of my neck against his waist. "Now lean into me."

He tipped toward me. I put my left hand in the center of his chest and my right between his legs, high on his thigh, then rocked him up on my shoulders. He was light, but not quite balanced. I wobbled as I stood, but I made it.

Lut-Gar cursed in my ear. "What did I tell you, you damned whore."

I shifted my left hand from his thigh to his nuts and gave a little squeeze. "Careful, meatneck, or I'll throw you on the floor, most of you anyway."

He froze up like a statue, which was perfect. I needed him stiff for the next part of the trick.

With a wink at the crowd, I pressed him over my head. I had to use my legs for drive, but I got him up.

The crowd gasped and cheered like crazy. I turned in a circle, grinning out at them, thinking, you ain't seen nothing yet. All my stage fright was gone. The reason we were here was gone. All I was thinking about was how I could top this, what my next trick would be. Maybe I'd lift a couch with a girl sitting on it next.

I ended my circle looking up at Kedac on his platform. He was staring at me, eyes wide and shiny, like wet glass. He licked his lips. Lut-Gar started squirming and kicking. I squeezed his nuts again to make him behave, but that only made him kick more. I lost my grip and dropped him a lot harder than I meant to.

He was up like a cat, drawing a dagger. He was so pissed his face was the color of raw meat. "I swore I would kill you."

He stabbed at me. I caught his wrist and stopped him cold. The crowd was shouting and standing. Shit! I was blowing it! This would ruin everything.

Lut-Gar swung his free hand. I caught that too and bent his wrists down and back. The men in the crowd were roaring and drawing their swords. Sai was beside me, clawing at my arm. "Mistress Jae-En. Mistress Jae-En, you must stop."

Lut-Gar yelped and dropped his dagger. The men were coming, swords out. I was going to get stuck like a pincushion. I kicked Lut-Gar in the bread basket and reached instinctively for my sword. It wasn't there. It was under a fucking boat by the river. I balled my fists. The swordsmen were closing fast.

"Hold!"

Everybody stopped. Kedac stood on his platform, arms raised. "Sheath your swords, gentlemen. There will be no blood shed here tonight. That is for... a time to come."

The men hesitated, still angry.

Kedac raised an eyebrow. "Must I command you?"

The men reluctantly sheathed their swords and forced themselves to relax.

Kedac turned to Lut-Gar, who was picking himself up off the floor. "You disobeyed me, Captain."

"Kir-Dhanan, she..."

"What she did is not my concern. I gave you an order and you defied me. It seems you need some lessons in obedience. Report to my ship tomorrow... as a deck-hand."

Lut-Gar went so white I could see his veins under his skin. He trembled for a second, frozen, then went down on one knee. "As my Kir-Dhanan commands."

He stood and walked back to his couch like all his joints were locked, but not before he shot me a look that would curdle milk at fifty paces. I curled my lip at him.

Kedac turned to me and I gave him a smile. Nice to have somebody stick up for me around here. Maybe he wasn't so bad after all. Sure he'd kidnapped Wen-Jhai and tried to kill Sai, but that was part of their culture, right? Maybe he was a decent guy at heart.

He smiled back and licked his lips again. It was a little creepy, but what the hell, maybe they were dry. Sai ducked behind me. Thanks, pal.

Kedac chuckled. "You truly are a wonder, Mistress Demon. Wherever you may be from." He reached out and squeezed my bicep. "So strong."

I tensed up, then tried to relax. After my little performance I could understand him wanting a feel. Happened every time I'd won an arm-wrestling match in a bar. Guys always want to touch my arms, like to convince themselves they're real or something.

He smiled again. Actually he hadn't stopped smiling. "And I've no doubt that you are stronger than you have shown us tonight. You lifted poor Lut-Gar with no effort at all."

I shrugged. I didn't know what to say. I wanted him to stop touching me now. Kedac turned to the crowd. "It would take a brave man to bed a woman like this, would it not?"

The crowd laughed a little too loud. They were still on-edge from the fight that had almost happened. I was a little on-edge myself. What was his deal?

Kedac looked back at me, suddenly all sly. His pencil-thin moustache slanted up on one side as he smirked. "If you are a woman."

I looked down at myself. It seemed pretty obvious to me, but I guess he wasn't satisfied. He reached out and pulled my bikini straps down over my shoulders so that my boobs popped out. I was so stunned I didn't move. No *way* did he just do that! Wasn't I just thinking that this asshole might be an okay guy? I expected the crowd to gasp. This was a party for Kedac's fiancée after all. Her relatives weren't going to like this.

They didn't bat an eye. They chuckled like it was all part of the act.

Kedac grinned as he checked me out. "Convincing. Impressive even."

I was just getting over my shock enough to start clenching my fists when he stunned me again. He stuck his hands under my boobs and hefted them like they were a couple of fucking cantelopes. He looked over his shoulder, playing to the crowd. "No wonder you're so strong, carrying all this around."

They laughed again. I was shaking. I'd killed men for less. Literally. That poor guy outside the Fly-By-Night. I was sorry I'd killed him. He was just an idiot. He hadn't deserved to die. But this fucker… I'd run him through a fucking tree-shredder with a goddamn song in my heart.

It was only the total insanity of the situation that short-circuited the orders my brain was sending to my hands to tear his motherfucking head off and shove it up his ass. I just couldn't believe it.

Kedac kept talking over his shoulder to the crowd while absentmindedly honking my boobs. "But I am not yet satisfied. Who knows what the men of 'Far Oopaloo' look like? I have heard of men from the jungles of Mir who sport two heads and a tail. So men who carry the comfort of a woman's bosom on their persons is not beyond the realm of possibility. However, there is one proof of femininity that I will not dispute—that is if one can call an absence a proof."

I froze again as I figured out what he was saying. He was *not* going to do that. Even after what he'd pulled so far I couldn't believe he was going to do that.

He did.

He stuck his hand down my loincloth.

The world turned red and black. My blood pounded in my ears like an air compressor. All I could see were the veins on Kedac's neck, pulsing. He was inches away, leaning into me as he felt around between my legs.

Nobody touched me like that. Nobody. I bared my teeth. I was going to rip his throat out. I was going to pull his heart out with my bare hands and eat it.

Far away, like a radio in another room I heard a voice. I couldn't hear what it was saying: the blood was too loud in my ears, but it was a voice I knew. I didn't want to listen. I wanted to kill, but some guardian angel part of me made me wait, made me keep my teeth clamped together. The voice got louder, like somebody had opened a door between me and the room with the radio. "Mistress Jae-En. Do no do it. I beg you. They will kill us."

I didn't know what the words meant. I didn't care. Killing was all that mattered. Tearing chunks out of that defenseless neck, ripping off that arm, gouging out those eyes, that's what mattered. Then the voice in my head had a name. Sai. Sai would die if I did this. I would die. I'd never get home. Never see the sun again. My sun. The right sun.

The red started to fade. I could see the whole room again, instead of just the individual hairs on Kedac's neck. The fire running in my veins turned to ice. My bloodlust became a calm, cold-blooded certainty that someday, somewhere, when the odds were a little more even and I wasn't babysitting some handsome prince, I would kill this motherfucker.

I relaxed. Blinked. Kedac was turned away, joking with the crowd. They were yukking it up like he was Dane Cook. How could he turn his back on me? Didn't he know? Didn't he understand how close I'd come to killing him? Wasn't he afraid I'd choke him to death?

I felt a hand on my arm. "Mistress Jae-En?"

"I'm fine, Sai. I'm fine."

I shifted my weight and felt something holding my legs together. I looked down. My loincloth was around my knees. Fucking Kedac had... I choked off my mad-on before it could get started again. Later.

Kedac turned back to me as I was pulling myself together. He beamed at me like we were best buddies. "Your performance... intrigued me. Tell Yin-Yir that I wish you to wait for me in my private apartments. I will join you after all this—"

The Sigouney Weaver chick stepped up behind him. She looked disgusted, though I couldn't tell if it was with me or Kedac.

"Cousin?"

Kedac's shoulders tightened like a kid who's been caught reading *Playboy*. "I regret to remind you that there is no time for private entertainments this evening. We have many people to speak with before the night is over. In fact, if we do not withdraw from the banquet now, we will not see all who we must..."

"Yes yes. You need not remind me of my duty." He gave her a cold look. "If you will allow me the merest of moments."

She nodded and stepped back politely, but her eyes were like ice bullets.

Kedac turned to me again, a little red in the face. He dug in his belt pouch and pulled out some coins. "It seems matters will keep me this evening, little giantess." He slipped a coin into my left bra cup. "But come to Ormolu in the next moon..." Another coin in the right cup. "And I shall pay you double this to test the limits of your strength." He gave me a dirty smile and slipped the last coin deep into my loincloth. I trembled with the effort to keep my thumbs out of his eyes. I think he must have read it as desire, because he grinned and winked at me as he turned back to the platform.

As he climbed the steps to his couch he started clapping. The whole room joined in, cheering and whistling. Coins started flying into the center of the U. One bounced off my head.

Eggplant was waving at us from the curtained doorway. I started toward him, motioning to Sai. "Let's get the fuck out of here."

Sai held me back. "Pick up the coins, mistress. They will know something is amiss."

All I wanted was to get out of that room—I never wanted to see any of those people again—but I saw his point. Street buskers who passed up their tips would look mighty suspicious. I picked up the coins as quick as I could, and almost ran through the curtain. I couldn't get Kedac's dirty leer out of my head.

CHAPTER FOURTEEN

TRAPPED!

"**M**istress Jae-En, do you hear me?"

I looked up. I was sitting next to Sai at one of the tables in the mess hall. I didn't remember getting there. Distracted, I guess. The place was still a madhouse. It was louder than a Fort Lauderdale sports bar during spring break. All the acts were still there, half of them waiting to go on, the other half waiting to get paid, and it smelled like a locker room with a clogged toilet.

I shouted at Sai. "Sorry? Say again?"

"Your plan. You said you had a plan."

I sighed. "Oh, yeah." I was going to have a hard time working up any excitement for the rest of the evenings festivities. I hadn't been big on this whole fuck-fest before, but now? Now all I wanted to do was sit in the dark and dream up new and interesting ways to kill Kedac.

On the other hand, if I copped out now, everything I'd been through tonight would be pointless. I would have kept my hands off Kedac's neck for nothing.

I scanned the room. What the hell had I been thinking way back fifteen minutes ago before I'd met the hate of my life? Oh yeah, the pom-pom lady, with the bat-pigs. This was going to be cake. Another quarter hour in this cozy little oven hadn't made anybody love those little bastards any better. It wouldn't take much.

I stood and looked down at Sai. "Follow me, but not too close."

Sai joined me. "What do you intend?"

"Don't worry about it. Just be ready to move."

"I bow to your experience, Mistress." Sai stayed about a car length behind me as I wandered through the room pretending I was just stretching my legs. Pretty lame idea if that's what I'd really wanted to do. It was more like tip-toeing through a crowded departure lounge when a plane's late. People were sprawled everywhere with their shit all around them.

As I passed the pom-pom lady, I stepped beside a bat-pig and slid a toe under its belly. Before it knew what I was doing, I hoisted it across the room.

It probably wouldn't have mattered much where I dropped the little bastard, but I picked the best place I could.

There was a snotty diva singer with a big, no-neck muscle boy for a helper. All night she'd been bitching to him—these guys were too close, those guys were too loud—and he'd go off and lean on whoever-it-was until they moved off or shut up. Needless to say they weren't the most popular act in the room. Perfect targets.

It was a good shot. I'd been aiming for the prima donna's chest. I got her face. The bat-pig wasn't real happy about taking its unscheduled flight and when it hit her it was a screaming claw-bomb, spitting and scratching like a bucket of wet cats.

The prima donna screeched and swatted at it. Her no-neck helper shouted and cuffed it across the room just as the pom-pom lady looked up. She screeched too, like a mom seeing her kid getting punked by the school bully, and charged toward No-Neck.

The bat-pig's next touch-down was in the middle of a bunch of acrobats practicing a trick. They crashed to the floor and came up shouting and wav-ing their fists. One of them pitched the bat-pig back at No-Neck. He ducked it and plowed toward them like a linebacker.

The pom-pom lady cut him off, and flailed at him with her spaghetti arms. He stiff-armed her into a bunch of midget wrestlers who threw her into some dancers.

No-Neck slammed into the acrobats and they swarmed him like pit bulls on a bear. The fight started rippling out in every direction. The whole room had been waiting for a trigger and this was it. Jugglers whaled on fire-eaters, cooch dancers high-kicked sword swallowers, contortionists tore into clowns, and the bat-pigs zipped around chewing on every ankle they could get their pointy little teeth into.

Finally, just like I'd hoped, the guards at the two doors waded into the crowd, shouting at everybody to sit down and shut up. That was my cue.

I grabbed Sai's wrist. "Come on. But don't run."

We headed straight for the door to the twisty hallway, stepping around fights and ducking flying bat-pigs. We passed a guard on the way. He was busy braining a dwarf with his scabbard and didn't give us a second look.

Nobody challenged us as we walked into the hallway. Nobody even noticed. I took a couple corners before I stopped and pulled Sai into an empty room. He grinned at me.

"Well planned, Mistress Jae-En."

"Thanks, but it's your show from here. Where do you figure Wen-Jhai is?"

He frowned, looking around to get his bearings. "I have never been here before, but a Dhanan of Ora dare not give his betrothed aught but the best. Wen-Jhai will be in the finest apartments the castle can provide, on the highest floor."

I gave him a look. "You sure about that? After that scene in the banquet hall I wouldn't be surprised if he stuck her in the cold-cellar."

Sai looked puzzled. "What mean you?"

"Well, seems pretty obvious to me that Kedac don't give a damn about Wen-Jhai."

"How so, mistress?"

I stared at him. "Weren't you watching? Loverboy had his damn hand down my loincloth. He made a goddamn date with me! Doesn't say much for his true love, does it?" I forced myself to unclench my fists. "Don't know why you held me back. Hell, I don't know why you didn't jump in ahead of me and kill him yourself."

Sai blinked like I was talking gibberish. "Mistress, I know not what your rank is in your homeland, but tonight you presented yourself to Kedac as a common actor."

"What the hell does that have to do with anything?"

Sai goggled at me some more. "Why, everything. How a Dhan or Dhanan relieves his animal urges with a member of the lower orders has no bearing on the affairs of his heart."

I turned on him. I could barely see him through the static in my head. "Are you saying I'm one of the lower orders?"

Sai backed away. "By no means, Mistress. As I said, you may be a Dhanshai in your own land. I only meant that you cannot fault Kedac for treating you as an actor when you have disguised yourself as such."

"And just because I'm one of the lower orders I'm supposed to take…"

"Mistress, I said you are *not* one of the lower order, merely that…"

I shook my head. He didn't get it. How could he not get it? "Okay okay, forget about how he treated me for a second. What about Wen-Jhai? You're saying that a guy can screw around on his fiancée as much as he wants as long as its not with his own class?"

"Exactly. Now you have it."

I stared at him. "And you don't think this is bad?"

"'Tis as the Seven intended."

"So, if you wanted to bump uglies with one of the lower orders tomorrow you'd do it, Wen-Jhai or no Wen-Jhai."

"If there was one I desired, yes. 'Tis unhealthy for a man to deny his urges."

Someone he desired. I guess that told me how I rated. So much for my letter to *Penthouse*.

I looked up at a noise. A servant went by in the hallway. I had a lot more I wanted to ask, but now wasn't the time. "Come on. We better get out of here. We go up, right?"

"Indeed, mistress. My goddess is, as ever, above me."

He could say that after admitting that he fucked everything that moved? "Hoo-boy."

"You spoke, mistress?"

"Never mind. Forget it."

***

I kept turning it over as we went up the stairs. Every time I thought I had these guys sorted, they threw another curveball at me. Here I thought they were a bunch of uptight prudes, and the whole time they're acting like it's baby-oil night at the Playboy Mansion. My brain felt like somebody was twisting it on a taffy puller. I couldn't decide if they were more advanced than Earth—if this was some kind of hippy-dippy, open-marriage, free-love thing, or if it was more of a Mandingo-have-that-girl-washed-and-brought-to-my-room thing. "How about Wen-Jhai. Does she get to fool around too? If she gets the hots for the cabana boy does she get to take him for a test drive?"

Sai stopped dead in his tracks, white as a fish belly. "You dare suggest that Wen-Jhai, the most pure, the most virginal..."

"Okay okay. Forget it. It was only a question."

That answered that. Just like back home, the door only swung one way.

Three floors up, we stepped out of the stairwell into a wide hallway lined with suits of fancy armor and statues of hunky naked guys. I rolled my eyes. Kedac seemed to take this macho stuff just a little too far. If I hadn't known better from personal experience I would have figured him for a man's man.

Sai started down the hallway. "Come, we must find another stair. We are still not high enough."

I followed him. I'm not sure why. Sai didn't seem to have any better idea where to look than I did. We nosed around that level for what seemed like forever, getting lost in the criss-crossing corridors. Twice we had to hide when patrols went by. Fortunately there was always plenty of marble muscle-men to duck behind.

Finally we spotted a stairway up, but just as we headed for it we heard footsteps and voices again. We had the drill down now. We crammed ourselves behind a statue of Mr. Olympia running Mr. Universe through with a spear. Nicely carved. Lots of detail. Both guys had their business hanging out. I didn't get it. If I was a dude, going into battle with my unit flopping around would make me feel just the tiniest bit vulnerable.

I eyed the corner, waiting. It wasn't guards this time. There were three or four voices, male and female, and one of them was music to my ears. I growled. "Kedac."

Sai peeked at me around Mr. Olympia's marble backside, wild-eyed. "Please, Mistress Jae-En, do not be impulsive."

I wasn't making any promises. This was too good an opportunity to pass up. I started climbing up Mr. Olympia's back so I could jump down on Kedac from above when his posse came around the corner. I groaned. There were guards after all: two in front carrying lanterns, and two bringing up the rear, with Kedac and Mai-Mar and his pals in the middle, six or seven nobles and navy types, all armed to the teeth.

My dreams of going jungle-cat on Kedac's ass popped like a balloon. Kill-crazy as I was I could still count. A baker's dozen sword-swinging tough-guys against me and my two fists. I gave Sai the mental finger again for talking me into leaving my sword behind, and froze on Mr. Olympia's chilly shoulders, holding my breath as they got closer.

Below me, Sai wispered. "Vawa-Sar." He was staring through Mr. Universe's legs.

I followed his gaze. Sure enough, pacing beside Kedac like a puppy trying to get a wolf's attention was Sai's sister's fiancé, the guy with the terrible fashion sense. He was kissing ass like a pro.

"Worry not, gracious Kir-Dhanan. We shall not fail you. Construction will be complete early next year. Already we have stockpiled enough simples and supplies for two years."

Kedac's voice was a manly rumble. "And the loan?"

"As soon as the wedding takes place."

Kedac nodded, all business. "Excellent. Your help in this matter will be rewarded, Dhan Sar."

Kedac walked right under me. I could have reached down and ruffled his hair—or snapped his neck. I squeezed Mr. Olympia's neck instead, just to keep my hands busy, while visions of Kedac's eyes popping out danced in my head.

By the time I'd come back from my happy little dream, Kedac and crew were around another corner. I climbed back down and joined Sai. He was frowning like a cheerleader taking a math test.

"Stranger and stranger."

"What's stranger. Vawa-Sar?"

We stepped out from behind Mr. Olympia and Mr. Universe and started up the stairs. Sai nodded. "How does he make loans to Kedac-Zir? His family is impoverished. They've not sent their sons to court in generations. In fact, Vawa long hesitated to ask for my sister's hand for fear the marriage be misconstrued as an act of charity. And why give money to the Kin-Dhanan? Save the Aldhanan himself, Kedac is the wealthiest man in all Ora."

"You're talkin' to the wrong gal, Sai. I ain't exactly up on Oran current events."

He nodded, distracted. "Forgive me. I do not mean to bore you with my family affairs."

That was a silly thing to say considering this whole shindig was all about his family affairs, but I let it go.

We were almost to the top of the stairs when we heard footsteps trotting up behind us. We hurried into the upper hall and ducked behind a tapestry.

The footsteps passed and we peeked out to see serving women carrying trays of food. Sai's eyes lit up. "This way."

He started after them. I followed, confused. "You hungry all of a sudden?"

"They carry menwah, the traditional pastry a suitor gives his beloved."

"Oh. A box of chocolates."

"I beg your pardon?"

"Never mind. We've got the same thing back home."

We followed the servants to a guarded door. The guards let them in, stealing some of the sweets as they passed. Sai and I watched from a corner. "That is where Wen-Jhai resides. I am sure of it."

"I suppose it would be too easy just to beat up the guards and go in."

"No no. Impossible. None can know we were here."

"Of course not."

I'm not going to bore you with more acrobatics. All we did was sneak into the room next to the guarded room, then I jumped from that balcony to Wen-Jhai's balcony and swung Sai across with the cord from a set of curtains. Easy. It made for a hell of an entrance though. We strolled in through the balcony door like we'd just come back from a cigarette break. Got a nice reaction too.

Wen-Jhai was on a couch, sipping something from a cup and munching a pastry. She turned at the noise and did a total, old-fashioned spit-take—drink spraying, cup smashing on the floor, cookie crumbling. Sai froze, a look of love in his eyes that made me realize how dead he'd looked the whole time I'd known him.

Wen-Jhai looked from Sai to me and turned paper white. "Ah no, truly now I know that you are dead, beloved."

Sai stepped forward, smiling. "But, my love…"

Wen-Jhai jerked back and shielded her eyes from him. She looked directly at me instead. "Have mercy, cruel demon. I beg you, return this shade of my beloved to the lands of the dead and torment me no more."

I wasn't sure what to say. Sai upstaged me anyway, arms outstretched. "Wen-Jhai, my heart. Be not afraid. I am no spirit. I live. Touch my hand."

Wen-Jhai uncovered her eyes and reached out shaking fingers. "Can it be? Are you truly flesh and not this time a dream?"

Sai took her hand. "Flesh, my dear, and yet this is a dream come true."

Sai's touch hit Wen-Jhai like a shock wave. She gasped. "Oh, Sai! It *is* you."

They slammed together in a hug. Wen-Jhai clung to Sai like kudzu.

"Beloved, you know not how I have wept, thinking you—"

Wen-Jhai's chin was over Sai's shoulder, and when she opened her eyes yours truly was front and center. She pushed away from him again. "But... but, Sai, if you be not dead, what demon is..."

Sai turned and remembered I was there. He giggled. "My love, Mistress Jae-En is no demon. She is a visitor from... from the lands beyond the sea."

So they *did* have big-ass pink chicks over there. Who knew?

Wen-Jhai's brow scrunched up. "She? This is a woman? But she is dressed like a fighting man."

I was getting tired of being talked about like I wasn't there. I was going to say something, but Sai stepped in. "And well that she does, for her fighting prowess saved me from the savage clutches of the Aarurrh and brought me here to your side."

Wen-Jhai still looked a little wary, but I didn't sense any girlfriend/strange-woman jealousy like I was afraid of. I guess I looked too freaky for her to worry about like that.

She bowed and crossed her wrists to me. "If that is the case, Mistress Jae-En of the lands-beyond-the-sea, then I am your servant in all things, for you have returned to me he who I believed forever... lost..." She choked up and clutched Sai again. "Oh, my love!"

They kissed. It went on for a while. I checked out the room. Kedac had done okay by her, although as usual he'd laid it on a little thick: flocks of pillows, battalions of sculptures, layers of velvet curtains with tassels and silk ropes and flowery shit. And there was food. Lots of food. It looked like the inside of Liberace's brain, with Elvis doing the catering.

Sai and Wen-Jhai came up for air somewhere around the five-minute mark and Sai held her at arms' length. He raised an eyebrow. "Wen-Jhai, you've..."

She yeeped, and tried to cover all of herself at once. "Look not upon me. I'm a fat ruktug! I... It was the only vengeance I could think of."

I suppose she had put on a few pounds. I hadn't been sure at first, but she was definitely not the slim sex kitten I remembered. She was still plenty hot. She'd just gone from Angelina Jolie-hot to Marilyn Monroe-hot, which for my taste was a step in the right direction. Sir Mix-A-Lot would have popped a stitch.

Sai was confused. "Vengeance?"

"On Kedac-Zir. For killing you. For wedding me against my will. I vowed to make myself ugly and fat, repulsive to him and an embarrassment to his position."

Poor kid. She had a lot of work ahead of her if she was aiming for fat and ugly. Even another twenty pounds would only make her Jayne Mansfield-hot, and I'd like to see the straight man repulsed by that.

She blubbed into her hands. "And now here you are alive and I have ruined myself. How can you love me like this?"

I rolled my eyes. I could think of plenty of ways.

Sai said the same thing, but fancied it up a bit. "Beloved, you have only added to your beauty. And does our love not go beyond the physical? Is not our love the love of souls and minds? Are we not twin spirits, separated at birth, yet destined to overcome every obstacle to be together at last?"

I was about to go into insulin shock, but it worked for her. She threw herself into his arms. "Oh, my love!"

"My heart."

My lunch. Did these people really talk like this? The closest I'd ever got to that shit was, "So, uh, you wanna get a beer or somethin'?"

Wen-Jhai suddenly flung herself away from Sai and collapsed on the couch. She seemed to fling around a lot. She had a lot to fling. I was surprised she didn't have bruises.

"Oh, cruel custom that separates us and makes might the arbiter of love. Would that tradition were overthrown and you and I could live and love as we would."

Sai knelt beside her and took her hand. "Beloved, with all my heart I wish it. Is it not the world we dreamed of in our youth? Is it not the land we vowed to found in the country beyond the moons? I love you with my heart, not the strength of my arm, and if the contest was a test of love and not steel, no man might best me."

Wen-Jhai looked a little worried. "But... But you will face Kedac-Zir for my hand. That is why you have come, is it not?"

Sai blanched, but he firmed up his jaw and opened his mouth to reply. He didn't get the chance.

"Your second helping of reah, my lady."

A maid was coming through the door with another platter. She saw us and screamed. The platter clanged on the floor. The guards rushed in.

I groaned. I *knew* shit would go wrong. I ran toward them, calling back over my shoulder. "Come on, Sai!"

The guards froze, halfway through drawing their swords. Good thing too since I'd forgot again that I wasn't wearing mine. I grabbed empty air and groaned louder. Too late now. I charged in with my fists like this was a bar fight back home.

The guards stepped back, staring. They were having the same reaction Wen-Jhai had. I went with it. I raised my arms over my head and screamed. I think I might have said, "Booga booga booga."

It worked. They froze. I hit 'em with a double clothesline, right out of the pro-wrestling play book. Their heads bounced off the floor like basketballs.

But I'd forgot the maid. She was running down the stairs already, screaming bloody murder.

I stripped the guards of their swords and looked around for Sai. He was still back with Wen-Jhai. "Time to go, your lordship."

Wen-Jhai disagreed. "No, Sai! Stay and fight! Take me from this oaf! Demand a challenge! Avenge me for this indignity."

There wasn't much time for discussion. We could hear thundering footsteps and the jingle of armor coming from all over the castle.

I ran back to the balcony doors, handing off a sword to Sai as I went. After lugging around the big Aarurrh blade, these little scimitar thingies felt like Wiffle ball bats. "Come on, Sai. Let's skedaddle."

Boots were running in the hall now. Sai was caught in the middle, sick with love, and pole-axed by fear. And when it counted, he did the wrong thing. Not that I blamed him. It made some sense, but, sensitive as he was, he didn't know women very well.

As he backed toward the balcony, Sai sobbed and threw out a hand to Wen-Jhai. "Beloved! Come away with me. Forget the old ways. Our love is above all this!"

Wen-Jhai recoiled like he'd hit her. "Come away? But... but you must win me! 'Tis the only way!"

Poor sap. In over his head, and not enough sense to stop thrashing and just float. "But did you not say you wished for tradition to be overthrown? For us to love as we would?"

Wen-Jhai was full of sadness and pity. "Only in dreams is that possible, my heart. In the land beyond the moons. Until we rule there we must live here, and we would have no place in Ora if you shamed me so."

With a roar, guards poured into the room in like an armored avalanche, swords out, arrows aimed.

I wasn't ready for this. I'd had one half-assed sword lesson from Lhan. Fighting ten guys and dodging arrows at the same time was not my idea of learn-as-you-do.

"Wave goodbye, lover boy." I grabbed Sai by the back of the harness and leaped ten feet onto the balcony. The guards gaped.

Sai shouted. "Wen-Jhai, my love!"

She stamped her feet. "Sai! Dare you leave? Come back!"

I knocked Sai's reply out of him along with his breath as I slung him over my shoulder. The guards ran forward, but too late. I hopped onto the stone railing and then across to the next balcony. They saw us duck in the adjacent room and ran back in, shouting to their pals in the hall to cut us off.

I ran across the room, locked the door, then ran right back onto the balcony. I wasn't going to get lost in those twisty hallways with the whole damn castle after me like some life or death game of Pac-Man. We were on the top floor. The roof was the next stop, and there were plenty of nubby decorations sticking out of the wall.

"Wait here."

Sai squeaked. "Wait here? But…"

I was already hopping up the wall. Two hand-holds and I was over the low lip and on the flat roof. There was a big barn-sized shack in the middle, an airship tethered on the far side, piles of crates and barrels stacked all over the place, and a row of things that looked like big empty bird cages.

"Hurry, Mistress Jae-En! They're coming!" I felt a "bang bang bang" through the soles of my boots. They were breaking down the door of the room below me.

I leaned over the lip of the roof and reached down to him. "Jump." He jumped, but I'd misjudged the distance. It had looked a lot less from down below. Sai didn't come within a yard of my hand.

"Fuck." I looked around again. There were coils of rope all around, attached to iron rings set into the roof: tethers for the airships.

I jumped to the nearest one, grabbed an end and ran back to the edge of the roof. Down below Sai was backing away from the balcony door. I heard bumping and scraping from under my feet.

"Mistress Jane!"

"Here. Grab on."

I dropped about ten feet of rope down to the balcony.

Sai grabbed. I hauled. Just in time. The balcony doors slammed open. The first guy out the door missed Sai's ankles by a gnat's ass. The guards shouted and leaped. A couple fired off arrows, but they whiffed past, straight up. I yanked Sai over the wall and we both fell backwards in a heap.

Sai rolled off of me and sat up. "Close, Mistress, very close." He looked around. "What now?"

Good question. I'd been so focused on getting away from the guards that I hadn't actually thought about where being on the roof would get me. Where it got me was treed.

I chewed myself out good. I'd always laughed at the idiots in movies who run for the roof when the badguys are after them, and here I'd done it myself. Stupid.

I glanced at Sai. He was looking at me with total trust. I guess I'd got him out of enough scrapes that he thought I had an endless supply of escapes in my back pocket. I was afraid I might have to disappoint him this time. "I... I'm working on it."

I peeked over the edge of the roof for a look at the courtyard. An arrow zipped up past my ear. Two guards were still on the balcony, and worse, two more were climbing the wall with crossbows on their backs. The rest had to be circling around. Time was running out.

I pulled my head back and stood, looking around at the outer walls. With a running start I could jump me and Sai to an outer wall, loop the rope around one of those whatever-you-call-ems—man, I should have paid more attention in history class—the square stone teeth between the gaps they shoot arrows out of. Battlements? Anyway I could hang a rope around one and rappel down into... the camp that surrounded the castle, where we'd be chopped to pieces by the entire navy. Okay, no, that wouldn't work.

I scanned the roof again. "Can we take the airship?"

Sai suddenly looked worried. I wasn't coming across with the goods. "Er... a ship of that size requires a crew of ten, mistress."

"Wonderful." Two strikes and I didn't see anything else to swing at. It sucked, but going back into the castle was my only option. "Where would they put a stairway up here?"

Sai pointed to the little barn. "Inside the skelsha roost, perhaps. But..."

I had no idea what a skelsha roost was, but if there were stairs in there we were going. "All right, let's go."

Sai's eyebrows went up in the middle. "But, Mistress..."

I grabbed his wrist and ran for the barn, dragging him behind me like a mom at an airport running to catch a plane.

Halfway there guards started pouring out of it, and these guys were ninety percent bow-men.

"Fuck!" I skidded to a stop. Sai bounced off me and collapsed. I jerked him up. "Back to the wall."

No dice. The guys who had been climbing the wall while I was sitting there with my thumb up my keister were on the roof now.

They fired.

The guards from the barn fired.

I tackled Sai into a jumble of cargo. Crossbow bolts thudded into crates and barrels.

We were fucked. In thirty seconds the crossbowmen would circle around our cover and turn us into porcupines. There was no way out, unless I could fly over the walls like goddamn Peter Pan. I kicked at another one of the coils of rope in frustration.

I froze. There was a way, but it was suicide stupid—a ninety-nine percent chance of instant death. On the other hand, just sitting here was a one hundred percent chance. One percent wasn't much, but I'd take it. I'd rather do anything than just stand around like a cow in a slaughterhouse waiting for the sledgehammer to hit. I chopped through the knot that tied the rope to the iron ring.

Sai looked up. "You have a plan, Mistress?"

I was too busy to answer. I worked the rope into a lasso. I'd always done well in the biker rodeos, roping beer kegs from my fat-boy, picking playing cards off the ground at thirty miles an hour. I'd never had any real-world use for that shit before. There's a first time for everything.

I could hear the crossbowmen running wide left and right. I spent a precious second getting my bearings. Which side faced the camp? Which side faced the town?

"Mistress, please."

The lasso was ready. "Get on my back and hold tight."

"But..."

"Just shut up and trust me."

He was a good boy. He slung his arms around my neck without another word.

The first crossbowmen were just clearing the crates and drawing a bead as I looped the rope coil over one arm and got into a crouch.

They fired.

I jumped. High. I wanted my first move to throw them off. It worked.

Bolts went everywhere, but nowhere near me.

I hit the roof running and went flat out, ten feet a stride, straight for the city-side edge.

The crossbow guys were well trained. Only half fired when I popped out of my trap. Now the rest fired while the first guys reloaded.

Something hit me on the shoulder hard enough the make me stumble.

"Mistress!"

"Not now."

No time for conversation. The edge was coming up fast. I gathered my lasso in my left hand, jumped up on the lip of the roof and sprang out as hard as I could. A flock of bolts followed me out into the wide black yonder. The outer wall was about thirty feet out and twenty feet down. I cleared it easy, even with Sai on my back, and sailed out into thin air over the three-hundred foot cliff that dropped straight down to the lights of the city below. Nice view.

Now came the hard part. Twisting in mid-air, I swung the lasso over my head and loosed it toward the battlements. If you think an old unbeliever like me can't pray, you ain't seen praying. I spread it around too; Jesus, his mom, Buddha, Mohammed, Krishna, the Seven. Yeah, them too. Something I've learned from traveling all over—never dis the local gods.

Maybe prayer works. My lasso looped over a big stone block neat as you please, and held tight as we dropped below the top of the wall. I noticed Sai was screaming and wondered how long he'd been at it.

We were arcing down toward the wall pretty quick. I let out as much of the rope as I dared, hoping to get down below the smooth walls to the cliff face where there were some handholds, before somebody upstairs got smart and cut the rope.

Sai's weight on my back made my landing a little harder than I liked. I landed feet first, flexing my knees like they taught us in Ranger rappelling class, but even in Waar's gravity my legs weren't strong enough. Not even close. They folded like a tent, and I hit the wall in sections, knees... elbows... tits... forehead. The world blinked white and fuzzy. When it snapped back, the rope was slithering through my fingers. I clamped down and left a ten-foot-long skin skid mark on the rope as the friction of stopping turned my palms to sushi. At least we stopped.

Sai had a choke hold on me that would have knocked out Hulk Hogan and there was only fifteen feet of rope left below us. I turned to tell him to let go and came nose to razor-sharp nose with a crossbow bolt sticking out of my shoulder piece. Blood was running out from under the armor. So that's what that knock had been. At least my arm was still working. Sai, on the other hand, was killing me.

"Sai. Sai, ease up. I can't..."

He let up a little and I sucked in a breath.

Sai whimpered. "Thank the Seven. Safe."

The rope went slack. We dropped like a stone. The bastards up top had done what I was afraid of and chopped it through. Fortunately we were already on the cliff face. Okay, maybe fortunately is too strong a word. I felt like a ball bouncing through a pachinko machine, but after a terrifying second I managed a one-arm grab that sprained two fingers and almost pulled my arm out of its socket. Then the rest of the rope fell on my head. Wile E. Coyote doesn't have days this bad.

I pulled myself to a better position and caught my breath, feeling for broken ribs. I glared over my shoulder at Sai. "Never say things like that! Never say 'thank god, we're safe!' You tempt fate like that, it's guaranteed to walk over and shit in your salad."

Sai didn't hear me. He was totally frozen in fear. Fine. At least he wasn't talking. I started down the cliff as fast as I could. The last thing I wanted was to find Kedac's welcome wagon waiting for us at the bottom.

CHAPTER FIFTEEN

DISGUISED!

Lhan gave us the silent treatment when we got back, but that didn't stop him from getting out his bandages and funny-smelling pots of goo and going to work on us. Silent was okay with me. I wasn't much in the mood for talking. I hurt so bad in so many places I didn't know which one to cry about. I had road rash and bruises on my forehead, elbows and knees from slamming into the cliff. All my muscles on my left side were wrenched from my one-hand save, and my hands were so raw I couldn't take off my own armor, which meant I hadn't been able to see what the crossbow bolt had done to my shoulder. And what was it all for?

Far as I could see Sai had nearly got us killed hoping to hear that Wen-Jhai didn't want him anymore so he could get out of his fight with Kedac. And then he wimped out and ran when he found out that she still loved him after all. At least he felt the same way himself.

"I have ruined everything! Wen-Jhai despises me now. She professed her love as fully and sweetly as the poets of old, and when she asked me to avenge her and claim that love, I... I asked her to run away with me, like a thief instead of a Dhan." He flung out his arms. "Oh, Lhan, bind not these wounds. Let me bleed to death as I deserve."

Lhan tied off a scrape with a little too much force. "First, Dhan Sai, you do not bleed enough to kill a linfa, thanks entirely to the valor of Mistress Jae-En, I have no doubt. Second, you have only to meet Kedac-Zir as you should, and you will be instantly redeemed in Wen-Jhai's eyes."

"But the opportunity has passed! Do not Kedac-Zir and Wen-Jhai leave to-morrow at sunrise on a ship for Ormolu? How can we hope to catch them?"

Lhan smiled wickedly. "Because we too leave tomorrow at sunrise on a ship for Ormolu. A trading caravan has assembled for safety around Kedac-Zir's naval escort. Anticipating your *failure*—" he really leaned on that *failure*, "—I booked passage on one of the merchantmen."

The sarcasm went right over Sai's pretty little head. He practically kissed Lhan, he was so grateful. And now that Sai was safely back on the path of honor—and suicide as far as I was concerned—Lhan was all smiles again. Weird people.

Lhan handed me a pot of goo and started unbuckling my armor while I smeared gunk on all my scrapes and cuts. It stung like Ben Gay, but smelled kinda like coleslaw. Ewww. As I moved one of my bikini-straps to get at my ribs, one of Kedac's coins fell out and clunked on the floor. Lhan looked at it, then at me, eyebrow raised like a question mark.

I blushed, which pissed me off. What did I have to be ashamed of? "Kedac liked my show."

Lhan's face tightened. "Oh."

I dug the second coin out of my other bra cup. "I'll have to get the third one later."

Lhan turned white. "The beast."

Sai didn't notice any of this. "But how do we reach our ship? Kedac's men will be watching for us."

Lan gave me an appologetic look and turned to Sai, Sarcastic. "Forgive me, Sai, for momentarily forgetting your plight. 'Tis true, Kedac will know it was you by now, and Mistress Jae-En is inconveniently distinctive in appearance. We shall need disguises."

Sai groaned and flopped back on the bed. "I am thoroughly sick of dis-guises."

Lhan shot him a look, but didn't say anything. I didn't say anything either, but it took some doing. The words "And I'm thoroughly sick of you," were knocking mighty hard against my teeth.

Lhan touched the shaft of the bolt that went through my shoulder armor.

"Does it pierce the muscle?"

I shook my head. "I don't think so. It doesn't catch when I move my arm."

"Good." He lifted the shoulder piece off. There was a jab of pain and a gush of blood. The bolt had passed through the armor at a shallow angle and mostly missed me. There was a pencil-size groove in my shoulder. Messy, but not serious.

Lhan started to patch me up.

Sai turned a little green. "Mistress!"

I don't know why, but that's where I almost lost it. I mean, there Sai was, feeling sorry for me, and for some reason it made me totally furious. Maybe it was because it had taken him until then to get over himself enough to notice that I was fucked up. Sai kept going. "I beg you to forgive me, Mistress. That my folly has caused you injury is more than I can…"

I put a hand in his face. "Don't start."

"But, I…"

"Just don't."

I almost walked out the door. Fuck Sai, the self-centered little fuck. All of a sudden I couldn't stand to be in the same room with him. There had to be someone else on this shit-ass planet who could help me figure out the teleport stones and get my ass home. What the hell did I need him for?

I sighed and let my hand drop. I did need him, dammit. Not just because he could hook me up with a way back to Earth, but now, after what had happened tonight, I needed to stick with him because sooner or later he was going to lead me to Kedac. Things had changed. I had something to do before I went home. I had to kill Kedac.

But, Christ, even that was Sai's fault. If he hadn't dragged me into the castle, Kedac wouldn't have got his greasy paws on me, and I wouldn't be planning my first premeditated killing. Yeah, I'd killed before—that poor bastard back in Panorama City, One-Eye, that other Aarurrh, but those had been crimes of passion or self-defence. Kedac? That'd be straight up cold-blooded murder. Sai had a hell of a lot to answer for, but I couldn't call him on it. Not if I wanted to get to Kedac.

I looked up. Sai and Lhan were eyeing me, worried. I shrugged. "Sorry. Uh, apology accepted."

Sai bowed his head and crossed his wrists. "My thanks, Mistress. You relieve me."

A twinge of guilt ran through me. From here on I was tricking Sai, pretending to help him. When we got to Ormolu for the showdown I was going to cut to the head of the line and kill Kedac before Sai got a chance.

For a second I felt like a heel, but there was more than one way to look at the situation. On his best day there was no way Sai could kill Kedac, right? So if I killed Kedac first I was actually doing him a favor. I was saving his life for fuck's sake—not to mention getting Kedac out of the way on the marriage front. Once the dust cleared and everybody had time to think about it, Sai and Wen-Jhai would thank me. They'd probably send me postcards from their honeymoon.

I let out a breath and put on a big smile. "So, okay. What about disguises?"

Lhan looked relieved that the tension was over. "Sai and I are easily disguised. A change of costume will be sufficient. You as I said before, pose more of a problem."

I pinched my arm. "Right. Wrong color."

Lhan smiled. "That is actually the least of our worries. There is a paste I know of from my service in the navy. Our spies used it to stain their skin a deeper shade when traveling incognito among our southern neighbors. The ingredients are easily obtainable and the formula simple."

"Great. So it's just everything else about me you can't fix."

He shrugged. "It requires some thought, is all."

Sai's head popped up. "Soldiers? Mistress Jae-En is certainly warlike enough."

Lhan shook his head. "True, but armor will not cover her more, er, feminine attributes."

Sai blushed. "Yes. Of course. Er, scholars? Surely a scholar's robes would cover, er, all difficulties."

Lhan's eyes lit up, then faded again. "A good suggestion, but no. Robes would cover everything but her height." He looked at me again. "And the color of her eyes. Hmmm, this may prove more difficult that I anticipated."

No shit. The problem was that there were just were no six foot women—and very few men—in this neck of the woods, no matter what color they were. I stuck out like a giraffe on a gerbil farm.

Sai raised a hopeful finger. "Circus performers?"

Lhan coughed. "You forget, Sai, that they are looking for circus performers."

Sai blushed. "Oh yes."

We all got quiet after that, trying to think. I don't know why I bothered. What I knew about Oran society you could write on the back of a matchbook. All I could think of was putting on a fake moustache and sombrero, but I was guessing there weren't many of those to be had around these parts.

Finally Sai groaned and threw up his hands. "'Tis impossible! What disguise will make her shorter and… er, smaller of frame? If only we could just put her in a sack."

I snarled at him. "Funny, I was just thinking the same about you."

All of a sudden Lhan clapped his hands together. "A sack! I have it!" He was grinning from ear to ear. He leaned forward. "Earlier this evening, while you were sneaking into women's bedrooms, I was drowning anxiety in a jar of tisol downstairs. Among my fellow imbibers were a group of Andag priests and their hulking guard."

Sai made a face. "But…"

Lhan turned to me. "Andag is a country of barbarians to the far north. Their priests wear sack-like masks and clothing that covers their entire bodies."

Sai pouted. "And they smell terrible."

"Which means they have a private room, since they're not allowed in a roost. And when I saw them last they were well on their way to unconsciousness."

***

The priests were sprawled out in their room like a crime scene photo. They were all big guys by Oran standards. Guess they grew 'em large up north. Lhan picked the two smallest and started to peel them. He pointed to their bodyguard, propped up in a corner and snoring like a freight train. He was gigantic. Well, about my size actually. I got to work.

It should have been Sai doing this. I hurt so much I could barely move, but Sai couldn't have shifted this big bastard with a forklift, so I got elected while Sai watched outside the door.

Ugly smelled pretty ripe even before I stripped him; equal parts piss, booze and herd animal, but when I got his armor off, a wave of B.O. that would have dropped a horse came up and smacked me in the face. I gagged. "You sure this is a good idea?"

Lhan grinned, wicked. "Think how much Sai will enjoy it."

I chuckled. After the shit Sai had put me through that night he deserved to stink, even if it meant me stinking too.

"Er, Mistress Jae-En?"

I looked up. Lhan was giving me a strange look.

"Mmm?"

He hesitated. I'd never seen him this nervous. "Er, I... once, in the past, I too had my person... violated against my will, and I know the shame and rage that follows."

I froze, what was he leading up to here?

He blushed. "I only want to say that I understand, in a small way, your anger, but hope, for Sai's sake, that you'll not do anything—rash."

My face got hot. I couldn't look at him. "Don't worry, Lhan, I'm over being rash."

Lhan let out a breath. "My thanks, Mistress. You ease my mind."

Christ. Now I was lying to Lhan. What a piece of crap I was.

***

Sai must have guessed that we were getting a little tired of his whining. He put on the priest's reeking rags without a word, but Lhan and I could see him shuddering. We could hardly keep from laughing.

Before I could get into my gear, I had to paint myself up. Lhan went out and came back about an hour later with the makings; fat black berries, some kind of alcohol, a special sort of clay. He mashed it all together in the chamber pot, but I had to do the painting by myself. Gentleman to the core, Lhan wouldn't think of laying a hand on me while I was naked, damn it.

He left the room with Sai and I smeared the stuff all over, even in my hair, which turned a dark maroon, making it at least a little closer to the usual Waarian purples and blacks. I had to bind my boobs too. Lhan had found a length of sailcloth and I strapped down as carefully as a butch taking a straight girl to a Baptist high-school prom. I ended up looking like I had Arnold Schwarzenegger's pecs. Good for intimidation I guess.

After a lot of groaning and swearing I finally got my banged-up and bound-up self dressed. The rags fit. Too bad they had a funk like a week-old dead cat. A long cloak went over a bulky, knee-length coat of leather plates like dragon scales. Under that I wore a shirt and leggings and boots that were a little too big. My mask was a curtain of fine chain mail mesh. I could look out through the links, but no one could see in, like standing inside a screen door on a sunny day.

I called Sai and Lhan back in. They were dressed in long robes so dirty you could barely see the twisting tribal designs embroidered on them, and witchy leather masks like something out of a goth fetish ball. We all had a good laugh at each other.

***

On the way to the shipfield at daybreak, Sai told Lhan about overhearing Vawa-Sar and Kedac. Lhan nodded, thoughtful. "So Vawa-Sar dabbles in politics? Likely 'tis your sister Shayah who pulls his strings. That rube has never had the sense of a krae, while she has always had an avaricious heart. Shayah would not be content with Vawa as he is, a rustic with an inheritance of rocks and cliffs. She would want him to make something of himself, and so sends him to play at court intrigue."

Sai tugged on his mask. He was having trouble seeing out the eye holes. "But what do they plan? What of all that talk of loans and construction and provisions?"

"Perhaps Vawa merely builds a hunting lodge for Kedac's pleasure. Game is the one thing Vawa-Sar's wasteland is rich in. As for the loan, 'tis not clear from your story who borrowed from whom. Vawa-Sar could be in debt to Kedac-Zir."

Sai seemed a little disappointed that he hadn't uncovered some kind of plot. "Well, it sounded mysterious."

Lhan patted him on the shoulder. "It may well be. We shall investigate once you settle your affairs with Kedac-Zir."

I couldn't see Sai's face through the mask, but he seemed to shrink at the mention of the fight. We went the rest of the way in silence.

***

The good thing about smelling like a diseased buffalo is that people leave you alone. There were navy thugs snooping all over that ship-field for Sai and me, but nobody came near the two filthy priests and their huge "man"servant. The bad thing about it was we almost didn't get our spot on the merchant ship.

The captain was a tubby, balding guy with a little fringe of hair that made him look like a monk. He sure didn't act like one. When we came on board

he was tearing everybody within earshot a new asshole; the guys in the rigging, the guys lowering cargo into the hold, the guys filling the gas bag with
"levitating air." His skin was a deep purple, but he got so red in the face
when he screamed that he looked like a black cherry. We were the last straw.
"I care not what your bill of passage says. I take no outlanders on this ship.
Especially no maku-sacrificing heathen priests, and particularly no stinking
lamlots who don't know what water and a scraper are for! Now get off my
ship before I report you for spreading the pox."

I balled my fists. I wasn't in the best of moods. I was still sore from last
night's panty raid, I hadn't slept, and the Andag armor was hot and heavy and
infested with things that bit me in places I only let very good friends bite me
in. I started forward, ready to twist baldy's fat, cherry head off.

Lhan held me back. He bowed and scraped like a bellhop. He put on a
funny accent too. "Accept, please, our basest apologies. We understand that
our sacred stench is less than pleasant to untutored pagan nostrils. Therefore
allow please some small restitution for your trouble in the form of honest
Oran gold."

The captain waved back his muscle boys, who had been closing in during
Lhan's speech. "How much honesty do we speak of?"

Lhan took out his money pouch. "Perhaps half again the original price of
passage?"

The captain nearly popped a blood vessel. "Half? Three times the amount
would barely repay the misery of my crew. Not to mention the cost of delous-
ing them all at journey's end."

Lhan bowed again. "Noble captain, it is against the precepts of our faith to
bargain, yet how can I pay more than I have?"

After five minutes of back and forth, we ended up paying double, and had
to settle for sleeping on the deck. The captain wouldn't let us go below decks
for any amount of money.

Afterward, there was time to watch the sky-caravan get ready for lift off.
The ship-field was a huge grassy meadow, crowded with all kinds of ships:
man-o-wars so big they needed two side-by-side gas bags to fly, smaller de-
stroyers with slim balloons and hulls like spearheads, that were mounted
all over with giant crossbows that looked like they used telephone poles for
ammo. There were fat merchantmen that didn't look like they could get off
the ground and little trading ships like ours, no bigger than a metro bus.
They were all packed so close together I couldn't see the sky. It looked like we

were in some huge room with gigantic pillows on the ceiling.

Under that weird marshmallowy roof guys scurried around like ants, loading cargo, food, water, and "levitating air," which came from huge brass tanks mounted on wagons and pulled by teams of krae. They looked like fire extinguishers the size of eighteen wheelers.

By the military ships, a crane was loading big cages onto the man-o-wars, the same cages I'd seen on the roof of Kedac's castle. They were filled with giant, scary pterodactyl-things with big leathery wings, heads like woodpeckers, teeth like crocodile's, and, like all the animals I'd seen here except for the men and the insects, a third set of limbs. On the pterodactyls they looked like some kind of steering system: little arms with flying squirrel skin-folds tucked under the big wings. The craziest part was, they all wore saddles.

"What the hell are those?"

Lhan looked where I was pointing. "Skelsha war birds. Skelsha cavalry ride point, looking for danger, and defend the big ships."

"Fighter planes."

Lhan raised an eyebrow. "You wax obscure, mistress Jae-En."

"Sorry. Don't mind me." My eyes wandered. Far from the warships, I spotted Vawa-Sar and a bunch of guys in hooded capes getting on board a ratty little ship that was being loaded with heavy crates and lumpy bundles. "Hey, Sai. Isn't that your brother-in-law again?"

Sai and Lhan looked where I was pointing. Sai nodded. "Vawa-Sar. Yes, so it is. You see, Lhan?"

Lhan bobbed around, trying to see through the rigging and people in the way. He turned to Sai. "There may be something in your suspicions after all, Sai. Though they hide 'neath cloaks, I believe I spy among Vawa's friends Korec-Bar, chief builder of Kedac's navy, as well as several of his aides." Lhan nodded to me. "Many thanks, Mistress Jane, for your sharp eyes. This is most interesting."

Sai looked eager. "Is this a weapon we can use against Kedac?"

Lhan gave him a sharp look. "The only weapon you will use against Kedac-Zir is your sword. Using politics to settle matters of the heart is beneath you, Sai. After your duel with Kedac-Zir, if he lives, then is the time to raise embarrassing questions at court."

Sai wasn't listening. He was staring past Lhan.

We turned. A column of marines, four abreast, was marching through the crowd to the biggest, classiest merchant ship. Behind the column came an open carriage. Wen-Jhai sat in the back, ramrod straight, as regal as the Queen of fucking Sheba. Beside her, all in black and purple, was Mai-Mar, Kedac's creepy cousin, and riding on a krae beside the carriage was Kedac himself, as smug as a Georgia state trooper. He was ruler of all he surveyed and he liked it, a lot.

I wanted to peel that smile off his face with my teeth. I had to physically hold on to the rail to keep from jumping ship and charging him. Not yet.

Sai stood up straight and stuck his jaw out. He turned to Lhan. "Should... I face him now, Lhan?"

Lhan grinned. "Loath though I am to dissuade you while your fire burns hot, I would not advocate it. The purpose of the duel is twofold; to defeat Kedac-Zir and to impress Wen-Jhai. Dressed and smelling as you do now, you would fail utterly in this second objective. Fear not, Sai. There will be plenty of opportunities for honor when we reach Ormolu."

I felt another sting of guilt. I was going to nip all of Sai's opportunities for honor in the bud and piss off Lhan to boot. I couldn't look at them. Instead I kept my eyes on Kedac and the carriage. At the ship Kedac dismounted and walked Wen-Jhai and Mai-Mar up the gang plank. He made his good-byes to his fiancée with a kiss on the cheek as dry as your Aunt Mirna's.

Lhan and Sai exchanged a glance as Kedac rode with his men back to the big man-o-war.

Lhan smirked. "Quite the romantic, this Kedac-Zir. Traveling separately from his betrothed so that their reunion will be all the more ecstatic."

Sai surprisingly came to Kedac's defense. "He merely looks to her comfort. There is little room on a man-o-war, and none of it suitable for an Aldhan-shai. Also, he is sensible of propriety. He travels apart from her so that the purity of the Aldhanshai will be unquestioned."

I could think of some other reasons. "Maybe she never floated his boat in the first place."

Sai and Lhan shot me a look. Sai looked annoyed. "Do you still harp on what we spoke of last night?"

I shook my head. "No no, you set me straight on that. A guy's gotta get his kicks. But what if maybe he just plain doesn't like her."

Lhan was shocked. "What you say is impossible."

Sai was horrified. "Then why would he marry her?"

Were they kidding me? "Well, she's a princess, ain't she? That's gotta be a rung up on the social ladder, even for a muckety-muck like Kedac."

Sai and Lhan turned white. Sai's voice was cold and hard. "Mistress Jae-En, here in Ora, love is the only reason to marry. Romance is our ideal, our second religion. This is why the Sanfallah is tolerated: because 'tis thought that no boundaries of wealth or clan should stand in the way of true love, and that a true lover is willing to fight and die for his love."

True love but you got to fuck all the peasants you wanted. Okay, whatever. "But didn't you tell me that the Sanfallah came down to the strength of your arm, not the strength of your heart?"

Sai looked grim. "There is that flaw. The old ways say that a man's love will make his arm strong. I… I am proof this is not the case. But that does not impugn Kedac-Zir's honor, just my lack of skill. Though my rival, I would not suggest that Kedac-Zir does not love Wen-Jhai, only that he cannot love her as I do."

Lhan spoke up. "To doubt a man's love is the greatest insult on Ora."

Well, that showed me. "This goes back to that thing you wear under your belt, right?"

Sai nodded. "The Balurrah. Honor demands that a man wear the colors of his true love whether her family be at war with his, whether she be another man's wife, an Aldhanshai, servant, slave, or whore. Any man not willing to risk the embarrassment of discovery cannot truly love. His lover would shun him."

I laughed. "Man, the divorce rate back home would be sky high."

Sai frowned. "Divorce? I know not this word."

"It's *my* homeland's second religion."

The man-o-war blew a signal and all the wagons and longshoremen backed away. Time to go.

The ground crews threw off the hawsers and the whole field of sky-ships rose like a school of whales surging toward the surface of a purple and gold sea. It was as beautiful as a movie. I stayed at the rail long after Sai and Lhan split to the upper deck for more fencing practice.

***

For two days that was pretty much the routine: me looking over the rail and watching the skelshas zip from ship to ship, carrying messages and passengers; Lhan and Sai hacking at each other on the top deck, out of the way of the airmen who were constantly climbing up and down the rigging and winching in and out the steering wings.

I wanted to join in the fencing practice, but I was still waiting for my palms to heal from the skinning they got sliding down the rope. Even if I'd been one-hundred percent I couldn't have played: not if we wanted to stay incognito. Sai and Lhan could strip down to their masks and undies and still be in disguise. But I was busted if I took off even one layer—busted by my bust—and I didn't feel like sweating into these rags anymore than I had to. I might start some kind of bacteria culture and kill the whole planet.

So I watched the landscape go by. It was worth watching. The shadows of the airships chased each other across the landscape like a flock of ghost sheep. We flew over a red, orange and blue patchwork of fields, dusty khaki areas of dry wilderness, and blue-black forests. Roads wandered through it all like the marks a kid makes dragging a stick through the dirt. The roads would come together now and then in a cluster of houses or a castle or a town, and then split apart again. Twice I saw one of the Seven's super roads, ruler-straight and running from vanishing point to vanishing point.

I finally saw a lake or two, though they were more like wide places in the rivers, and once, at sunset, way off on the horizon, a silver flash that might have been a sea. So little water. It made me wonder why the whole damn planet wasn't a desert. How did the plants grow? Did it ever rain?

***

Boy, did it rain. I found that out the hard way the second night out. I woke up to horns blowing and a spatter of raindrops on my face. There were airmen rushing all around, shouting, and horn lanterns swinging on hooks where the torches usually were. A cold wind hummed through the rigging. I was surprised. Even as high up as we were it had been pretty warm both day and night. Now I was shivering.

Sai and Lhan woke up too. Lhan grabbed a passing airman. "What goes on?"

"Storm!"

"But storm season doesn't start for two quarters."

"Tell that to the wind."

The storm had come up fast in the fourth dark when both moons were out of the sky. The airmen hadn't noticed it until too late. The normal procedure in storms was to drop to the ground and tie off until it blew over. Trouble was, if you started down too late you could get dragged across trees and rocks and smashed into mountains.

That's what had happened to us. Some ships were halfway down and just now realizing it was too late to go further. All of them were battening hatches and tying off the steering sails, hoping they'd be able to ride out the storm in one piece.

With a roar, the sprinkle of rain turned into a fire hose. Everything went gray. I couldn't see. It was like a TV station suddenly going to static. The wind kicked up so hard that the downpour was blasting left to right across the deck. The ship tipped like a bike leaning into a turn. Lhan, Sai and I started sliding toward the rail.

Lhan shouted, clutching his pack. "We must go below!"

I grabbed the rest of our stuff and we hunched our way to the nearest hatch, holding on for dear life. A boson stepped in our way. "You don't go below, remember, priest?"

I grabbed the guy's harness and picked him off the deck one-handed. "We go below or you go over."

His eyes bulged out. "Go and be damned, then."

I dropped him and we went below. Snarling airmen and merchants pushed us out of every cabin and hidey-hole we found, shouting, "Stinking priests, find your own place!" and, "Filthy vermin, no room!" It was just like being a biker.

We ended up down in the ballast, as far from the rest of the passengers and crew as we could go. This was a stuffy, black pit below the lowest deck, filled almost to the top with crates and rocks. We were wedged into the gap between the shifting crates below and the creaking beams of the deck above.

I didn't like it. I *really* didn't like it. I couldn't see. I couldn't breathe. I couldn't even roll over. My claustrophobia kicked in big time, and having my chest strapped up wasn't helping. I felt like a goddamn python was putting the squeeze on me. It took every ounce of restraint I had not to start thrashing and screaming like a shock treatment case.

It got worse when the ship started bucking like a drunk rodeo bull. The hold was hotter than Baton Rouge in July, but I was sweating ice water. My breath came in little Chihuahua pants. I puked. It did nothing for the atmosphere.

Lhan's voice chuckled in my ear. I flinched. "Have we found your weakness at last, Mistress Jae-En?"

"Fuck off."

He slipped his hand into mine. "I know you are strong, Mistress, but you may squeeze as hard as you like until your panic passes."

He didn't know what he was offering. I could have crushed his hand like a bag of pretzel sticks. It was even money I would rip his arm out of its socket. But it's funny. Squeezing helped. Human contact—okay, almost human—and the concentration it took to keep squeezing, but not too hard, took my mind off where I was and gave me something to do. Maybe he did know what he was offering.

***

I must have fallen asleep. The next thing I remember was Lhan pulling his hand away. The ship was still and quiet. The wind had stopped. A line of flickering light appeared overhead as Lhan pushed up the hatch and peered into the gangway above us. An airman was passing by. Lhan hailed him. "All clear?"

"Aye. Now get back on deck where you belong, filthy mountain trash."

Fly the friendly skies, my ass.

We crawled up on deck. I took so many deep breaths of cool, clear air I nearly passed out. Sai and Lhan looked around. After a minute with my head between my legs I joined them. We were under gray clouds and over craggy mountains. There were only two other airships with us, a big merchantman and another little trader like ours, both as tattered and smashed as we were. The navy was nowhere in sight.

"Where are we? Where are the other ships?"

Sai ignored me, staring at the merchantman.

Lhan answered. "The storm appears to have dispersed the convoy. We are separated from our escort."

Sai pointed. "Wen-Jhai's ship! That is Wen-Jhai's ship! We must…"

Lhan interrupted. "I would not approach Wen-Jhai before facing Kedac, Sai. She might again misconstrue…"

"Yes, of course. But then we must reunite with the rest of the ships as quickly as…"

An airman shouted from the rigging. "Pirates!"

CHAPTER SIXTEEN

PIRATES!

The whole ship turned to look. Dropping out of the clouds, like black ghosts sinking through a gray ceiling, were four evil-looking air ships, with spear head hulls and long, football-shaped balloons, all painted up with snaky red designs.

The ships made a bee-line for the fat merchantman.

Sai screamed. "Wen-Jhai!"

Our ship and the other trader were in the clear, for now, and our cherry-headed captain was bellowing for evasive action. Sai jumped to the helm. "Attack! You must attack!"

"Fall away, priest! You're mad! All sails out, lads! Due west. It's our only hope!"

Lhan grabbed the captain's arm. "You think you can escape? You cannot match speed with those cutters."

"Watch me try!"

Sai shook him. "No, you mustn't!"

The captain flailed away and drew his short sword. "Will no one free me of this plague of priests?"

But Sai, for once, was quicker. He put his blade to the captain's neck, eyes crazed. "Attack or die, Captain. The choice is yours."

The captain swallowed. His Adam's apple touched Sai's blade. "Attack, lads! Due east! It's our only hope!"

Personally, I was kinda with the captain on this one. It was going to take the pirates a while to take care of the big ship. We'd be miles away before they came after us, and with all the cloud cover they might never find us. But since I didn't have a hope in hell of convincing Sai not to attack the pirates, and since I wanted my chance at Kedac, I had to stick with Sai's script. I sighed and stepped behind the captain and tried to look menacing.

The ship wallowed around, barely able to steer because of its crippled sails, and headed for the pirates. The other ship followed our lead. I don't know if they did it 'cause we did, or if their captain was braver than ours.

Sai and Lhan tore off their masks and priest cloaks. I ripped off my junk too. I could hardly move in the damn stuff. Some of the airmen stared, but this wasn't the time for disguises. I would have stripped off my shirt and leggings too, but we were closing too fast. I unwrapped my Aarurrh sword.

Grappling hooks snaked out from the pirate cutters and bit into the merchantman's rails. The pirates pulled their ships close on all sides. Sword-waving silhouettes leaped the gaps and poured onto the merchant's deck, but just before the whole ship was overwhelmed we saw a skelsha dive from the aft rail with someone on its back. The pirates shot arrows and spears after it, but it was a dot against the clouds in seconds.

Sai gasped. "Wen-Jhai?"

Lhan shook his head. "Mai-Mar."

"She abandons her charge?"

Leave it to Sai to put the worst face on everything.

"Maybe she's going for help."

Sai looked at me and touched his heart and forehead. "May you be right, and may The Seven help her find it." He turned and glared over the rail. "Now, by the black blood of The One, why do we move so slowly?"

I was amazed. Sai was positively itching to get into this fight. Was this the same guy who curled up like a pill bug at the thought of facing Kedac?

Five minutes later, our ship and the other trader mashed into the pirate cutters. Sai leaped to a pirate deck, leading our wimpy charge of about fifteen guys, mostly terrified airmen and a few merchants who had their bottom line to motivate them.

Lhan and I exchanged a glance and hurried after Sai. He might have grown a pair, but he still wasn't much use in a scrap. We were going to have our hands full keeping him alive.

There were no pirates to fight on the cutters. They were all on the merchantman, cutting up an outnumbered squad of Oran Marines. A pirate lookout saw us coming and called a warning. Half the raiders turned to face us, and by the time we'd crossed the cutter's deck, the rail of the merchantman was a solid wall of pirate steel.

Sai leaped at them like a berzerker. He was dead meat, unless...

I kicked off the rail and jumped ahead of him, unslinging my Aarurrh sword in a big circle as I came down. The blade rang off swords, armor and helmets like a shootout in a bell tower. The pirates fell back, some of them bleeding. I'd bought us about ten square feet of beachhead. "All right, motherfuckers, who's next?"

Now I really felt like Schwarzenegger.

Sai and Lhan landed behind me, along with the rest of the trader's crew, and the two sides slammed together like surf on rocks.

When he paid attention Sai almost pulled his own weight, but half the time he was looking over the pirates' heads, scanning and shouting for Wen-Jhai, and when he got like that he was scarier than a three-year-old with a butcher knife. Not only did we have to keep him alive, we had to avoid getting winged by one of his distracted backhands. Lhan and I ended up staying wide to his left and right and clearing a big ring around him.

I'd like to tell you that I felt sick and disgusted committing multiple murders. I didn't. Not right then at least. When it's second to second and kill or be killed, it's a pretty easy decision.

Actually I was more than all right with it—I felt great. Free. This was what I was made for. Somewhere deep inside of me, my filthy, kilt-wearing, cattle-thieving ancestors were singing a Cumberland war song. My blood pounded out the beat. I could hear bagpipes. My brain turned off and pure animal instinct turned on. See threat, block it, break it, throw it over the side. See opening, stab it, kick it, kill it. I was laughing, giddy as a kid on a tilt-a-whirl.

After all that I'd also like to tell you we won. Sorry. Didn't happen. Sword to sword I could have gone all night. Lhan was right. I wasn't going to meet too many swordsmen in his class. These guys were lumberjacks with cutlasses. I was knocking 'em all over the shop, but I was also the biggest target on the deck, and I got so carried away playing Conan the Barbarian

I didn't even think about arrows until there was a yard-long shaft through my right shoulder—yes, same fucking shoulder as before—and two more dangling from my shirt. I would have kept fighting even then except my sword wouldn't lift anymore. I fell back, trying to switch hands, and tripped over a body. I landed on my butt.

Without me guarding his left, Sai took a club to the head and dropped. Lhan stepped over him and snatched up a second sword. I struggled to get back up and help. I had too much invested in the little turd to let him die.

The pirates smelled blood and moved in, but a voice shouted behind them. "Stop! Enough! Dead meat don't pay like live slaves! Take 'em whole."

The pirates stopped. Lhan and I stayed on guard, ready to fight to the end. None of the pirates looked like they wanted to be the first to try and take us alive, but then the owner of the voice, a little rat-faced dandy in a green leather harness pushed to the front. "Unless you want to look like a spinefish, you'll drop those weapons right quick."

He gestured up. The rigging was filled with archers, all aiming at me and Lhan. "Don't be fools. Your mates are dead or surrendered. You can't win."

Lhan and I looked around. Rat-Face was right. Our merchant buddies were on their knees behind us. Pirates were rounding up the airmen and passengers from the other ships: men, women, even a few children. Others were throwing open hatches and cargo holds. We exchanged a look and put down our swords.

The pirates swarmed us. They tied our arms, then jerked us onto a cutter with the other prisoners. Rat-Face hopped aboard and his crew cast off; unhooking the grapples, dropping a couple tons of ballast through holes in the hull, and rising into the clouds.

As we climbed, I watched the pirates below transfer the cargo from the two smaller ships to the other cutters. The big merchantman they didn't bother unloading. They just replaced her crew with pirates and prepared to make sail. The last thing I saw before we were sucked up into the gray clouds was Wen-Jhai being led out onto the deck, proud and defiant.

I looked at Sai, sagging beside me. He'd seen her too. There were tears in his eyes.

We came up out of the clouds into a sushi sunrise: raw and pink. Hanging in front of it was a pirate ship as big as Kedac's man-o-war, with two more cutters tucked by its sides like baby dolphins sticking close to mama. The big ship was a two-balloon job, with the hull painted same red and black color scheme as her attack ships. The twin balloons, however, were purple, and maybe it was just me and my dirty mind, but from the front, they looked like a huge pair of tits.

***

On board the big pirate galleon, Rat-Face lined us up on the main deck. Lhan, Sai and me ended up parked pretty close to Wen-Jhai. Sai kept shooting longing glances her way, but she wouldn't give him the time of day.

The arrow through my shoulder, which I hadn't even felt during the fight, was killing me now. It was one of those layered pains. A deep ache in the muscle that pulsed all the way to my fingertips, a steady branding-iron burn where it went in and came out, all topped off with zesty, eye-blinding spikes of agony whenever I moved or bumped the shaft. I stood real still.

When we'd all quieted down, a big guy with gold fringe all over his harness stepped forward. He was my height, and twice as beefy, with a big beard and a thick mane of hair. He had a big smile too, and a big voice.

"Welcome, friends! You may have heard that we corsairs of the air are a bloodthirsty lot. 'Tis a view we encourage. But in truth we're fair men when it comes to trade and promises kept. We only kill fools. The rest get a choice. Three choices, really."

He looked at a group of merchants. "Those of you who have rich relations or associates in your homelands may ask to be ransomed. You will find our rates reasonable and our accommodations comfortable."

He turned to the airmen from the merchant ships. "Those of you who yearn for freedom and adventure, not to mention generous shares in all spoils, step forward and join us! And we speak to the women among you, too. The law of your fathers holds no sway here. In the sky we are free of all laws, and many a merry messmate swings a pair of tits as well as a sword."

To prove his point he pulled a little spike-haired chick with a brace of daggers in her harness out of the gang behind him and put a rough arm around her neck. She elbowed him in the ribs with a grin. I gaped and looked around. Sure enough, about one in fifteen of the pirates was a woman. And now that I thought back, there might have been some women fighting on the merchantman. I'd been so focused, anything but swords and spears had been a blur. My heart pounded. Finally on this planet of naked Victorians I'd found people who thought like me!

The burly pirate was still in mid-spiel. It was suddenly hard to listen.

"Sign our articles and all is forgiven. You'll get a place in the crew to match your skills and a share of all spoils. But those of you who find freedom not to your liking, and who are not fortunate enough to have wealthy friends have a third choice. Our next stop is the slave market of Daest, where freedom will no longer trouble you."

That got everyone jawing. Most of the merchants and first class passengers started signaling Burly to cut ransom deals. Some of them must have done this before. They acted as bored and business-as-usual as smugglers at the Tijuana border. As for the merchant airmen, I was surprised how many stepped forward to join the pirates, considering how hard they'd fought. I guess for airmen a ship is a ship, and the thought of slavery was one hell of a motivator.

It was all I could do to stop myself from stepping forward with them. I'd already had my share of slavery on this planet, and I bet human masters would be worse than the Aarurrh could ever be. On top of that, I was starting to think of these pirates as my people—space bikers, outlaws who couldn't stand the bullshit daddy-culture of this planet any more than I could.

On the other hand, they were slavers, and I've got what you might call issues with the idea of freedom, and losing it. Besides, I still had unfinished business to attend to.

I leaned in to Sai. "You tell me what to do and I'll do it. We've got to get you back to Kedac and get your marriage back on track."

Lhan gave me an uncertain look. "Your selflessness is admirable, Mistress." He said it like he hoped it was true.

I shrugged, uncomfortable. The guilt-knife poked me in the short ribs again. "Yeah, well."

Sai was in a tizzy. "We must think first of Wen-Jhai. That she should become a slave. I would die six hundred deaths before I let it happen."

Lhan nodded. "Well spoken, Sai. But there is another concern. If Wen-Jhai is ransomed and we are not, the pirates would deliver her into the arms of Kedac-Zir, and your suit and your hopes would be at an end."

"But surely, Lhan, there is no doubt that we will be ransomed."

"Is there not? What if our dear fathers refuse to pay? You can be sure that Kedac-Zir has taken care to spread word of your plea to Wen-Jhai to run away with you without facing him on the field of honor. If your father hears that, you are damned in his eyes. And I have fled my rustic banishment against my father's direct command. We may find ourselves orphans with living parents."

Sai's pop must have been a pretty hard son-of-a-bitch, 'cause Sai's face drained white like a frosted glass when somebody sucks all the grape Kool-Aid out of it.

Lhan didn't stop with the bad news. "And we cannot be sure of Wen-Jhai's release either. The ransom of nobles and wealthy merchants is common enough. The ransom of the Aldhanshai of Ora is another thing entirely. She may be too dangerous to ransom. This is a situation that must be handled with delicacy. If I might suggest, I know a certain wealthy Oran, er, gentleman who could be persuaded to ransom me as his son. You and Wen-Jhai we might pass off as brother and sister—my noble, orphaned cousins—and Mistress Jae-En, Wen-Jhai's faithful barbarian body-servant. Through this deception we may return to civilization together and yet remain in possession of Wen-Jhai."

Sai looked as relieved as a guy who finds out it's not herpes after all. "By the Seven, Lhan, you are a wonder."

I coughed. "It is if you can count on your pal to come across with the dough. I've had plenty of 'best friends' flake on me when they were supposed to bail me out of the hoosegow. And we're not talking chump change here. You're asking this guy to come across for four people."

"If this were a mere acquaintance, it might be as you say, Mistress Jae-En. but I trust this friend implicitly. We are… very close."

I wasn't convinced. "Why don't we sign up with these guys 'til we find some chance to make a break? They gotta touch down some time to stock up on groceries."

Lhan smiled. "A bold plan, Mistress, and were it not for Wen-Jhai, one I would not hesitate to adopt. However, it may involve fighting, and I would not subject Wen-Jhai to that risk."

Sai piped up. "I favor Lhan's plan."

Well, of course old Lily-Liver liked it. I shrugged. "Okay, I'm in."

Lhan looked over at Wen-Jhai. "Now it only remains to convince the Aldhanshai. Quickly, Sai. Go to her."

Well, there's a hitch in almost every plan, and Wen-Jhai was it for this one. I saw her stiffen as Sai sidled over to her, and then freeze up entirely when he started whispering in her ear. That didn't last. Once she heard his pitch she went from glacier to volcano in a second and a half.

"You cowardly insect! 'Tis because of you that I am in this predicament at all. If you had faced Kedac-Zir as I begged you to, we would be wed by now!"

Heads were turning. Wen-Jhai didn't care. Lhan was starting to sweat. He stepped beside her. "My lady. Please lower your voice. For the safety of us all."

She ignored him. "No more will your pretty blandishments tempt me from the path of honor! Ransomed under a false name? How dare you suggest that I be ransomed at all?"

Then she went and did it, and at the top of her voice too.

"I am Wen-Jhai, Aldhanshai of Ora, daughter of Kor-Har, Aldhanan of Ora, commander of the greatest armies of Waar! The only payment these revolting flesh traders will receive is in good Oran steel when they feel upon their filthy necks the mighty blade of my beloved betrothed, my warrior Dhan…"

I could see Sai hoping against hope that she was going to say his name. But it was no dice. This whole act was about making Sai feel like a worm. She wasn't going to change her tune mid-solo.

"…my noble hero, the Kir-Dhanan of all Ora, Kedac-Zir of Kalnah!"

Sai deflated like a popped balloon. He looked like somebody had scooped his insides out with a spatula. All kinds of things were happening around him, but he wasn't interested anymore.

Wen-Jhai's speech had made a hell of an impact on the pirates, too. They were all talking at once and grinning like sharks. I heard one whispering behind me.

"What a catch! We be rich, lads and lasses. Old Kor-Har'll give up half his treasury to win his daughter back. We'll never have to raid again."

The chatter was reaching high school lunch room volume. All the pirates were laughing and cheering and raising their fists like they'd just won the Super Bowl.

"Fools!"

The jabber cut off like somebody'd closed a stone door. The pirates looked toward the top deck. They mumbled around me.

"The captain."

"Now you'll see, you rogues. Now you'll see."

I don't know what I was expecting. Hell, I thought the captain was the burly guy with the gold fringe. But if that wasn't him, well, maybe he'd be some guy in a fancy red coat with a moustache and a big hat, or maybe I'd drank too many bottles of spiced rum in my time.

It wasn't a guy in a red coat. It wasn't even a guy.

Swaggering up to the rail and sneering down on all the pirates like they were the biggest bunch of chowderheads she'd ever seen was a wiry, sharp-eyed woman who reminded me of this tough Latina cop I'd tangled with once; cool, handsome, and hard as nails. She was so flat-chested she could have passed for a guy, except for the lush lips and the dark slanted eyes. Her bootie was a dead give away too. Jennifer Lopez would have died of envy to see it. She had it encased in skin-tight black leather leggings that tucked into heavy boots. Over a pointless black and silver bikini top she wore a short, fur edged jacket cut like bullfighters wear 'em. It was red, but that was as close to Captain Morgan as she got.

"Fools, your greed makes imbeciles of you all! We might, *might*, if we were more clever than we've ever been, if all the winds and gods favored us, if the Aldhanan was as blind as a cave fish and the Kir-Dhanan couldn't fly his way out of a spring rain, we might exchange the Aldhanshai for her ransom and get away. But think you that we could remain safe?"

The pirates hung their heads like school kids caught shooting spitballs. The captain's eyes flashed. Any questions I had about how a little chick like her could ride herd on all these tough hombres went right out the window. A look from her and the Abominable Snowman would tuck his tail between his legs. If he's got a tail.

The captain didn't slow down. "Think you that the Aldhanan would let an insult like this go unpunished? Think you the Kir-Dhanan of Ora, commander of the greatest air fleet on Waar would suffer the scruffy band of sky-pirates who kidnapped his betrothed to live? His reputation would not allow it. Ora is ruler of the skies. We would be on the run for the rest of our days, which thankfully would be very few indeed. You see what fools you are?"

The pirates cringed like whipped dogs. She let 'em off the hook and turned those laser eyes on Wen-Jhai. "But fools though you be, you are nothing compared to this one. Pirates can be excused for thinking first of gold. This one has no excuse for her actions."

Wen-Jhai raised her chin. "You may not talk of me this way."

The captain ignored her. "This one, if she had thought at all, would have realized what speaking her name would mean. She would have realized that we could not dare ransom her, that we could not even return her to Ora unharmed and with all apologies without facing the wrath of her father and her betrothed. She would have realized that once she spoke her name, the only safe course we poor pirates could take would be to forget ransom, to give up the potential gold that we would have exchanged for our noble prisoners, and instead wipe out all trace of this fateful encounter as if it had never happened."

The prisoners were getting nervous. The whispering sounded like a hundred skillets frying bacon.

"She would have realized that we would have to burn the ships that we had captured so none would ever know their fate, that we would have to destroy the cargo and the treasures we discovered, and, we would have to throw over the side both her and her loyal subjects, so that they could never bear witness against us."

The deck was as quiet as a morgue. All the prisoners were turning to give Wen-Jhai the fish-eye and she wasn't taking it very well. The speech had got to her, too. Her face was maggot-white and her mouth was opening and closing like a brook trout.

"I... I... I didn't..."

If she'd said, "I didn't realize," I think the crowd would have torn her apart. But the captain interrupted her.

"Fortunately for her, or perhaps not, I am neither safe nor sane. Like you, friends, I am greedy. Like you it would please me to see an Aldhanshai taste life on the other side of the whip."

She let them have a dirty little chuckle, then started up again. "There is no way we can make what we should from this fine catch. The Aldhanshai has made sure of that. But there is a way that we might make a slight profit and still rid ourselves of her before she burns our fingers."

The pirates pricked up their ears. So did I. If there was an option to being thrown over the side I was all for it.

The captain went on. "We were to sail for Daest, to sell those who chose to be slaves. But Daest is too friendly with Ora. Our nobler guests might manage to return home to tell tales to the Oran Navy. But far to the south, in the jungles of Mir, is the City State of Doshaan, sworn enemy of Ora since it threw off the imperial yoke sixty years ago. There, buying Oran slaves is not just a matter of economy, but of revenge. Let us sell our wares there. *All* our wares."

And she smiled like poison candy at Wen-Jhai as the pirates cheered.

Sai snapped out of his funk. "No! You mustn't! How dare you treat an Aldhanshai of Ora this way! You will be burned alive for this! By the Seven I shall…"

The captain rolled her eyes and turned away. "Lock them up."

Burly signaled the pirates and they started herding all of us down below decks. Every single one of the prisoners gave Wen-Jhai dirty looks as she passed, me included. Because of her I was going to be sold as a slave. Because of her my chances of getting revenge on Kedac were melting away faster than a Popsicle on a hotplate. Because of her I might never get home. Being thrown over the side was starting to sound not so bad, as long as I could take Wen-Jhai with me.

***

There were two large cells below decks, one for men, one for women. Sai struggled as Wen-Jhai was led away from him. "Wen-Jhai my heart! Be brave!"

She turned up her nose at him like a cheerleader snubbing a nerd. "Braver than you."

He slumped, boneless. The guards shoved him into the men's cell. My disguise must have been holding up despite all the cuts in my shirt, because they threw me in after him.

For a little while it was quiet. We were too busy stewing about this latest shitty turn of the wheel to talk. Then a plump little woman came in with a basket full of bandages and patched everybody's wounds.

When my turn came Lhan offered his hand to squeeze. "It helped you before."

I waved him off. "Naw, I'm good."

The woman snipped the head off the arrow with what looked like a pair of sheep shears, then drew the shaft out by the tail.

I should have taken Lhan's hand. It was over in five seconds, but so is a car wreck. It felt like she was drawing a red hot heater coil through my arm. I was shaking like a rock star in detox by the time she was through. Then she smeared some herbal muck on the wound and the fireworks really started.

She covered it all with a bandage and patted me on my good shoulder.

"There now, my brave lad, all done. Any other wounds you're not showing?"

One or two, but if she did anymore checking she'd find out I wasn't a lad at all. I told her to beat it.

After she left I joined Sai and Lhan in a corner. "Okay, so Wen-Jhai blew it. What now?"

Sai couldn't take that lying down. "Dare you accuse her? 'Tis we who are to blame. Had we fought more valiantly…"

Lhan smoothed the waters. "What's done is done. We must think of the future."

Just then there was a rattle of keys and the cell door opened. The burly pirate crooked a finger at me. "You. The strapping lad. The captain requests the honor of your presence."

What the hell did that mean? I'd killed enough of her men that she had plenty of reason to hate me. Was she going to string me up? I looked to Sai and Lhan, uneasy. "What's this shit?"

Lhan shrugged. "I know not, but do nothing rash unless your life is at stake. Perhaps you can win us some advantage."

Burly barked. "No talking! Come."

Refusing wasn't going to do much good. I went.

***

Burly showed me into an empty cabin about the size of an LA studio apartment—room to swing a cat, but only if it was a little short in the tail. Aside from the size, it was a pretty snazzy pad. Rich draperies hung around windows made of some clear, thick membrane stretched tight. They looked out on to dark clouds and the last red line of the sunset. Paneled walls curved up into a beamed ceiling. The furniture was all wicker—to keep the weight down I guessed, and the shelves were covered with nets so things wouldn't fall off. Horn lanterns hung from chains, and pulling aside a curtain, I found a little bed in a closet.

"So eager already?"

I spun around. The Captain stood in the doorway. "Don't look so nervous, lad. I'm not always the fire-breather you saw on deck. I am Kai-La. Men call me Queen of the Air if they're being polite, "That damn she-skelsha," if they're not. You may call me anything but another woman's name." She laughed. I must have been pretty beat from all the fighting because I didn't get it.

She patted a wicker chair. "Sit down, boy. You look nigh on to death."

I sat. Sitting was good. Kai-La gave me a long look as she crossed to a cabinet and took out a wide-based jug and two short mugs. She licked her lips.

"There certainly is a lot of you, isn't there?"

I was catching on now. "Uh, more and less than you know."

She sat down in the chair beside mine and handed me a mug full of something sweet and powerful. She was suddenly serious. "Listen, friend. You are not Oran. There is no need for you to share the Orans' fate. I'm prepared to offer you again the choice they have lost. Will you join us?"

My heart jumped, but... "I... I don't like slavers."

She smirked. "And yet your friends are slave owners."

"What?" I was shocked. Were they?

"My poor bumpkin, were you born under a rock? Are not they not Oran land owners? Who tills their fields? Makes their food? Wipes their behinds?"

It hadn't even occurred to me. I mean I knew they had servants, but I'd assumed they were paid or something.

"Truly, lad, what land do you hail from that knows no slavery? 'Tis a place I'd like to visit."

I snapped out of it. "From parts unknown."

She laughed. "Half my crew hails from there. So, do I change your mind?"

It finally occurred to me that this was my chance. This was the advantage Lhan wanted me to win for us. And I'd almost turned it down, twice. "Uh, why not. Beats being a slave."

Kai-La paused, then laughed. "You were not born a liar, lad. Your thoughts crossed your face just now as clearly as if written on a scroll. You mean to join my crew in the hope that you will gain an opportunity to escape."

"No, I..."

"Cease. My offer is withdrawn, no matter what you say." She sighed. "A pity. You killed many men, men that must be replaced. And from what I heard, it seems you could almost replace my crew entire."

"I'm sorry." And I was, too. If things were different... But they weren't, so fuck it. I gulped down my drink.

Kai-La joined me. "No matter. You and your friends will fetch enough coin to replace them another way, though not so much as you would have had that evil slut had kept her mouth shut."

"What's your beef with Wen-Jhai? She's an idiot, but I wouldn't call her evil."

Kai-La looked surprised that I was talking back, but Wen-Jhai had her all worked up, so she let it go. "The nobility are like drunken giants. They may mean no harm, but every blind stagger crushes hundreds, thousands. You saw her. She gave no thought to the rest of you. Her pride was wounded, so she spoke and doomed you all. I know too well the carnage that trails in the wake of 'noble' idiots."

She stared out the window like I wasn't there, then snapped out of it and leered at me. "But enough history. On to more pleasurable pursuits." She put down her cup and stood. "I always like to sample my wares, to make sure I never sell second-quality merchandise."

She circled me, running light fingertips across my collar bone and shoulders. "And I have a penchant for big, strapping boys." She caressed my jaw. "Particularly those with such smooth, youthful…"

I hated to piss on her parade. "Er, listen, sister, I…"

She frowned playfully. "You demur?"

"Um, it's not that. It's just…"

"Then why do we wait?"

And with that she ripped my shirt open—and came face to face with my sailcloth binding. She frowned. "What's this? Were you wounded so badly?"

"Uh, not wounded, exactly."

Before I could explain, she drew a twelve-inch pig-sticker and sliced open the canvas with one swipe. All that was missing was a cartoon *"sproing!"* My boobs split the cut wide and bounced out to fill my shirt.

She stared. "You're… You're…"

"I tried to tell you."

She looked up at me, a strange quirk in her brow. "And so strong as well? It truly is a pity you cannot join us. You will find no happiness elsewhere as you are. I have traveled this world over. I know."

I had the feeling she was right, but that didn't matter as long as Sai came through on his promise of a ticket back home.

She sighed and saluted me with her drink. "My apologies if your appetites run in that direction, but you just won't do. Right now I need a fat cock to fill my cunt and empty my brain." She stood. "A pleasure and a wonder to meet so strong a sister. May slavery not break your spirit."

She ushered me out and told Burly to put me in the women's pen. He did a double take, then grinned. As he was leading me away she called after him. "Send up the pretty one. And have him washed. This one smelled like an Andag priest."

I almost turned back and told her she was wasting her time, Sai didn't go for bad girls, but why bother? I didn't owe her any favors. She'd find out soon enough.

CHAPTER SEVENTEEN

LOCKDOWN!

Sai and Lhan were waiting at the bars of the men's cell, eyes full of questions, but Burly pushed me past too quick and threw me in with the women before I could say anything.

A second later I heard Lhan and Sai protesting when Burly pulled Sai out. Sai called back as he was dragged down the hall. "Lhan! Protect Wen-Jhai if I die! Save her! Goodbye, my friend!"

I looked at Wen-Jhai. She was staring blankly at the wall.

The women's cell was less crowded than the men's—Wen-Jhai, me, some merchants' wives and serving girls, and a top-heavy temptress in a gaudy peek-a-boo loincloth bikini who had sex-worker stamped all over her. She had that hard, eyes-on-the-prize look you see in strip clubs all across America.

It was as tense as a courtroom on sentencing day. The women were giving Wen-Jhai hard looks and sniffing like they smelled something rotten. I'm guessing Aldhanshais weren't used to getting the silent treatment. Wen-Jhai did her best to pretend there was nobody else there, but her knuckles were white and her jaw was quivering. The only one who wasn't looking daggers at her was the boom-boom gal. Maybe she knew what it was like to be shunned.

I wasn't real happy with Wen-Jhai myself, but she looked so lost and pathetic that it was hard to keep my mad on. I gave her a smile to let her know not everybody was against her, but she made like she hadn't seen me. Maybe since I was Sai's pal she was tarring me with the same brush.

Things didn't get any more comfortable when, a little later, we all heard, coming through the plank ceiling, the voices of Sai and our lusty captain Kai-La rising in pornographic ecstasy.

Wen-Jhai froze like Lot's wife. The other women clammed up and didn't know where to look. I glared at the ceiling. I know Sai had told me just the night before that fucking lower class chicks didn't mean anything, but goddamn, he'd only called a tearful goodbye to Wen-Jhai less than half an hour ago. Didn't he need a little time to switch gears? I snorted, disgusted. Maybe Oran guys wore those little love tokens around their waists to keep track of which chick they were supposed to be in love with.

Wen-Jhai was leaking quiet tears now. For some reason this pissed off the other women even more. They curled their lips. I heard one say, "Not fit to be an Aldhanshai."

Wen-Jhai's jaw started to quiver. She was about four seconds from bawling her head off. She jumped up and flounced to a corner, then kneeled down facing the walls like a school kid who's being punished. The whole room watched her shoulders shaking. Her sobs clashed with all the huffing and puffing coming from upstairs. I wanted to cover my ears.

The worst part was, the shagging didn't stop! Sai and Kai-La panted and gasped and screamed an hour, then after ten minutes of quiet, when I'd begin to hope it was over, they started the whole circus all over again! Little punk was Captain Viagra on top of everything else? It wasn't fucking fair.

After a while the dancer—her name turned out to be Shae-Vai—crawled to Wen-Jhai and started petting her hand and murmuring in her ear. I lay down and tried to go to sleep, but I couldn't. All the noisy night long I kept myself awake thinking one thing. "What has she got that I ain't got? What has she got that I ain't got?"

A full head and an empty cunt is what I had—the exact opposite of what the captain was getting. The bitch.

***

The trip went on for days. So did the schtuping. Sai was giving it to Kai-La every night, all night, which meant that Wen-Jhai was weeping every night, all night. She and Shae-Vai became bosom buddies. They would talk together in a corner, mostly about Wen-Jhai's horrible fate. More than once I overheard her say, "I know the sort of slave they will make of me. I'll not do it! I shall kill myself before they take my honor."

Shae-Vai was always sympathetic. "Poor, brave Aldhanshai. I, alas, had my honor taken from me long before I knew its importance."

It got worse. One night while the orgasm Olympics were going on overhead and Wen-Jhai was weeping in Shae-Vai's arms, I noticed Wen-Jhai's moaning changing tone. I raised my head.

It took me a minute to make out shapes in the darkness, but finally I saw Shae-Vai and Wen-Jhai in the far corner. Wen-Jhai's back was arched across Shae-Vai's knee, grabbing the rough boards of the wall, while Shae-Vai's hand moved between her legs. Goddamn it, everybody was getting laid but me!

Shae-Vai winked at me. I groaned and closed my eyes. I didn't want to know. Shae must had pulled a fast one, moving from soothing Wen-Jhai to seducing her so smoothly the little fool hadn't known what was happening until Shae's "comforting" had started blowing her mind.

I couldn't take it. Here I was, alone on an alien world in the middle of a fucking porno movie with only my hand for company. I don't know if I was frustrated, or lonely, or just plain pissed off, but all of a sudden my eyes were wet and my throat closed up. Dammit, I missed Don! I wanted his big arms around me so bad it felt like somebody had my heart in a vice.

I frigged myself to sleep. It didn't do a damn bit of good.

***

Unbelievably, the next day was worse. Shae-Vai was asleep in a corner, worn out from corrupting virgins no doubt, and the rother women were in their own corners whispering. Wen-Jhai was pacing, as edgy as a cat in a rocking chair factory. I ignored her, doing pushups and trying to remember all the words to "Folsom Prison Blues," until she sat down beside me.

"You are called Jae-En?"

"Close enough."

"And you have traveled with Sai-Far since—since my capture?"

I had half a mind to snap at her. Some shit about "now that you're a sinner like the rest of us you can finally lower yourself to talk to me?" But I was a little lonely for conversation myself. "Uh-huh."

She bit her lip, then kept going. "Believe you that... that he loves me?"

"It's all he ever talks about."

A little sob flew out before she could stop it. "But why then...?"

She hid her face in her hands. I quit my pushups with a sigh and sat beside her. I obviously wouldn't get any peace until we'd had this conversation. "What's the matter? Sai told me that it didn't mean anything—as long as it was with trash, that is."

Wen-Jhai raised her head and sucked in a big breath. "He is correct. By law and custom it means nothing, a mere release of animal urges that touches neither heart nor mind. But though I try, I cannot..."

She buried her face again. Tears leaked through her fingers. "Look not upon me. I am ashamed, ashamed."

I scowled. "You? Whadda you got to be ashamed of?"

She swiped at her tears with the backs of her hands. She looked like a kitten washing its face. "An Aldhanshai must be the epitome of Oran womanhood. She must uphold our sacred traditions of matrimonial fealty and be above petty envies. She should not be roused to jealousy by her Dhanan's dalliance with outland *filth*!" Her little fists clenched at her sides. Her knuckles stood out against her purple skin like they'd been dotted with white paint. "And yet... and yet..."

I patted her arm. Probably a breach of etiquette, but she looked like she needed it. "Hey now, don't beat yourself up. 'Matrimonial fealty' is great in theory, but when your man is bonking some bitch right over your head it's kinda hard to be objective."

I guess I struck a nerve. She beat her fists against her thighs. "How could he! Even the most debauched of Dhanans has the courtesy to be discrete. Here he embarrasses me in front of... merchants! And with her! The witch who condemns me to slavery."

I had to agree with her, and not just because it wasn't me Sai was giving it to. I know guys think with their dicks, but this was ridiculous. This was a world class lack of class.

Of course she hadn't exactly been chanting her rosary, had she? I nudged her and grinned. "Well, at least you got a little revenge last night, right?"

Her purple got about five shades lighter. "Ah, no. You heard?"

"Uh, I've got good ears."

She started leaking again. "The Seven have mercy. The shame! I know not what came over me."

"I've got a vague idea."

"Please, Mistress Jae-En. Can you make light of my disgrace? I can no longer call myself Aldhanshai. I have given in to the most base, vile…"

I rolled my eyes. "Oh get real, girl. Who threw the first stone here anyway? How can you feel guilty with Sai going at it like the Energizer Bunny upstairs? Hell, if my old man was bonin' the chick next door, I'd be ridin' another bull before you could say 'saddle up.'"

That couldn't have translated, but she caught the gist. "But… but that's horrible."

"Why?"

"Why? Women don't… It, it is different for men. Men must slake their animal fevers or go mad."

"And women don't have animal urges? Sure they do. Better believe *I* do, and the captain sure as hell can't get enough of it."

"Women of breeding, I meant. You wouldn't…" She had the decency to look embarrassed. "Only women of the lower classes enjoy this. A noblewoman is pure. Her love is the love of the soul."

"Honey, the love of the soul only goes so far. You can't have true love without a little true sex thrown in."

Wen-Jhai recoiled. "You defile the word, mistress."

I leaned back, staring at her. "Oh, come on. Are you honestly telling me you're not supposed to like it?"

Wen-Jhai started shading toward pink. Her voice changed like she was quoting. "Only the love of her noble Dhan, within the bounds of holy wedlock shall spark the flame of desire within the breast of a true Dhanshai of Ora. All other… hungers are unnatural and depraved."

I smacked the floor. "That's crap! You're acting like you're a whole 'nother species. You may have been born with a silver spoon in your mouth, but you got the same 'hungers' as every other woman on this planet."

Wen-Jhai's eyes flashed. "How dare you suggest that I have kinship with…"

"Come on, sister. Wise up. You're your own proof."

"What… what do you mean?"

"You're a princess, right? An Aldhanshai? Who's got more breeding than you?" She looked uncomfortable.

"So, can you tell me you didn't like playing Jiffy Lube with Shae-Vai last night? And even though you're mad at him, don't you get a little turned on when Sai and the Captain are hitting the high notes?"

"Stop! Stop!" She covered her ears. "'Tis a disease. My father's physician said it was a disease. He made me take cold baths and drink salt water."

"Fucking... It's not a disease! It's nature!" Goddamn backward planet. Back on Earth—well, actually, back on Earth there were still places where women weren't allowed to show even their faces, and they had their clits cut off so they couldn't enjoy sex. Maybe I didn't have room to talk after all. Where were the good planets? "Come on, Wen-Jhai, why should men have all the fun and women all the shame when they're both the same animal?"

I turned away. Maybe I should have been more patient with her. It takes people a while to get around shit they've been told all their lives. Try telling a gun nut they're more likely to get shot if they own a gun than if they don't. I started doing pushups again. I'd only done five hundred so far that day. I was falling behind.

Somewhere around rep eighty I felt a delicate finger tracing the line of my tricep as it flexed and relaxed. I stopped and looked up. It was Wen-Jhai. She wouldn't look at me, just kept watching her finger as it trailed along the cords of my arm.

"Mistress Jae-En?"

"Yeah?"

She started again. Maybe she'd lost her place. "Mistress Jae-En?"

"Still here."

"Mistress Jae-En. You know so much of all this. You seem to know both sides of... of it. You seem to... *be* both sides of it. You have the strength of a man, and the... ripeness of a woman..."

That other shoe was going to drop any minute now.

"Mistress, I wondered if... if you might teach me..."

Christ. All it needed was this. I restarted my pushups. Almost pushed myself to the goddamn ceiling. "Sorry, Princess. I'm... I'm not inclined that way, but I'm sure Shae-Vai will be more than happy to give you another lesson."

"I... Forgive me."

She hurried off, blushing. I felt like a jerk.

***

I did a lot of pushups that day. It was the only way to keep my mind off... other things. What with all the whoopie being made all around me, I was horny enough that the crack of dawn was starting to look good, and Wen-

Jhai had looked so sad and snuggly that I wanted to eat her up with a spoon.

The problem was, even though I'd poured all that free love crap in Wen-Jhai's ears, the idea of diddling the future wife of my oldest friend on the planet was more than the little red-haired angel on my shoulder could stomach. It killed me that me, the bad-ass biker chick, with more notches on my bedpost than Mae West, was acting like the biggest prude on board this goddamn love boat.

I didn't get any sleep again that night. Sai and Captain Kai were hard at it upstairs, and down in our little nest, Wen-Jhai and Shae-Vai were tickling each other's fancies and being none too quiet about it. Wen-Jhai was making up for lost time. She had Shae-Vai wailing like a siren.

I turned to the wall and covered my ears, pissed at Waar and Sai and Wen-Jhai and everybody else who'd been part of getting me into this fucking situation, but mostly at myself. I knocked my head against the floor.

"I've created a monster."

CHAPTER EIGHTEEN

SLAVES!

Doshaan was the wettest place I'd been to on Waar—a swampy pit of a town with blue-green moss growing on gray stone buildings and big, ferny trees out of a dinosaur book. It stank like low tide in Galveston.

The buildings, at least the ones I saw through the bars of the rolling cage the pirates loaded us into for our trip from the shipfield to the slave market, were wide and flat, with windows like mail slots and pitched swamp-grass roofs. Even though they looked like jungle shacks, they felt more like home to me. I finally realized it was because they were rectangles instead of hexagons.

The city was crowded with more different kinds of people—races, I guess—than you could shake a stick at. Back in Ora everybody had pretty much looked the same, which made folks like the Andag priests stand out. Here, nobody would have given them a second look. The locals were thin, maroon guys who wore dark blue togas, but I saw folks with skin tones from lip-gloss white to eggplant black, hair from straight to kinky, bald heads, bristle heads, braid heads, big noses, little noses, hawk noses, tall thin guys, short square guys, big round guys, all in wild costumes: Oran harnesses, kilts, robes, leggings, tunics, loincloths, furs, culottes for God's sake, and more silly hats than a shriner's convention.

I couldn't understand them all either. Most of these guys spoke languages not included in my traveler's translation package.

The slave market was a big square in the center of town. On a pedestal in the middle was a twenty-foot statue of some fat lady whose tits had eyes instead of nipples and whose belly had a mouth full of shark teeth. I bet the kids in these parts ate all their vegetables and didn't sass back.

Around the edges of the square, rickety wooden stages had been set up. Some were big and fancy, some were small and dingy. Each had a duded-up barker shouting his lungs out in front, and cages around the back to hold the merchandise. That is, us.

The pirates paid some guy to rent a stage and hung out colorful banners and curtains. Burly, dressed up in a yellow and red caftan as subtle as a Vegas neon sign, did his best used car salesman act, raising his big voice to call in the suckers. The rest of the crew took care of the details like writing up bills of sale and collecting the money.

Captain Kai wasn't in sight. None of the pirate gals were. I wondered if they ever left the ship. I could see why they wouldn't. Doshaan was different from Ora in about every way possible, but not as far as women were concerned. They followed behind their men just like in Ora. They swept and washed. They traveled in packs for safety when they went out. In the sky, the pirate gals were equal partners. Down on the ground the rules of Waar were back in full effect.

Burly said the pirates almost never came this far south, so we pulled a good crowd just on the novelty factor. Half the square stopped to check us out. There were lookee-loos, window shoppers, serious customers, professional buyers looking for wholesale lots, rich folks killing time, and social climbers desperate to buy some class. There's nothing that says you've arrived like owning someone.

They pushed me on stage with the rest of the goods. I didn't like it. Okay, that's an understatement. I hated it. I hated being looked at like a piece of horseflesh. I hated the pirates for being the coolest guys around and evil, slaving fucks at the same time. I hated the buyers, who talked about you right in front of your face. I hated Sai and Wen-Jhai for cursing the pirates and whining about being slaves when they had slaves of their own back home.

But the thing I hated the most was that, when they opened the bidding I felt insulted when I wasn't picked. I started tensing my arms to show off the muscle and sucking in my gut anytime somebody gave me the once over. I was putting on a fucking show, for Christ's sake!

Up to then I hadn't felt any shame about being sold, but when I realized I was playing up to the damn buyers I turned so red my ears burned. Didn't stop flexing though. I couldn't help it. I felt horrible. Only time in my life I've ever called myself "whore!"

But though I didn't sell, Sai and Wen-Jhai were snapped up right away, both after some serious bidding wars. Two heavy hitters fought over Sai; a tubby, fortyish woman in jewel-caked pajamas who was carried around in a chair by four sweating Chippendales dancers, and a frail old man in a rich carriage whose hands shook when he made his bids.

Burly worked the price up into Cadillac territory, and was trying to drive it up to Rolls-Royce. "Two thousand golden Tolnas says the lady. Do I hear two thousand five hundred? Two thousand five hundred for this handsome, well-bred house slave. A Dhanan of Ora, he has impeccable manners, a classical education, and the face and figure of a Batu votive statue."

The old geezer flapped his hand, twice. Sai flinched. Burly smiled. "A double bid! Three thousand golden Tolnas from the Dhanan in the carriage."

Lhan groaned. It was the most anyone had bid all day.

Sai was trembling. "Lhan, in the name of the Seven, what shall I do?"

"You must be brave, Sai. I will deliver you if I can."

I snorted. "And who's going to deliver you?"

"Three thousand golden Tolnas! Can no one improve on three thousand? Madame, will you not rise to the challenge? No? Anyone? Anyone to bid three thousand five hundred? No? Three thousand going once."

Sai whimpered.

"Three thousand going twice."

Lhan cursed.

"Sold to the noble Dhanan in the jeweled carriage." The geezer's eyes gleamed. He looked at Sai the way Kitten had when she first saw him—that "oh-boy-a-new-toy" look.

Sai choked out a sob. Lhan hissed through his teeth. "The filthy old profligate!"

The old guy's bodyguards collected Sai as one of the pirates crossed to the carriage with a handful of papers.

I looked at Wen-Jhai. She'd been weeping in Shae-Vai's arms since the pirates had pushed them on stage. Now she just cried harder. That was nothing compared to Lhan.

I was amazed. I'd never seen Lhan like this. He's taken everything that had happened to us so far as cool as James Bond. Now he was straining at his chains like a gangbanger's pit bull. "Unhand him, you debased bravos! Dare you give an innocent over to such evil? Such lecherous…"

Burly cuffed him on the ear with a hand the size of a catcher's mitt. "That'll do, noble heart."

Lhan picked himself off the stage as Sai was dragged away, weeping. Lhan shouted after him. "Courage, Sai. Let him not—"

Burly knocked him flat again. The old guy's bodyguards put Sai in the carriage and it pulled away.

I helped Lhan to his feet. "Come on, bro. Don't take it so hard. He'll be okay."

I wasn't actually sure about that. The old guy gave me the creeps. It wasn't so much that he was obviously as queer as a three dollar bill—I switch-hit myself and I've got no problem with whatever two consenting adults get up to in the privacy of their own homes—but there wouldn't be any consenting going on here. This geezer would take what he wanted, and wouldn't bother to ask Sai for his okay.

Lhan shrugged away from me, his eye never leaving the carriage. "Leave me be."

I let him be. I wasn't sure why he was going off the deep end. I remembered he'd told me somebody had violated him once. Maybe that was it. Whatever his trouble was, it was my professional opinion that he needed to be hugged until he squeaked, but if he wanted me to let him be I was fine with that. Really.

Next it was Wen-Jhai's turn. She and Shae-Vai must have looked cute together, because two playboy-types started digging deep into their bank accounts bidding on them as a set. They finally went to a brawny guy with a top knot. He looked like an ex-bodybuilder who'd gotten too friendly with the dessert tray lately. He would have been one scary motherfucker except he was wearing more make-up than Wen-Jhai and Shae-Vai put together. Actually, that made him scarier.

Wen-Jhai shrieked and struggled when they loaded her and Shae-Vai into his coach. Shae-Vai took it in stride and tried to calm her down. For once I was glad Wen-Jhai had her around.

After that the pirates pushed Lhan and me and a bunch of the tougher prisoners to the front of the stage. They'd held us out to show to the gladiator schools.

Burly went down the line, giving us each a big build up. Lhan was first. "The pick of the lot, gentlemen, an Oran Dhan of noble stock, trained from boyhood in sword, dagger, lance and bow. A fighter of style and grace with the looks and dash to bring in the ladies as well as the men."

Lhan didn't look exactly dashing just then. He stood with his head down, fists clenched, not paying attention to anything.

Burly grunted, annoyed, and stepped to me. "Next, a one-of-a-kind curiosity, sure to bring the crowds. Behold the savage Jae-En, barbarian giantess from beyond the Andag mountains in the frozen north. Never before has a woman such as this walked the face of Waar. Note her powerful legs, the thickness of her arms, the muscles of her torso, and, disbelieve me if you will, noble lords, she is stronger than she looks. With my own eyes I have seen her slay six men with a single sweep of her man-high Aarurrh sword. Can you afford to let an attraction such as this go to your competitors?"

Burly could have sold sundials in Seattle. *I* would have bought me after that pitch. He moved down the line and started the snake oil all over again with the next guy.

There were about five gladiator schools checking us out, all with names like The Shining Axe School, and The Glorious Victory School, but there was really only one that counted. The Twin Blades School appeared to be the big leagues down Doshaan way. The other schools just hung around to fight over the scraps they didn't want.

Twin Blades took the winning bid on both me and Lhan, as well as seven other hard cases. Our buyers were a couple of thin, sad-looking guys in dark blue togas. They looked so much alike they had to be brothers; both balding, hawknosed and stringy necked. They sat in a open coach mumbling to each other, pointing from slave to slave, and sending a tough, dark purple goombah with pig-tails and a face like an all-weather tire to do their business for them.

Pig-Tails felt my arms, checked my teeth and my legs as bored as a housewife squeezing produce in a supermarket, but he gave a dirty chuckle when he honked my tits. "Deadly weapons indeed."

Even chained up I could have got him, but Burly must have read the tension in my back. He came up behind me and talked me up to Pig-Tails while pressing his knife between my shoulder blades. "She be spirited as well."

"Aye. Well, we'll break that."

I played shy and wouldn't let him look me in the eye. If I had he would have known I was going to kill him. Another one added to the list. What the hell was I turning into?

***

The brothers bought us along with our weapons and armor. We were packed in rolling wooden cages and taken on a long ride across the city. I tested the wooden crossbars, but there were plenty of guards riding beside the cages to keep me from getting any ideas.

Lhan was still cursing under his breath like a street loony. "Filthy slavers! To sell an Aldhanshai and her noble Dhanan like mere kraes. Have they no respect? No compassion? Poor, innocent Sai."

Maybe I should have left him alone to be miserable, but some of the stuff Captain Kai had said was twisting around in my brain and when it bumped against the stuff Lhan was saying it made my head hurt.

"Lhan, you own slaves, right? And so does Sai?"

He was only half listening. "Yes."

"So what's your beef with the slavers? You're as guilty as they are."

His eyes flared. "I have never bought or sold the Dhans or Dhanans of any land. Nor would I."

"That's not what I meant."

"Then I fail to understand you."

"Slavery. You're guilty of slavery."

He raised a confused eyebrow. "Yes, I am guilty of slavery, and of breathing, and of wearing a beard on my chin. Are these things prohibited?"

"I... well, don't you think they oughta be? Er, slavery I mean. Not that other stuff."

"Why?"

"Why?" I didn't have an answer ready. I mean, like every American, I'd been told since I was born that slavery was bad. Nobody'd ever asked me to explain why before. "Well... well... men shouldn't own other men. All men are created equal, and all that stuff. You and Sai sure as hell don't like it much now that it's happened to you."

Lhan smirked. "No man likes it when his fate turns on him, and really I rage more for Sai and Wen-Jhai, who are of a more delicate nature than I. But this curious notion that all men are created equal? Perhaps 'tis true in your lands, but not here. Yes, one soul in the great sea that all return to in death has as much chance of being reborn an Aldhanan as a peasant. But once the Life Giver judges you and choses your birth, you are entitled to the privileges or shackled with the misfortunes that come with your place in life. One of the privileges of a noble birth is that, though we may be ransomed or killed, there is an unwritten law among civilized peoples that we are never enslaved."

"And you're okay with this?"

"'Tis as the Seven intended."

I shook my head. "Sorry. I mean you're the nicest guy I've met on this shitball planet, but at the same time you're a whip-cracking slave driver. It just don't add up."

Lhan's head jerked up. "Lady, no slave of my family's has ever been beaten. Well, not since the time of my grandfathers. We are a modern family. We treat our slaves with firm kindness, as we would any livestock. If they are incompetent they are sold. If they provide good service, we free them after eighteen years and give them money to start a life, if that is what they wish."

I looked around at our fellow slaves to see if they were buying any of this stuff, but they just stared out through the bars, oblivious.

Lhan wasn't done. "You seem to think of slavery as some unbearable hardship. While 'tis true 'tis not easy, and I cannot say I am happy to have become a slave, 'tis often a better life than that of a free peasant in some destitute backwater. In fact there are educated men from impoverished lands who sell themselves as tutors or house servants on the promise of later living free in Ora."

I tried to get my head around it. "So you're telling me all the slaves in Ora are happy as clams and all the masters are big, friendly sugar daddies who pat their slaves on the head and hand out lollipops?"

Lhan hesitated. "Again your metaphor eludes me, mistress, but I take your meaning. No, I would not go so far as to say that all slaves are happy. Cruelty is not unknown. There are bad masters everywhere, but Ora is more enlightened than many lands. Here in Doshaan, of an instance, I hear that their royal smiths cure the steel of their swords by running them through slaves while the blade still glows from the forge."

He shivered, horrified. "Poor Sai. Poor Sai."

I sat for a while. I didn't know what to think. I tried to work up a hate for Lhan as a slave-driving fuck. It didn't work. It was like trying to hate Thomas Jefferson for owning slaves. It was part of his culture. Lhan didn't think he was evil, and by Oran standards he wasn't. He was good to his slaves and hated people who weren't. What was I supposed to do? If I stopped being his friend because he owned slaves, who else was I going to pal around with? Who on this planet was any better? Everybody who could owned slaves. Even the slaves were just hoping to get free and rich so they could buy slaves of their own.

I gave up. I wouldn't go as far as, "When in Rome." No way was I planning on owning slaves myself, but until someone started a revolution and freed 'em all, I'd just have to lump it.

Maybe you think I compromised my morals or something. Maybe you wouldn't have hung out with slavers. I ain't saying you're wrong. Maybe I was taking the easy way out. Just don't give me shit for it 'til you've had *your* vacation on Waar.

CHAPTER NINETEEN

GLADIATORS!

We got a bath as soon as we got to the school, and my new bosses, Sketh and Skir, got a surprise. My purple washed off. It was the first wash I'd had since we'd put on the stinky priest robes, and weeks of sweat and dirt must have loosened the dye. I went in a grimy purple gray, and came out pink with red hair again. I thought the jig might be up, but the brothers, when Pig-Tails called them in to have a look-see, were happier than pigs in shit. They'd already planned on billing me as the Savage Barbarian Giantess. Now they could call me the Savage Demon Giantess. I'd doubled my freak appeal with one bath. As far as they were concerned they'd pulled a fast one on the pirates.

They gave us simple beige tunics to wear—the local version of prison blues, and once we put them on, Pig-Tails, whose name was Hesh, by the way, herded me, Lhan and the other new recruits out to bake on a hot, sandy practice area while our new owners figured out where to put us. Just like boot camp. Hurry up and wait.

I cased the joint.

The school was a square, high-walled compound, with grass-roofed bunk-houses built around the central training ground. There was a cookhouse on one side with a mess tent next to it. The trough where we'd had our splash and scrape was behind it. The trainers lived in a stone building where the weapons and armor were stored.

Over the walls of the compound I could see the arena, just across the street. It was a gray stone hexagon about the size of a minor league baseball stadium. It made me shiver. It felt like some huge animal staring down at me, waiting to eat me up.

Hesh got Lhan and the rest of the new guys squared away pretty quick, but I was a special case. The school had never had a chick gladiator before, so of course they didn't have a woman's bunkhouse. Personally I wouldn't have had a problem bunking with the men. I'd spent years sleeping rough with bikers, and some of them had no manners at all. If these guys bothered me they'd draw back a stump. But the brothers—the same guys who trained people to kill each other for entertainment—had *some* morals, and they wouldn't think of it. They put me in what I ended up calling the Ho House.

This was another one-story shack with a grass roof, wedged between the cookhouse and the guard's quarters, and it was filled with sluts.

Gladiators who won their fights got a fuck bonus, the "Reward," they called it. The brothers kept a small stable of whores to cook, clean, and service the men.

Pig-Tails led me to the shack. "You will sleep with the comfort women."

I almost laughed out loud. I had to stop myself from saying, "You bet I will."

He was putting a cat in the pigeon coop. I've known a few streetwalkers in my time, and when they're off the clock they're usually pretty sick of men. At this point, so was I. After all the frustration I'd been through I was finally going to get some.

Or so I thought. Sometimes things don't work out like you plan 'em.

***

Me and the girls got off on the wrong foot right from the start. Hesh barged into the room, dragging me by the wrist. All the cots were taken. He didn't care. He found me one by dumping some poor girl out of hers and throwing her stuff across the room. He shoved me at the empty cot. "You sleep here."

"Aw man, you didn't have to do that. I don't need a bed. I'm used to—"

He slapped me. "You do not speak. I speak. Gladiators need good sleep. If

I find you on the floor, you'll regret it."

I nearly clocked him right there, but he was already heading for the door. He looked back. "Rest. Tomorrow you begin training."

Then he left.

It got real quiet. I turned to the women. Even though I'd just had a bath, the way they looked at me, I felt like I needed to wash again.

I stepped forward. "Listen, I'm sorry. That was totally…"

They shrunk back like I was a leper. I moved toward the girl Hesh had dumped on the floor. "You alright? You need a hand or—-"

She crabbed backward, screaming.

I stepped forward again. "Wait. Stop. I ain't gonna hurt you."

She crammed herself against the wall, shrieking like I was peeling her skin off.

A woman at the back barked something, and the rest stepped in to defend the chick on the ground. One of them had a knife made from a sharpened wooden bed slat.

I raised my hands in surrender. "Goddamn it, stop! Listen to me!"

A little one leaped on my back and stabbed me in the trapezius with some kind of pointy hair stay.

"Fucking bitch!" I grabbed her and slammed her one-handed against an overhead crossbeam, knocking the wind out of her with a squeak like stepping on a mouse.

The rest fell back, eyes like Ping-Pong balls. I was doing something impossible. I *was* something impossible; a chick strong enough to lift a girl to the ceiling one-handed. They were paralyzed.

I put the girl down, using the most non-threatening movements I could. "Listen, I'm sorry—"

Hesh had heard the screaming. He slammed in with a couple of guards. They saw blood running down my back and weapons in the women's hands and started laying into them with long paddles like frat-boy pledge-wallopers, cracking heads, shins and asses.

Hesh screamed at them. "You dare damage the masters' property! I'll have you diced for this. I'll shave your heads and make you fuck vurlaks for a copper rill!"

I stepped to him. "Dude. Hesh. Sir. Please. It's only a scratch. Leave them alone."

"Silence!" I got another slap for my trouble. "Those who damage the masters' property must be punished."

Pretty funny coming from a guy who was giving the masters' property a world class smack-down. Every girl got a head-to-toe beating, and the girl who stabbed me got double. The paddles didn't leave a bruise, but they smacked as loud as firecrackers and left red welts that must have stung like bejezus.

When it was over, Hesh and his stormtroopers left without a word. You thought it got quiet the first time I was alone with these chicks—this time it was quieter than a funeral home after quitting time. The women stared at me like those kids in *Village of the Damned.* I tried again. "Listen, I'm sorry. I didn't want…"

As one, they turned their backs and started taking care of their wounds. Welcome to the sorority.

***

Needless to say, I wasn't feeling real friendly toward my owners the next day. Lucky for Hesh, he was front office. He didn't have anything to do with training the gladiators. He would have been dead before we got through roll call.

I was afraid our trainer was going to be worse than Hesh, but the bosses obviously cared more about the fighters than the whores. Zhen was an old ex-gladiator with one arm, and so many scars he looked like a patchwork quilt. He was short, even by Waarian standards, but he stood up ram-rod straight and walked with a bounce even though he had a limp and a cane. He was clean and tidy and as brisk as April in Alaska, talking fast in a voice that hissed like a high pressure air hose. You could see why. His neck looked like somebody'd got ninety percent done beheading him awhile back. He reminded me of my boot camp drill sergeants who, even when they were bawling you out in hundred degree heat, had a crease on their khakis you could slash a tire with. I liked him as soon as I saw him.

After a ten-minute breakfast of grain mash, rare meat and fruit, they lined us up on the practice ground—newbies in front, old hands at the back. Zhen reviewed us like a general, scowling. "Great fire from the sky, what gutter trash have they saddled me with now?"

He went down the row, ticking off our faults one by one. "Blind. Fat. No spirit. Weak. Clumsy." He sneered at Lhan's perfect posture. "School boy." Moved on. "Lack wit. Yellow guts." And then he got to me. He stepped back and stared. "Tits? Tits on a gladiator? And what can you do, my dainty darling?"

Like I said, I was in an ornery mood. I decided to show him. I jumped over his head. The rest of the school gasped. Zhen just raised an eyebrow. "So, a demon in strength as well as appearance, eh? Well, don't let it swell your head. Do it again. Jump!"

I jumped over him again, and faster than a nail gun he cracked me on the foot with his cane so hard I couldn't stick my landing. I face-planted in the dust. He turned to the class, ignoring my howls. "There's always an opening. Even a demon has to land sometime."

I ended up being the practice dummy. Anytime he needed to demonstrate a move I was the one he picked. By the end of the day I was black and blue and as burnt as a match head. I didn't learn anything Lhan hadn't already shown me, not that first day, but here I *really* learned it. This wasn't a few tricks I'd tried one night and half remembered. Zhen drilled us into the ground; the same moves over and over until they became reactions, instinct.

He made me wear the heaviest armor he could find, and wouldn't let me jump. "You find yourself in a tunnel? A low room? What good is your leaping then, eh, waifling?"

"You got low rooms in the arena?"

He slapped me for sassing back. "Many's the gladiator buys his freedom with valor. Half the bodyguards in this city felt the sting of my cane. Life has many turns, little one, if you live long enough to walk 'em."

Which was my only clue that he thought I had potential. The rest of the time we were all scum, fools, stumble-bums and vurlaks. Even Lhan got his share, and he was the best newbie by far. "Save your fancy ruffling for your Oran boudoirs, dandy lad. Your guard is as weak as a prostitute's virtue, and will get you stuck just as often, but for no pay. Back to basics. Now on your guard!"

And so on for two cycles—different weapons, different styles—swords, axes, spears, nets, spiked gloves, maces, and wild weapons I'd never seen before. Zhen taught us how to kill and maim, and more importantly, how not to kill and maim. I was surprised. Maybe all those old Steve Reeves gladiator movies were wrong, but here, most fights in the arena weren't fatal. It was a lot more like pro-wrestling. The idea was to put on a good show and not kill the other guy. The matches usually went to submission, that is, where one guy couldn't continue or the other guy had him at sword's point. The suckers wanted to see a wild fight and a little blood, and if you made 'em happy, everybody got to live.

That's not to say there was never any killing. Even though it was kind of fake most of the time, Zhen demanded that we know how to fight for real. Guys sometimes went psycho when they got too hurt, and a fake fight would turn into a real one. Sometimes you had to fight prisoners of war or condemned criminals who had no reason to play by the rules. Sometimes the bosses just got tired of you and told your opponent to get rid of you. If you came out on top in a match like that the bosses might change their mind.

None of that happened very often. It wasn't in a promoter's best interests to slaughter his top fighters. It wouldn't pay him back for all the training and the food we ate. So a good promoter hired a guy like Zhen to make sure the gladiators knew what they were doing and to put together fights that made the crowd stand up and shout. He had his work cut out for him. The arena regulars were connoisseurs of fighting. They knew when guys were going through the motions and they wouldn't stand for it.

The fights weren't fixed, exactly. In fact, there was a bonus for the winner—food, money and his pick of the Ho House, but there was a lot of showboating along the way, extra-fancy sword work, a jump or flip to get a cheer out of the crowd. The way Zhen explained it all, I almost thought I could hack it, no pun intended.

I wasn't so sure about Lhan. Ever since the slave market he'd been less than his cheery self. He was still pleasant, but he'd gone all grim on me, going through his training as focused as a cat stalking a bird, and when I tried to cheer him up, I could see him building his smile one piece at a time.

We didn't have much chance to talk in private for the first few days, but I managed to pull him aside at dinner one night. "How you holdin' up, bunky?"

"Well enough, mistress, though much concerned for our friend and his betrothed."

I chuckled. "You kidding? They got cush gigs compared to us. We could die here."

"'Tis not a laughing matter. Perhaps they do not face death, but their persons are in danger of a worse violation. I mourn for their virtue. We must escape this place as soon as possible."

After the hi jinks on the pirate ship I didn't think Sai and Wen-Jhai had enough virtue left between 'em to fill a shot glass, but I didn't say that. I leaned in like I was in a Cagney prison picture. "Whenever you say, Lhan. We could go over the wall tonight. It ain't that…"

"No, Mistress Jae-En. I applaud your eagerness, but with no knowledge of this city 'twould be suicide. We can't bumble around like the blind. We must know where we go."

"So what's the plan?"

"I have yet to form it, but for all else to work we must first be valorous here. We must live long enough to discover where Sai and Wen-Jhai are held, and how to make good our escape once we deliver them."

I had more questions, but a guard heard our whispering and looked our way, so we left it at that. I trusted Lhan. He had the gift of gab. He'd be able to talk the info out of somebody.

***

Pretty soon it became obvious that Lhan and I were being groomed as head-liners. Lhan was the best new fighter in the school, and I was second best, even without my leaping. The brothers came out and watched as Zhen made us fight each other, and I could see 'em mumbling together, excited as a couple of record executives who think they've got the next Britney Spears.

They had armorers and costumers take our measurements, and Zhen finally let me work on leaping and flipping and practicing with my big old Aarurrh sword as their in-house blacksmith made me a new one to match my new armor. I had a blast, throwing myself around, figuring out all kinds of wild spins and swerves I could do using the sword as a counterbalance.

Their biggest problem was finding me an opponent. The established guys didn't want anything to do with me. I was a no-win situation. Beating a chick didn't get them anything. To the audience it would be a big, "So what, she's a chick." And losing to a girl? Unthinkable. At the same time, they couldn't match me with any of the new guys. I was too strong. It wouldn't be an entertaining fight.

They ended up doing the worst thing possible, at least as far as me making any friends went. The bosses told all the main-eventers that they had a quarter-moon to shape up and start pulling their weight. At the end of the quarter, the guy who was still sucking in the arena had to fight the freak in her debut match. This didn't exactly win me a lot of pals on the practice field. The old hands hated me because I was a threat. My classmates hated me because I was the teacher's pet, and the girls back at the dorm? Well, things weren't exactly rosy in that department either.

I might have become queen of the sawdust circle, but back in the Ho House I was still the weird new girl nobody would talk to.

The top ho was a cold bitch named Fae-Ah, who I think was afraid I would take over. She did everything she could to keep the rest of the girls turned against me, telling them—in front of my face no less—that I was a spy for the bosses, that I had diseases, that my skin color was contagious. They swallowed her shit hook, line and sinker. Half of them thought I was a man in disguise anyway, why not the rest of it? Fae-Ah froze me out of all their conversations, jokes and stories. When I got close, they went dead quiet, and stayed that way 'til I left.

Yaj, the little chick who'd stabbed me that first night, a wild thing with her hair all down in her face, acted like a guard dog, always watching me, always keeping between me and the others. She was a weird kid. Never talked. Not a word. She reminded me of gals I knew back in reform school, cute and wiry, but so balled up from the shit sandwich life had fed them you couldn't get near them.

I kept my distance. She'd already cut me worse than anything I'd got on the practice field. But one day, when I went back around the cookhouse to take a quick dunk in the trough, I found her hunched over a bucket, washing vegetables, and crying all over her hands. I couldn't help myself.

"Hey, what's wrong?"

She looked up, then away as soon as she saw who it was. She wasn't fast enough to keep me from seeing that she was sporting a pair of black eyes and a fat lip. She looked like a raccoon after a three day bender, and her arms were black and blue too.

"Who did this?"

She threw a tuber at me. Hit me in the ear. I know when I'm not wanted. I ignored her and had my bath.

***

A couple nights later I was spending another evening twiddling my thumbs in bed while the hos gabbed on the other side of the room. Suddenly Hesh came in.

The chatter stopped like flicking a switch. Hesh smiled. He liked being feared. He beckoned to Yaj, who still had yellow-edged smudges around her eyes. "Dal-Far says you failed to please him after the last games. You must be retrained, again."

I saw Yaj pale. She shrank against the wall. The hos held their breath. Hesh raised his paddle. "It'll be worse if I have to force you."

Yaj went, trembling. One of the women burst into tears as soon as they left.

My fingernails were biting into my palms. I can't stand bullies. I never ran with a gang who picked on the weak. Oh sure, we'd steal a Benz for beer money, but that's robbing the rich. We never hit mom-and-pops and never beat on anybody who didn't throw the first punch. In fact, most of my assault raps were for sticking my nose in when some big fucker was beating on some squirt who couldn't fight back.

The bosses didn't let us out at night. There was a guard on the yard who watched the bunkhouse doors. We pissed in a bucket if we had to go after lights out. My blood might have been up, but I wasn't totally suicidal. I knew I'd get it if I went out the front door. I looked up. The roof was swamp-grass thatch laid over a wooden frame, angling to a peak over a roof beam. Worth a shot.

The women stared as I rolled off my cot and leaped straight up to the crossbeam below the roof beam. The thatch-frame was just open enough for me to slip through. All I had to do was push up through the grass.

I braced against the roof beam one-handed and used my other hand to knife through the dry grass. It was thicker than I thought, and rustled like a paper suit. I hoped the guards were talking or sleeping down on the ground.

I got one hand through and grabbed the roof peak, then snaked my other hand out and pulled.

There's an old expression being dragged through a hedge backward. Well, it ain't much fun forward either. I felt like I was pushing my head through a giant broom. I scratched my skin from shoulders to ankles, but finally I was lying flat on the peak of the roof and holding my breath. The yard-bull had heard something, all right. He was looking all around, but he couldn't pin-point the sound.

I waited for him to settle again, then went on fingers and toes to the end of the roof closest to the trainers' house. It was only a twelve foot gap, but another story up. I could have cleared it easy except I didn't dare take more than a three step run. Any more and the guard would get a bead on the noise.

I ran hard and kicked off the very end of the roof like a switchblade snapping open and cleared the lip of the trainer's house roof by inches. I landed rolling, trying to hit as soft as I could. Another freeze to listen for trouble, then I started inching my way around the roof, eavesdropping above all the windows. I found what I was listening for pretty quick; a dull smack of flesh on flesh, and a whimper like a dog being smothered under a blanket. The hairs on my neck rose like a ridgeback's.

There was no glass on the windows—I hadn't seen glass anywhere on Waar—and the shutters were open. It was easy to grab the lip over the window and swing down to the sill.

Hesh was too busy to notice me. He sat on the bed, naked, his legs wide and little Yaj bumping and grinding between them like a lap-dancer, but with a horrible strained smile on her face. Every time that smile slipped, even a hair, Hesh slapped Yaj so hard her head bounced around like a bobble-head dog in the back window of a car.

Blood rushed in my ears. I didn't decide to attack him. There wasn't any decision involved. I just launched.

I clotheslined him across the shoulders. We hit the floor hard enough to skid and he cracked his head against the baseboard.

If that had knocked him out I'd have had some options. He wouldn't have known who hit him. I could have let him sleep it off and everything might have been okay. But he was a hard-headed son-of-a-bitch. I'd only stunned him. He saw me, and that was the point of no return.

It occurred to me—*now* it occurred to me—that I had to kill him. Yeah, I'd sworn to kill him before, but it's one thing to say you're going to kill a guy and another not to have any choice about it.

I felt trapped, like I'd been buried alive. I couldn't breath. What the fuck had I done? Not only did I have to off the guy, I had to be subtle about it. If I stabbed him, or broke his neck, or threw him out the window, Yaj would probably be blamed and end up swinging from a rope. I sobered up faster than a drunk with flashing lights in his mirrors. My mad was gone, replaced by a sick panic.

Hesh was shaking it off, opening his mouth to shout. I clamped a hand over his face and sat on his chest, pinning his arms with my knees. I looked around, thinking like crazy. Yaj was so out of it she hadn't done much more than step back, eyes focusing slowly. What the hell was I going to do? How was I going to kill him without leaving a mark?

Hesh started struggling, turning purple as he tried to suck air through my fingers, and kicking against the floorboards. I waved at Yaj. "Hold his legs!" She was just with-it enough to sit on his knees.

I finally got an idea. The phone book trick. A cop pulled this on me once when I wouldn't suck him off in the interrogation room. You take a hammer and a phone book. You lay the phonebook against your victim and hit it with the hammer. The phone book spreads out the impact so you don't leave a bruise, but the shock transfers, and shakes up the victim's insides. Use a sledgehammer and you can kill a man without a mark on him. Well, I had a pair of sledgehammers, right on the end of my arms. All I needed was a phone book.

On a table next to me were Hesh's papers. There was a thick ledger at the bottom of the pile. Perfect. I laid it on his chest. He looked at me, confused, veins starting to break in his corneas from lack of air.

I cocked my arm back. Hesh saw what I was up to and struggled harder. I unleashed. Wham! The floor shook. I wasn't worried. I was sure the guards were used to all kinds of noises coming out of this room.

Hesh 'yurked' and spasmed, his eyes rolling up in his head. I gave him one more just to make sure, then checked him for bruises. I was lucky. There was no mark where his head had cracked the base board. I felt his neck. No pulse. I got up off him. Yaj was staring at me, eyes big as silver dollars.

I put the ledger back and lifted Hesh's body onto the bed, then turned to Yaj. "You all right? You understand me?"

She nodded, scared.

"All right. Count to sixty, then start screaming like a banshee and calling for help. They'll think he had a heart attack. Got it?"

She nodded again. I hoped she was reading me. I was going to need a distraction to cover the noise of jumping onto the Ho House.

I slipped out the window and up to the roof. A few seconds later Yaj went off like a cheap car alarm. Good girl. Guards came running from everywhere.

I jumped the gap. No shouts. I pushed down through the roof and combed the grass back into place with nobody but the women the wiser.

They stared as I dropped to the floor. I put a finger to my lips and got in my cot, pulling the covers over me to hide the fading scratches I'd got from the thatch. "Yaj is safe. Pretend you were asleep."

Ten minutes later the guards burst in and threw Yaj to the floor. They looked around suspiciously, particularly at me. "Did anybody leave this room tonight?"

I held my breath. The women could betray me and get off scotfree. I hadn't thought of that.

Fae-Ah shook her head. "No one has come in or out that door."

I almost cracked up, clever bitch. Instead I sighed with relief. That lasted until I tried to sleep. As soon as I closed my eyes the reaction hit. I couldn't breathe. It felt like Hesh was sitting on my chest.

I'd murdered him. It wasn't self-defense. It wasn't in the heat of battle. It was murder. Cold-blooded, premeditated murder. Turned out vowing to kill someone wasn't the same as actually doing it after all. Fucking idiot, thinking before that wanting to kill someone made me a murderer. Wanting to kill someone sure as hell hadn't made me feel like this.

I'd done it now. I couldn't go back to who I was before. I couldn't think of myself as sweet little Jane any more. I couldn't hold my self above the scumbags and pretend I was some kind of knight in black leather.

Sure I had an excuse. All us killers have an excuse. I'd had to protect Yaj. I'd had to protect myself. But if I hadn't gone to save her, Yaj would have survived, Hesh would be alive, and I'd be able to look myself in the mirror in the morning. Not that the school had mirrors. At least that was a blessing.

The next day we were introduced to the new overseer—one of Hesh's underlings—and that was that. I don't think even the brothers were too upset. Hesh had been a little too eager to dish out punishment. The rest of the school shrugged off his death. Nobody cared. Nobody but me.

I couldn't get those bloodshot eyes of his out of my head.

***

Things changed in the Ho House, but not that much. It wasn't like the girls instantly became my friends or anything. They still kept to themselves. I still wasn't part of the group. But now there were little kindnesses. They smiled when they fed me in the meal tent, and gave me choice cuts. They'd lend me hair ties and bath scrapers, and when I came back from practice my cot would be made up with fresh rushes. Little Yaj didn't stop keeping an eye on me, but now her scared cat look was mixed with a cocked-head, curious dog look.

***

After another half moon, my big debut came at last. I was nervous, but I was almost looking forward to it too. My opponent was a pug-ugly crank named Shir-Lat, who'd given me shit since I came in the door—tripping me, "accidentally" nicking me in practice, letting me know that the only position I should be filling here was flat on my back with my legs spread, and I was too ugly even for that. I wasn't exactly unhappy to be kicking his ass. My new fighting gear helped get me in the mood too.

Okay, yeah, I'm vain, but the armorers really did right by me. My armor and helmet were enameled steel, dark green with black trim, to play up my light skin, and glazed so it all shined like emeralds. Each overlapping plate sewn on my sword-arm sleeve was the color and shape of a jungle leaf. My loincloth bikini reversed the color scheme, butter-soft black leather with green trim.

The frosting on the cake was the sword, as long as the Aarurrh one Handsome had given me, just a finger slimmer, but with the same weight and better steel. It was balanced perfectly too. I felt like I'd been born with it in my hand. And it looked as good as it felt: an over-the-shoulder sheath that matched my outfit, a green jewel the size and shape of a chicken's egg for a pommel and, just like the original, a slightly curved tip. I felt like a million bucks.

***

The gladiator school was connected to the arena by a tunnel under the street for security reasons. The school and the arena were one big prison. We were never outside the walls, so supposedly we were never tempted to run. I was tempted every day. Only knowing that Sai and Lhan were still my best hope of getting back to Kedac and going home kept me from jumping the walls.

On the day of the big fight, they marched us through the tunnel into the guts of the arena, all dark and twisty, and reeking with the stench of the wild animals that were killed for the kicks of the crowd. The hallways were low and narrow. They made me nervous. All of that stone on top of me. Yeesh!

Lhan put a hand on my shoulder. "Worry not, mistress. We'll soon be out in the light where all will be speed and action and release." Did this guy know me or what?

They stuck us in a kind of gladiator locker room, a slant-roofed hole under the stands beside the big door that led out onto the arena floor. We settled down to wait. There were a lot of other acts on before us.

I watched through the gate as frightened men in rags were pushed out into the hot sun. Right behind them came a pack of vurlaks: those van-sized pit bull things we'd steered clear of back on the prairie, all teeth and muscle. The sound from the arena was horrible. I nearly got sick. Maybe those poor guys were murderers, but Christ.

I cheered up when the fights started. Steel on steel and the roar of the crowd. Maybe it was all those berzerkers and borderers in my bloodline, but the sound pumped me up.

After each match the fighters came back, limping, bleeding, sometimes on stretchers, but nobody died, and the crowd didn't seem disappointed. That made me feel better. I didn't mind giving Shir-Lat a hiding. He deserved that, but I didn't want to feel again like I had after I'd killed Hesh any time soon. I might be a killer now, but I wasn't so hard yet that I could kill some poor slob just because somebody told me to. I hoped I never would be.

Lhan went out ahead of me and I held my breath, but he came back without a scratch on him. His opponent was limping from a gash on the leg.

Zhen slapped Lhan on the back. "Not bad, fancy boy. You got the crowd with you, and you made it look like a fight. We'll make a gladiator out of you yet."

Lhan shrugged. He didn't give a damn about being a gladiator.

Then it was my turn.

*****

I thought it was going to be easy. I was wrong. I almost thought it was going to be fun. I was dead wrong.

It started off great. They announced me with horns and drums, and I swaggered out, doing my best Stone Cold Steve Austin impersonation. The brothers had talked me up big-time, saying I was a Savage Demon Giantess with powers beyond the ken of mortal Tae, so the crowd was itching to see for themselves. From the nervous murmur I heard in the stands I guess I lived up to the billing.

Shir-Lat was waiting for me, the sand around him stained with blood from the earlier massacres. His eyes were wild and scary. Gossip around the practice yard said he'd been coasting for years. Now his laziness had bit him in the ass. He was being forced to fight his worst nightmare, a woman he knew was better than he was. He did not want to lose.

The sound of ten thousand people all talking at once rolled over me like Malibu surf. I'd been in the arena before. Zhen had brought us in on off days for some practice fights to get us used to it, but it was different filled with people. The stands were a waterfall of color and movement, rising up to a gigantic canvas donut stretched out over long poles that stuck in from the outer walls to keep the sun out. The cheap seats were on the side where the sun angled in, the better seats were in the shade, and the best seats were at ringside: ritzy boxes, tented to keep out the sun and the nosy eyes of the poor. They were filled with expensive furniture and expensive slaves to wait on the fatcats with the big bucks.

All those eyes on me, waiting for me to amaze them. I got a little dizzy. That's when Shir-Lat attacked.

I heard his footsteps at the last second and jumped. He nicked me, but it wasn't much: a long scratch on the back of my leg.

The crowd gasped when they saw my ten-foot hop, but I was too busy chewing myself out for being such an idiot to pay much attention.

It was obvious pretty quick that Shir-Lat wasn't following the script. He attacked like he was on PCP, screaming insults and trying every trick he knew to kill me and kill me quick. "Go on, slut. Let me slip it in you."

"Fuck off, Shir. You're blowing the gig."

"They want blood, don't they?"

I tried to play it the way Zhen wanted me to, putting on a good show, leaping and diving, and making wild attacks and last minute blocks, but every time we clinched, Shir tried to run me through with his dagger and I had to parry and dodge like crazy.

The hardest part was not killing him. He was taking insane risks trying to reach me, leaving openings a blind man could have got in on. I had to pull attacks left and right or I would have cut him in half. Then he laid the knuckles of my off hand open to the bone and I decided it was time to slow him down.

It's tough doing things by halves when you're swinging a blade that could decapitate an elephant, but Zhen's training paid off. I took Shir apart like a boxer: piece by piece.

On our next pass he lunged. I blocked his blade and slid mine along his chest, slicing though his armor like it was a birthday cake and cutting a thin line in his pecs. He didn't take the hint. He came in again, swinging high. I ducked and surged up under him, planting my shoulder in his gut, then shot-putted him with my bloody left hand.

He landed like a bag of bones twenty feet away, but was up and charging again before the crowd's cheers died away. He was like that knight in the *Monty Python* movie, the one that wouldn't stop fighting even with all his arms and legs cut off. He wasn't going to submit. If I put my sword to his throat he'd walk into the point rather than say "uncle" to a girl. I had to figure out a way to take him out without killing him, and still make it look good.

First I stabbed him though the leg, hoping he'd stay down. Didn't work. He pulled himself up with his sword, tears in his eyes, and he limped toward me again.

The crowd had mostly been on my side at first. Shir was old and boring, a mid-card palooka they'd seen a hundred times. I was new and different. They liked seeing me jump around. But the longer the fight went on, the more I looked like a cat playing with a mouse, and the more they started to side with Shir. They were cheering him now, but he couldn't hear it. All he could think of was the shame of losing to me.

On his next attack he practically fell on my sword, flailing like a drunk swinging a beer bottle, as his wounded leg gave out. If I didn't end it now one of us was going to die. I swung a brutal cut at his head—brain surgery if I connected with the edge—but at the last second I turned it and caught him with the flat. He dropped like an ox taking a sledgehammer between the horns.

The crowd was silent until Shir-Lat moved a little and I bowed to him the way Zhen had taught me. Then they cheered, and kept cheering. They cheered Shir for his bravery, for never backing down even though he was totally overmatched, and me for my sportsmanlike conduct and for respecting his courage.

I ate it up. I felt like Rocky at the end of a movie. I raised my arms and got more cheers. I got so carried away with my own chivalry I did the stupidest thing I could have possibly done. I decided to carry my fallen comrade out of the arena.

I didn't realize how stupid this was until I heard laughing. The crowd were pointing and giggling. Even then I couldn't figure it out. Then it hit me. It was one thing for Shir to be beaten by a woman, the crowd had accepted that because it was pretty obvious I wasn't just a woman—I was a woman who could lift a wagon. Some of them probably half-believed I was a demon for real. It was another thing for him to be carried like a baby in his mother's arms. I'd already knocked a hole in his manhood, but this—I might as well have put diapers on him and stuck a bottle in his mouth.

There was nothing I could do. It was too late. Even if I put him down the damage was done. Halfway through the walk back, Shir came to enough to figure out what was happening. He looked at me and my heart sank into my socks. "Bitch."

The locker room felt the same way. The guys took Shir-Lat from me like I had the plague. He might have been an equal opportunity asshole, but even his worst enemies didn't look happy with me. I could see their wheels turning, all thinking that next time I'd do the same thing to them.

Zhen shook his head at me with a "boy-did-you-fuck-up" look on his face. I looked at Lhan for support. He shrugged. He didn't know how to fix it either.

CHAPTER TWENTY

JUMPED!

That night all us winners got a special dinner, with Texas-size slabs of meat, rich side dishes, wine and tasty treats, and then for our bonus, our "reward," we each got to pick a whore and take her to a private room in the trainer's house. Well, all of us except me.

I got the dinner all right, though I didn't enjoy it much. The rest of the table kept giving me the fish eye all the way through, all except for Lhan, but somehow we found it hard to make conversation. But after dessert, when all the rest of the winners went off with their chosen hos, I wasn't given the option. I didn't speak up either. Somehow this didn't feel like the time to find out how easygoing this society was about "alternative lifestyles."

What I hoped would happen was that Lhan would think of it and ask me, but he didn't even pick a whore. Maybe he was used to a better class of pro back in high society Ormolu. I didn't get to ask him. When lights-out came, me, Lhan and the losers were all locked back in our separate bunkhouses just like every other night.

It was pretty empty in the Ho House. Most of the girls were working. Three girls who hadn't been picked were chatting in their cots. Yaj, who was still a little black and blue from Hesh's love taps, had the night off too. She stared at me like she always did.

Not exactly congenial company. I wasn't in the mood to make new friends anyway. I was feeling miserable and wiped out from too much fighting and food and the tension of fucking up, so I just turned over and went to sleep.

***

I jerked awake with somebody's hand on my cheek.

"Who...?"

Yaj was sitting on the edge of my cot, petting my face like a cat does in the morning when it wants you to wake up. It was after lights-out. The other whores were asleep.

I knocked her hand away, nervous. I remembered her hair-stay shiv in my back.

"Whaddaya want?"

She stood up, never taking her eyes off me, and shrugged out of her shift, revealing her tiny, bruised body. "Reward."

Man, I almost cried. It was the first word I'd ever heard her say, to anybody. I didn't know what to say. "I thought... I thought..."

She sat down again and put her hand on my lips, then reached her scrawny arms around the barrel of my ribs and hugged me tight, burying her head between my breasts.

Now I did cry. I got tears all over her hair. I wrapped my arms around her and crushed her to me, but not too hard. I had to be delicate with Waarians, especially little ones like this.

After a bit she craned her head like a cat stretching, her lips seeking mine. I pulled her up, feeling her wiry curves slide across my body, a heat starting to build up between my legs, and—

A noise. The door. We both froze, like teenagers caught necking in the den. I looked around. A pale slant of moonlight picked out a piece of floor, the corner of a cot. Dim silhouettes crowded quietly through the door. Men with clubs and sharpened stakes. No question who they were here for. They were squinting around, trying to get their eyes used to the dark. I only had a second.

I lifted Yaj to the floor. "Hide in a corner."

They heard me and turned. I shoved Yaj away.

They came at me like dogs after a bear, swarming around the cots and knocking them aside, swinging their makeshift weapons. Were they nuts? Didn't they know what I could do by now? Then I saw a pattern twisting at me in the darkness. A net! The one weapon Zhen didn't lock up at the end of practice.

It dropped over me like a heavy coat. I fell back, half on, half off my cot, as six guys held down the edges of it with all their weight. I thrashed. I just got tangled. I couldn't get enough leverage to throw them off.

A seventh one jumped on my chest. It was Shir. He hissed in my face, raising a brass serving spoon that had been honed into a razor sharp spade. "Demon bitch! You will shame no more men in the arena!"

As he slashed down, something blurred behind him and suddenly he was screaming and trying to pull something off his neck.

Yaj! She stabbed at Shir's head and shoulders with her hair-stay. Before he could get her off, the other three whores were tearing at his guys, breaking their concentration and their grip on the net.

It was all I needed. I got an arm free, caught a guy by the belt and slammed him into two other guys. They fell, turning a cot into kindling. I sat up, but not fast enough. Shir stabbed back over his shoulder with his spoon blade and Yaj fell back, shrieking.

I clobbered Shir on the ear, then shoved him off and staggered up. The net was still tangled around my right arm and leg with two more dragging on it, trying to pull me back down.

The last guy jumped at my back, but I spotted him and jabbed back with an elbow. I heard a crunch. He dropped.

I stepped toward Shir, but the three guys I'd thrown were up again and stabbing sticks at me, and the guys holding the net gave up and joined them. I don't remember what I did next—I had my mad-on, and my brain was as red and hot as a branding iron—but when it was over two of them were across the room, standing on their necks, another was ass-deep in the wall, his head and shoulders hanging out in the cool night air, and two more were draped over the crossbeams above me like wet bed sheets.

I didn't notice. I was looking down at little Yaj, sprawled like a broken doll on the plank floor, a river of red pouring from a divot in her neck as big as an orange slice. My heart froze up like a lump of cold lead pressing down on the rest of me.

Something chunked into my back. No pain. I turned calmly. Shir was raising his ridiculous, murdering spoon for another chop.

I broke his neck.

The screaming of the women finally brought the guards. They found me kneeling in the blood on the floor, holding Yaj's little body in my arms. I was rocking back and forth and crying like a baby.

***

I woke up woozy the next morning to Zhen slapping my face. I tried to stop him, but I couldn't move my hands. I was in the infirmary, strapped to a cot.

Zhen stopped slapping. "Good. The brothers wish to see you." He turned to a pair of guards. "Let her up."

The infirmary was in the basement of the trainers' house. I vaguely remembered being brought down the night before. The saw-bones had given me a slug of booze that smelled like rubbing alcohol, and then went to town on my back with a needle and thread. Luckily I'd stopped Shir's spoon with a rib, so it hadn't done any internal damage. Not that I felt real lucky after thirty stitches.

The guards undid my straps and hauled me upright, as gentle as roustabouts. My head felt like somebody had tossed it in the spin cycle. Zhen led the way out of the room.

Two dizzy flights up they plopped me down on a backless chair in the brothers' office. This was the ritziest room in the school—heavy wood furniture, blue walls, sunlight streaming in through stone lattice-work high up near the ceiling, and bronze sculptures of famous gladiators all over the place.

The whole scene reminded me of a parole review. The brothers sat behind a long table, staring at me. Even though they had plenty of room to stretch out, they stayed hip to hip, heads together and whispering. They looked like Heckle and Jeckle with Rain Man's disease.

Sketh blinked at Zhen. "The damages, Fightmaster Zhen?"

"Yes, damages?" Skir echoed him.

Zhen clicked his heels together. "Sirs, Shir is dead. Broken neck. The others have only minor wounds. Nydin is worst off with a broken nose. All can work."

"And the circumstances?"

"Yes, tell us the circumstances."

Zhen looked at a spot on the wall over the brothers' heads and recited like a flat-foot on the witness stand. "Sirs, Shir and his companions paid off the bunkhouse guard, broke into the comfort house and attacked Jae-En with makeshift weapons. With the help of the comfort women, Jae-En defended herself and inflicted the aforementioned injuries."

The brothers did their whispering act again. Finally Sketh looked up at me. He reminded me of the principal at my second reform school, a long, thin Ichabod Crane motherfucker who always peered over his glasses at me like I'd let down the whole human race by smoking behind the gym.

Even without glasses Sketh looked like he was peering over his glasses. "It is against the laws of this school for any gladiator to strike another gladiator without permission."

Skir piped up. "Even in self-defense."

I rolled my eyes. "Yeah, wouldn't want any violence around here."

Zhen backhanded me. I was still too swacked from the doc's Mickey Finn to even flinch.

Sketh continued like nothing had happened. "The punishment for striking a gladiator without permission is sixty lashes. The punishment for killing a gladiator is death."

Skir chimed in again. "Yes, death."

I sighed. "Better and better."

Another smack from Zhen.

"However," Sketh put the tips of his fingers together and looked at me again. He really was just like that idiot principal. "We are aware that you are in many ways the injured party in all of this…"

Skir picked it up like they'd rehearsed it. "Even though your provocation of Shir *was* severe. Your actions against him were a deliberate insult."

Back to Sketh. "Regardless, in light of the complexities of the case, we have determined that there is only one way to be fair to all parties." He paused for dramatic effect. Lost on me. I could barely keep my head up.

Skir delivered the punchline. "Trial by combat. In the arena. You versus the surviving members of the attack."

That got through the fog. It even made Zhen cough. I did a little addition. "Me against… two, three, six guys? You call that fair?"

Zhen put a warning hand on my back. Sketh and Skir were babbling.

"Such insolence! Certainly is it fair."

"Eminently fair."

"There is no other way."

"None."

The interview was over. Zhen muttered to me as he led me out of the office. "Not the only way. Only the most profitable."

I nodded. Ask Don King. A grudge match always means big box office.

***

I didn't much care what they did with me. I was still pretty broken up over Yaj. It's not like she was my type, hell I probably wasn't hers, but she'd been so brave, and so loyal—protecting me, protecting the other girls. And she'd been the first person on this shit-ass planet that wanted to hold me, even out of pity. Oh sure, Wen-Jhai had come on to me on the pirate ship, but that had been about her, not about me. Yaj had hugged me. She'd wanted to give *me* pleasure. And I didn't just miss her because I'd been so horny lately. I missed her because I missed her, dammit! What I hadn't let myself admit—because I'm big, tough Jane, who never lets anything get to her—was how fucking lonely I was.

Ugly as I am, I've had plenty partners back on Earth, and believe it or not, more than sex, I missed human contact. Holding someone, having someone's arms around you on the back of your bike, curling up together on the couch watching a Vikings game. Yaj's little hug had made me miss that stuff so much it felt like my heart had grown spikes and was stabbing into the rest of me.

Poor little Yaj. In her weird way I think maybe she'd liked me. She saw me lying by myself when all the other fighters were getting their "rewards" and felt sorry enough for the big pink freak to give herself to me. That knocked the wind out of me. Think about giving yourself to a space alien because you thought it was lonely. And if that wasn't brave enough, the stupid little bitch went and died for me! All she had to do was hide in the corner and nothing would have happened to her! I couldn't think about it without choking up again, and I spent my nights replaying the scene in my head, thinking of all the ways I could have saved her if I'd really tried.

CHAPTER TWENTY-ONE

DEATH MATCH!

They still let me train and eat with the other fighters leading up to the big show, but to keep me safe at night they put me in a room in the trainers' house. I appreciated the gesture, but now that me and the Ho House girls were finally on good terms it was a little frustrating. Broke up as I was over Yaj I wouldn't have said no to a little comforting. But not a chance.

When Lhan heard the deal with the death match he was pig-biting mad. "But this is not just, Mistress Jae-En. Six against one? They only find a new way to murder you."

We were practicing together in the yard. Nobody else would work with me, either because they hated me too much, or they were afraid of pissing off the gang of six. "Hey, I beat 'em once."

"But not in the arena. Not all armed with their favored weapons and on their guard. And did you not have help before? Were you not saved by..."

"Don't twist the knife, Lhan."

"My apologies, Mistress, that was cruel, but I make my point. Even gifted as you are, six are too many, and these are better fighters than Shir. You are in need of help."

"Try telling the bosses that."

He lowered his sword, a funny look in his eye. "Indeed. I believe I shall."

He strode off. I followed, nervous. I didn't like that look. "Lhan, wait. What are you gonna do?"

He didn't answer, just bee-lined for Zhen, who was chewing out a couple fighters, as usual, and stopped in front of him. Zhen cocked an eyebrow. "Something troubling you, Fancy?"

Lhan bowed. "Sir, I wish to be Mistress Jae-En's partner in her upcoming bout."

The fucking idiot. "Lhan! What the fuck! Don't do that! There's no reason—"

Zhen cut me off. "Sorry, Fancy. You're too good an investment to risk in a suicide scrap like that."

"But is not Mistress Jae-En an even better investment? Want you such a prospect to die against such unfair odds?"

"What I want matters not. Your masters feel Mistress Jae-En is more trouble than she's worth. She has divided the stable, made trouble with the whores, and killed a gladiator with many good years left in him. If Jae-En wins, she removes the men who hate her most and things may settle down. If she loses, the source of the trouble is gone."

"But 'tis unfair! I demand…"

"You demand? You forget you're a slave now, Dhan Ruffler. I sympathize with you, and with Jae-En. Never have I had two better students, but I haven't the power nor the inclination to put you in that match. That match is punishment for killing and attempting to kill gladiators out of the arena."

Lhan smiled, sad and grim. "Then you have no choice but to put me in."

"For what?"

Before I knew what he was doing, Lhan slapped Zhen across the face. It was so loud, half the yard turned and stared.

Lhan bowed. "Consider it my feeble attempt to kill you."

Zhen stood stock still. His head had barely moved when Lhan had slapped him. Now he was as rigid as a sword. The whole yard held its breath.

Finally he spoke. "I will inform the brothers of your crime. They will decide your fate."

He turned and walked to the trainers' house, back straight as a Mountie's. On the way he told his seconds to take over, but didn't tell anybody to lock Lhan up. I hoped that was a good sign.

I turned on Lhan. "What the hell was that? What were you thinking?"

"Could I leave you to die, Mistress?"

"But what about Sai and Wen-Jhai? How are we gonna save the if both of us are dead?"

"We won't die. We two are more than a match for six."

I nearly hit him I was so mad. "That's only if they put you in the match! What if they decide to cut your throat? Or put you in your own death match? Did you think of that?"

That brought him up short for a second. Then he shrugged. "What is, is. Honor would not have allowed me to do otherwise."

"Has it ever occurred to you that sometimes us damsels in distress don't need saving?"

He smiled at me, the bastard. "Never, Mistress. Never."

***

Zhen made us wait a whole night to get the decision, and I didn't get a wink. My head was full of escape plans which always stopped short once I got over the wall. It's hard to make escape routes when you don't know where you are.

Next morning at line-up Zhen called me and Lhan aside. The rest of the school got so quiet you could have heard an ant fart. Zhen turned and barked at them. "Have you all lost your tongues? Is the art of conversation dead?" He turned back when the fighters reluctantly started talking about the weather and who got hurt last week.

He stabbed a look at Lhan. "You're a brave fool, Fancy. Fortunately for you, I was a brave fool myself once, or you'd be swinging at the end of a rope. Instead, I convinced the brothers that a noble-friend-comes-to-the-aid-of-his-lover story would bring in more women. You have your match."

Lhan stiffened. "Lover? You insult Mistress Jae-En this way?"

I wasn't a bit insulted, but now wasn't the time to mention it.

Zhen looked like he was going to hit Lhan. "You do not want the match?"

Lhan relaxed and bowed. "My apologies, sir. You are kinder than I deserve."

"Very true, Fancy."

Zhen went back to the class. Lhan and I exchanged a glance. He smiled. "You see?"

"Oh, I see all right. Now I'm gonna have to watch out for your ass as well as my own."

***

We'd already killed two of them when Lhan stopped dead beside me, staring up over my shoulder. "Sai!"

I couldn't look. The big guy with the cornrows and the super-size spear and the little guy with the chain mail catcher's mitt and the razorblade boomerangs were making things hot for me right then.

Lhan had been right. Six-on-one would have sucked. They had me scouted, but good. They knew all my tricks and had come up with some countermoves I didn't like one bit. The maneuver that was a pain in my posterior at that particular moment was where Corn-Rows would trap me against the arena wall with that long-ass spear, and the little guy would hook those fucking boomerangs around him like a curveball buzzsaw out of nowhere. If I blocked a boomerang the spear jabbed in at me. If I blocked the spear the boomerangs got in my face.

Even leaping out of trouble was tough. If I jumped I'd either get a spearhead up my poop-chute or get picked off in mid-flight like a spooked duck. But just standing there wasn't working either. I was starting to look like the world's worst paper cut casualty. My whole body stung.

Lhan had his hands full with his two guys too. One was a whip-thin killer with a slim sword. The other was a bouncy guy with a long pitchfork. Lhan's strategy was to keep moving so they got in each other's way, but that meant constant running, and he was starting to get winded.

And now he had Sai to distract him. Great.

Corn-Rows' spear shot toward my heart. I blocked it, but kept my eyes on Mr. Boomerang. He snapped off another throw and it winged over Corn-Rows' left shoulder, right into my strike zone. Idea! Instead of deflecting it like the others, I swung at it like Mark McGuire and connected. The boomerang linedrived right back at Corn-Rows and buried itself deep in his forehead. His eyes rolled up and he sagged.

Boomerang whipped his last two kangaroo killers at me, desperate. I grabbed Corn-Rows as he fell and held him up like a human shield. Two jolts jarred me as the boomerangs bit into his back.

Mr. Boomerang ran to a dead guy, trying to get a weapon. I heaved Corn-Rows at him and knocked him flat. The crowd cheered. They were behind us all the way this time. They always loved the underdog, and two against six was as underdog as you could get.

As I ran to help Lhan I took a quick glance where he'd pointed. It was Sai all right. He was dressed in a dangerously short toga and painted up like a geisha, but I'd recognize those mopey shoulders anywhere.

He was in one of the private boxes, sitting beside his skinny, prune-faced owner. There were two hunky bodyguards behind them. The old perv was looking down at the action with shiny eyes. He seemed to like watching sweaty, naked men fight. Sai looked comatose, like he was on a heroin nod. But he wasn't entirely out of it. When prune-face put a hand on Sai's knee I saw him shudder. Then it was time to stop looking.

I'd done a stupid thing throwing Corn-Rows' body at Boomerang. I was taking the Pitchfork guy off Lhan's hands when a boomerang ricocheted off my helmet. Duh! I'd given the little fucker back his arsenal! Now I was back where I'd started, one guy stabbing, one guy throwing. And worse, Lhan wasn't on his game. He was fighting as well as always, but he wasn't capitalizing on his advantages. Every time he won some breathing room, he'd sneak another look at Sai and Prune-Face instead of pressing his attack. He could have nailed Swashbuckler twice over if he'd been trying.

I shouted to him. "Come on, Lhan! Get it over with!"

"The filthy, corrupting cadaver! He…"

I parried a boomerang like Luke Skywalker blocking blaster fire. "Worry about him later. I could use a little help here."

I leaped a pitchfork thrust and we drifted apart again. I had to flip in mid-air to dodge another boomerang. Pitchfork ran under me, hoping to shish-kabob me, but I pulled my trick, throwing the weight of my sword out and snapping myself into a lopsided twist. I landed behind him.

He twisted and stabbed with his pitchfork, desperate. I batted the shaft away barehanded and ran him through, right up to the hilt. He puked blood on my armor. I shuddered.

A boomerang bit into one of my shin guards. No time to be sick. I spun, not even trying to pull my sword free, and threw the dead guy's pitchfork at Boomerang, blind.

It wasn't a good throw, but it was good enough. As the pitchfork wobbled past him, a barbed tine pierced his forearm. Not a killing blow, but he couldn't throw with that fork hooked through his arm. He was out of the fight.

I turned to help Lhan. He'd kicked Swashbuckler to the ground, but instead of running him through, he was stepping toward the stands, shouting. "Sai! Beloved! Unhand him, you…"

I followed his gaze, thinking, 'Beloved?'

In Prune-Face's private box things had reached a climax, so to speak. Prune-Face had his hand under Sai's loincloth and was fiddling about.

This was more than Lhan could stand. He threw his sword in Swashbuckler's face, snatched up the super-spear from Corn-Row's body, and chucked it as hard as he could toward the box. Prune-Face took it in the gut and flew back, pinned to the back wall like a butterfly.

The crowd gasped. Hell, I gasped. This was not good!

Everybody roared to their feet. The brothers screamed for the guards. Swashbuckler swung a brutal swipe at Lhan and cracked him on the head so hard his helmet spun off.

Lhan dropped. Swashbuckler turned on me. I backed up, totally panicked. I screamed. "Lhan! You okay?" No answer.

What now? Fuck! A gladiator who killed a spectator, especially a guy rich enough to get a private box, was killed on the spot—no explanations, no trial. We had to get out of here, but how? Through the stands? Not a chance. The crowd had turned into a wolf pack, howling for our blood. Through the tunnels? Nope. The big iron gate that locked us into the arena was down.

No wait, it was going up. A squad of guards was forming up behind it, ready to march out and kill us. If I timed it right I just might be able to…

But what about Sai?! If I left him now, how would I find him again?

That cleared my head. I leaped over Swashbuckler's lunge and kicked straight for Prune-Face's box. I pulled myself up a few yards of stone work one handed, hopped the rail and landed beside Sai, sword at the ready. Prune-Face's bodyguards stepped forward, drawing.

"Sai! quick. My hand!"

But Sai was moving in slow motion, still staring at Prune-Face, whose life was running in red rivulets down the shaft of the super-spear.

The bruisers swung at me. They must not have been watching the show. I knocked their swords away with one swipe and opened them both up with the back hand.

The crowd was tearing at the thin walls of the box. Hands ripped through like something out of a Living Dead movie. I scooped up Sai and jumped back down into the arena.

Swashbuckler was waiting for me, sword up, but before I could even begin to parry, two feet of steel exploded from his chest. He crumpled.

Lhan stood behind him, swaying. The back of his head was a red mess of sticky hair.

I landed. "Lhan! Thank god! I thought he'd got you."

Lhan only had eyes for Sai. "Sai! Are you unhurt? Has he befouled you?"

Sai's head lolled.

"I think he's drugged. Come on." I sheathed my sword. I was going to need both hands.

The iron gate was just cranking all the way open as we turned. The guards poured out.

I took Lhan by the wrist and ran right at them. They raised their spears to throw. Just as they did, I grabbed Lhan by the belt, cinched Sai tighter under my arm and leaped, carrying both of them over the guards' spears. A guard looked up, amazed. I kicked off his face, and sprang through the gate into the darkness inside.

There were more guards in the staging area, but they dove clear as we landed. I dropped Lhan and Sai and drew again. Lhan went on guard too, only weaving a little. The guards recovered and turned on us. The guards in the arena were tripping all over themselves trying to do an about-face.

I looked at Lhan. "You good to fight?"

"Good is not the first word that springs to mind."

If he could put together a sentence like that I wasn't too worried. "Watch Sai then."

I hopped to the cable that raised and lowered the gate, and chopped through it with one blow. The gate dropped with a crash that shook mortar out of the ceiling.

The guards in the arena screeched to a stop.

Lhan was fending off five guards. I jumped back to his side and brushed them back with a spinning slash. A captain shouted into the gladiator locker room. "Help us, you scum!"

But as I scooped up Sai and we started backing down the ramp into the innards of the arena, I heard Zhen. "My apologies, captain. But I can't risk my employers' property without their permission."

The captain cursed him. I looked back, amazed. I swear Zhen winked at me.

***

We ran through the catacombs like blind rats, me with Sai over one shoulder like a sack of potatoes, Lhan leaking blood like a sieve until he tied a piece of his loincloth around his head like a bandana. It made him look like an eighties action hero, but it stopped the bleeding.

I knew the way back to the school, but that was no good. We had to find a way to the street.

Guards poured down every stairway, and we had to double back from them and from dead ends half a dozen times.

We ran past the animal pens, a long comet-tail of guards right behind us. The animals got pretty stirred up, snorting and hollering when we crashed by, and so did the keepers. They jumped in front of us with whips and clubs, but we fanned 'em back with our swords. Then I got an idea.

"Lhan, the cages!"

We leaped to the cage doors, ripped the locking pins out, hauled them open and ran. The keepers screamed, terrified, and tried to close them back up, but the animals bulled their way out—the huge vurlaks, the saber-toothed shikes, the slinky, black ki-tens. Behind us, the guards ran into a seething mosh of teeth and claws. We couldn't outrun the sound. Horrible.

Unfortunately, there were more guards where those came from. As we started up a spiral staircase, a squad spotted us and surged after us, their spear points poking at our heels.

I popped out onto the next floor, banging Sai's head on the doorframe. He moaned. "Sorry, Sai."

Lhan was panting beside me. I wasn't exactly fresh myself. Sai felt like he weighted a fucking ton. There were barrels stacked by the wall. I tipped one on its side and rolled it into the stairwell just as the first guard reached the top. He went down twice as fast as he'd come up, and took his buddies with him. It sounded like a whole kitchen full of Revere Ware bouncing down a hillside.

Finally, at the end of a long hall, we saw a big loading area, with crates, barrels, cages, props and pieces of scenery, including what looked like a fully functioning warship, oars and all, stacked up along both walls, and at the far end, a huge doorway, big enough to drive a double-decker bus through, with beautiful, dazzling sunshine pouring through.

Unfortunately, another squad of guards was waiting between us and the door, and these guys had bows.

They let go a volley as we ran in. We hit the brakes and scrambled back into the narrow hallway. I felt a couple arrows glance off sleeve plates and then a weird tug in my side.

We ducked around a corner where they couldn't hit us and I looked at myself. There was a bloody trench along my ribs. An arrow had slit me open like an envelope as it passed. It wasn't deep, but it burned like a hot tailpipe and bled like a faucet. Lhan leaned against the wall beside me.

We were pinned down, and I mean *pinned*. They couldn't get us, but we couldn't get out. I looked at Lhan. He was bent over, pulling an arrow out of the bottom of his boot.

I raised an eyebrow. "You alright?"

He put his foot down gingerly and nodded. "An inconvenience only. But what of you?"

I set Sai down and ripped strips off his toga. "Gotta bind this up and I'm good."

Lhan limped forward to help. His right boot left bloody footprints.

I pointed. "You got a funny definition of inconvenient."

He shrugged and wrapped the strips around my ribs. "We have more pressing concerns at the moment."

The rags were soaked in blood instantly, but they slowed the flow. I gritted my teeth as he pulled them tight. "Yeah, we're going to have reinforcements crawling up our ass any second now. Any ideas?"

Lhan scanned the hallway, then pointed to a row of giant decorative ceramic vases, each as big as a phone-booth and almost entirely filling the side passage they were stored in. "Mistress, what are the limits of your strength?"

Moving cover. Great Idea. "Well, let's find out."

It took a second to worm my way behind the first vase, and my new wound complained as I twisted and stretched, but once I got in position, the thing wasn't much harder to push than a refrigerator. The smooth stone floor helped. I almost started shoving it toward the big room when I got an idea.

I picked up Sai, groaning. Every move felt like somebody putting the arrow back in the wound and twisting it around. I hoisted him to my shoulders anyway. There was just enough room between the top of the vase and hallway ceiling to lower Sai inside. Now we wouldn't have to come back for him.

Lhan and I pushed the big vase toward the loading area. The two of us together really got it moving. I could hear arrows chinking off its far side through my hands as we raced closer.

We exploded into the room behind the big vase and shoved it at the guards as hard as we could.

They scattered. Before they could reorganize I jumped up over the vase and dropped down into the middle of them, swinging my sword in a circle like a giant lawnmower blade. This was turning into my favorite tactic. Lhan stayed behind the vase and ran through anybody who came around it. We cut 'em down like weeds.

At least at first.

After a second, the survivors fell back, their captain screaming orders. He got his bowmen behind his spearmen. That was bad. Running straight at them wouldn't work. Their spears would hold me off long enough for the archers to pin-cushion me. I turned to Lhan. "Stay behind the vase."

He nodded, tired. He looked like staying behind the vase was all he could handle right then. I felt about the same. The pain in my side had stopped jarring me every time I moved, and had settled down to a continuous dull toothache agony. I wanted to lie down.

Instead, I leaped up onto the pile of junk against the left wall. I heard a sound like twenty guys all swinging Wiffle ball bats at the same time and rolled behind a giant papier-mâché prop head just ahead of a barrage of arrows. Shafts stuck out of the the head's face like whiskers.

I looked around. There was a stack of crates beside me, each about the size of your average TV. I hefted one. Heavy, but manageable. I heaved it blind over the giant head in the general direction of the archers.

Crashes. Screams. Bingo! I sent another one flying. More screams. I heard the captain shouting orders, and then the clink and clunk of guys in boots and armor climbing the pile of junk.

I tried to kick the giant head down on top of them. Too heavy. It must have been weighted inside. I pressed my back against the crates behind me and put both feet on the back of the head like I was on a leg press machine. I pushed. It didn't give. Then, with a crack, it did. I landed on my butt, but the head toppled, and started an avalanche of junk that knocked the guards to the floor. A barrel exploded beside them, gushing out some kind of liquid. Lamp oil from the smell of it. The guards couldn't stand up in it. Most of them were too hurt to try, anyway.

Lhan charged out from behind the vase and started poking the guys I'd missed with my aerial assault, his sword flashing every which way. He kept his feet out of the lamp oil by using the bodies of the downed guards like stepping stones in a river.

The captain was rallying the last survivors and I heard shouts echoing from the corridor. Reinforcements. Time to go.

I jumped to the lip of the huge vase, then dropped down inside where Sai was curled up like a baby. Little punk had slept through the whole fight. I threw him over my shoulder again, and kicked my way out of the vase. It shattered into a hundred pieces.

Lhan and I ran for daylight, hop-scotching over the downed guards, just as the reinforcements ran into the room. We could hear them skidding and crashing in the lake of oil behind us.

The door led out to an enclosed yard: stables, a blacksmith's forge, feed bins, and a gate that opened onto a busy street. We sprinted past a clump of cowering slaves and through the gate with the shouts of the guards following us.

The street was a mess of wagons and porters and slaves all trying to get through the same narrow roadway at the same time, and everybody screaming and waving their arms and cracking whips. Perfect. We dove into the crowd, me playing linebacker to Lhan's fullback, clearing a path through the surging, shouting chaos.

The guards were close behind, but losing ground, busting heads and shoving, and getting shoved back for their pains.

We made a corner and got out of line of sight. The street ahead was as crowded as it was behind us. Time to change directions. Up seemed like a good choice.

We were in front of a two-story building with a flat roof. I put Sai down and laced my hands together, holding them low. "Lhan, run and jump."

"But... but 'tis two stories high!"

"You better hope I don't toss you three."

He laughed, nervous, but ran and planted his foot in my hands. I heaved. He flew, arms flailing, and disappeared over the lip of the roof. There was a thump and a scream.

"Shit."

I got Sai on my shoulder again, leaped up, kicked off a nearby wagon, and sailed up to a balcony, then up a clay drain pipe to the rooftop. Lhan was tangled in some lady's laundry line and she was giving him what for. She started screaming all over again when she saw me.

I heard shouts from the street. I looked down. People were pointing up, showing the guards where we went. They charged into the building. "They're coming up. Come on."

Lhan pulled free of the clothesline and we did the hand-boost trick to a higher roof, then building-hopped our way to freedom. Though maybe freedom isn't quite the right word for it when you're running and wounded in a hostile city you don't know your way around in, being hunted for multiple murders with no idea how to get home.

CHAPTER TWENTY-TWO

RESCUE!

We finally found a place to hole up a few miles from the arena. It was a half caved-in three-story building. The stairs to the second floor had collapsed, so no one was going to walk up there and find us by accident.

I laid Sai down. Between me slinging him around like a backpack for the past hour and whatever dope he had in his system, he was as droopy as a rag doll. I made sure he had a pulse, then turned to Lhan. "Lemme look at those wounds…"

I had to stop there. My vision was going black around the edges. I sat down, dizzy. I hadn't realized how wiped out I was. A six-on-two fight in the arena, a running battle, bloodloss, pain, and a flat-out sprint across the city by rooftop—I was running on fumes.

Lhan was no better. He couldn't even get out his usual noble martyr bullshit. "Look to yourself, mistress. I… am…" He slid down the wall.

I crawled over to him, pulled off his boot and undid the bandage on his head. He was too pooped to protest.

His head was a mess. The helmet had saved his life, but not by much. There was a ragged gash slanting across the back of his skull where Swashbuckler's blade had chopped through the bronze skull-bucket. It was crusted with blood and hair. He winced when I touched it. "My apologies, mistress."

"Hey, you patch me up. I patch you up."

"And I thank you for it, but I was apologizing for my precipitous actions, which began this desperate journey."

"Hey, we escaped, right? Now shut up and let me work."

The room we were in was half open to the sky. By the far wall were a few cracked clay bowls in a pile of assorted garbage. I crossed to them. Good thing we were in Doshaan where it rained all the time: the bowls had water in them. Most of them had other stuff too; rotten beans, soup bones, some black gunk I didn't want to stir up, but one was clear all the way to the bottom.

I carried it back to Lhan, then ripped more strips off Sai's fancy toga. His clothes were the cleanest, and besides, I was always looking for an excuse to get that boy naked. I soaked the strips and cleaned and bound Lhan's head wound, then had a look at the arrow wound in his foot. For once Lhan hadn't been downplaying things. It really was nothing—a shallow but bloody puncture.

I patched that up too, then both of us sat back and just breathed for a while.

After about twenty minutes, Lhan raised his head. "We need food and drink. I must go out."

I scowled. "You? You're the worst off of all of us. You're lucky your head's still on your shoulders."

"And yet it must be me, mistress. Sai is in no condition to move, and you… would be spotted in an instant."

I didn't like it, but he was right. "Don't you get tired of being right all the time?"

He smirked. "'Tis occasionally wearisome."

A thought occurred to me. "Wait a minute. You got any cash? How are you gonna buy anything?"

Lhan frowned. "Hmmm, a point, yes. We could sell our weapons and armor, but…"

"Not on your life, pal."

"No. In our present situation that would not be wise."

I glanced at Sai. Prune-Face had loaded him down with a jewelry store's worth of gold. He was swimming in rings, necklaces, bracelets, and ankle chains.

"Hey, problem solved. We could buy the whole supermarket with this stuff."

Lhan had a look. "Yes. Unfortunately, just one of these baubles could indeed buy a market. Any attempt to buy a meat bun or a jug of wine, even with the smallest of Sai's rings, would be met with suspicion and most likely arrest."

"Then what the hell are we gonna do?"

Lhan grinned. He looked like the devil from a fifties hot-rod magazine. "I think 'tis time to leave honest commerce behind and turn to more underhanded methods."

"Uh, you mean steal something?"

"Precisely."

***

It took a quarter-hour of roof hopping for me to find and liberate a long enough length of laundry line, but then we were in business.

Lhan and I worked out a little whistle code, then I roped him down to street level and off he went—the man, bringing home the bacon, while I stayed home and took care of baby Sai. How domestic.

Sai was still far out of it, so I had some time alone to think, but it took a little while for my brain to quiet down. The whole damn day had been fight, jump, run, hide, steal, kill. When I finally throttled down I spun back to what had started today's craziness—Lhan screaming 'beloved,' and putting a spear through Sai's pervy master.

Beloved? Lhan loved Sai? Lhan was gay?

The more I thought about it, the more it made sense. That's why he had been so upset when Sai had been sold to Prune-Face. That's why his "appetites" had got him sent down to the country, and why he'd been so happy to join Sai on this wild goose chase. That's why he hadn't taken a whore when he'd won his match in the arena. That's why he didn't have the hots for me—though who knows if that would change if he was straight. It made me feel better anyway.

But it didn't explain everything. If he was gay, why was he so hot to get Sai married to Wen Jhai? You'd think he'd be trying his damnedest to turn him against her.

I was pretty sure Sai had no idea how Lhan felt. It had never come up, but I got the feeling that Ora was a pretty tight-assed, homophobic, men-are-men-women-are-women society. Lhan would probably be hung from the nearest cottonwood if he came out, and Sai would be the first to denounce him.

Poor Lhan. It's tough enough for dykes and fags and undecideds like myself back home, but here? Shit. I'd rather wear a Gay Pride shirt in Lubbock than come out here. Sure, guys like Prune-Face could get away with it. The rich can always get away with it, but to admit you love your best friend? Suicide.

I thought I was lonely here. How lonely was Lhan?

***

Sai opened his eyes a while after Lhan got back. We'd got a little fire going and the smell of roasting meat woke him up. He was so hungry, he was shaking. His arms wouldn't hold his weight. Lhan was at his side instantly, feeding him like a baby. Sai wolfed it down, practically crying. "By the Seven, I have missed this. You have no idea how long—"

Lhan's knuckles went white. "Did the demon starve you as well?"

Sai flushed and looked away. "Dhan Hijan, demanded... things of me I would not give."

Lhan snarled. "The brute."

"When I fought back, he thought to make me more compliant by starvation and wine laced with lunom. Also I was not allowed to sleep."

Lhan was foaming at the mouth. "Degenerate torturer."

"But I never gave in. At... at least my soul never did. I am ashamed to admit that my flesh sometimes... betrayed me."

Lhan was getting all hot and bothered just thinking about it, but covered it up with anger. "The decrepit lecher! I mourn that he died so quickly."

There was an uncomfortable silence after that. I broke it before anybody made a confession they might regret later. "So, uh, whadda we do now? Get the hell outta Dodge? Look for Wen-Jhai?"

Sai looked up. "I have seen Wen-Jhai. Not a quarter moon ago."

Lhan brightened. "But this is excellent news. Know you where she is held?"

Sai frowned, thinking. "Dhan Hijan brought me to a gathering at the palace of one of his... intimates, for a night of unspeakable entertainments. Wen-Jhai was serving wine, dressed in a costume of shocking depravity."

I wondered how much more depraved a costume could get around here, considering that the women on this planet went around ninety percent naked already.

Sai continued. "I attempted to speak with her, but even here, a captive in a barbarian land, she would not acknowledge my presence. Truly she must hate me more than death."

Bummer. But where was she working? "Uh, Sai, the dude whose joint this shindig was at. What did he look like?"

Sai made a face. "A degenerate monster. Strong as a vurlak, and wearing a manly top-knot, yet painted like a woman."

I shot a glance at Lhan. He nodded. "'Tis Wen-Jhai's master. We saw him purchase her at the slave market. Good. Remember you where he resides?"

Sai waved a vague hand. "By a lake. With many other rich palaces. But where that may be from here, I know not. Hijan's carriage traveled with curtains drawn, at least when I was his passenger." He shivered again. "I saw little of the city."

Lhan pressed him. "But would you know the house, were you to see it again?"

Sai sneered. "Oh yes. The man's degeneracy carried even to the walls of his estate. I would know those foul facades, never fear."

Lhan smiled. "Then we are halfway to success already. I have but to discover the location of this lake and we may begin to plot our escape."

***

The first part was easy. Over the next few snack runs Lhan got directions to the lake and even a rough idea where Lord Top-Knot's house was. Part two of the plan, where we escaped Doshaan and got back to Ora safe and sound, was a little trickier.

Captain Kai-La had been right about selling us all the way down here in the tropics. There was no trade between Doshaan and Ora. None. First off they hated each other. Doshaan had once been an Oran colony and had fought a rebellion to get free. Second, there was half a continent's worth of jungles, pirates, deserts and hostile kingdoms between 'em. Even if they'd wanted to trade, it would have been tough.

In the end, after hanging out in shady airmen's bars, Lhan found a captain who would take us north no questions asked as long as we paid his outrageous price. He was flying to some desert trading town halfway between Doshaan and Ora, where supposedly we'd be able to find a northern lunom runner who'd take us the rest of the way. Lhan didn't like the deal—it cost almost a third of Sai's jewelry—but it was the best he could find.

The ship was sailing during the third dark a couple days later. Northbound ships left at night because Doshaan always got a strong south wind after dark. We planned to snatch Wen-Jhai and get to the airfield just in time for take-off, and Lhan had promised the captain a big enough backend that he said he'd wait for us.

Our biggest stumbling block was, as usual, me. A big pink monster couldn't just walk across the city to Lord Top-Knot's palace. There were wanted notices for us painted on public buildings, with pretty good sketches of us too—though mine made me look fat—and patrols were searching the city for us. We'd killed an upstanding member of society. We were wanted men—and woman.

Lhan solved the problem. He bought a pony-cart, or, I guess, a birdy-cart—a little, one-krae crate with a bed the size of a mini-truck's. He got armor and a sword for Sai, and native costumes for both of them. Doshaani carters kept the sun and rain off with wide straw hats that looked like upside down woks. Perfect for hiding your face. For me, they got a tarp and bundled me in the back. Lhan grinned at me. "Just try to think like a sack of bulbauts."

I didn't like the arrangement at all; riding around in the dark, holding perfectly still for hours under a heavy canvas without any air-holes, bumping and rocking through sounds and smells without being able to see, never knowing if something was coming for me. How could I protect myself? I was sweating before Lhan even got the tarp over my head.

He saw me panicking and gentled me like a horse, massaging my shoulders and whispering in my ear. "Fear not, Mistress. No harm will come near but I will call out. Keep your hand on your hilt if it calms you. Be our hidden protector."

Man, was he good. What a waste. I got under the tarp with only a whimper and we headed on the long, bumpy, ride to the lake.

Lhan had been smart with the disguises. We looked just like a hundred other merchants dragging their goods across town. Fortunately, the main road to the shipfield went right past the lake, so there was a constant flow of traffic going to where we needed to go. Unfortunately, there were no roadside inns on that stretch. The rich bastards didn't want anybody loitering in their backyard I guess, and there were more patrols along there than anywhere else in the city. But things went off without a hitch. We faked a breakdown, pulled off the road, hid the cart in the soggy jungle and changed into our armor in no time.

Then it got bad. That jungle nearly stopped us before we got started. It was thicker and swampier than we expected, and we wandered around lost for way too long. I was worried we'd miss our flight. Finally we found a little stream and followed it to the lake.

The palaces were on the other side, and we trudged for fucking forever through mud and bushes with thorns like piranha teeth until we got to civilization. The going was easier on the feet here, nice blue lawns and gravel paths, but more dangerous. Those big shots all had house guards, and we spent a lot of time hiding behind ornamental shrubbery before Sai finally whispered. "There it is. With the disgusting reliefs on the walls."

They looked all right to me, but then I never claimed to have any taste. My idea of decorating is tacking album covers and Harley posters on the wall. It *was* a little explicit—naked couples banging each other in really uncomfortable positions, monsters and demons, all hung like Johnny Wadd, copping feels from winged chicks with curves out of a '50s *Playboy*. And it got more triple-X once we got over the wall. It was like Larry Flynt's garden in there— all the way down to the big penis-shaped shrubberies.

I did my usual second story job to get us into the palace proper, giving Sai and Lhan a hoist to a balcony and leaping up after them. The place was all carved wood, winged roofs, painted beam ends, latticed windows and studded doors, all spread out like some fancy island resort. Covered walkways twisted through ponds and gardens and connected different bits of the house together.

"Does this place remind you guys of a tiki-style steak joint?"

Lhan looked around at me. "A what, mistress?"

"Naw, never mind. I guess it wouldn't." I tapped a wooden pillar. "But why is everything made of wood? I thought rich guys liked to build in granite and marble."

Lhan chuckled. "In Ora we build in granite and marble because we have few trees. At home this palace would be an obscene extravagance. Here 'tis a show of status. Doshaan is one of the few lands wet enough to support great forests. The trade in precious wood is the foundation of their wealth."

"Oh, I gotcha. Like a Ford dealer driving a Crown Vic."

"Er, if you say so, mistress."

The palace was a ghost town. There were hardly any guards, and we didn't see any slaves or happy home owners. I didn't like it. I kept saying, "This is too easy. This is too fucking easy."

Finally we ran into a pudgy little slave who squealed when he spotted us and tried to run. I tackled him and clamped a hand over his mouth. Lhan put his sword to his neck and Sai whispered in his ear. "Where is the slave Wen-Jhai held?"

I let him open his mouth. He was smart. He didn't scream. "She… she is with the master, in the crimson pavilion."

"Lead us there, villain."

He did. We still didn't meet any guards. I got nervouser and nervouser.

The crimson pavilion was a hexagonal two-story lake-side cottage that looked like a hat from the Elton John collection. It had lanterns and decorative beams sticking out all over the place. The second story over-hung the first, and had so many open floor-to-ceiling windows that it was basically a porch. There were flimsy red curtains billowing out of the windows, so we couldn't see anything inside, but as we got closer we could hear a woman wailing like she was being taken apart with an ax.

Sai sprang forward. "Wen-Jhai!"

I hauled him back. "Wait. We all go together."

He struggled, desperate, but I made Lhan hold him until I tied up our guide and hid him behind a statue of a woman getting groped by a six-armed snake. Reminded me of my Uncle Dean.

I wanted to stage manage this thing just right. This was our big chance to get Sai back on Wen-Jhai's good side by showing him as the hero. This meant I couldn't just heave him up over the balcony. What if he tripped? It could blow the whole thing.

So we went in the front door. There were a couple guards, but I flattened 'em before they could even draw. Lhan and I tied and gagged 'em.

It sure was crimson in there all right. Everything inside was painted shades of red and pink and maroon. The first floor had a dining area looking out over the lake, with a low table made from one huge red crystal, and a library of purple and red leather books and dirty pictures on the walls. In the center a spiral staircase twisted up to the second floor.

I put Sai in the lead—it had to look like he was in charge—and we tip-toed up.

We came up in a fancy bathroom, open on three sides to the garden. Steam rose from a painted porcelain tub that looked like a giant tea cup. A cloud of red paper lanterns surrounded it, hanging from the ceiling. Make-up tables and closets full of flimsy clothes were butted against the inside wall. A curtained doorway led to where the screams were coming from. They were a lot louder up here. They made my toes curl.

Sai charged for the curtain. I let him go. "Do your stuff, loverboy."

He drew his sword with a fierce shout, threw open the curtains and charged in, blade first.

And stopped dead.

Lhan and I weren't planning on going in unless Sai got into serious trouble. This was his show, so we hung back, but we could see what Sai saw by peeking through the curtain. It was stop-in-your-tracks stuff all right.

Wen-Jhai was bent over some kind of custom-made leather pommel-horse, naked and dripping with sweat, while her beefy owner, Lord Top-Knot, painted up like a Bangkok bar girl, slammed into her from behind like a piston. Shae-Vai, Wen-Jhai's buxom gal-pal, lay face up on a low bench under the pommel-horse, her head between Wen-Jhai's legs.

Sai's jaw dropped. So did mine.

Wen-Jhai was as taut as a guitar string. Her hands white-knuckled the pommels and she screamed like a police siren. Finally, Lord Top-Knot's thrusting pushed her over the edge. She started bucking and screeching like a horse in a burning barn. "Oh, yes! Harder! Don't stop! By the Seven, don't stop!"

Lhan and I couldn't look at each other. Sai was dead white. The tip of his sword drooped to the ground with a clank.

Lord Top-Knot looked up. His eyes bulged. He jumped back out of Wen-Jhai with a yell. "Who dares? Who dares?!" He grabbed a sword and waved it at Sai—kind of redundant if you ask me.

Wen-Jhai raised her head. Her eyes went wide. I watched her face turn three colors in three seconds: white with shock, pink with shame, then gray with horror when it hit home how this was going to fuck up the rest of her life.

But the next second her face turned a forth color. She went red with anger as Sai, stiff as starch, turned away from Lord Top-Knot's attack and walked back through the curtain.

I knew he wasn't turning tail. He'd walked away because he was disgusted, but Wen-Jhai didn't see it that way. As far as she was concerned this was twice now Sai had come to rescue her and chickened out when it came down to the big fight.

Lord Top-Knot started after Sai, shouting, but just then, I kid you not—and this is the kind of bullshit coincidence that makes me walk out of movies, so you gotta know I wouldn't put it in if it wasn't true—who comes swinging through the window on a rope ladder, but Kir-Dhanan fucking Kedac-Zir.

Sai was already out of the room, so Kedac didn't see him. Instead, he hopped off the ladder and went after Lord Top-Knot.

Sai turned back when he heard the clash of swords and froze. Lhan and I were frozen too. My heart was pounding against my ribs like a battering ram. My brain was screaming. "It's Kedac! It's Kedac! It's motherfucking Kedac!" But I was so fucking stunned I couldn't move an inch.

Lord Top-Knot just wasn't ready for so many surprises. Kedac beat his blade aside and ran him through with one lightning thrust. Top-Knot crumpled. Kedac called to Wen-Jhai. "Come, betrothed, my airship awaits."

With a snooty sneer in the direction of the curtain, Wen-Jhai ran to Kedac and hugged him like he was her conquering hero and she was his virgin bride, like she hadn't just cum like a run-away freight train ten seconds before.

"Yes, beloved. Save me from this den of cowards."

Kedac scooped her up in one arm, stepped through the window, and started up the rope ladder. Shae-Vai was right behind them.

I finally snapped out of it enough to realize I was missing the perfect opportunity. Here was Kedac, without any muscle around him, thousands of ilns from home, and I was ten times the swordswoman I'd been the last time we were face to face. Now was the time. Now!

I charged through the curtain and ran to the windows, drawing as I went, but before I got four steps, the rope ladder started rising and Kedac disappeared out of sight.

I ran onto the balcony and looked up. The end of the rope ladder was already fifty feet over the pavilion, being reeled up into an Oran warship that hung in the sky and blocked out the little moon.

I howled with rage, as much at myself as at Kedac. If I hadn't froze up I could have had him. What the fuck was wrong with me?

CHAPTER TWENTY-THREE

PURSUIT!

Me, Lhan and Sai walked out of Top-Knot's palace as easy as we had walked in. Kedac's raid had been as silent as ours, so nobody raised the alarm. Good thing too. I wasn't paying attention like I should have. I was still busy watching the instant replay inside my brain—Kedac swinging through those curtains, me just fucking standing there. I cursed myself out something fierce.

Sai wasn't much better. He dragged along like a whiny kid at the end of a trip to Disneyland. "Lead me not a step further, Lhan. Let me cast my worthless self in this lake and have an end to misery."

For once I knew just how he felt. I was ready to jump in a lake myself. But that wouldn't get me my revenge. If Sai decided going after Wen-Jhai wasn't worth it after all, I'd lose my ride back to Ormolu and Kedac. So, shitty as I felt, it was time to play cheerleader.

"Come on, Sai. You were taken by surprise. We all were. You'll get him next time. We just gotta get to Ora."

Lhan nodded approvingly. "Well spoken, mistress. Heed her, Sai. There is always another day."

Sai bleated like a sheep with a head cold. "But why fight when I no longer desire the prize? By the Seven, to think I might have wed such a depraved harlot."

Lhan and I exchanged a look. I didn't know what to say. Lhan didn't either. He coughed. "Er, we will speak more of this on board. Regardless of all else, our home and our hopes all lie in Ora. We must make that ship."

That's what I wanted to hear. We marched Sai back to the main road, then all the way to the Doshaan Airfield.

The ship was still there. It was even smaller than the one Kai-La's pirates had nabbed us on, and it looked like it would fall apart if you looked at it wrong. Its balloon was patched like a clown's pants.

The captain, a fat, moon-faced guy who dressed more like a pirate than the pirates had, bowed us on board. Lhan had paid him so much he didn't give me a second look. In fact he was so happy to see us he wouldn't leave us alone. He followed us around, grinning like a Tijuana strip-show tout until Lhan gave him one of Sai's gold bracelets to make him go away.

Our cabin was smaller than an Arkansas jail cell. Lhan and I weren't about to spend more time in that closet with Sai moping and moaning than we had to, so after we took all weapons and sharp objects away from him and locked him in, we went up on deck to wait for him to fall asleep.

Captain Happy was just casting off. We leaned on the rail and watched Doshaan drop away from us in the double moonlight.

It wasn't like flying over an American city. There was hardly any light, just the occasional soft glow of a torch or a cooking fire in some courtyard. The moons were so bright the fires were practically invisible anyway. The silver of the rooftops against the deep black of the alleys made it all look like some huge, cubist black-velvet painting.

Funny how a little mood lighting made me goofy for a festering snake pit that had treated us like shit and tried to kill us. Kind of like seeing your psycho ex in a bar and thinking, "What a hottie," before you realize who it is. Happened to me on Waar time and again. For every nightmare situation it threw at me, it would show me something so beautiful that I wished these medieval morons had invented the camera already.

Lhan's sigh brought me out of dreamland. "They must be wed. Apart they are a danger to themselves and others."

"No kidding."

We stared into space some more. I had a question, but I was nervous about asking it. I did anyway. "But wouldn't you rather have Sai stay single, and… available?"

Lhan froze. "I… I know not what you mean."

"Come on, Lhan. You gonna tell me 'beloved' has more than one meaning in your lingo?"

Lhan gripped the rail. He looked straight ahead. "Will you betray me?"

"Betray you? Why?"

"Things must be different in your land."

"Not as different as you'd think."

He shook his head. "'Tis an impossibility here. Even if Sai shared my… sickness, we would have to hide our love or be killed. And I'd not hide it. I'd shout it to the world." He chuckled. "No, they must wed, you see? Once he is safely removed within the walls of matrimony, honor will not allow me to make an adulterer of him. I will no longer be in such danger of indiscretion."

He grinned at me. "Know you how close I came to kissing him when you rescued him in the arena?"

I nodded. "But they hate each other. What if they don't get together? You gonna be able to resist temptation forever? Aren't there other guys you could…?"

He waved a hand. "Men, women, it makes no difference. I take my pleasure with both equally. That is not the problem. The problem is that there is only one Sai, and until he and Wen-Jhai are joined forever, I will be as a blossom, unable to turn my gaze from the sun."

My heart lurched in my chest. Lhan was a switch-hitter too? Suddenly I was all for Sai and Wen-Jhai tying the knot. That is if Lhan would even look at me after I betrayed Sai and killed Kedac. My guts went sour as I forced a smile. "Well, then pardner, you and me got some work to do."

***

We started in on Sai the next day, tag-teaming the poor guy so hard we made his pretty little head spin. Lhan sat him on his bunk and looked him in the eye. "She doesn't love him, Sai. In your heart you know this."

"Then why did she run to his arms?"

"To spite you, of course. To fan the flames of your jealousy. She wants you to come after her. To save her from her fate like a true Dhan of Ora should. Twice now you have failed to rescue her. Yet all will be made right again when you…"

"Rescue her? From what, pray tell? She enjoyed it! By the One, she was wallowing in it, like a filthy, depraved animal. Aldhanshai or no, no man can marry a woman who has… so spectacularly thrown away her virtue before marriage."

My turn. "Just like you wallowed with Captain Hot Pants."

"That… that was different!"

"How?"

"I but tried to win our release. I used the only weapon at my command to try and soften the captain's heart."

I pushed the image of that weapon out of my head. He was right. That *was* different. That was almost honorable. "Well, yeah, but… but maybe that's what Wen-Jhai was doing."

That caught him. He looked a little unsure of himself for a second, then he came back strong. "But she enjoyed it!"

I laughed. "You didn't enjoy it?"

"Certainly I enjoyed it. Am I not a man?"

Here we went again. "And Wen-Jhai is a woman. What's the problem?"

"'Tis different for men. We must slake our animal natures or… go mad. Women are innocent creatures who…"

"Captain Hot Pants was an innocent creature?"

"She's not a woman. Not a lady. Ladies do not…"

"Oh yeah? Ain't Wen-Jhai a lady?"

"She… that decadent corrupted her. He turned her into a lustful animal."

I nudged him, buddy buddy. "Isn't that how you want her to be with you?"

"I… but within the bounds of matrimony all is permissible."

I turned on him like a trial lawyer. "Ah-ha! So you're not mad at her for becoming a lustful animal, you're mad at her because she didn't wait for you to be the one who did it to her. So really you're just pissed at her for being unfaithful, and you ain't got a leg to stand on there, bucko."

Sai was practically in tears. "Mistress Jae-En, you make me dizzy. I know not what I think anymore."

Lhan's turn. He patted Sai's shoulder like the good cop. "All she means, Sai, is that we have all sinned. Are any of us above reproach? Forgiveness is the greatest virtue of an Oran gentleman. And the hardest won. Can you not do this noble thing?"

"Gentleman? Can you call me that after all my failures? Perhaps *I* am not worthy of *her*. Twice have I let courage fail when brought to the test. No Lhan, I am no gentleman. I am the lowliest insect. Kedac-Zir is a true man.

What a hero he looked, swinging to her rescue."

Man, Sai squirmed more than a centipede on a hot plate. I was ready to give up on the little piss-ant, but I thought about losing my chance at Kedac and dove back in. "Who's more of a hero? The guy who brings the whole navy with him, or the guy who tries the impossible, with just a sword and his pals to back him up?"

"The hero is he who succeeds."

Well, he had me there, but I kept at it. "Okay, he's a hero, but he's a hero with tap water for blood. Did he call her beloved? True heart? My love? Did he even call her by *name* for fuck's sake? No, he called her 'betrothed.' Did he kiss her? Nope. Did he hug her? Only to carry her up the ladder. I still say he doesn't love her."

Even now he wasn't buying it. "Mistress Jae-En!"

"Sorry, Sai, he comes half way around the world to rescue her and then doesn't even swap spit with her? It just don't add up."

Lhan raised an eyebrow at that, but Sai put his hands over his ears. "Please do not slander an Oran gentleman. He must love her. He would not marry her else."

"Yeah? Well, if that's a sample of his love I'd hate to see his blank stare."

"And yet she went with him."

"Because you didn't do the job."

His shoulders slumped, but I could hear the gears grinding. Lhan and I exchanged a glance. Would he or wouldn't he? Finally…

"Well, *if* we meet again, and *if* she will speak to me… then I will speak to her."

The only reason Lhan and I didn't high-five behind Sai's back was because Lhan didn't know how.

Now we just had to make it to the church on time.

***

We switched ships in a little patch of desert that had apparently been an Oran naval outpost back in the day. The only thing left was the plant that made the "levitating air" and the shipfield, which made it a perfect place for smugglers from the north and south to gas-up and trade.

Our layover lasted six endless days. Sai and I chewed our knuckles to the bone. If Kedac and Wen-Jhai got married while we were stuck in the ass-end of nowhere it was over for both of us.

But finally, after I'd given up for good a hundred times, a scruffy ship came over the horizon and touched down to drop cargo before heading back to Ora.

Lhan closed the deal with the smuggler while me and Sai hid in the local bar. Lhan wanted Sai out of the way so he wouldn't say something stupid and blow the deal. Me? Well, you could never tell what people were going to think of me. The guy was happy to take three passengers, particularly when Lhan didn't bat an eye at his asking price.

But later, when he had us standing on his deck he changed his tune. The problem was that he knew who we were.

He was a meek-looking old geezer with a mousy beard. It made me wonder how he had the cajones to be a smuggler. I decided to call him Captain Mopey.

He shot me a nervous glance, then bowed to Lhan. "My apologies, noble Dhanan. I knew not who you were until I spied... er, until this moment. Know you that there be a price on your heads in Ora?"

Lhan stared. "A price? For what?"

The captain looked embarrassed. "Forgive me. You are charged with aiding the Pirate Kai-La in the kidnapping and enslavement of the Aldhanshai Wen-Jhai. In addition to the Aldhanan's bounty, Kir-Dhanan Kedac-Zir personally offers a fortune to know your whereabouts. 'Tis not worth my life to carry you."

Lhan gave him the hairy eyeball. "How much of a fortune?"

The captain named a price. Lhan gave him half of Sai's jewels and let him see the other half. "Here is double that. And likely six times what your life is worth. Now what say you?"

Mopey practically licked Lhan's boots. "Noble Dhanans, we will slip into Ormolu like ghosts. None will know of your presence."

Lhan scraped him off with a couple "thank yous" and smiled at me. "A man is so obliging when he knows you have more left in your pocket."

I was more worried about the price on our heads. "What's this bounty shit? Who's been telling lies about us kidnapping Wen-Jhai? Who even knows we got attacked by pirates? Did anybody get away?"

"One person. Kedac's cousin."

"Who? Oh yeah, the She-Wolf, but why would she make shit up?"

Lhan looked lost in thought. "I am beginning to wonder, Mistress Jae-En, if there is not some substance to your suspicions about Kedac's wooing."

CHAPTER TWENTY-FOUR

BETRAYED!

We came down over Ormolu at sunset eight days later. It was amazing—a huge honey-gold city in the middle of an endless patchwork of fields, all red, purple and aqua. The Ormoluans—Ormolunians? Ormolites?—had built the city at the junction of a river and three of the Seven's super-highways. It was walled, but the walls couldn't hold it all anymore. Whole neighborhoods of chunky, colorful houses spread out beyond the massive fortifications like hexagonal Legos spilling out of a toy box.

There were crumbling shacks, tenements, ritzy townhouses. There were swarming open air markets where you couldn't see the cobblestones because the tents and stalls and shoppers were packed so tight. There were arenas like the one back in Doshaan, race tracks, parks, gardens. There were wide streets, twisty little alleyways, and the super-highways which, once inside the walls, became high-rent, tree-lined boulevards lined with swanky shops.

But the thing that made my jaw hit the deck was the tower at the meeting point of the three roads. It was huge! Bigger than that Eiffel Tower thing in Vegas, but shaped like a six-sided, art-deco rocket ship—lots of fins and flanges, all stepping back as it got higher, until it came to a point, which was topped by a steel needle half again as high as the whole thing. It had no windows and it was as shiny and white as a showroom mini-van. The super-highways formed a mile-wide traffic circle around it, and inside that circle was a large park dotted with the biggest, richest palaces in town. They looked like mice surrounding a great Dane. There was no *way* these bow-and-arrow bone-heads had built that tower.

I grabbed Lhan's arm. "What the hell is that?"

He smiled, proud. "That is the temple of Ormolu, High Lord of the Seven. 'Tis for His temple that our city is named, and what permits us to claim the honor of being the greatest city on Waar."

"But... but you guys never built that!"

"Of course not. 'Tis a relic of the Seven. Each of the seven holy cities is built around a temple, but this is the temple of the High Lord; the largest and finest."

"Man, these Seven guys had the toys, huh? So, you pray in there? It must hold a million."

Sai looked shocked. "None but the priesthood may enter, and then only those of the highest level. We pray at the chapels in the temple grounds. That is where Wen-Jhai's... wedding will take place, if it hasn't already."

I watched the thing as we sailed by it. Silhouetted against the sun it suddenly looked like a giant prick casting its shadow across the city. You might think, after all my whining about not getting any, that I'd see that as a good thing, but I didn't like it. It seemed to sum up the whole Oran daddy-knows-best culture in one big phallic "fuck-you" middle finger. It gave me a weird, big-brother-is-watching-you feeling. The feeling you'd get if you had a nuclear missile for a next door neighbor—or a police station.

***

We landed just as the sun went down, in the largest shipfield I'd seen yet, a mile square if it was an inch, with ships rising and sinking all over it. In the purple sunset it made me think of a giant lava lamp.

When we went to leave the ship, Captain Mopey came up, hemming and hawwing. "Er... beware, gentle sirs, there is danger for you in Ormolu. You have been most generous for my small kindnesses in the past. Let me take you to a safe place while I scout out the lay of the land for you. Whatever information you require, I can obtain it for you."

Lhan smiled. "For a price, of course."

Mopey bowed. "The Dhanan is most kind."

Sai frowned. "You have already been paid double for our passage. Can you want more?"

Lhan pulled Sai aside. "He offers a valuable service, Sai. Unjustly accused though we may be, we are still wanted criminals. Until we know where and when Wen-Jhai's ceremony takes place we must remain hidden. If having won this far we are stopped at the very gates of happiness…"

"This happiness you speak of is a presumption I can't share, but if you wish it…" Sai shrugged.

Lhan turned back to the captain. "Lead on, sir."

***

Mopey drove us out hidden in a cargo wagon, so at least I had company under the tarp this time. He put us up in a second-story rat-trap over a barrel-maker's place in a shabby slum near the shipfield. There was an air-men's tavern on the corner. We could hear them singing dirty songs.

Lhan gave Mopey another fraction of Sai's jewelry and told him to find out when and where the royal wedding was taking place, or if it already had, and where Wen-Jhai and Kedac were staying. Mopey went away promising news and food within the passing of a moon.

We settled in to wait, and wait. It was cramped up there, two rooms with nothing in 'em except one chair and a three-legged table that was supposed to have four. The windows on one side looked out on the street, but Mopey told us we'd better keep the shutters closed. I thought it was overkill, but Lhan agreed, so we didn't even have a view.

There was nothing to do. We should have slept, but we were all too busy thinking. Could we get to Wen-Jhai or Kedac the wedding? Was it already over? Would we have to crash it?

Sai was probably worrying about whether he could beat Kedac, and Lhan was probably worrying about whether Wen-Jhai would actually talk to Sai even if he did. What I was worrying about was whether I was going to go through with my plan at all. Now that Kedac was almost in reach I was feeling guiltier than ever. All that bullshit I'd told myself about Sai thanking me for killing Kedac went right out the window. Sai would hate me. Worse than that, Lhan would hate me. Sai might be a weenie, but Lhan and I had become friends. We got each other's jokes. We'd gone through hell together.

How was I going to look him in the eye after I'd jumped ahead of Sai and cut Kedac in half?

I tried to tell myself it didn't matter. I'd be catching the next train back to Earth as soon as I could anyway. But would I? Once I killed Kedac you can bet Sai would put the kibosh on hooking me up with his father-in-law the Aldhanan pretty damn quick. Shit, the guy probably wouldn't even *be* Sai's father-in-law if I killed Kedac. If Sai didn't do the job himself would Wen-Jhai even give him the time of day? The more I thought about it the more I realized how much killing Kedac was going to fuck everything up. Everybody would hate me and I'd be back at square one as far as getting off this boondock planet went. I went back and forth about it so much I wore a trench in my brain.

To kill the time, Sai and Lhan taught me a game they played when they were kids. It was a cross between horseshoes and marbles. You drew a circle on the floor, then stood across the room and tossed pebbles at it. Everybody started with the same number of pebbles, but once you threw all you had, you could only start the next round with the ones you'd managed to land inside the circle. The last guy with pebbles left won. Lhan won every time, the bastard.

When a moon-crossing passed and Mopey still hadn't come back we got too fidgety even to play games, so we just sat around doing nothing and looking up every time we thought we heard him coming up the stairs.

Finally, way into the third dark, we did hear steps on the stairs. Too many steps. There was somebody on the roof, too, and more on the back stairs.

Lhan drew his sword. "Friends, we are betrayed."

The doors and the windows exploded as guys rushed in from the stairs and swung down from the roof. We were up to our asses in assassins, all wearing dark cloaks over their harnesses and leather masks that covered their whole heads.

Our rep must have preceded us, 'cause they brought the whole gang. There were more than twenty guys swinging steel in that tiny room, with fucking Captain Mopey on the sidelines whining, "The jewelry! You promised me their jewelry!"

It was a little tough getting busy at first. They were so tight around us I couldn't swing my sword without backhanding Lhan or Sai. The assassins had the same problem. I decided to do everybody a favor and clear a little space. I picked up the three-legged table like a shield and bulldozed a handful of guys straight at the smashed-in window.

Damn place was such a shit-box that I didn't just push them out the window, I pushed the entire window out of the wall. The whole frame, plus a shower of bricks, plaster and men smashed into the street below. I almost went with them, but I caught the broken edge of the wall and hauled myself back in.

Some joker took advantage of my precarious position and poked me in the backside. I yelped like wolf in a trap and spun around, swinging my sword blind. I cut the poor bastard in half.

That stopped the show. The assassins stood there staring from me to the body, bug-eyed behind the peep-holes of their masks. Sai and Lhan took the opportunity to get in a few free swings.

That's all it took. The assassins ran like the devil was on their tails, that backstabber Mopey with them.

We stood in the ruins of the room, looking at half-a-dozen maimed and dismembered bodies as the sound of the assassins' footsteps pitter-pattered away down the street. The guy I'd cut in two was turning one corner into a red lake. I spit and swallowed, trying to force down the queasy, swimmy feeling I still got after killing people. I'd cut a guy in half!

I put on my tough chick act to cover my hands shaking. "So... so who are these ninjas? The local vigilante gang?"

"Let us discover." Lhan knelt by a guy who still had his head and cut off his mask.

Sai gasped. "Can it be? No!" He pulled aside the guy's cloak, and peeked at the insignia on his shoulder armor. He turned pale. "I know this man. 'Tis Dal-Var, one of my sister's household guard."

Lhan and Sai checked the rest of them. Half wore Sai's sister's insignia, half wore Vawa-Sar's.

Sai was all a-twitter. "But what means this treachery? Why does my sister try to kill me?"

"Only one way to find out." I jumped out the window.

The tallest building around was across the street. I sprang to a first-floor balcony and monkeyed up to the roof. I leaped up on a little shack and scanned in all directions. Our assassins couldn't be more than a few blocks away, but which way?

Finally, through a gap between two buildings, I saw some shadows flicker across a wall. I ran to the edge of the roof and leaped across the alley behind it, then started hopping from roof to roof like some super-villain from a Spider-Man comic. It cleared my head. I started feeling better. In fact, I felt great. What a blast. Without Lhan and Sai I could really travel. I was practically dancing, touching down with just a toe here, a heel there.

I spotted the assassins running down a side-street with Mopey wheezing behind them. I kicked off a brick chimney to change direction, then hopscotched after them. One of them seemed to be the boss, shouting at the others to hurry up. That's the one I wanted.

Unfortunately, just as I caught up they crossed a wide avenue and I ran out of roof tops.

I screeched to a stop. I was a little leery about dropping down to street level. According to Mopey I was on Ormolu's ten-most-wanted. Hell, even if people hadn't seen my mug shot, they'd hunt me down based on my freak factor alone. Had to be done though.

I jumped down two stories and landed in a three point stance in the middle of the street. People turned, gaping.

I stood and howled like a redneck at a Lynyrd Skynyrd concert. "Yippie-kai-yay, motherfuckers!"

It worked. People ran like cats from a vacuum cleaner. Mothers grabbed their children. Women hid behind their men. Men hid behind their women.

"Monster!"

"Demon!"

I charged across the avenue into an alley after the assassins. The last two looked back. They shouted and scattered. The others turned.

I jumped into a flying kick and planted both boots square on the bossman's chest. He skidded ten feet in the alley muck. I rolled and came up standing.

The assassins faced me, eyes wide, whiteknuckling their swords, on the knife edge between fight or flight. The boss man was behind me. I stepped back to haul him up. Bad idea. The assassins read that as a retreat and charged.

The alley was too narrow for me to get a good swing in, and I'd had my fill of cutting guys in half for one night. I sheathed my sword, heaved the bossman over my shoulder, then jumped up and grabbed a drain pipe. Swords chipped sparks off the brick wall all around my ankles. I climbed hand-over-hand to the rooftop. Good thing none of those fuckers had bows.

***

Back at the hovel Lhan tore the guy's mask off. Sai gasped again. It was a big night for gasping. "Shao-Lar?" He turned to us. "'Tis my sister's personal bodyguard." Then back to Shao-Lar. "What is the meaning of this, villain?"

"I'll never talk."

I reached under his loincloth and squeezed. "You'll never talk in that octave again."

He squeaked, but kept his mouth shut. Brave man.

Lhan leaned in. "We know much of it already. We know Vawa-Sar has dealings with Kedac-Zir that hinge on his marriage to Wen-Jhai."

Sai opened his mouth to disagree. Lhan elbowed him. "Come, Shao-Lar. Or shall Mistress Jae-En make a boy of you again?"

Shao-Lar groaned and turned to Sai. "It... It was your sister's plan. Hers and Vawa-Sar's."

"My sister? You lie, sir. Shayah is a..."

Lhan interrupted. "A conniving harridan, and always has been, ever since she told on us to your father for plucking the tail feathers of his favorite krae. Say on, Shao-Lar."

He nodded and turned to Sai. "Vawa-Sar covets your father's land, since his is rocky and barren. He knew that unless you were dead Shayah would not inherit. Together they conspired to cause your death, so that when they married, Vawa-Sar would inherit your father's lands as well as his own."

Lhan spit. "Vile fratricide. I always did detest her."

Sai waved at him to clam up. "And so they sent you here to kill me? They dared?"

"No Dhanan, this was but a desperate measure when it was discovered that you had escaped Kedac-Zir's blade."

Sai paled. "Kedac-Zir? He truly is involved in all of this?"

Shao-Lar blinked. "You said you knew of that."

I laughed. "We guessed. Now spill it."

He hesitated. I gave his nuts another honk. He spoke right up. "Kedac-Zir was key to it all." He looked at Sai. "Knowing your... lack of martial prowess, and seeking a way to kill you that would bring no investigation or retribution, they concieved a plan where someone would bride-nap Wen-Jhai under protection of the Sanfallah and kill you in the process. But for the plan to succeed it must be someone so rich and well-connected that no political motive might be construed. They contacted Kedac-Zir and he agreed, in exchange for some favors, the nature of which they have kept secret even from me."

I gave Sai an I-told-you-so look. "See?"

"No! I refuse to believe it. No Oran gentleman…"

Lhan laughed. "Even now you defend him?"

"Perhaps he agreed to their plan, but only so that he might follow his heart."

"Once again, Sai, your charitable nature does you credit, but with the evidence of Mai-Mar's lies, implicating us in the kidnapping of Wen-Jhai, I begin to suspect…"

Sai stood, straighter than I'd seen him in days. "You are right, Lhan. If there is even a suspicion of doubt we must confront him. I would have the testament of his love from his own lips, that I might judge its fervor for myself." He looked down at Shao-Lar. "Where stays Kedac-Zir?"

"He is billeted at the Naval barracks."

"He keeps Wen-Jhai at a barracks?" Sai was outraged.

"No, she stays with Kedac-Zir's cousin, at his townhouse."

"See?"

Sai glared at me. "We shall see indeed. When is the ceremony?"

"Tomorrow, at dawn."

Sai gasped again. I told you, lots of gasping. "Then we must leave at once. The forth crossing already begins."

Lhan motioned out the window. "But we are wanted criminals. These cursed relatives of yours have made sure of that. We shall be stopped before we get half way."

I looked around at the masked corpses. "Uh, guys. I hate to even suggest it, but…"

***

And so, for the umpteenth time on this planet, I had to play dress-up.

When we were ready Sai made to kill Shao-Lar, but Lhan reminded him that a true gentleman was merciful, so we mercifully tied Shao-Lar up and mercifully dumped him in the garbage heap behind the building with the other vermin.

Even though I'd suggested it, I wondered how inconspicuous we'd be wearing masks in the street. Lhan told me not to worry. Vendetta and assassination were a penny a pound around here. People were used to seeing guys running around dressed up like masked wrestlers.

We talked over ways to get into the navy stockade as we hurried across the city, but everything came up short. Lhan had served at this camp and knew how they ran things, which was tight as a drum. I wasn't going to be jumping the wall here. Navy issue crossbows could stop a charging vurlak. I'd be a pincushion when I landed.

We couldn't just disguise ourselves as airmen either. The gate guards had lists of who went in and out. Besides, an airman's harness wasn't going to cover my, uh, more recognizable features.

Our ideas got wilder and wilder; hide in a wagon full of supplies, ride in on the underside of an airship, start a fire, start a riot.

I groaned. "Why don't we just get ourselves arrested. At least then we'll be inside the damn place."

Lhan stopped dead and turned to me with that crazy Clark Gable grin of his. "Mistress Jae-En, truly you are divinely inspired. You have found the way!"

"Huh? Whaddaya mean?"

"I mean we give ourselves up."

"Lhan, I was kidding! It was a joke!"

Sai stared. "Truly, Lhan, are you gone mad? They will kill us."

"Not on sight. We are not such barbarians here in Ora that the authorities would deny us the formality of a trial, even if only to parade us before our peers before they beheaded us. Convening such a trial would take several days. In the meantime they would lock us in the barracks brig."

Sai rolled his eyes. "Ah, cast in a dungeon. Of course. The advantages are obvious."

I wasn't exactly catching on either. "Come on, Lhan. Where the hell does that get us?"

Lhan leaned in, excited. "I shall explain. While stationed here, I, on more than one occasion, became intimately acquainted with that brig. 'Tis not a dungeon. 'Tis but a wooden lock-up, the primary function of which is the punishment of junior officers who have been arrested for public drunkenness. 'Tis a homey, accommodating jail, which while more than strong enough to contain young fools who can't hold their tisol, should be no match for a phenomenon such as Mistress Jae-En. And once free inside the camp, it will be nothing to reach Kedac-Zir's quarters."

Well, I had serious doubts it would be as cake-and-pie as all that, but it was the only plan that even got us to square one. "You're the boss, Lhan. And I want you to know I wouldn't go to jail for just anybody."

Sai bit his lip. "It seems foolhardy to me."

Lhan nodded. "Indeed. But have you a safer, quicker plan?"

"Er, well…" Sai shrugged. "Lead on, Lhan. Your follies seem to succeed more often than do mine."

CHAPTER TWENTY-FIVE

TREASON!

At the gate, Sai looked down his nose at the watch commander and did his prince-of-the-blood act. "Be so kind as to inform Kir-Dhanan Kedac-Zir that Dhan Sai-Far of Sensa wishes to meet him on a matter of honor."

Guards were circling around behind us. That was fine. All part of the plan. I hoped.

The watch commander stared, dumbfounded. "My pardon, sir. Your name again?"

"Lout, I am Sai-Far, son of Shen-Far, Dhanan of Sensa and these are my companions, Lhan-Lar of Herva and Mistress Jae-En of... elsewhere."

The guy was torn. You could see it. He was used to kissing ass to guys like Sai, but he was also looking at three walking wanted posters. "Your pardon Dhanans and—" He gave me the once over again, just to make sure, "And Lady, but I must place you under arrest."

Sai stuck his nose in the air as the guards moved in. "You insult me, sir, but as you have an advantage of numbers if not quality, I will go quietly."

He surrendered his sword belt. Me and Lhan did too. This was the part of the plan I liked the least. What if they put our weapons in another building?

What if they didn't just lock us up, but chained us too? I was strong, but breaking out of chains might be pushing it.

They marched us through the camp, a huge hexagonal layout of big, twelve-man hexagonal tents. One wedge-shaped sixth of the camp was filled with permanent buildings; a big stone joint with skelshas coming and going from its roof that Lhan said was Naval HQ and Kedac's private quarters, a cookhouse, a stable, some other administration buildings, and the brig, which was a one-story wooden hexagon with tiny barred windows and guards outside the door.

It was pretty much like Lhan said, a front room with a desk, a burly jailer, and a door to the cells behind. It reminded me of the hoosegow in a TV western, except there were torches on the walls, and a little hibachi in the corner where the jailer was barbecuing lizard kebabs—I don't remember Marshall Dillon ever barbecuing lizards. The jailer was a barrel-chested pug-ugly with a five o'clock shadow all over his skinhead dome. He gave us the once-over and curled his lip at me with the, you-ain't-so-tough sneer I've gotten from lock-up bulls all my life. I just seem to bring it out in 'em. I don't know why.

He threw our weapons and armor into a chest that was bolted to the floor and locked them up, then took us to the cells.

We had a surprise waiting for us back there. Lhan's "sleepy little lock-up" was packed to the rafters. I counted eight thick wooden doors, four on each side. Each door had a narrow, barred window, and six of the eight windows were crammed with faces, all pushing and shoving for a look.

I recognized some of the faces. There was a big burly guy with a full beard looking out of one, and a swarthy chick with a square jaw and long thick eyelashes. It was Captain Kai-La and her crew! Guess they hadn't ducked Kedac after all.

I almost said something to Kai-La as we passed, but Lhan nudged me. Smart boy. No need to let our jailor know we were all old pals.

The pirates didn't speak either. They just stared. I locked eyes with Kai-La for a second. Her face was as blank as an unplugged TV.

Ugly put Sai and Lhan in one cell and me in another. Damn prudes, keeping boys and girls separate. Now I had to break out of two cells.

The room was built from the same heavy wood as the door, with one small barred window on the outside wall which looked just big enough to squeak through. I was pretty sure I could rip out the door or the window no problem. The hard part was going to be noise. If I kicked open the door, pug-ugly would come running, which wasn't a bad thing. It would save us going after him. But he'd probably send those guards outside the front door for back-up, and that was suicide.

As I was eyeballing the door up close, Kai-La's voice echoed down the hall. "It grieves me to see you captured, friends. For I believe we were the cause of it."

Sai snarled back. "Speak not to me, slaver."

Lhan was more polite. "Mean you some other cause than selling us in Doshaan?"

"Aye. When we were captured, they tortured us to know your whereabouts. Not all of us were strong."

I heard a thump from Sai's direction, like he'd thrown himself against his door. "'Twas you who put Wen-Jhai in Kedac's hands? 'Twas you who…"

Lhan cut him off. "Sai, you must stay quiet." His voice rose slightly. "Mistress Jae-En, what keeps you?"

I sighed and looked up from the door. It was hopeless. The lock was buried deep behind hard wood and metal straps. "I can't figure how to blow this joint without waking up Ugly. I can break down the door, but I ain't gonna be able to get to him before he screams for help."

"Hmmm, think you that you can open the door with one blow?"

"I'll give it a shot, but it's gonna make a hell of a racket."

"Worry not. Just be ready to act."

"When?"

"You will know."

I sure as hell hoped so.

I jumped as Lhan started shouting. "You cowardly cuckold! 'Tis you who has gotten us into this fix. If you had even enough spine to stand upright we'd be celebrating your wedding now, instead of rotting in durance vile."

Sai screamed back. "Blame me, viper that I was fool enough to once call friend? Who was it that lifted not a finger when I went to challenge my rival singlehandedly in his mountain fortress?"

"There was no challenge, you lying…"

They started to wrestle around, shouting and banging into the walls. The door to the front slammed open and Ugly rushed past my cell. "Belay that noise, you filthy ructuks, or I'll flay you alive!"

That was my cue. I heel-kicked the lock as hard as I could. The door frame splintered, but didn't break.

Ugly's face appeared in the peep hole. "What's this? You try to trick Las-Har?"

How could I resist? I kicked the lock again. The door caught Ugly right between the eyes. He slammed against the far wall and sagged to the floor. I stepped out. He was out like a light. I took his keys and unlocked Sai and Lhan's cell.

Lhan smiled at me. "Well done, mistress. Often have I wished to do that very thing."

We bound and gagged Las-Har, then tiptoed down the hall.

Kai-La spoke through her window. "You appear to have a plan, friends."

Sai glared at her. "And it does not include you."

We snuck into the front room, listening for the guards out front. All quiet. Another key opened the weapon lock-up. I felt a hundred percent better once I strapped my armor and sword back on.

Lhan grinned. "Now we take our leave."

We went back to my cell and looked at the window. The bars were set into a steel frame that was built into the wooden casement. If I just ripped it out of the wall somebody was going to come running. We had to pull it apart piece by piece.

I tried, but my fingers weren't strong enough. Lhan drew his sword. "Perhaps this?"

I drew mine and slid the tip into a join. "Even better." It made a perfect pry bar.

As we got to work, Kai-La's voice followed us again. "Sai-Far, bedmate, can you be so cruel? Have you no fond memories of our time together?"

Sai sneered. "They are obscured by the memories of you leaving us to die."

"But we did not. In fact you may recall that we went to great lengths to not kill you."

"For your own profit."

"You do not feel that being allowed to live has been profitable?" She sounded as sincere as a casket salesman.

Sai wasn't buying it. "As a slave? Your charity is most meager, pirate."

Kai-La didn't give up. "And meager charity is all we ask of you. Unlock but one of these doors and you may leave us to our fate. We ask not to be saved. We ask nothing that we did not do for you. Merely give us opportunity to save ourselves."

Sai snarled. "You waste your breath, skelsha."

I pried the last piece of frame away and lifted the bars out. As I set 'em gently on the floor, Kai-La spoke again. "And you, the she-Dhan, can you leave a sister of the sword to the noose of Oran justice?"

I blushed, but kept my mouth shut. I didn't know what I wanted. Kai-La had fucked us something fierce when they'd sold us down the river in Doshaan, but that didn't stop me from liking her for some reason. Next to Lhan she was the sharpest cookie I'd met here. On top of that I saw, the way Sai would never be able to, how Wen-Jhai had forced her hand.

Kai-La kept talking. "We two both know how close you came to joining us. Can you now turn your back on us?"

Sai and Lhan shot me a surprised look. I shrugged, sheepish. Sai glared. "Heed her not, mistress. We must go."

I gave him a flat look—he was such a weenie sometimes—then shrugged. "Right. You first. Let us know when it's clear."

I hoisted him up and he slipped through the window like a weasel. He was so thin he had room to spare. "All clear, mistress."

My turn. I had to be second because I was the most vulnerable going through. I needed Sai outside and Lhan inside in case someone came by and caught me with my ass hanging out like a horse stuck halfway over a fence.

Lhan offered me a hand up. I hesitated. I looked at the ring of keys on the floor, then at Lhan. "Any objections?"

He shrugged. "On a purely pragmatic level, their escape will draw attention from our own."

"Good point. " I grinned and snatched up the keys, then dodged back into the hallway.

I unlocked Kai-La's door. She smirked as I opened it. "As always, one must look to a heart other than that of a Noble Oran Dhan to find Nobility."

I tossed her the keys. "Yeah, whatever. Just give us a head-start before you make your run."

Kai-La bowed and crossed her wrists, but she didn't stop smirking. I ran back into my cell. Lhan laced his hands together and I heaved myself up to the window.

Now that I was trying to get through it, it seemed tinier than ever. Getting my shoulders and boobs through was tough. My hips were tougher. Luckily I'd slimmed down and toned up since I'd landed on Waar. If I'd tried this trick my first week here I'd have needed a crowbar and axle grease. As it was I had scrapes down both hips that rubbed against my sword belt every time

I moved.

Sai looked around, nervous, as he helped me out. "What delayed you, mistress?"

"My conscience got caught on something."

He started to ask me what I meant, but just then two airmen came around a corner. We ducked into the shadows. They didn't see us. Lhan slid out as soon as they were gone. I gotta hand it to the pirates. They didn't make a peep once.

We reconnoitered. Kedac's HQ was at the end of a row of buildings just behind us. There weren't many people around this time of night, so it was pretty easy going. We kept to the shadows and ran low, commando style.

HQ was another story. There were guards at the front doors and two pairs of guards patroling the perimeter at regular intervals.

We circled the place at a distance, looking for the weak point. There was a big first-floor window open around back, but it was about eight feet up and there wasn't enough time between patrols for all of us to run over and for me to lift them in then climb up myself. We couldn't make it all at once, but one at a time...

I went first, sprinting over the open ground and springing through the window in a head-first dive. I skidded across a polished marble floor and banged my head into a table leg, then jumped up, dancing around and rubbing my head and biting my fingers so I didn't scream. When the pain wore off a little, I unbuckled my sword belt and gave the guys the high sign.

They waited until one of the patrols had just disappeared around the corner, then Sai ran full-tilt for the window. I lowered the buckle end of my sword belt to him. He grabbed it and I hauled him up, right before the second patrol came around the other corner.

We did it all over again with Lhan and we were in. The room looked like an officers' mess, with a long table down the center loaded up with fancy plates and goblets. We listened at the door, then peeked out. Nobody. Lhan tip-toed down the hall, found the stairs and gave us the all-clear.

On the second floor we checked around again. It was almost deserted—only two guards posted outside a door. Guess where we needed to go.

Lhan pulled back around the corner. "That will be Kedac's quarters." He looked at Sai. "I believe the time for subtlety is past. Once you confront Kedac-Zir and confirm to your satisfaction that he is indeed complicit in your sister's foul plan..."

Sai couldn't let that pass. "He may yet prove himself a man of honor."

Lhan smiled. "Then we will have nothing to fear, for being a man of honor, Kedac-Zir will see how cruelly you and Wen-Jhai have been tricked. He will bow gracefully out of the marriage and restore to you your freedom. If, however, he fails to live up to your hopes for him, then it becomes an affair of honor and none will dare interfere until you win. After that we give ourselves up and, armed with the knowledge of Vawa-Sar's treachery, throw ourselves on the mercy of the Aldhanan's justice."

Sounded a mite too happy-ever-after to me. "I hope the Aldhanan's justice is less bent than Arkansas justice."

Sai bit his lip. "This all supposes that I win. If I fail?"

"Then we will all die gloriously."

I groaned. "I knew there was a hitch somewhere."

Lhan patted me on the shoulder and strolled around the corner like he owned the place. What the hell was I doing running around with these lunatics? One was too chicken for his own good, the other was too brave for mine. Sai and I exchanged a glance and followed reluctantly.

Lhan waved a cheery salute to the guards. "Ahoy, lads. How passes the night?"

They weren't buying it. "State your business, sir."

Lhan bowed toward Sai. "Dhan Sai-Far of Sensa desires audience with the Kir-Dhanan."

They flicked a glance at me and tightened their grips on their swords. "How came you here?"

"The lads below passed us up. Kedac-Zir sent for us."

They started to draw. "The Kir-Dhanan is not here. Put up your arms!"

Lhan and Sai drew too. Not good. Steel on steel would bring marines out of the woodwork like cockroaches. I slung my sheathed sword off my back and reached it over Sai's shoulder as he parried his guard's attack. I rang the guy's bell with the flat, then back-handed the other one. They sagged into Lhan and Sai's arms. Lhan motioned with his chin. "The door!"

It was locked, but the first guard had the key. I unlocked it and we dragged them in, then tied and gagged them. Kedac's apartments were his castle all over again, lots of weapons and armor on the paneled walls, statues out of a Nazi whorehouse, a heavy desk and chairs, an eating area with chaise lounges and a simple bedroom through an arched door. But like the guard said, no Kedac. None of us had counted on that.

"What now? Somebody's gonna miss those guards before long. We gotta find where Kedac is and skat. Like pronto."

Too late. There were voices in the hall. "Ur? Sil? You louts, what was that banging..."

"Where have they gone?"

Lhan leaped to the door and turned the bolt. Just in time. Somebody rattled the handle, then...

"Something's amiss. Rouse the guard. I'll wait here."

"Yes, sir."

"And find a key!"

Now we were up the creek. Lhan and Sai ran to check the windows. I started searching for a closet to stash the guards in. For all the guys in the hall knew, Ur and Sil could have snuck off to get drunk. The longer it took everybody to realize that they'd been jumped, the longer it would take for them to start looking for us.

It was hopeless. Fucking backward Waarians hadn't invented the closet yet. All Kedac's crap was in wardrobes and trunks—too small to hide a couple of big marines in. I kept looking. Maybe there was a latrine. Some of the classier joints I'd been in had indoor plumbing. I pulled aside curtains and looked behind hangings.

The fifth tapestry I tugged on wouldn't pull. It seemed to be attached at the bottom. I looked down. The lower left corner was stuck in the wall. Not tacked to it, but *in* it. I looked closer. There was a hairline vertical crack in the paneling . A secret door.

I just barely remembered to whisper. "Guys!"

Sai and Lhan came and had a look. Lhan immediately started pressing all the bits of decoration on the paneling near the door, looking for the catch. "A fortuitous discovery, mistress. There were guards below the window. Escape that way is nigh impossible. If this is a way out, we may yet survive the night."

But nothing he pressed did anything. Sai and I joined in, poking every knob and bump in reach. No help.

A herd of footsteps came from the hall.

"No-one's seen them, sir. But nothing untoward either."

"Well, if 'tis nothing then they'll be court-martialed. Let's have that key."

We went nuts. We pressed everything within five feet of the crack, hands flapping around like pigeons on crack. Then I looked up. There was a decorative molding along the top of the wall, all bumps and curlicues, all dusty. All except one bump. I pushed it. It sank in like a pinball flipper. There was a click. A section of the wall swung in an inch or so.

The key was turning in the hallway door. The guy outside was saying, "Swords out, men. Expect the worst."

Lhan shoved the panel open. I grabbed the marines by their belts and walked them in like matching suitcases. Sai and Lhan crowded in and closed the door with a quiet click, just as we heard the door from the hall slam in.

"Ur-Nar? Sil-Tar? Right then, search the room."

We put blades to the necks of the guards, in case they got stupid, and held our breath. What if the searchers knew about the secret door?

They didn't. Either that or the boss guy didn't want the grunts to know about it. Anyway nobody tried it, and after about five minutes they all trooped out again. The last thing we heard was, "You two stand guard until we find them. The rest of you search in pairs."

Silence. We let out a big sigh of relief. Lhan smiled. "One doom avoided. Now let us discover if this place is our passage to salvation."

We all turned. The space was pitch black. Lhan stumbled around until he found a lamp and lit it. We looked around. It was a little disappointing. Just another room just like the one we'd left, but a lot plainer, and with no windows; a big table, some chairs, and papers all over the place.

Sai sighed. "Maybe there is another door. Or a trap in the floor."

We hunted around. There was a map laid across the table, held down with cups and plates, and scattered with what looked like tin soldiers. I didn't give it a second glance, but Lhan saw it and did a double-take. "By the Seven and The One!"

Sai turned. "What is it?" Then he pulled the same face Lhan had.

I hate being the last to know. "What? What's the big deal?"

Lhan turned to me, a terrible look in his eyes. "This... is a map of Ormolu."

I didn't get it. It looked like Kedac was playing out a battle around Ormolu. But so what? "So maybe he's planning defense strategies or something."

"The attacking pieces wear his colors."

"Maybe he ran out of bad guy pieces."

"Perhaps." He and Sai started digging into the piles of paper. I joined in. I hadn't had many chances to test it, but I could read their gibberish too, though nothing complicated.

I didn't need any extra vocabulary for what I found. It was plain as day. The first thing I grabbed was a letter from some Dhanan which said, "You have my support and a thousand men. Too long have we suffered under the yoke of this money-mad tax farmer." Another scrap read, "Once the marriage takes place there will be no stopping us. With the Aldhanshai's blood joined to yours, your legitimacy will be beyond question."

Lhan gave a gasp. "Sai, listen. 'The barracks and storage facilities will be ready in six cycles, and I look forward to our new titles and lands under your glorious reign. Long live the new Aldhanan.' 'Tis signed Vawa-Sar. That vile sister of yours isn't just your betrayer, but the betrayer of the entire kingdom."

But Sai was staring at the parchment in his hands like he could have burned holes in it. Lhan stepped toward him. "What troubles you, Sai?"

Sai handed him the parchment, silent and cold. Lhan read it aloud. "Beloved, Weh-Jhai yet lives. Through the pirate that attacked us I have traced her south to Doshaan. She is the slave of the Doshaani Dhanan Jur-Shim. The plan proceeds at last. I know how it irks you to pay suit to that brainless child, but once you wed her and take the throne as your destiny dictates, we will find a quiet little palace in the country for her and she will pass out of your mind entirely. How glorious will it be, you the ruler of all Ora, and I, your ruler of the bedchamber. Patience, beloved. Your devoted cousin, Mai-Mar."

Sai looked like a statue of himself, as cold and hard as marble. I'd never seen him like this. He was almost intimidating. "He does not love Wen-Jhai. He must die."

***

When we stepped back into Kedac's study the windows were glowing a little. Sai went from fury to despair in one sharp drop. "Dawn! We're too late! The marriage will start at full light. How can we cross twenty ilns of city in an instant when we have yet to even escape the camp?"

Lhan grinned. "We must look to those above for the answer."

Sai was indignant. "You jest, Lhan? Not even the Seven can help us now!"

"Not the Seven, the skelshas. Come."

There was no time to be clever. We just clobbered everybody we met. The guards outside the door were easy. Lhan jerked the door open, I grabbed 'em before they could turn, dragged them in and banged their heads together. We tied 'em up with the others.

There was another pair at the stairs to the roof. I ran at them ten feet a stride. They looked up at me like deer in the headlights. I clotheslined 'em out of their boots. We used their loincloths for gags and their swordbelts to hog-tie 'em.

Going up the stairs was scarier. We didn't know who was up there, or how many. It turned out not a lot, but they were enough. They almost wrecked the whole thing.

We came up into a barn that stank like the world's biggest bird cage. There was a wide aisle down the middle with a big open door at one end and caged-in roosts down either side. Behind the cage bars the huge dark shapes of skelshas rustled and murmured on stepped-back rows of roosting poles. They looked like the Spanish Inquisition in leather robes. I didn't much care for the long jaws full of alligator teeth. Who ever heard of birds with teeth?

We were just peeking out the barn door, checking for guards on the roof, when we heard a voice behind us. "Who is it now? Who needs to fly at this Seven-cursed hour?"

We spun around. A bent old guy was stepping out of a room at the back, sleepily strapping on his harness. Lhan walked toward him, talking fast. "We do, old fellow. Three of your swiftest skelshas."

The guy squinted in the dark. "Captain Nar? Is that you? I'll need a written… You're not Captain Nar."

But Lhan had already reached him. He slammed the old timer to the ground, knocking the wind out of him. "Sorry, friend. Stay still and you're in no peril." He gagged and hog-tied the old man.

I checked the roof. The three lookouts I could see hadn't heard us.

Lhan rolled the old guy to one side. "Quickly. The roost doors."

We helped him open the doors. The skelshas got restless, but Lhan moved through them whispering and stroking and they calmed down again. He untied three of them and led them out one at a time as Sai took saddles and bridles from a rack and started saddling them.

I'll be honest. The idea of riding one of these things gave me the willies. I'm not afraid of heights, and I've ridden damn near everything from a rodeo bull to a blown-fuel Buell drag bike, but I've also wrecked just about all of them once or twice climbing that old learning curve. That wasn't exactly an option here—once we got airborne the pavement was a long way down. I listened real careful as Sai gave me the crash course, so to speak.

We were so focused we didn't hear the little bastard behind us until it was too late. He was just a kid, a stable boy. He must have been sleeping in the same room with the old guy. We forgot to check.

I caught him out of the corner of my eye, sneaking for the stairs. "Hey! You!"

I jumped up and ran at him, but he went like a rabbit, and started screaming like a banshee. "Murderers! Spies! Assassins! Help! Help! Help!"

Lhan called me back. "It is too late! We must fly, now!"

He was right. There were shouts coming up from below, and running footsteps out on the roof. Lhan and Sai cinched their saddle straps tight and mounted up. I tried to do it like they did, but my skelsha rolled his eyes and flapped aside like a skittish window shade. He could tell how freaked out I was and that freaked him out, which was freaking me out. It was freak-out feedback.

Lhan's skelsha started to pump its wings and run. Ours began to follow. I hopped along beside mine, one foot in the stirrup, one foot skipping off the ground. "Hold still, peckerhead!"

The big bastard was catching air now. "Fuck! Stop!" I hauled myself up into the saddle by brute force.

The guards from the roof ran in, aiming crossbows, but Lhan dug his heels into his skelsha's neck and it shot its wings wide, right in their faces. They fell back, firing blind and missing by a mile. We sailed right over their heads as marines poured out of the barn behind us, shouting and shooting.

My stomach lurched when we went over the edge of the roof and the ground dropped away. Christ, I wasn't ready for this. Wobbling around in the sky without a good idea how to work the controls wasn't my idea of a good time, particularly with crossbows blasting away at me. Lhan and Sai missed getting hit because of speed and skill. I dodged 'em 'cause I was all over the damn sky. That skelsha didn't like me and I didn't like him. He was turning loop-de-loops, the fucker. I almost lost my lunch when we whipped around in a big climbing circle and headed east. The marines kept shooting, but we were too high. Their bolts arced under us like sand-fleas hoping to catch a seagull.

CHAPTER TWENTY-SIX

COUP D'ÉTAT!

The sun was rising behind the temple of Ormolu. We rode along its long shadow like we were flying over a black carpet until we reached the ginormous traffic circle that surrounded it, then Lhan started angling us down. Below, the morning light was creeping across the gardens of the big park area within the circle and lighting up the white marble palaces that filled it like they were glowing from the inside.

My skelsha and I had finally ironed out our differences. Well, actually I'd just given up trying to steer and it did what it wanted. Good thing it seemed to have that duck instinct and flew in formation behind its pals.

We were dropping toward a high, gold-roofed temple with a humongous Oran warship hanging over it. I recognized the ship. It was Kedac's, and for a second I panicked. I thought maybe he somehow knew we were coming and had brought out the big guns. Then I noticed that the ship was covered with colorful streamers. I relaxed. It was the Oran version of the wedding limo. Kedac and Wen-Jhai were going to fly off to their honeymoon on a warship. Symbolic, huh?

We came in low, aiming for a wide courtyard attached to the temple, when suddenly a bolt of blue light, bright as the sun and thin and straight as a pencil, shot over our heads. Our skelshas panicked, squawking and flapping. I did too. Shit, wouldn't you? Outside of a *Star Wars* movie I'd never seen anything like that in my life.

Lhan forced his skelsha into a dive. Sai followed suit. I banged on my bird's skull. "Down, you idiot! Holy shit! What the fuck was that?"

Lhan shouted over to me. "Holy indeed. A holy relic. A wand of blue fire. With it the Aldhanan's guard protects him from all attackers, even those in the air."

"But that was... that was..."

"Holy."

"If you say so."

We touched down in front of the temple's marble steps. A squad of guys in fancy red enameled armor, finned helmets and flapping white capes raced out to us.

"Now what?" I'd had enough confrontation lately.

They looked like extras from *Ben Hur*, except the three guys in front were carrying ordnance out of another movie altogether: long white tubes with pulsing lights down the side. They looked like something Casio might have made in the eighties. My head hurt looking at 'em. It made the whole scene seem wrong, like seeing King Arthur on a cell-phone or Beethoven slinging a Fender Strat.

Lhan and Sai jumped down from their skelshas and raised their hands like terrorists at the end of a stand off. I did the same. I don't know about you, but wands of blue fire scare the piss out of me.

Sai started shouting, "Let us through. I am the groom. I am here to claim my bride."

The captain stopped in front of him as his men surrounded us. He had one of the white plastic tubes and a pom-pom on his tin hat to let you know he was in charge. It bobbed in the wind. "Kir-Dhanan Kedac-Zir is bridegroom here. Who threatens the Aldhanan at his daughter's wedding?"

Sai made a formal bow, crossing his wrists. "No one threatens the Aldhanan, noble captain. I merely make haste to my wedding. I am Dhan Sai-Far of Sensa, lawful betrothed of Princess Wen-Jhai. Kir-Dhanan Kedac-Zir kidnapped her. I demand the right to fight for her hand."

The captain sparked at the name. "Sai-Far of Sensa, I have orders for your arrest."

Lhan stepped up. "And who gave those orders?"

"Kir-Dhanan Kedac-Zir."

Lhan sneered. "A coward's way to protect his bride."

The captain frowned. Sai saw where Lhan was going and picked it up, pouring it on. "Can this be? Does an Oran gentleman stand in the way of true love? When has the Sanfallah ever been decided by orders of arrest?"

That seemed to make up the captain's mind. He turned to his men. "Search them and take their weapons." Sai started to protest, but the captain stopped him. "Make your challenge and you will have your sword."

They frisked us and took anything even remotely like a weapon. I let 'em. I was in shock. This was the loopiest thing that had happened yet in this whole damn adventure. Forget coming to another planet. Forget getting shot at by death rays or fighting for my life in an arena straight out of a gladiator movie. A cop who'd bend the law for true love? If we were back in LA we'd all be on the ground getting Rodney-Kinged for sassing back. For the first time since I got here I wondered if it was all a dream.

They led us through the hexagonal temple, a big echoey place with high, arched ceilings, all gold and white, and out a side door into the courtyard. There was a big crowd out there. They sparkled like the headdress on a Vegas showgirl—all wild colors and big chunks of silver and gold and jewels hanging off fancy harnesses. The gaudiest get-ups were in the front row: the royal family. On a stage a priest was doing some holy calisthenics with the crowd following along. It looked like fancy dress aerobics.

The altar behind the priest was a miniature version of the Temple of Ormolu's rocket-tower. The real one loomed up directly behind the back wall like the Jolly Green Giant in a white suit. Kedac, the fucker, was over at stage left, looking smug. It made my hands itch just looking at him. Opposite him, Wen-Jhai stood with her jaw stuck out like a ship's prow, defiant and brave, but I could see her eyes were wet. Right next to the altar dangled a rope ladder, hanging from Kedac's ship. An airman with a bugle stood at attention beside it.

The priest looked like he was winding up for the big finish when we pushed in, boots stomping and harnesses jingling. Sai jumped up on a bench at the back. "Stop this farce!"

Everybody turned. The priest dropped his arms. Kedac glared around, looking for the interruption. Wen-Jhai stared. Near the front, that creepy she-wolf Mai-Mar looked back, worried. She was sitting with Vawa-Sar and a woman who looked like Sai, only not so pretty—Shayah, his backstabbing sister.

Silence. Sai had everybody's attention.

Now was my chance. Nobody was looking at me. It was an easy two hops to the stage. I could break Kedac's neck and be over the back wall before anybody knew what was going on.

At least I could have if it wasn't for Sai. I looked up at him and couldn't do it. Not without giving him his chance. But would he actually take it? He was as pale a lavender toilet paper. He wasn't saying anything.

Kedac sneered like he thought Sai was blowing it. Sai saw the sneer. His back stiffened. Finally!

"Kir-Dhanan Kedac-Zir, you have stolen my bride, and not for love, but for the basest reasons. I challenge you for the hand of the Aldhanshai Wen-Jhai!"

With his chin high, Sai hopped down off the bench and marched through the crowd, flanked by the royal guard. So much for my revenge. How could I jump in now when Sai was doing so well? I followed him, walking beside Lhan. We exchanged a proud look. I felt like a mom. My little Sai, a man at last. Of course, he was still going to get slaughtered. Maybe I'd be able to jump in and save his life. I'd sure as hell avenge him.

The crowd whispered like a snake pit. I could see Kedac's jaw tighten like he was going to do something rash, but instead he just rolled his eyes and turned to complain to the priest.

The priest nodded and faced Sai. "You come too late, Dhan Sai. The ceremony has already begun. The time for challenges has past. Remove yourself."

Sai snarled. "Kedac-Zir, will you hide behind ceremony to avoid me? Are you such a coward that you will let a priest save you?"

That got a gasp from the crowd. Point for Sai, but Kedac parried it. "Who is the coward here? Who tried to steal Wen-Jhai dishonorably, without facing me? Who tried to corrupt her with his craven philosophy and his modern ways?"

He turned to a guy in the front row. This was the richest-dressed dude there, with a robe that looked like it was made of solid gold and a purple gem on his forehead as big as a baseball. "My Aldhanan, let not this coward defile this holy day. Arrest him."

The Aldhanan stood and turned. He was a big, powerful older guy who carried his heavy cloak like it was made of air. He looked like one of those sixty-year-old triathletes you see in vitamin commercials. "Sai-Far, you embarrass yourself here. You disgrace this court and your family. Leave now or face arrest."

"My Aldhanan, I apologize, but I will not."

"You defy me?" The Aldhanan signaled, and the guards who'd led us in drew swords and started to close in on us. I balled up my fists. Damn it, I knew we shouldn't have given up our swords.

Lhan put a hand on my shoulder. "Not here."

Sai dropped to one knee like he was signaling a fair catch. "My Aldhanan, I beg of you, indulge me but a moment. I may have lacked physical courage in the past, but unlike this kidnapper I have never been a traitor."

The crowd gasped again. The Aldhanan stared. Kedac was white-knuckling his sword hilt. The Aldhanan held up a hand to his guards. "If this is some dissembling attempt to advance your suit you will not die quickly. Now speak."

"My Aldhanan, you may do with me as you wish. I only speak in hopes of protecting you. While seeking Kedac-Zir at his headquarters last night in order to face him, I discovered a secret room in which there were plans laid out for an attack on…"

Kedac squawked, like a parrot. I don't think he meant to. "My Aldhanan! Must we listen to this drivel…"

The Aldhanan held up a hand and waved for Sai to continue.

"An attack on Ormolu, my Aldhanan. And in his papers were correspondence from various Dhanans, some here today, offering men and gold to finance his overthrow of your throne!"

Another big gasp from the crowd. The Aldhanan raised an eyebrow. "You have evidence of this treason?"

Sai whipped out a handful of papers from his pouch. "Letters, my Aldhanan."

A guard took them to the Aldhanan, who read them, scowling. Kedac twitched on the stage behind him. He couldn't keep quiet.

"My Aldhanan, whatever papers those may be, they are fabrications, forgeries, meant to discredit me in your eyes. They are the unmanly weapons of a weak-hearted twister of words, without spine enough for an honest challenge of steel and blood."

"I challenge you now, blackguard."

"When it is conveniently too late." Kedac played the crowd like a politician. "Look at him, my Aldhanan. Who will you believe, the commander of your navy, who has served you faithfully all these years, or this mewling half-man in his uncared-for armor, with his disreputable companions—an outlander giantess who apes the dress and manner of men, and a degenerate with a history of deviant scandal?"

Thanks pal. Thanks a whole bunch.

The crowd seemed to be leaning toward Kedac, and insults aside, I could see their point. There he was, square jaw, white teeth, shining gold armor. He *looked* like the hero. We looked like the circus had come to town—a big pink freak, a boy that looked like a girl, and a smarmy ringmaster. We hadn't washed in weeks, our armor looked like it had been dragged behind a city bus, Sai and Lhan were unshaven, and I was having a class five bad hair day.

Sai didn't back down an inch. "My Aldhanan, you have but to go to the navy barracks to see for yourself the truth of my story. I…"

Kedac cut him off again. "Miserable conniver, you will do anything to delay the inevitable. Go if you will, my Aldhanan, but I suspect a trap, a ruse to draw you from the safety of the temple. Come, arrest him. A marriage conducted after the first hour of dawn becomes inauspicious. Will you let him spoil your daughter's happiness?"

The Aldhanan looked tired. We were annoying the hell out of him. We were ruining everything. "I begin to believe you are right, Kir-Dhanan. Guards."

The guards moved in. Sai looked from Lhan to me, desperate. I shrugged. So did Lhan. We were fresh out of ideas, but suddenly Sai's eyes flashed. "My Aldhanan! My Aldhanan, one more moment! I beg you! What if I could prove Kedac-Zir's treachery right here, out of his own mouth?"

"You have had your say, quisling. I have said that dissembling would be your doom and so it shall. Take him away."

The guards grabbed us and dragged us back toward the door, but Sai kept shouting. "My Aldhanan, Kedac-Zir does not love your daughter! He marries her solely for political gain, and I can prove it!"

"Stop!"

It was Kedac who'd shouted. His face was red with fury. He turned to the Aldhanan. "My apologies, my Aldhanan, but I must beg to take from you the pleasure of killing this excrescence. No man may insult an Oran Dhan's most sacred honor and go unpunished. By your leave, bring him forth."

The Aldhanan waved his okay and the guards carried Sai forward, but not us. They held us where we were. They lifted him onto the stage, handed him his sword and left him in front of Kedac.

Kedac drew his sword and curled his lip. "Now speak your so called proof or answer me with steel."

Sai turned to the Aldhanan. "My Aldhanan, you may discount my evidence, but there is evidence not even Kedac-Zir can deny that his wooing of Wen-Jhai has been a sham."

The Aldhanan grunted, impatient. "Speak or draw. Time grows short."

Sai bowed and turned back to Kedac. "I ask but one question of you, Kir-Dhanan Kedac-Zir." He paused for effect. "Who's Balurrah wear you?"

The crowd went dead silent. Even the Aldhanan started to pay attention. Kedac was tofu-white. My heart pounded. Boy howdy, he'd done it.

Kedac turned to the Aldhanan. "My Aldhanan, no man shows his Balurrah to any but the woman he loves."

But the Aldhanan had seen Kedac's fear like the rest of us. "And yet, Admiral, to prove your innocence, and your loyalty to me, a tradition might be bent."

"No, my Aldhanan. In all things but this am I loyal to you, but this is a private matter between the Aldhanshai and myself."

The Aldhanan smiled, grim. "Then you will have no objection to showing her, here. Now."

Kedac looked nervous, but bowed. "Very well." He held out a hand to Wen-Jhai. "Beloved."

She crossed to him, hesitant. Suddenly her grabbed her and put his sword to her neck, glaring at the Aldhanan. "Fool!"

The crowd babbled. Kedac backed toward the rope ladder. Sai shouted and jumped for him. Kedac kicked him into the front row, but lost his grip on Wen-Jhai.

That was my cue. I shook off my guards, ripped my sword out of another guy's hands, kicked off a bench and arced over the Aldhanan. I landed on the stage and launched again, catching Kedac in a crossbody block as he lunged again for Wen-Jhai. We crashed to the stage. I drew my sword and slit Kedac's harness up the back. It took a lot of will power not to slit his back up to his neck.

The crowd was backing away, freaked out by my leap. The guards were surging forward. The Aldhanan was shouting. I stood Kedac on his feet and ripped off his harness. He stood there, naked except for his loincloth and his balurrah. The medallion was decorated with Mai-Mar's colors and symbol.

Even the Aldhanan gasped this time. Wen-Jhai shrieked and collapsed. The Aldhanan shouted to his guards, pointing at Kedac. "Arrest him!"

The guards climbed the stage. Kedac slashed back with his sword. Stupid me, I'd forgot to disarm him. He almost disarmed me. His blade chopped through my armored sleeve and bit into my arm. I fell back, clutching myself and seeing colors.

Kedac ran to Wen-Jhai and hauled her up, fanning back the guards with a slash of his sword. He dragged her to the rope ladder and shouted to the airman with the bugle. "Rise! Sound rise and fly!"

The guards with the wands of blue fire drew down on Kedac as the airman blasted out three short notes. Kedac jerked Wen-Jhai in front of him and stepped backward onto the ladder as it rose into the air. The guards didn't have a clear shot.

The Aldhanan shouted up at Kedac. "Stand down, traitor. Release my daughter."

Kedac laughed. "You command me no longer, tyrant! No more will you tax the Dhanans and steal our power." He saluted the crowd. "Rise, Dhanans, rise! Our destiny is unaltered. The axe merely falls earlier than anticipated. Hold the despot here and the navy will hold the city within a crossing."

The Aldhanan and his guards turned to see who he was talking to and were suddenly face to face with a sea of blades. All the naval officers and a lot more Dhanans than I expected were drawing steel and starting for the royal family.

Instant chaos. Everybody started fighting everybody else. The loyalists in the crowd tried to help the guards. Other guys were dragging their wives and children out of the way. The guards were trying to aim their magic death wands without hitting any of the good guys.

Kedac and Wen-Jhai were above the wall now. The bottom of the ladder dragged across it.

The guards with the wands were hanging fire. They couldn't shoot at Kedac for fear of hitting Wen-Jhai, and they couldn't gun down the big ship because the balloon would explode and the whole flaming mess would crash down on everybody. They couldn't stop Kedac.

I could.

I pulled myself up and tested my sword arm. It hurt like dammit and was stiff from shock, but I could move it. I raced across the stage, jumped up on the altar, kicked off the scale model of the rocket-tower, and launched up for the last rungs of the rope ladder.

Unbelievably, with all the other shit he had to concentrate of, Kedac saw me coming. He kicked the ropes with his heel and made the ladder swing under his feet.

The rungs danced through my hands like a fumbled pass. I crashed down on top of the garden wall, knocking the wind out of myself, and slammed down onto my back behind the altar. I whited out for a second and sucked air like a ruptured hose. It felt like a truck had parked on my chest.

I needed a time out. Not a chance. Kedac's bugle boy ran behind the altar and jumped at me, sword raised. I stuck a foot up and caught him in the nuts. He curled up like a hedgehog and crashed to the stage beyond me. I staggered up, trying to remember how to breath, and weaved out from behind the altar.

The temple garden was a moshpit with swords. Bodies slammed into bodies everywhere I looked. By the stage Lhan was pulling Sai to his feet. Sai shouted something I couldn't hear and shook his fist as Kedac's rising ship. I staggered to them.

Lhan looked up. "A noble attempt, mistress, but I believe 'tis time for our skelshas. We must catch Kedac before he reaches the naval base or all will be lost."

He started for the door. I followed, groaning. The last thing I wanted to do was hop back on one of those fucking goony-birds, but if it would have got me another crack at Kedac I'd have hitched a ride on a bottle rocket.

CHAPTER TWENTY-SEVEN

FREE FALL!

We ran down the steps to where Lhan had tied up the skelshas. My bird bitched and snapped at me, but I got on him at last and he looped up into the sky after Sai and Lhan like a wounded duck. I swear he was deliberately trying to make me lose my lunch.

Lhan spurred his skelsha straight for Kedac's ship. It hadn't got far. The wind was blowing from the direction of the naval base, so Kedac had to tack back and forth to make headway.

We caught up to him about halfway across the city. Lhan tried to bring us in high and out of the sun, but they still spotted us. As soon as we got within range crossbow bolts came spitting from the deck of the ship. They buzzed by like angry bees.

We angled off again, climbing up out of their line of sight. I jockeyed my bird alongside Lhan's. It was spooky quiet that high up. I couldn't hear any ground sounds at all. "Can we come down on top of them and poke a hole in their balloon?"

Sai yelped. "No! Do you mean to kill her?"

Lhan shook his head. "'Tis still too unpredictable. Sometimes a holed envelope rips wide and the ship plummets like a stone. Other times it takes hours to sink. The first we cannot risk, and the second would not serve us."

"Okay, you tell me."

Lhan pointed. "If we swoop down on all sides, one of us at least should gain the deck, and in the confusion that followed, the other two would find their chance."

I made a face. "Sounds like suicide for the first one in, and not much better for everybody else."

Lhan shrugged. "Kedac has not a full compliment of men. This was to be a honeymoon, not a raid. Besides, to save the nation and the Aldhanshai? Could a true Oran do less?" He caught himself. "Ah, but forgive me, Mistress. This is not your fight. You are welcome to retire."

I laughed. "And let that fucker Kedac win? Not a chance, bucko. I just don't want to die for nothing."

Sai gasped and pointed across the city. "We are lost! Another ship comes to Kedac's aid."

Lhan and I turned. Sure enough, rising from the naval base was a sleek little cutter with the Oran colors flying.

Lhan tugged on his skelsha's reins. "The we must act swiftly. Come." He angled himself over Kedac's ship. We joined him, circling like vultures over roadkill. Sai looked as gray as paste, but his jaw was set. I felt like he looked.

Lhan dropped his fist. "Now!"

Lhan and Sai jerked the reins of their skelshas down and back, forcing them into steep dives. I did the same, but my skelsha fought me for a second before I muscled his head down.

We whipped down past the airbag so close that I could see the individual strands in the ropes that held the balloon to the ship. I came down portside. Lhan was to starboard, and Sai tried to land on the back rail.

It didn't work. They were ready. A whole fucking swarm of bolts shot at me as soon as I dropped below the balloon. My skelsha screamed as he took two in the chest and one through the left wing. He thrashed away and down, squealing and losing altitude fast. Ormolu pinwheeled up at me. I hauled on the reins. "Up, you bastard! Up!"

He leveled off a little, but he couldn't climb. Flapping his wing hurt to much.

A shape streaked down past me, then arced up under. It was Lhan. He'd got off easier than I had. At least his skelsha had. The bird didn't have a scratch. Lhan had a bolt through his thigh.

"Hold him steady, mistress."

I tightened up on the reins as Lhan inched up under me. What was he thinking? I was lighter than I looked in Waar's gravity, but there was no way a skelsha could carry the two of us—not in a dogfight, that was for damn sure. And what was he doing helping me? Where the hell was Sai?

I looked up. Sai's skelsha was circling over the balloon again. They both seemed unwounded until I noticed a couple bolts dangling from his skelsha's landing gear.

Lhan looked up, two yards below me. "Step down to me, mistress. Carefully now."

"It won't work. I'm too heavy."

"'Twill work for long enough. Now hurry. Your bird is dying."

He was right. I was dropping lower every second. My skelsha could barely hold his wings out anymore. If I didn't go now I'd be crashlanding in some Ormolu backyard. I waved him closer. "Come up. Come up."

Lhan eased his bird higher. He was practically carrying my skelsha piggyback. I threw my right leg over my bird's neck, then slid off.

For a second I had that sick feeling like when you drop from a wall in the dark and don't know how far it is to the ground, but then I landed square on the skelsha's back, right behind Lhan. My bird's cry of relief came right on top of Lhan's bird's squawk of surprise. We dropped fifteen feet in a second and I thought we weren't going to stop, but then Lhan hauled on the reins. "Pull beloved! Pull!"

I held on to him like I was in the chick seat of a Harley. "What now? This poor bastard ain't gonna last two minutes."

"Well I know it. We must land quickly."

I looked down. "It'll take too long. We're gonna do the last thousand feet in nothing flat."

"That is why we go up."

Up? Was he going to fly us to one of the moons? "Whaddaya mean? Where are we going?"

He didn't answer. I held on, terrified. Lhan stayed out of range of Kedac's ship as we climbed. A couple guys took potshots at us, but the bolts arced down under our skelsha's belly. The poor bastard flapped for all he was worth and we slowly climbed back into the sky. It was killing him. He was wheezing and gagging against his bit. My wounded skelsha spiraled down below us, barely flapping.

Finally we were over the balloon. Lhan waved to Sai and angled toward Kedac's ship. I grabbed him. "What are you doing. That didn't work the first time!"

But instead of diving for the deck, this time he aimed his bird for the top of the balloon. The poor thing almost collapsed as it landed. Sai's skelsha *did* collapse. Its wounded legs couldn't stick the landing and it crashed beak first, throwing Sai from the saddle.

Lhan bellowed, terrified, as Sai flew toward the slope. He hopped off his bird to try and catch Sai, and nearly fell himself as Sai hooked the netting with a one-hand grab. His bird bounced past him and tumbled off the balloon into freefall.

We watched as it threw out its wings, caught an updraft, and got riddled with crossbow bolts as it came back up to deck level. The poor fucker spun down toward the rooftops like a broken umbrella.

Sai and Lhan helped each other back up the curve of the balloon as I hopped off Lhan's skelsha. I pulled them up the last few feet. "This is great. Now we got one skelsha for the three of us."

Just then a screechy horn blew from below and Lhan's skelsha raised its head. Lhan cursed and ran toward it, but before he could catch it, the thing spread its wings and dove down toward the deck.

I stared. "What the fuck?"

Lhan's shoulders slumped. "The homing horn, to call back riderless birds in battle."

I groaned. "Well, that narrows things down, don't it? We're stuck, and climbing down to rescue Princess Poo-Poo Pants is gonna get our asses stuck full of arrows. I think we gotta pop this puppy and take our chances with the drop."

Sai yelped again. "No!"

Lhan glanced over the side. "'Tis too late for that. We are nearly over the base now. They will land in their own shipfield and we will be lost."

I kicked the balloon. "Well, what the fuck do we do, then?"

He drew his sword, looking over my shoulder. "It seems we fight."

I turned. Clambering up the netting like so many monkeys came a squad of marines.

Sai squeaked. "There are more here!"

We spun back. We were being surrounded.

Funny, for a second it cheered me up. You can't fight ifs and maybes. You can't kick a possibility in the nuts. At least these guys I could do something about.

Then the fuckers pulled out bows and ruined the whole thing. The marines stopped just high enough to watch us, but too far down for us to get at them without practically hanging off the balloon. Behind them, a line of crossbow guys drew down on us. Smart fucker, that Kedac. He wasn't about to play king-of-the-hill with us. He'd just stay out of range and snipe at us.

Let me just take a second to say how much I fucking hate bows. And guns, and bombs, and all that long range stuff, stuff that makes it easy for some schmuck to kill you from far off without having to think about what he's doing. A guy can drop a bomb from a plane and he doesn't have to picture what's going on below him. Imagine if the guys in the *Enola Gay* had had to personally chop the heads off all the people they killed in Hiroshima—even the little babies. You think they might have felt a little twinge after a while?

Lhan shouted, "Down!" as the first bolts zipped by us. I had a better plan. As Lhan and Sai fell flat I drew my sword, flipped it around and stuck it point down into the leather of the balloon. "Next guy who shoots, we all go down!"

The bowmen hesitated. They looked to their sergeants. I pushed the point a little deeper. "I got nothing to lose. I'll rip it wide open, whether you hit me or not."

The sergeants called down the balloon for new orders. A few seconds later, they waved at the bowmen. They lowered their crossbows, but kept them at the ready. The marines stayed where they were, watching us.

Sai and Lhan raised their heads. I motioned with my chin. "Get your swords out. We gotta make this look serious."

They sat up and drew. There were some shouts from the marines, but nobody shot at us. Sai made cow eyes at me as the three of us knelt in a little circle, swords point-down like some picture from a King Arthur story. "Once again you save my miserable life, Mistress."

Lhan grunted. "But for how long. This standoff ends once we land. They know all they have to do is wait."

That was true. I hadn't bought us much time. We were practically over the base now. The fortifications were slipping beneath the mass of the balloon. The other navy ship was below us too, turning our way but still a good thousand feet down. I grinned, queasy. "Well at least we don't have to worry about that other ship. They can't risk firing on us anymore than these guys can."

Lhan didn't return my smile. "Yes, but unless we can invent some new course of action, we will be dead regardless. The first casualties in a bloody civil war."

I was only half listening. The other ship wasn't rising. It was staying at its own level, passing under Kedak's ship and out of my line of sight as it continued south. They weren't coming for us at all. Why was that?

I stood and looked closer, not at the balloon, but at the deck. There were tiny faces peeking out from under, looking up. I spotted a flash of red. A short-cut red jacket. Kai-La! And there was Burly beside her. The old she-skelsha had managed to get out of the Navy camp after all.

My heart jumped. "The pirates!"

Sai and Lhan followed my gaze just as their ship vanished under ours, but they had seen too. I wanted to run to the side of the balloon and wave and shout. They were our rescue—the United States Marines coming over the hill in the nick of time—except they weren't. They were heading for the horizon as fast as their little balloon could take them.

Not that I blamed them. If I'd just lifted off from a navy base in a stolen ship, the last thing I'd want to do would be to stop and chat with the flagship of the whole fleet. They didn't know what was happening up here. And even if they did they wouldn't come to the rescue. Sure, I'd busted them out of jail, but we weren't exactly bosom buddies, were we?

A hissing burst from below snapped me back to the here and now. The airmen were venting gas. We were starting our drop. The only way out of this high-flying bucket of shit we were in was to get some help, and fast. If we could talk the pirates into teaming up with us we had a chance. But how? What I needed was a skelsha so I could fly down to them, or...

I pushed the idea away. Too crazy, even for me. But was it? They were directly below us. Their balloon was bigger than a trailerpark double-wide. Pretty good-sized target. Little fingers of fear started creeping up my neck and choking me. I shook them off. If I was going to do this I'd have to do it so fast my brain wouldn't be able to catch up with me before it was too late.

I sheathed my sword and looked at Sai and Lhan. "Keep poking the balloon. I'm going for help."

Sai frowned. "You go to do what?"

Lhan had figured it out. "No, Mistress Jae-En. 'Tis is too dangerous."

"It's better than wating to get picked off like a fish in a barrel. See you in a minute." I turned to the left side of the balloon—the side Kai-La's ship would be coming out from under—and started running. Sai and Lhan called after me. I ignored them. I had to keep moving.

The marines shouted as I charged toward them, and the archers raised their crossbows. The balloon started to slope down beneath my feet. I kicked off like a cliff diver and leapt over their heads, as flat and far out as I could with crossbow bolts whizzing all around me.

As the curve of the balloon dropped behind me and the whole city of Ormolu spread out below me like a satellite photo, my brain finally caught up with me.

What the *fuck* was I doing?

I was freefalling four thousand feet up without a goddamn parachute, that's what I was doing. And the crazy part was, I hadn't been able to see my target before I jumped. The bulk of Kedac's balloon had been in the way. I'd jumped blind, and now I was fucked.

The pirates had sailed a lot further out than I'd thought. They weren't below me. It was hard to judge at this height, but they seemed to be twenty or thirty feet beyond my fingertips and the gap was widening. There was nothing between me and the ground but air.

I fought off the impulse to curl up into a ball and scream. I'd been an Airborne Ranger, damn it. I'd trained for this. Chute failure was boot camp basics. I threw my arms and legs out wide and held myself rigid, trying to catch as much wind resistance as possible. The air beat at me like water from a fire hose. It forced my eyes closed and got under my heavy leather armor and made it flap like silk. I slowed up. Not much, but more than I expected. I forgot! I was lighter on this planet. I wasn't falling as fast. I had maybe fifty seconds instead of forty before I went splat. Hooray.

I could feel the limits of my control like a skateboarder feeling how far she can lean into a turn before her wheels slip. I could even use my arms and legs and big fat ass to steer a little.

I aimed myself as best I could at Kai-La's stolen ship. It worked. I angled closer. But fast enough? I rode the edge. If I didn't push hard enough my dive would be too steep and I'd fall short. If I pushed too hard, I'd lose resistance and drop like a stone.

I arched my body like a bow. The gap was closing, but I was falling faster than I was turning. The ship rushed up to fill my vision like a speeding truck, blocking out half the city below it, but I wasn't coming down on top of it. It was still off left. I could see faces. Faces was bad. That meant I could see under the balloon. I was too far out. I arched further. Reaching out with my hands.

My brain was screaming. I'm going to miss it! I'm going to drop right past!

Suddenly I could see the netting and the seams in the skin in the balloon, zooming-in like I was looking through a telephoto lens. I threw my arms up and tucked. I smashed into the flank of the balloon, elbows first. Fireworks exploded behind my eyes.

If I'd come in straight I would have broken my arms and neck. Luckily, I hit at a shallow angle, so all I got was a major case of rope burn and Excedrin Headache Number 1006. That was the good part. The bad part was that I glanced away again.

What was it my science teacher said? The angle of something or other is equal to the angle of some other shit. In other words I bounced off at the same angle I hit, away from the balloon. The city and the sky whipped across my vision, then something hit me hard in the guts and I folded up like a wet rag over a laundry line. I heard a crack. My ribs? I couldn't tell. Everything hurt.

I slipped off the hard thing and fell again. Something white flew up in front of my eyes. Something else caught my shoulder. I jerked to a stop. I wasn't falling anymore, but I didn't know what was happening either. The pain in my stomach and my shoulder and my head was making me fade in and out like a light on a dimmer switch. Where was I? My whole world was white. It was all I could see. Was I in heaven? I never thought heaven would hurt so much.

The white flapped forward and hit me in the face. It was cloth, heavy and stiff, like canvas. Canvas!

There was a rope under my armpit and a thick spar of wood over my head. The steering sail. I'd hit one of the ship's steering sails. I was safe.

Safe-ish. An arrow ripped through the sail next to my head and dangled there. Shit! "Don't shoot! It's me! It's Jane! Stop!"

I heard voices below me. "Show yourself."

I was hung up. I reached up and grabbed the spar. I groaned. Every muscle in my body ached. I pulled up and slipped my other arm free of the rope. The pain almost made me black out. Every joint in my body screamed. I needed a masseuse and a chiropractor, stat.

I inched my way to the balloon, then grabbed the rigging and climbed down. Every move was like getting poked by blunt needles. When I got under the curve of the balloon the whole deck was looking up at me.

Kai-La cracked a smile. "Quite an entrance, lass. You might have joined us in the lock-up and saved yourself some trouble."

Burly and another pirate helped me down to the deck. My legs buckled under me and I slumped against the rail. "Not here to join you. You gotta join us."

One of her eyebrows arched. "Join you? What mean you?"

I pointed up. "Help us take that ship."

Kai-La and the pirates burst out laughing. Kai-La folded her arms. "I may be called the Mad She-Skelsha, but I'm not as mad as all that. That's Kedac's flagship, pride of the Oran Navy."

I shook my head. "It's not crewed-up. He was going on his honeymoon. Only a squad or two."

Kai-La chuckled. "Most reassuring. We will defeat Kedac only have the entire Oran Navy after us for the rest of our lives. My apologies, girl, but tempting as it is to teach the blood-thirsty vurlak a lesson, I'm afraid I still decline."

I waved a hand. "Wait. Listen. Kedac's gone renegade. Tried to overthrow the Aldhanan. He's kidnapped Wen-Jhai. We gotta stop him before he raises the whole navy." Kai-La stared at me. I dropped the other shoe. "You pull this off, you save the country. Probably get a goddamn medal. At least a fat payoff."

Kai-La and Burly exchanged a glance. Kai-La kneeled beside me. "Is this true?"

I held up three fingers. "Scout's honor."

Kai-La looked at Burly again, then crossed to him. They whispered back and forth. I raised my voice. "Hurry it up, will ya? They've already started dropping. My pals are gonna get poked full of holes."

They talked for a second more, then Burly turned and started shouting at the crew. "Drop ballast! Turn about! All hands prepare for boarding!"

Kai-La grinned down at me, as cold as a freon enema. "You had best be telling the truth, Lass."

I showed her my three fingers again. "Scout's honor. Scout's honor." Then my head flopped back and I closed my eyes.

CHAPTER TWENTY-EIGHT

VENGANCE!

Somebody was shouting. I opened my eyes. It took a second for my brain to claw through the fog and figure out what was going on. Kai-La. Ship. Lots of pain. Okay. Up to date.

Kai-La's rat-faced third in command was standing at the rail, dressed in a kir-dhan's uniform and calling to Kedac's ship. "Ahoy, the *Triumphant*. Are you in need of assistance?"

I looked around the deck. Half a dozen pirates were also standing around in airmen's loincloths and officers' uniforms, but most of them were hiding below the rail, grappling hooks in hand.

Good plan. The pirates had a navy ship. Why not use it to get as close to Kedac as possible before pulling off their false moustaches and shouting "Boo!" Last thing they wanted was to exchange artillery fire with a ship five times their size. Kedac had four huge, telephone-pole-lobbing, super-crossbows running down each side of his ship. We had three total and they were toothpicks compared to the wood Kedac was packing. He'd turn us into sawdust and red paste.

I peeked over the rail. We were fifty feet straight out from Kedac and drifting closer. I looked up, worried, but Sai and Lhan were still poking the balloon with their swords, and the marines were still watching them like coonhounds under a treed possum.

Now we were thirty feet out. A kir-dhan from Kedac's ship shouted back. "Give the code of the day, kir-dhan!"

Rat-Face put on a puzzled look. "We already gave the code. Did you not hear it?"

Kedac's kir-dhan started to look suspicious. "Repeat it or come no further." Kedac stepped to the poopdeck rail, looking at us.

Rat-Face nodded. "Certainly." He turned to a pirate dressed as an ensign. We kept drifting closer. "Ensign, the code of the day."

The other pirate saluted and stepped to the rail. "Yes sir, the code of the day."

Kedac's kir-dhan was looking back and forth between them. The marines behind him were starting to mutter. They knew something was wrong now. Kedac's kir-dhan waved his hands. "Back! Stay back."

Kedac barked from the poopdeck. ""Turn them away, kir-dhan!"

The ensign-pirate grinned. We were in range. "The code of the day is... *attack!*"

Like a squad of jack-in-the-boxes, the pirates popped up from behind the rail. Half of them chucked grapples at Kedac's ship, the other half shot arrows into the marines. Only a few grapples hit, but they were enough. The pirates hauled on the ropes and the gap between the ships got smaller.

Kedac's marines started screaming and shouting and running around like crazy, caught off guard. Half of them were still in the rigging, hemming in Sai and Lhan.

Kedac stayed calm though. He called orders from the poopdeck like a waiter reading off his ticket to a cook. "Arbolasts, hole their envelope. Marines, clear those grapples. Crossbowmen, return to deck and fire at will."

It worked like magic. With orders, Kedac's crew started moving like clockwork. Marines jumped forward to hack through the ropes. Crossbowmen dropped to the deck and lined up behind the marines. Four details broke off and started prepping the big crossbows, swinging them up at our balloon and cranking back their wrist-thick bowstrings.

The pirates came back with a barrage of arrows, picking off marines and brushing them back from the grapples.

The gun-crews were protected though. The humongous crossbows were so big the pirates couldn't get a bead on the guys working them. If we could close the gap fast enough, we'd be able to overrun the crews, otherwise we'd be heading south PDQ.

The marines returned fire, mowing down half the pirates who were pulling us closer to Kedac's ship. We were going to lose the race. The marines would fire their big guns and sink us before we got to them. At least they would if Mrs. Carver's little girl didn't get off her freckled pink ass and do something about it.

Up 'til then I'd been trying to decide if I wanted to sit this one out. My heart wanted in on the finish. If I didn't get a piece of Kedac this whole trip would be for nothing, but my body was telling me that I needed a breather, maybe even a short stay in hospital. The cut Kedac had given me had stiffened up my arm so much it felt like I was wearing a concrete cast, and the rope burn where the sail-rigging had caught me felt like somebody had got after my armpit with a belt sander, and I was pretty sure I had a broken rib.

Take a break, my brain said. You've already done the impossible. You got the message to the pirates. Let somebody else take it from here. But nobody else could do this. If I didn't go, they'd pop our balloon and we'd freefall to pavement.

The gun-crew to my right was getting closest to ready. I got into a crouch. My muscles told me to lie down again. I told them to fuck off. I had to shout.

I hopped onto the rail and kicked off into a somersault dive over the closing gap. A couple of crossbow bolts zipped by. I landed off-balance on the stock of the giant bow and swung lamely at the crew with my sword. I missed by a mile, but they jumped back anyway, surprised.

Then I had a thought. Taking out the gun crew wasn't going to do much. New guys would just take over as soon as I jumped to the next one. What I needed to do was to put the crossbow itself out of commission.

Nothing easier. I backhanded the heavy crossbow string with my sword.

Stupid!

The cable split no problem, but I forgot about the recoil. When it parted, that baseball bat-thick rope snapped back like a whip and cracked me across the thigh and ass-cheek.

Nothing has ever hurt worse—swords, clubs, gunshots, ditching my Harley naked—don't ask—nothing. It hit me like a club, knocking me off the crossbow and bruising me down to the bone, but worse, it laid me open like it was made of barbed wire and broken glass. I fell down under the nose of the bow, writhing and screaming, my leg covered in blood and greasy sweat.

"Fuck! Fuck! Fuck!" The pain just kept coming. It felt like my ass had been napalmed.

Shapes were moving above me. The gun crew, working their way around the bow, trying to get at me with their swords. I could barely see them through the tears in my eyes. I had no idea where my sword was. Hell, I didn't have a real good idea where my hands and feet were.

A crew man swung at me. I tried to roll and kick. I have no idea if I connected, but the fact that I'm telling this story proves he missed. The rest were closing in. Their swords went up.

I'd like to tell you that my life flashed before my eyes and I apologized for all the crappy things I'd done, but all I can remember thinking was, "Well, shit."

Then one of the guys was twisting and screaming, and the rest were turning. The screaming guy flopped on top of me and the arrow sticking out of his back poked me in the tit.

The other guys fell back as a wave of pirates came over the rail, swinging steel and screaming bloody murder. They'd made it.

I wanted to get up and help, but my parts weren't talking to each other yet. My leg and ass were giving off too much static.

Something blocked out a big chunk of the sky. I thought it was another marine and groped around for my sword. It was Burly. He laid my sword across my chest and patted me on the shoulder. "Smartly done, lass. We've cleared the other ballisti. Join us when you're ready."

Ready, hell. A gang of marines were stabbing at us right now. Burly knocked one sword aside with his armored sleeve and kicked another guy's legs out. I fumbled my sword up in front of my face in time to stop another guy's chop an inch from my nose. Ready or not I was in the fight.

I grabbed my attacker's ankle and pulled. He fell into the guy next to him. Burly skewered a third guy and stood. I tried to join him. White-out again. I fell against the big crossbow, blind with pain. Marines dropped from the rigging. Burly fought them off. I couldn't help. I was too busy heaving.

When the bile stopped rising, I swung my leg a little and put some weight on it. The pain jacked through me again, but I was ready for it this time. It only made me scream.

"Goddammit!"

There was no time for this. Burly was getting swamped. He had a cut over his eye. I stabbed with my sword and gutted one of his attackers, fighting another blackout. Two more turned on me. Less for him to worry about, but too much for me. I fought 'em off through a haze of agony. The pain made everything else harder to focus on, like having a woodpecker tapping on the back of my skull.

With Burly's help I cleared two guys and we took as quick look around. Things weren't so good. The pirates had the marines outnumbered two to one, but these were Kedac's crack troops we were talking about here. They were his elite personal guard. Not only were they better fighters, they were more organized. We had some seriously tough hombres on our side, but they didn't work together like marines. A cold sweat of panic made my palms slick. We couldn't lose it all now. There had to be some way to level the playing field.

I looked around for Kedac. If I could take him out of the fight, that might take the fight out of the marines.

He was up on the poopdeck fighting with Kai-La and the rat-faced pirate, but as I watched, Rat-Face spun away from Kedac, spraying blood every-where, his throat cut to the spine. Kedac turned his full attention on Kai-La. She backed to the rail, sweating like a whore on dollar-day. And she wasn't the only one. We were getting our asses handed to us all over the deck.

Wait a minute! Level the playing field?

Burly saw Kai-La getting slammed and started forward. "Captain!"

I stopped him. "I'll go. I've got an idea for you. What would happen if you dropped some ballast on the little ship?"

Burly's eyes clouded as he thought it through, then he grinned. "Brilliant, lass. I'll get some lads on it and spread the word."

"Aces."

I turned back toward Kedac and almost swallowed my tongue. Kedac was turning Kai-La into Swiss cheese. She was bleeding from a handful of cuts and he had her bent back over the rail, making gnat's-ass parries.

There was a deck full of brawling bodies between us. I'd never make it un-less I took the highroad. My leg was still burning like I'd soaked it in battery acid, and cramping so bad I could barely stretch it out straight, but it would only get worse if I stood still.

I jumped and kicked off the shoulder of a marine, ruining his swing at a pirate, then sprang off another super-bow and arced toward Kedac, raising my sword overhead. "Death from above!"

I snagged something with my sword and stopped dead just as I cleared the poopdeck rail. I crashed to the boards. The pain of jumping was nothing compared to the pain of landing on my leg. Jet engines roared behind my ears.

When I could think again, I looked up to see what I'd hit. There was a two yard rip in the underside of the balloon. The edges were fluttering as the levitating air escaped. Oops!

I pulled myself up, hissing through my teeth, and stepped toward Kedac, but somebody jumped in front of me—a huge, bullnecked son-of-a-bitch in a deckhand's loincloth, his eyes shining like a street crazy's. "I swore vengeance upon you, demoness, and the Seven have delivered you to me at last!"

He swung a sword at me. I fell back. Who was this guy? What was he talking about? Then I remembered. He was the dude I'd lifted over my head at Kedac's shindig, the guy who Kedac had busted down to deck-hand, Lut-Gar. I hardly recognized him without all his medals.

I groaned. Not now! Kai-La was halfway over the rail and losing blood like a sieve. I tried to knock Lut-Gar aside and get to Kedac, but even though he was dressed like a deckhand, he still fought like an officer. He dodged my blade and lunged. I had to twist sideways to miss getting poked.

I swung. He parried, binding my blade. Fucker was strong. He stopped me cold. I kicked him in the chest. That worked, though I almost fainted from using my leg. He bounced off Kedac's back, jarring his sword arm.

Kedac glanced back, glaring. "Mind your swing, curse you." Then did a double take when he saw me. "You!"

Kai-La swung at him, but even distracted, Kedac was too fast. He blocked, but at least she managed to stagger clear of the rail and reset herself.

Lut-Gar stepped between me and Kedac like a jealous boyfriend at a high-school dance. "I have her, Kir-Dhanan. I have her. Fear not."

Kedac looked like he was going to say something, but Kai-La swiped at him and he had to get back to work.

I blocked Lut-Gar's swing and chopped at him, but again I underestimated him. I was so worried about stopping Kedac I wasn't thinking about the fight I was in. Lut-Gar punched me in the temple. My knees sagged. I saw double.

He beat my blade aside. It bit into the rail and got stuck. I tugged at it, but my brain was a million miles away from my hand. Lut-Gar raised his sword, eyes glowing in triumph. "At last I am avenged! At last I make recompense for the indignities you have suffered upon me!"

If he'd shut up he might have got me, but suddenly the deck tilted—a twenty degree sideways list. Burly had come through. Dropping ballast from the little ship had shot it higher, pulling Kedac's ship up on one side by the grapple ropes. Lut-Gar stumbled backward, downslope, tripped over Rat-Face's body, fell against the siderail, and flipped up and over, ass-first into the wide blue yonder. Dignified to the end.

I staggered up and turned toward Kedac. The tilt had taken him by surprise. Hell, it had taken *me* by surprise and I knew it was coming. He was pulling himself upright. Unfortunately it had caught Kai-La off guard too. She was on her knees, clutching her bleeding forehead. She'd brained herself on the rail. Kedac moved in.

I dove forward, sword first, and shouldered Kai-La sideways as Kedac's blade shot out. His steel screeched off mine and passed a quarter-inch to the right of Kai-La's ear. She was too gone to notice.

Kedac turned on me, eyes burning with hate. "You meddle too often in affairs not your own, demon bitch."

He slashed down at me. I blocked one-handed and hauled Kai-La out of the way with the other. I shoved her toward the stairs. "Get out of here! Go down and help your pals."

Kedac nearly cut my head off before I got back on guard. You couldn't do two things at once around Kedac. If you weren't one-hundred percent focused, he'd slip something by you and come away with your liver. My plan was to keep him busy until Sai got down off the balloon and challenged him like it said in the script, but right then I was too busy just keeping his sword out of me to worry about plans.

Christ, he was fast! Not even in gladiator school had I faced somebody this good. And I wasn't exactly fighting fit. This wasn't how I dreamed about facing him. Beat to shit. I couldn't jump. I could barely fucking walk—especially not on this slanting deck. This sucked!

Kedac, glared at me over our swords. "To think I found you arousing, putting Lut-Gar in his place. I would have paid you handsomely for the pleasure of mastering you. Instead you defy me at every turn."

I laughed. Even that hurt. "How are you supposed to master me if I don't defy you once in a while?"

"You were to defy me in private! Instead, you continue to humiliate me in public. You reveal my coup before time, and worse, expose my nakedness and the inner secrets of my heart in front of the flower of Oran nobility!"

"Yeah? Well, after what you did to me, we still ain't even."

He actually looked confused. "I? What have I done to you?"

He didn't know? "You stuck your finger up my cunt in front of a roomful of laughing yahoos, asshole!"

His face turned red. He looked like an angry plum. "And you found the attentions of a noble Oran insulting? You were offended that the Kir-Dhanan of all Ora favored you with his touch?"

I couldn't believe it. He was actually pissed that I wasn't thanking him for groping me. "Nobody touches me without asking first."

Kedac laughed. "And should I ask my krae if I may mount her too?"

There it was, stripped naked. The fucker might be talking to me man to woman and fighting me warrior to warrior, but when it came down to it, I was an animal, an educated parrot that could talk but wasn't really human. That's when I really got mad.

I know you're supposed to give people from other cultures a break on shit that they've grown up with—I'd cut Lhan and Sai some slack on the whole slave-owning thing, but Kedac was an asshole. Sure his culture didn't treat women too well, but Sai and Lhan came from the same culture and they'd treated me like gentlemen. Kedac enjoyed humiliating me. That night at his party he'd got off knowing that no matter how strong I was, because he was an Oran noble, he could fuck with me anyway he wanted and I couldn't fuck back. He was a bully.

Have I mentioned how much I hate bullies?

The red boiled up in my eyes like I'd put on blood-colored sunglasses. Everything except Kedac went away—the battle going on around us, my wounds, my pain, my exhaustion. Five minutes before I'd told myself I'd save Kedac for Sai. I'd honor my promise and let him have his shot. All that went away too. Fuck honor. Fuck promises. Fuck Sai, Lhan and going home. None of that mattered. Consequences were for afterward. The only things in the whole world were me and the fool in front of me. I'd never seen a man more in need of killin'.

I was so focused that Kedac seemed to be moving in slow motion. I watched him start moves and knew exactly where to be to stop them. My big sword moved twice as fast as his thin one. It took him longer and longer to parry my cuts. He was blocking inches away from his body now, and I'd opened up little gashes in his forearms and thighs. Blood was running across his fingers, slicking the handle of his sword. His grip was slipping.

But the best part was his face. It had a new expression on it. One I'd never seen there before. His eyes were wide. His teeth were clenched. His forehead was drenched in sweat. He was afraid!

My heart soared like an F-15. He knew he was going to die. Better than that, he knew that it was me, a low-class, outlander slut, an animal—worse, a *female* animal—who was going to kill him. Swallow *that*, fucker!

I batted a thrust aside like it was a fly and kicked him in the chest. He slammed back against the aft rail, arms thrown wide. He tried to get his sword in front of him. I chopped it near the guard and knocked it out of his hand. It pinwheeled down toward the city, flashing in the sun with every turn. Some lucky Ormoluian was getting a gift from heaven. I hoped it didn't kill 'em.

I put my sword to Kedac's throat. He was helpless—too scared and breathless even to beg. I smiled. I won. He was mine. A flick of my wrist and he'd die guzzling his own blood.

But not yet.

I grabbed his harness. I was going to do him like he'd done me. I was going to strip him naked and make him shake his dipstick in front of all his troops. I was going to stick my goddamn thumb up his ass.

He read it in my eyes, and his fear turned to horror. He knew I was going to destroy him, his rep, his macho, and he was more scared of that that he was of dying.

I smiled like a wolf, all teeth. "Time to dance, sweetcheeks."

I ripped his harness off like it was made of Play-Doh, and was reaching for his loincloth when a hand touched my shoulder.

"Mistress, stop."

I shrugged the hand off. I was busy.

"Mistress."

The hand was there again. I shrugged it away again and turned, snarling. "Get the fuck away from me!"

It was Lhan. He was standing behind me, calm and quiet, like a butler in an old movie. "Mistress, Sai waits to make his challenge."

Sai stood a few feet behind him, looking angry and noble.

I turned back to Kedac. "Well, he's too late. I got here first." All my shrugging had caused my sword to write a red line across Kedac's Adam's apple. It made me think I should just kill him now before Lhan could bother me anymore.

"Will you truly betray the trust of your oldest friend in this world? Will you snatch away his one chance for happiness?"

I clenched my teeth. "You don't understand. You don't know what I owe this guy!"

Lhan leaned close, whispering in my ear, exactly the way he did with a frightened krae. "But I do understand. He stole your dignity. Violated your person. Your vengeance is indeed justified. It has happened to me."

"Then leave me the fuck alone and let me finish what I started." My hand was shaking from holding my sword to Kedac's throat for so long. The motherfucker's eyes were zipping back and forth between me and Lhan with a look of hope that made me want to beat him up all over again. There was no way I could let him go. No way.

Lhan's voice came over my shoulder again, as soft as ever. He was getting on my nerves. "And yet, Sai's need is greater."

"Bullshit!"

He talked right over me. "For while you fight to avenge a wrong from the past, Sai fights to assure his future, and that of his bride."

I slammed Kedac back against the rail and reset my sword at his throat. I don't know why, but I was almost crying. It was hard to get the words out around the lump in my throat. "I don't give a rat's ass about the future! 'Til I beat this motherfucker, nothing else matters!"

Lhan chuckled, soft. "But do you not see, mistress? You have already beaten him. Look in his eyes. He has died a thousand times these last moments. Though you have not killed or humiliated him as you might have wished, there is no way for him to erase the knowledge that you could have, and would have, and he could not have stopped you. You defeated him utterly the moment you saw fear in his eyes. All else is redundancy."

My lower lip was quivering. There were tears in my eyes. "But... but..."

Lhan touched my shoulder again, but this time it wasn't to stop me. This time is was a friendly squeeze. "Come, Mistress Jae-En, you have had your victory. Let Sai have his."

I held my sword to Kedac's throat a few seconds more. All I had to do was lean forward, or trip. Yeah, trip! It could be an accident. I could just slip and it would be all over before anybody could do anything. What could they say? They might think I'd done it on purpose, but they'd never know for sure. Not for sure.

But I'd know. I'd know that Lhan had been right: that I'd already won, and gone ahead and ruined Sai's chances out of spite, like a spoiled kid who breaks a toy rather than share it with his baby brother.

I shrugged like it didn't matter, and lowered my sword. Kedac curled his lip. I could almost hear him thinking "weakling." I slapped the taste out of his mouth.

He crashed to the deck, lip bleeding. I turned away and looked Sai in the eye. "Take him apart."

Sai bowed and crossed his wrists. "Thank you, Mistress Jae-En."

Lhan gave me a grim smile. "Your restraint ennobles you, mistress."

I grunted. "Just get it over with." I stepped past him and slumped against the rail, all my aches and pains catching up to me all at once. Down on the main deck things had changed. The battle was over. The pirates had won. I guess my deck tilting ploy had done the trick. All the surviving marines were kneeling in a little cluster surrounded by pirate guards.

I noticed vaguely that the ship was level again too. The pirates had cut the grapple ropes. We were on even keel, but sinking fast. The rip I'd made in the balloon was twice as long now and I could feel the ship dropping through my feet like I was in an elevator.

Lhan was talking behind me. "Dhanan Kedac-Zir, custom and courtesy demand that we offer you time to rest and recover from your recent exertions, but in light of your almost certain arrest when this vessel touches the ground, we must insist that you honor your obligation to Sai-Far now."

Kedac sneered. "The little fop will only face me after your demoness has weakened me? Pathetic."

Lhan ignored him, but I saw Sai stiffen up. Lhan continued. "There is at least one advantage to facing Sai-Far now. You will have the chance to avenge yourself upon the author of your downfall. Once on the ground even this will be denied you."

I peeked over the side. We were still a thousand or so feet up, but the ground was coming up fast. I was amazed to see that while we'd all been fighting, the wind had pushed us all the way back to the Temple of Ormolu. We were going to set down not far from the temple where we'd started. I could see a crowd of people running along below us, looking up. Their faces were getting clearer every second.

Lhan's voice pulled me back to the deck. "Gentlemen, when you're ready."

As I turned back to watch, something caught my eye on the main deck. Kai-La, with her head bandaged like a turban, was pushing Wen-Jhai out from below decks, and not being real gentle about it. Wen-Jhai looked around bug-eyed, probably afraid that she was a prisoner of the pirates again. Then she saw Sai and Kedac squaring off on the poopdeck and stopped dead. She clasped her hands together like the heroine out of a silent movie. I couldn't tell who she was worried about.

I turned to watch the fight.

Sai spun his sword through the loop-de-loops of a fancy salute, but before he was done, Kedac lunged forward, trying to gut him where he stood. Sai jumped aside with a squeak and the fight was on.

Lhan sniffed. "So much for honor, noble Kir-Dhanan."

Kedac barked a laugh. "And will honor save me from the noose?"

He laid into Sai like a combine harvester. I winced. This was going to be quick. I looked at Lhan, nervous. He made a "don't worry" motion with his hand.

When Sai was still alive after thirty seconds I started to hope he might be right.

Something had happened to Sai. He was fighting like a totally different guy. He was fast and precise, and more important, he wasn't choking. He was still nowhere near the fighter Kedac was, but unlike all the other times I'd seen him fight, where it looked like he was trying so hard to remember what to do next he couldn't do what he needed to do now, here he was totally focused. He wasn't berserk with anger. He wasn't afraid. He wasn't frustrated. He was calm, determined and patient. He took what Kedac was dishing out, and let him wear himself out hacking away like a weed-whacker.

On the other hand, thanks to me and Kai-La, Kedac was tired and beat to shit. And he was fighting like a crazy man, trying to end it before we hit the ground. He was the one who was distracted. He kept glancing over the side to see where we were and who was waiting for us.

A minute later the ship touched down on top of a low tree with a bump, and tipped slowly over to one side. The pirates and marines saw it coming and were ready. Almost all of them jumped clear. The wounded who couldn't jump rode the ship down, holding on to whatever they could. Luckily the roll-over was so gentle that nobody got seriously banged up, even Wen-Jhai, who came down safe in Burly's arms.

Sai and Kedac were another story. They were so focused that the wreck took them by surprise. As I hopped down to the blue lawn with Lhan, I turned and saw them both skidding sideways and slamming against the rail. Sai pitched over the side and landed hard on his shoulder and neck next to a bush. Kedac fell on the other side of it.

Before either of them could get up we were surrounded by the gang that had been running along under us.

I was a little worried about who the welcome wagon would be. When Lhan, Sai and me had run out of the temple it had been fifty-fifty whether Kedac's posse or the Aldhanan's guards were going to come out top dog. I was happy to see the red armor of the guards lining up around us, and right in the middle of them, the Aldhanan himself. I wasn't so happy to see that they were pointing all their zap-guns at us.

The pirates went on guard, swords out and bows up. The guards did the same, screaming. The pirates shouted back. Too many fingers on triggers. Things were getting out of hand.

Lhan raised his arms and stepped forward, shouting over the noise. "My Aldhanan, these selfless privateers helped Sai-Far capture Kir-Dhanan Kedac and his renegade crew. Please, if it is your will, reassure them they will not now be shot for their valiant efforts."

The Aldhanan waved his men back like it was an afterthought. "Where is my daughter?"

Wen-Jhai stepped around Burly. "Here, father." She ran to him. He caught her in one arm and turned to his guards. "Now, place the traitor Kedac-Zir under arrest and bring him before me!"

Lhan took another step. "By your leave, my Aldhanan, Dhan Sai-Far and Kedac-Zir are at the moment engaged in the Sanfallah. The challenge was made on board and has yet to come to a definite conclusion."

The Aldhanan made a face like he'd bit into a bad oyster, but he held up his hand. His guards stopped. "Then we will wait until the finish to arrest him."

Nice to see what he thought of Sai's chances.

So while Sai and Kedac recovered, the guards formed a ring around them, and all us lookee loos—which included the whole wedding party by now—crowded in behind them.

Kedac was up first, pulling twigs out of his hair. He limped around the bush toward Sai, who was on his hands and knees like a palooka after a knock-out punch. Damn it, get up, you little idiot!

I must have stepped forward without knowing it. Lhan put a hand on my wrist. "You must not. The Sanfallah is as sacred as marriage in Ora. None may interfere, not even the Aldhanan."

I groaned. It was over. But no, Kedac tripped on some fallen rigging. Sai heard him coming and got his sword up at the last second. Kedac's blade screamed across his guard and he staggered past, hissing and favoring his left leg.

Sai grunted to his feet and they were back into it.

I felt helpless. Fuck tradition. We were just going to stand here and let Sai die? By now everybody knew he was innocent and Kedac was guilty. They should stop this.

Nobody did. We all just watched. I held my breath. Sai was a mass of cuts, but he was still fresh. It was Kedac's third fight in ten minutes. He was limping and blowing like a linebacker in double overtime.

In the end though, I don't think that's what got him. I think it was mind stuff that messed him up. He kept shooting glances at the ring of silent faces surrounding him. I think he was starting to realize that his world had already ended. His face twisted up into an angry pout like a baby who can't reach a toy.

He screamed at Sai. "You cannot win! How can you win? You are no man!"

He bashed Sai's blade aside and caught him a hell of a whack on the thigh. It bit deep. Sai's leg collapsed under him. He went down screaming. The gash showed bone and meat.

Kedac shouted, triumphant, and raised his blade for the killing blow. It never landed. Half blind with pain, Sai somehow managed to stab up from the ground and ran Kedac right through the heart.

Kedac looked as surprised as the guy who's just walked into the wrong restroom. He sank to his knees, wrenching the sword out of Sai's hand, then collapsed to the grass. Sai joined him.

The crowd stared, totally silent, then there were twin shrieks and two women pushed forward. Mai-Mar threw herself prone on Kedac's body, wailing like the sword was in her heart, not Kedac's. Wen-Jhai ran to Sai and cradled him in her lap, blood and all, totally ruining her wedding get-up. She stroked his face. "Sai, my heart!"

Sai smiled weakly. "Wen-Jhai, beloved."

Then he fainted.

CHAPTER TWENTY-NINE

TRUE LOVE!

So everything was happily ever after. We all got patched up by the Aldhanan's own personal surgeon, and one quarter later Sai and Wen-Jhai got married in the same white and gold temple, but with even bigger crowds than had been there the first time. Everybody wanted to see the guy who'd single-handedly stopped the plot to overthrow the Aldhanan.

Lhan and I did a graceful fade about that. Let Sai have all the glory. We didn't have reputations to uphold in the first place. Besides, the Aldhanan came across with some fabulous parting gifts for our troubles—new armor, clothes, weapons, cash, krae, and swanky digs at the palace while we were in town.

Kai-La and her pirates got some of booty too—a new ship, a cargo hold full of gold, jewels, and Oran trade goods, a free pass to the Oran border and a quarter-cycle head start. The Aldhanan wanted them gone as quickly as possible. It "wouldn't be prudent" to let the man on the street know that the government had its collective ass saved by a gang of hooligans.

Before they left, Kai-La once again offered me a spot on her ship, and once again, I gave it a miss. If I'd been stuck on Waar I would have taken her up on it in a hot second, but I was going home, so I just wished her well and watched her sail into the sunset. Wish I could have brought her home with me. She'd have made one hell of a biker chick.

The conspirators were all rounded up and beheaded, Mai-Mar included. Justice didn't drag its feet in Ormolu. Their properties were confiscated and Sai and Lhan both got a share. I passed on mine, for the same reason I skipped being a pirate.

Sai's sister Shayah was arrested along with the rest, but at Sai's request she was turned over to his custody. From the look on his face when he talked about her, I got the feeling she'd have been better off on the chopping block.

I wish I could have been a fly on the wall when Sai and Wen-Jhai kissed and made-up. She was apparently at his bedside 24/7 while he was recovering from his leg wound. I bet they had plenty to talk about. Although, on second thought, it probably wasn't all that interesting. They were both such little tight-asses that they probably used words like "past indiscretions" and "intimate relations" when they meant to be saying "screwing around behind your back" and "fucking like a crazed beast."

Anyhow, the wedding went off without a hitch, and Lhan and I both breathed big sighs of relief. About damn time as far as I was concerned. Of course, we didn't totally relax until the next morning at the palace when the newlyweds came down to breakfast two hours late with a glow on you could have seen in the dark. Whew!

***

After that, though, shit started getting a little weird. I reminded Sai that he was going to ask the Aldhanan about finding me a way home and he said he'd bring it up, but it might take a few days. I didn't mind. Lounging around the palace was no hardship. I spent the time boiling myself in their hot spring spa and getting my hips back chowing down at the palace buffet, but then I started seeing priests hanging around. There were priests in the palace all the time anyway. These guys had all-access passes as far as Oran high society went, so it was no big deal to see 'em hanging out. But I was seeing a lot of them, and they all seemed to be following me. They were like my little orange and white shadows.

Then one day Sai and Lhan hunted me up as I was stepping out of the palace's steam room after my morning work-out and sauna—I tell ya, it's a hard life being the Aldhanan's favorite. The boys had big fake smiles on their faces, like kids with water balloons behind their backs.

I scowled at them. "All right, guys, what's the gag?"

Lhan laughed in a strangled sort of way. "Gag? We plan no joke, mistress."

Sai showed me all his teeth. "We merely invite you for a day of foolery and frolic."

"You gotta be kidding me."

Lhan bowed. "'Tis truth. The Aldhanshai Wen-Jhai bids you join her for picnicking and merrymaking. Her carriage awaits without."

I gave them a look. Even for them this was a little fruity. "What's with you guys? You look like a couple of moonies on a recruiting drive."

Sai giggled, nervous. Lhan elbowed him. "Nothing is amiss, Mistress. Truly. Come, we will breakfast on the way."

I sighed. "All right, I'll play along. Just let me go to my room and…"

Lhan practically jumped. "No need for that. All is provided for."

"But…"

"You mustn't keep an Aldhanshai waiting, mistress."

"Okay okay. Whatever. I bet I'm gonna regret this, but let's go."

They led me out to the front gate. I was sure the whole way that I was going to get a pie in the face or a dunk in the fountain at the end of it, but when we got to the drive, there was Wen-Jhai, waiting in a gold and green carriage, complete with a coachman and big wicker hampers strapped to the back. She had a couple guardsmen for escort, and Shae-Vai by her side, looking like she'd been a respectable lady's maid all her life. What an actress.

The carriage wasn't big enough for all of us, but there were two thorough-bred krae all saddled up and ready to go.

Wen-Jhai waved a queenly hand. "Greetings, Mistress Jae-En. You honor us with your presence."

That was the politest thing she'd ever said to me. Something was definitely up.

Nobody was telling, though, so I just mounted up and joined the small talk as we rode out of Ormolu up into the low orange hills to the north. If they wanted to keep a secret, let 'em. I wasn't going to beg.

***

We finally stopped in a high meadow carpeted in thick blue grass and splotches of day-glo flowers. The view was incredible. The meadow looked down over Ormolu and the whole crazy-quilt river valley. The sun turned even the shittiest parts of the city into gold, and made the blue-tiled towers blaze like sapphires. It looked like a music box miniature of itself.

The guardsmen rolled out a big rug—the same kind the Aarurrh big shots held their pow-wows on—and Shae-Vai laid out a spread that would have fed the starting line up for the Green Bay Packers. There were cold meats, hard boiled eggs, fruits, hot drinks, chilled wines, salads, breads, pastries, jellies and jams, cold soups, candied insects—not bad if you closed your eyes—patés, and something that looked exactly like a four winged fried chicken.

I nudged Lhan. "What's this?"

"Jekjek. A game bird, known for its robust taste. Try it."

I tried it. It tasted just like pork.

So, after a whole afternoon of eating and drinking, and—if you want to get technical about it—frolicking and merrymaking, I'd almost forgot about the way Sai and Lhan had acted that morning. But then, as Shae-Vai packed the dirty plates and glasses, Lhan and Sai gave each other a look.

Lhan stood and turned to me. "Mistress Jae-En. Will you walk with us?"

I looked up from polishing off the last jekjek leg. The frolicking was over. Sai and Lhan were as grim as hangmen.

I got up. "So, you're finally gonna tell me what this is all about?"

Lhan shot a glance over at Wen-Jhai and Shae-Vai, who were telling the guardsmen how to lift the hampers into the carriage. "We merely wish to walk."

"Oh. Right. Gotcha." I gave him a wink. "A walk. Sure, let's walk."

We wandered to the middle of the meadow, out of earshot. I took another bite off my jekjek leg. "So what's with all the cloak and dagger stuff?"

Sai leaned in, shifty eyed. "It was necessary to get you out of the palace on some innocent pretext. The walls of Ormolu have ears."

I groaned. "I thought we were done with all that shit. Kedac's dead. You and Wen-Jhai are married. Everybody's happy."

Lhan nodded. "All is well with Sai and the Aldhanshai. 'Tis you we are concerned about."

I frowned. "What happened? Did I step on somebody's toes or something?"

Lhan exchanged a look with Sai. Lhan looked grim. "In a way. You have aroused the interest of the temple."

"I *thought* I'd been seeing a lot of those little creamsicles. Whadda they want with me?"

"That is also a mystery, though I would wager it has to do with your strength, your leaping, the color of your skin, which though not the gold spoken of in the sacred texts, is nonetheless decidedly not within the mundane spectrum. Perhaps you begin, at least in their minds, to tread on the War God's sacred territory; to impinge upon his divinity."

I didn't know what that meant, but it didn't sound good.

Lhan lowered his voice, even though nobody by the carriage could possibly hear us. "Sai has learned that the priests mean to invite you into the temple tomorrow."

"Is that bad?"

"None but priests have ever reemerged from the temple."

I glanced out at Ormolu, glowing red in the sunset. The light was turning the big white skyscraper temple a fleshy pink. Made it look even more like a dick. I shivered. "I knew I didn't like that place."

I looked back again. "So you're saying I should split town?"

Sai nodded. "It might be the wisest course."

I sighed. "Well, you know I was planning on leaving anyway. Uh, have you seen the Aldhanan about getting me back to..."

He looked guilty. "I'm sorry, mistress. With the priests asking questions I deemed it unwise to bring your problem before the Aldhanan. It might be unsafe for him to help you."

"Ain't that gratitude. How safe was it for us when we were helpin' him out?"

"Fortunately, I recalled another source. An old tutor of mine with a fascination for forbidden knowledge. He collects legends and stories of the days before the Seven ascended. I went to him and asked him for help locating a... a living stone." Sai looked around like he was afraid priests were going to jump out from behind the bushes, then continued. "He was reluctant to confide in me, for to speak of these things is heresy, but I paid him well and gave him my word that I would not betray him. He said he might have record of such a stone among his volumes and papers. Some rumor from grave robbers who raid the abandoned cities to the east."

Well it was *something* to go on. "Uh, has he got a map? Or is this going to be a snipe hunt?"

"He searchs for a map as we speak. I will have it sent to you as soon as he brings it to me."

I didn't get it. "Sent to me? Just drop it by my room. We've still gotta go back and pack, and..."

Lhan coughed. "You are already packed."

"Huh?"

"That is the second reason for this picnic. Sai and I fear priestly intervention if you return to the palace. If you are willing, you may accompany me to one of my old… haunts. We shall stay there until your map is found."

I frowned. "After the big thank you and all the swag we got from the Aldhanan, you really think we got something to worry about here?"

Lhan nodded. "Unfortunately, yes. The Aldhanan is the ultimate worldly power in Ora, but the Church of the Seven bows to no law but that of Heaven. Though the Aldhanan might protest if you were to disappear, he would be powerless to question the Temple as to your fate."

"Man, there's nothing like a church to fuck up a good religion. I feel like swatting somebody!" I threw the bones of my jekjek leg in the general direction of Ormolu. Some picnic this turned out to be.

Lhan put a hand on my shoulder. "I am truly sorry, Mistress. You should be riding out the triumph gate to the cheers of the multitudes, not sneaking off like a thief in the night."

I shrugged, trying not to show how bummed I was. "You guys did all you could. As long as you get me that map and show me which dot is Ormolu I'll figure it out from there. It's just kind of a drag starting again all the way back at square one, that's all."

Lhan smirked. "You need only be alone if you wish it so."

I looked up. "What?"

He bowed. "I would hate to intrude where I am not wanted, Mistress, but city life already begins to bore me. I long once more for the open road. If you can again bear my company, I would travel with you."

I nearly jumped for joy. "If I wish? Hell yeah, I wish! I wish like dammit."

"Once again your syntax astounds me, Mistress, but I take it to mean that you agree."

"You betcha."

"Quite."

We laughed. Then we stopped. It was quiet for a second.

My heart gave a little lurch. I turned to Sai. "So, uh, I guess this is goodbye, huh?"

He nodded. "Your packs and weapons are hidden under the seats of the carriage."

We crossed back to were we'd parked. Lhan and I strapped on our swords and tied our packs to our krae. Wen-Jhai joined us, Shae-Vai following a respectful distance behind her.

Sai gave me a manly handshake. "My thanks to you for all you've done for us, Mistress Jae-En. Wen-Jhai and I would not be here and alive were it not for your courage and valor."

"Come off it, Sai. We got enough of that mush at the banquet."

Wen-Jhai gave me a hug and a smile that was halfway between shy and sly. "Thank you, Mistress Jae-En, for returning my beloved to me, and for… everything."

I flushed. They were making me feel like the hero at the end of a western. I kicked the dirt. "Aw shucks, ma'am. It weren't nothin'."

Behind her I noticed Shae-Vai smirking at me, eyes twinkling. I smiled back. If Sai somehow grew an open mind, He and Wen-Jhai were going to have a very interesting marriage.

Lhan and I mounted up. I looked down at Sai and Wen-Jhai. "You kids be good to each other."

Sai nodded gravely. "On my honor you have that promise, Mistress Jae-En, if in return you promise me that you and Lhan will take care of one another on your journey."

Lhan and I looked at each other, embarrassed.

"Sure."

"But of course."

We waved good-bye, then rode down the hill to the main road and away from the city. It was a beautiful day for a ride.

"So where's this hide-out of yours, Lhan?"

"Not far. A friend from my wild days has a country house nearby. 'Tis much accustomed to clandestine meetings."

"Well, let's not take any shortcuts, all right?"

***

Late that night Lhan and I lay around on a couple of chaise lounges in a private suite of rooms in Lhan's friend's plush pad. There was the remains of a meal and a couple of bottles of high-octane Oran wine on the table next to us, but we weren't exactly relaxed. Sai's messenger was supposed to have been there hours before, and we hadn't heard back from the servant our host had sent out to find him.

A couple of cell phones would have taken care of everything in about two seconds, but we would have had to wait two thousand years or so before these numbskulls got around to inventing weekend minutes. So we just lay there, watching the candle flames dance in the warm breeze from the open windows, a little too anxious to kick back entirely, but not quite ready yet to be really worried. After a while I remembered that I had a question I'd been meaning to ask Lhan since the wedding.

"You all right about Sai getting hitched?"

Lhan sighed. "He is in love, and content at last. That is all I've ever wanted for him."

"Man, you put the noble in nobleman, don'tcha? I'd be jealous as hell."

He chuckled. "I am a little. But mostly of his happiness."

I snorted. "Tell me about it."

"Pardon?"

"Huh? Oh, nothing. Never mind."

We lay silent again for a while. I don't know what he was thinking about, but I was thinking about Big Don. Not the big stuff. Not the sex, or the road trips, or the diamond ring. The little stuff—sitting around the kitchen table in the morning, going grocery shopping, taking the dogs to the vet.

Lhan spoke up. "You and I are two of a kind, are we not, mistress?"

"Uh... Whaddaya mean?"

"You come from another place. This is not your home. And though I was born here, I sometimes feel that there is no place for me on this world."

"I know just how you feel. I've felt like that on two worlds now."

"Then... you must be truly lonely."

I clenched my fists. "Brother, if you don't shut up I'm gonna start bawlin', and that ain't pretty."

He shut up, but after a minute I felt his fingers slip around mine.

"Mistress Jae-En, there is a balm for loneliness. 'Tis imperfect and temporary, but while it lasts 'tis soothing."

I raised my head. He was up on one elbow looking at me with those dark purple eyes as serious as a judge. My heart started thumping like a kick drum. I closed my big fingers around his long, slim ones. That must have been what he was waiting for, 'cause he leaned in and kissed me.

Wow.

I didn't know how bad I'd missed that until I got it. It felt like Lhan was filling me with cool, clear water from the toes up. I pulled him over to my couch and held him tight and kissed him like I was dying of thirst. It felt so good it hurt.

But after a minute a rotten little thought came up and tapped me on the shoulder. I pushed Lhan back and looked into his eyes, searching.

"If this is some kind of pity fuck, I… I'm gonna throw you out that window."

He shook his head, solemn. "If it is, mistress, then 'tis you who take pity on me."

Well, if you think I could resist a line like that you're out of your ever-lovin' mind. I took pity on him all right. I took pity on him until the candles burned out.

At some point we moved from the chaises to the bed in the next room. At some point after that I finally wore poor Lhan out and he drifted off.

I wasn't quite sleepy yet. I stared up at the ceiling, a big stupid smile on my face, trying to remember what the hell I wanted to go home for, anyway.

There was a prison cell waiting for me back in California. If I somehow ducked that, I had a couple years of construction jobs ahead of me before I'd have the dough for another hog. And god knows how long I'd have to hang around in bars before I found another Mr. Goodbike, if I ever did. And where did we go once I got him? I'd been to all the continental forty eight and Alaska too. Sure there was plenty left to explore, but nowhere some Good Sam in his RV hadn't been before—no place that didn't have a write-up in some Triple A guidebook.

I was on the lam here in Ora too, but I was guessing the Orans were about as close to inventing extradition as they were cell-phones. Once I got clear of Ora's borders there was a whole new world to explore. And with Lhan riding beside me, I'd have somebody to share it with, which is all I've ever asked for.

Lhan was one hell of a somebody too. I wasn't sure I was in love. He was no Big Don. Who could be? I wasn't even sure love was what I wanted right then anyway. It was just nice having somebody to hold now and then.

I looked over at Lhan and smiled. Maybe we wouldn't go looking for magic stones after all. Maybe in the morning I'd ask him if he'd rather just take a road trip instead.

Somewhere around there I started to drift off. My eyelids drooped and my brain got fuzzy. I rolled over and spooned against Lhan, purring like a cat.

I thought I heard a noise through the fog. Had Sai's messenger finally come? I was almost too tired to care, but I lifted my head. It felt like it weighed a thousand pounds.

There were shadows in the next room. Candle flicker? No. The candles were out.

I tried to shake off my sleep. I couldn't. Something was wrong. The room smelled like butterscotch pipe tobacco.

There were shadows over the bed. Shadows in orange and white robes. They reached for me.

CHAPTER THIRTY

BANISHED!

I woke up on a rock floor with the mother of all hangovers drilling for oil in my head, and an elephant sitting on my chest. At least something was squashing me into the ground and crushing the air out of my lungs. I could hardly breathe. Wherever I was, it was dark, but the way my gasping echoed I knew I wasn't outside.

I tried to lift my hand to find out what was on my chest. It was heavy as lead. Was I wearing a chain mail shirt? It was an epic struggle just to raise my arm, and when I finally dragged it over my body I touched naked flesh. And there was nothing on top of me. What was this fucking weight?

"What the hell is going on? What the fuck did those creamsicles do to me?"

I got to my feet. It took a while. It felt like I was giving Andre the Giant a piggyback ride. A faint green light was coming from somewhere and after a bit I could make out some details. I was in a high-roofed cave, standing on an uneven stone floor. It was dry and hot and empty.

I turned to see if I could find the source of the green light. Behind me a translucent stalagmite was glowing a pale, lemonade green. By the time my tossed salad brain figured out where I'd seen a light like that before it was starting to fade.

I stepped toward it. I was so damned weak I could barely move. The stalagmite dimmed and went out. I touched it anyway. Nothing. Cold, smooth stone.

"Fuckers! Where the fuck have you dumped me now, you fucking fucks?"

I really shouldn't have screamed. My head throbbed like a hive full of bees. My stomach headed for the exit.

When I was finished puking I looked up again. Now that the green light was gone, I could just see a dim pink light coming from the left. I stared until the highlights and shadows turned into a picture. A narrow passage. Somewhere down it was the pink light. There was no guarantee that whatever the pink light was would be better than this cave, but people tend to walk toward light and I'm people. I walked.

It felt like I was slogging waist deep in a peanut butter swamp. I clumped along like Frankenstein. The passage led to the mouth of the cave. I peeked out.

The cave was in the side of a cliff, looking over a landscape from a Mars lander photo; sand everywhere, huge skyscrapers of stone all over the place. The sky was blood red and the air was hot enough to curl your nose hairs.

"Hell, they've sent me to hell."

Something moved in the corner of my eye. I ducked back, ready for anything. Far across the sandy plain some kind of weird vehicle with wheels on the roof was racing down a long, straight road. It got closer. I squinted at it.

It was a Chevy mini-van with a pair of kids' BMX bikes racked to the roof.

I watched the mini-van drive out of sight again.

I laughed.

I couldn't stop.

I cried.

I couldn't stop that either.

I was back on Earth.

Now that I knew that, I knew where I was. This was Monument Valley. The weight on my chest was Earth gravity. The blood red sky was an Arizona sunrise.

I was home. I was where I'd wanted to be all along, away from a shit-hole world full of slaves and gladiators and naked sexists and killing, in one of the most beautiful places on the planet, one easy hitch-hike away from a bottle of beer and a Marlboro, and all I could think was...

I want to go back.

AFTERWORD

There were a few more things on the last tape—directions about sending the money, if I made any, to her Aunt Cici in Florida, "The only family I ever had that was worth a shit," a warning not to try and find her, that sort of thing, but that was all there was of the story. I don't know where Jane is, if she made it back to Waar, or if she's still here, or if the whole thing's just a big hoax, but you can be sure that if I do make any money, I'll do exactly what she wants. The thought of making Jane angry, even if she's light-years away on another planet, is not one that appeals to me.

Her last words on the tape were this. "Later, bro. I hope you can do something with this crap. I got a bus to catch."

Acknowledgements

Ten years ago, I brought a sloppy parody of a planetary romance to a writing class taught by Emma Bull and Will Shetterly. I thought, in my hubris, that it was ready to be published. Emma and Will showed me otherwise, then opened my eyes to what *Jane* could be, if I took her seriously. Without them, this book would not be in your hands.

Nine years ago, I showed the newly reworked *Jane* to my friends Sue and Grey, who both gave me sharp, insightful criticism and kept me on the straight and narrow. Without them, this book would not be in your hands.

One year ago, I dug *Jane* out of its dusty drawer and showed it to Howard Andrew Jones, hoping he would tell me it was good enough to e-publish. Instead, he told me it deserved a proper publisher, and passed it on to his agent, Bob Mecoy, who also saw something in it. Without them, this book would not be in your hands.

Six months ago, Ross Lockhart at Night Shade Books read *Jane*, and... Well, you know the refrain by now. Without him, this book would not be in your hands.

Night Shade Books is an Independent Publisher of Quality Science-Fiction, Fantasy and Horror

ISBN: 978-1-59780-397-7 ❰ $14.99 ❰ Look for it in e-Book

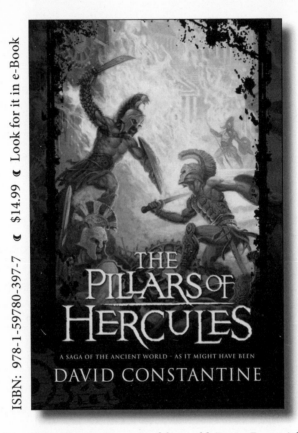

THE
PILLARS OF
HERCULES

A SAGA OF THE ANCIENT WORLD - AS IT MIGHT HAVE BEEN

DAVID CONSTANTINE

Alexander, Prince of Macedon, is the terror of the world. Persia, Egypt, Athens…one after another, mighty nations are falling before the fearsome conqueror. Some say Alexander is actually the son of Zeus, king of the gods, and the living incarnation of Hercules himself. Worse yet, some say Alexander believes this…

The ambitious prince is aided in his conquest by unstoppable war-machines based on the forbidden knowledge of his former tutor, the legendary scientist-mage known as Aristotle. Greek fire, mechanical golems, and gigantic siege—engines lay waste to Alexander's enemies as his armies march relentlessly west—toward the very edge of the world.

Beyond the Pillars of Hercules, past the gateway to the outer ocean, lies the rumored remnants of Atlantis: ancient artifacts of such tremendous power that they may be all that stands between Alexander and conquest of the entire world. Alexander desires that power for himself, but an unlikely band of fugitives—including a Gaulish barbarian, a cynical Greek archer, a cunning Persian princess, and a sorcerer's daughter—must find it first… before Alexander unleashes godlike forces that will shatter civilization.

The Pillars of Hercules is an epic adventure that captures the grandeur and mystery of the ancient world as it might have been, where science and magic are one and the same.

Night Shade Books is an Independent Publisher of Quality Science-Fiction, Fantasy and Horror

ISBN: 978-1-59780-394-6 ☙ $14.99 ☙ Look for it in e-Book

Enormity is the strange tale of an American working in Korea, a lonely young man named Manny Lopes, who is not only physically small (in his own words, he's a "Creole shrimp"), but his work, his failed marriage, his race, all conspire to make him feel puny and insignificant—the proverbial ninety-eight-pound weakling. Then one day an accident happens, a quantum explosion, and suddenly Manny awakens to discover that he's big—really big. In fact, Manny is enormous, a mile-high colossus! Now there's no stopping him: he's a one-man weapon of mass destruction!

Enormity takes some weird turns, featuring characters like surfing gangbangers, elderly terrorists, and a North Korean assassin who thinks she's Dorothy from *The Wizard of Oz*. There's also sex, violence, and action galore, with the army throwing everything it has against the rampaging colossus that is Manny Lopes. But there's only one weapon that has any chance at all of stopping him: his wife!

about the author

Nathan Long is a screen and prose writer, with two movies, one Saturday-morning adventure series, and a handful of live-action and animated TV episodes to his name, as well as ten fantasy novels and several award-winning short stories.

He hails from Pennsylvania, where he grew up, went to school, and played in various punk and rock-a-billy bands, before following his writing dreams to Hollywood—where he now plays in various punk and country bands—and writes novels full time.